Keep Away From The Windows

Martin McGregor

Keep away from the windows.

A collection of short stories by Martin McGregor

First published in the UK in 2016 and 2017 by MDM Publishing

ISBN Number 9781521221983

Copyright © Martin McGregor 2017

The right of Martin McGregor to be identified as the author of this work has been asserted by him in accordance with the copyright, Designs and Patents Act 1988.

All rights reserved. No part of this publication may be reproduced, stored in or introduced into a retrieval system, or transmitted in any form, or by any means (electronic, mechanical, photocopying, recording or otherwise) without the prior written permission of the publisher. Any person who does any unauthorised act in relation to this publication may be liable to criminal prosecution and civil claim damages.

 This is a work of fiction. Names, characters, businesses, places, events and incidents are either the products of the author's imagination or used in a purely fictitious manner. Any resemblance to actual persons, living or dead, or to any actual events, is purely coincidental.

Original cover photograph by Daniel Diaz

This book is sold subject to the conditions that it shall not, by way of trade or other means, be lent, re-sold, hired out or otherwise circulated without the publisher's prior consent in any form of binding or cover other than that in which it is published and without a similar condition including this condition being imposed on the subsequent purchaser.

While MDM Publishing make every effort to see that no inaccurate or misleading data, opinion or statement appears in this book or any other affiliated publications. MDM Publishing wishes to state that the data in this book and any other affiliated publications are the responsibility of the author concerned. MDM Publishing and their officers and agents accept no liability whatsoever for the consequences of any such misleading data, opinion, or statement.

I began writing short stories for these books back in 2013. Four years later I have completed a trilogy. Much has happened in those four years, and all in all, the world feels a much less safer place. As you grow older, politics seeps into your life and you find yourself angry at things you have very little hope of changing.

I write to occupy my mind. I write to keep myself from going insane. I write because someone may enjoy the messed up scenarios that play out in my head. I can actually visualise all of characters in the flesh, and I base a lot of the stories on real life situations. I guess that is why quite a few people seem to relate to them.

I decided to combine all three books together to make my writing more accessible, and to provide value for money. At the end of the day, we are all just trying to get by. I hope that you find something within these pages to entertain you. I am sure that there will be a story or two that you love or hate. I try to cater for all tastes. Looking back, there are a few stories which seem weak, but it would be unfair of me to strip then away.

Once again I would just like to take the time to send you a personal thank you for purchasing this book. It is appreciated that you spend your hard earned money on my stories, and in truth, you the reader make all of my efforts worthwhile. There are a number of different shorts here, all on varying themes. In these pages you will encounter demons and ghouls, zombies and monsters in different guises, all in equal number. I hope that everyone will have a favourite, and it will make you smile or shiver for a few moments. If it stirs an emotion within you, then I have done my job.

I love writing, and hope that you enjoy reading these stories too. I still hope that one day this may well become a full time job. Until then, I will keep on writing, and I will never give up trying. Thank you once again for your continued support. I wouldn't be here without every single one of you

Martin McGregor 2017.

This book is dedicated to all of my family, especially my mother Brenda and to my sons, Nick, Chris, Jordan, and Owen, and my grandson Fredster. Also I would like to thank my readers and fans, especially Giovanna, Shona, Nigel, Sharon and Michelle. Also to those who endure my constant requests for a review or to read one of my draft stories. Please take this as a personal thank you to each and every one of you, as without your continued support and encouragement I know that I would have given this up long ago.

Cover photograph by

Contents

1. The Clown.

2. Reboot.

3. Emma's Ghost.

4. The Reckoning.

5. Helter Skelter.

6. The Spread.

7. Lady Ice Part 1.

8. The Red Devil.

9. What Goes Around.

10. The Banshee Dream.

11. Zombie Horror!

12. The Unwanted.

13. The Storm Riders.

14. One Night Stand.

15. Mother Nature.

16. Our Saviour.

17. Lady Ice, Part 2.

18. The Test.

19. The Rainmaker.

20. Before My Eyes.

21. The Hidden Agenda.

22. Animal.

23. Take a bow.

24. Enemy Mine.

25. We Float.

26. The last days of Martusa.

27. The End Game.

28. Multiverse.

29. New Years Eve.

30. To Stop My Bones from Rotting.

31. Rewind.

32. When the bough breaks.

33. The Dream Collectors.

34. The Sin Eater.

35. Lady Ice Part 3.

36. Never meet your heroes

37. Sleep won't come

The Clown

Today Tegan was feeling much older. It had been her fifth birthday and she now knew that every year, she would be one year older. Never younger, never the same age, never again would she be four. She was so big now, that she could even sleep with the lights off! She knew of all the things in the house that were dangerous, and all the things that she could and could not touch. Tegan was a clever girl. Her mother had always told her that.

Now it was her time for bed, and that was the one time of day, that she never really liked. Today, as it was her birthday, she had been allowed to stay up late. It was now half past eight! Her tummy ached from eating so much cake earlier in the day, and she was still smiling about all the fun she had with her friends at her party. Her mum had even hired a magician to show them amazing magic tricks, but best of all, she had lots of lovely presents to open and keep.

It had been snowing all throughout the day. It had begun to settle in the afternoon and it was still gently flowing as she made her way up to bed. Her mother held her hand and they walked up the stairs together. They were a special team. Daddy hadn't been to see her today, they both hoped he might, but Daddy now had Emily to love, and they lived a very long way away. Tegan sort of understood why he never came around to see them anymore, but she still didn't like it.

As they reached the bedroom door, Tegan slowly pushed it open, she was always wary in case someone might be on the other side, just waiting in the room. Her mother switched on the light, and walked into the room with her. Tegan had once seen something on the television a few months back that had given her a little scare. Now every night before she would go to sleep, she had to be reassured that her bedroom was safe.

"Monster check mummy!" She told her mother, and she would not enter the room any further until her mother had complied with her request. Her mother shook her head.

"How many times do I have to tell you honey, there are no monsters." Her mother still continued to shake her head in disbelief, but now she was smiling as she did so. She was only twenty seven, but the last few months had been hard on her. Tegan would often hear her cry when she was alone in her room at night. It was worse the last time Daddy came, there was a lot of shouting, and Nana had to come and collect her. Now small wrinkles had started to appear on her mother's face around her eyes and forehead. Tegan didn't like them. They made her look more like Nana.

The first place to check was the wardrobe. Her mother opened the door and moved the clothes from side to side. "Let's see. In here….no monsters." She stated. Then she knelt down on the floor, and looked all under the bed. She beckoned Tegan across the room to join her.

"Come look, and see for yourself. No monsters are under here either." Tegan peered under the bed, and carefully looked from side to side in the shadows. Once she was satisfied that she was safe. She jumped up on to the bed.

"Check out of the window mummy!" Tegan shouted. Her mother, now familiar with the nightly pattern, was already walking toward the window, ready for the third and final check of the night. She pulled the curtains slightly apart, and saw that the snow now covered the landscape for miles.

"No monsters outside either." Her mother concluded.

The house that they lived in stood alone in the heart of the country. The next house was about half a mile away across a large field. It was lonely here sometimes, but at least it was peaceful. The snow continued to fall; only now it seemed as if it were becoming heavier once again. The sky was white and the glow of the white clouds seemed to light up the room. Tegan liked it being light outside at night.

"Can you leave my curtains open please mummy?' She asked. 'I want to see the snow falling!' Deciding it wouldn't do any harm, her mother left them open and walked back over to Tegan's bed.

She tucked her snugly in, and kissed her on the forehead.

"Goodnight my baby girl. I hope that you had a great day?" She said.

"I had the best day ever mummy, thank you!" Then she reached up and squeezed her mother tightly around the neck. Her mother gulped her own saliva backward into her throat, and swallowed hard. She was immensely proud of her daughter, but she knew she was sad her father hadn't come. She kissed her on the forehead once more, and then made her way out of the bedroom, and she closed the door behind her.

Tegan was not yet ready to go to sleep just yet though. It might have been the bright light of the skyline keeping the room lit up, or maybe it might just have been those sugary treats she ate so many of earlier, but an hour later, she was still awake. She played quietly with her dolls whilst sat upright in the bed, she was ready just in case she heard her mother coming up the stairs, already prepared so that she could dive quickly back under the covers. She sang simple little songs to herself that only she knew all the words to.

At ten o clock, she had grown bored, and now she was just laid down whilst fidgeting in her bed. Try as she might though, she could not go to sleep; such was the excitement of the day.

As Tegan lay still, she placed her hands behind her head and cupped them together. She placed her head back down on her hands and looked up toward the window. The snow was still falling. Then something magical happened. In the window, there appeared a bright red balloon! She closed her eyes and opened them again, but she wasn't dreaming. It really was a balloon that she was seeing! Then another balloon appeared, but this one was blue. Both appeared to hover at the same level, right outside of her window.

It was simply too much for an inquisitive mind to ignore. She sat upright in her bed, and slowly pushed her covers over to one side. She then carefully dropped her feet down to the floor. It was important her mother did not hear her walking around, or she might get in trouble. Slowly she walked across the room until she reached the window. It was a little too high for her to see out of, so she took the books from her bookshelf and gathered them into a pile under the window. Then she climbed on top of the books.

The balloons weren't floating. They were being held on strings, the strings were being held by a clown. He saw Tegan's face appear at the window and he waved to her. Tegan instantly ducked down out of sight, but after a few seconds of caution she felt brave enough to stand up again. The clown waved at her once more. This time Tegan gently waved back to him.

The clown then started dancing around in the snow. It wasn't like a normal dance though; this was a really silly clown dance. It made Tegan laugh. The clown could see her laughing away, and this made his dancing even more silly. At times he would even fall over on to the cold white floor. Then the clown put his hand to his mouth and said something. With the window closed, she couldn't hear him, so she decided to open the window to hear what the Clown was saying to her.

The window would only open a little way, thanks to a safety device that had been fitted, but it allowed her just enough room for Tegan to talk to the clown.

"What did you say?" She asked. The clown made an insane giggling noise, that made Tegan smile even more, and then he responded.

"Hey there little girl, Do you want to come out into the snow and play?" He asked. Tegan could feel the temperature outside was cold, but not too cold. "Will you help me make a snowman?" He asked, and then he pretended to fall over in the snow once more.

The clown laid still, he was face down in the snow. Tegan watched him for a few moments more, expecting him to move, when he remained still, she called out to him.

"Mr. Clown! Are you o.k.?" She shouted, as loud as she dared. The clown did not respond.

She was only five, but she knew that if someone didn't move, they might be in trouble. It was just like the time when Granddad fell down and went to heaven. The decision was then made, she had to go and help him. She slowly crept down the stairs descending them one by one in almost silent steps. Her mother was asleep in her reclining chair in the front room. An empty bottle of vodka and a single glass was on the table next to her. There was no point trying to wake her mother now, she had to help Mr. Clown.

She put on her coat and shoes, walked to the front door, and she reached up for the latch. She had to stretch up to reach it and it took two attempts, but on the second try, the latch twisted round, and it allowed her to pull the door open. It was heavier than she remembered; not realizing the amount of snow which that was already piled up on to it. Some of it fell into the hallway.

She ran across the slippery snow, over to where the clown lay. She shook his shoulder and was startled as the clown jumped up.

'Boo!" He shouted and then he began laughing. Tegan initially held her breath from the fright, but then she laughed along with him.

"You scared me!" She said giggling away. The clown then stood up.

"Can we go make a snowman?" He said.

"Sure!" Tegan replied. She was happy that she had found a new friend out here, and that he was alright.

"We need to go to where the really good snow is, just across that field. Will you walk there with me?" The clown asked.

Her mother had told her, she was never to walk off with strangers. This wasn't a stranger though. It was a clown. He made her laugh, he was funny! She looked back at the house, and then she remembered what her mother had told her earlier. There are no monsters. The words made her feel safe and she decided that she was alright, now she was five, she was all grown up, and she should go.

"Alright, but we can't be long. One snowman, then it's time for me to go to bed. "Tegan stated.

The clown then took her by the hand and they started to walk across the field together away from the house. When they were far enough away from the house, he picked up the child. There was no one close enough to hear her scream. Her tiny body wasn't able to struggle against his strength at all. He put the funny smelling handkerchief over the child's mouth and after only a few seconds, the child was unconscious.

Earlier that day he had already scouted out the entire area. It wasn't far to the old woodshed from here. He knew the child was inquisitive. He knew that she would easily be lured, if necessary, he would have taken care of the mother too. It had been easier than he imagined though. After he had finished with her, he could dispose of the body and get away from here quickly without ever being seen. His four by four was parked close by. He turned toward in the direction of the woodshed and as he did so, he dropped the child. He experienced the strangest sensation of the world around him fading, and then he found himself falling into darkness.

The pain he felt in the back of his head was intense. He was in the woodshed, but he had no recollection of how he got there. The child was close to him, but she was laid on the floor a few feet away. She was faced away from him, and still unconscious. Behind him he heard movement, and he turned his head startled by the sound. The clown mask was then ripped from his head, and the magician who had entertained Tegan and her friends earlier in the day, was exposed as the man who was hidden behind the mask.

The child's mother then walked from the shadows and stood in front of him. She was wearing a stained leather smock. He tried to stand up, but he had been tied down fast to what appeared to be a table.

"I wasn't going to hurt her, I swear!" He began to plead.

"Please. Save your breath. I know what you are." She angrily stated. "Tegan's father once tried to take my daughter away from me. I learnt back then about how cruel men can be. Today I saw the way you looked at my child. I've seen that look before. I have seen it ever since I was a child myself." The mother was carrying something in her hand. It looked wooden, and it was almost like a baseball bat, but not quite. In this level of light, it was difficult to tell.

"Please let me go. I know I was wrong, I know I need help, please..." He pleaded.

"Her father tried to take her, but I couldn't let him take my daughter. I had to make sure...I had to make sure he never came back again. Not him or his new whore. I ended them both with my father's gun and took them out to the field. Tegan will never know. They are both buried deep."

The magician had a sudden moment of realization, there is no greater power in nature than a mother, forced to protect her young. As the metal head of the axe glimmered in the dim light of the woodshed, he knew that his fate was already sealed. He lost all sense of control and as his body shivered he emptied his bladder across the wood chopping table.

"And you know what makes this worse you sick piece of shit? I fucking hate clowns." Her voice was calm, and unexpected, especially as at that very moment it was in full swing and the axe was swung down. The impact severed his leg completely at the top of his thigh. The screams were few and short lived, as blow after blow reigned down, next the other leg was removed, and then both of his arms, and then finally the severed head which rolled from the table and fell down on to the blood splattered floor.

Tegan had been feeling strange all day. Perhaps the excitement of yesterday had been too much. Now it was her bedtime again. Her mother carried out the usual checks, but tonight, the curtains would have to remain closed. Her mother had insisted.

"Mummy, last night I had a dream, and there was a funny clown in it!" She said. Her mother knelt down next to her. She then began stroking her daughter's hair.

"Don't worry baby, it was just a dream. Now you need some sleep." Her mother smiled as she kissed her forehead.

"Mummy... Are there really any monsters?" Tegan asked.

"No Tegan. There are none, none that will ever hurt you, not my little baby. No one will ever take you away from me I swear." She replied. As she left the bedroom, she turned off the light, but she left the door slightly open. There would be no vodka tonight. Instead she would sit quietly in her chair and wait for anyone who would even dare try to hurt her daughter. The axe was clean, freshly sharpened, and ready.

The woodshed was locked. It would remain so until she had time to take Tegan for a trip to her mother's later that week, and then she would clean up the mess. His car was another matter. That would have to be either driven into a lake or burnt. No other cars were coming near the house anytime soon, the snow would ensure that. She would work out what exactly what to do with the car later. The ground would have to thaw before she could dig deep enough to bury the corpse. Until then, the insects could feed, and the clown could rot.

It was two days since her husband had gone missing. His magician's kit sat on the side exactly where he had left it. She comforted her two young daughters as best as she could. She tried ringing his phone again, and it went straight to voicemail, she chose not to leave another message. This wasn't the first time the magician had disappeared, but unknown to the family of the great Mysterio; it would certainly be his greatest ever disappearing act.

Reboot

It was only last night that the clocks had gone back one hour, and it was annoying to say the least. Today, things had felt just a little bit on the strange side. It was an eerie feeling that could not be shifted. Before the clocks had changed, itt had been getting dark at around 6.30 p.m, but now at almost 9 p.m. It could almost have still been daytime. The night sky was eerily bright, and yet there was no rational explanation.

There was a bit of a commotion outside. Everyone was starting to spill out onto the streets to witness this strange phenomenon. At first the gathered crowd had thought that it might have been some sort of strange weather pattern, but as the crowd grew greater in number, so the brightness of the sky above became even more intense.

This wasn't like normal daylight though, far from it. The sky was eerily white, and even had hints of pale green patches in some areas. The crowd were almost silent as they looked skyward, almost hypnotized by the sea of light that flooded throughout the previously dour looking sky. Daniel Davies had just come out of the bath and walked into a living room that was illuminated so brightly that it dazzled his eyes. He looked out of his conservatory window, wondering just who the hell was shining such a bright light near his back window at this time of night. He peered out of the windows and once he saw the bright colour of the sky and was astounded to find that it was not the light of a torch or from a car's headlights at all.

He stared at the crowd outside for a few moments and then shrugged his shoulders. He walked back into the living room, and switched on the television. Annoyingly, none of the channels appeared to be working. Instead, the screen was full of static, all except for a single word that was located directly in the middle of the screen. Try as he might though, even with his glasses hastily thrown on, he could not for the life of him make out what the word was.

Daniel flicked through the channels once again, and each and every channel contained the same static appearance, and that same single word directly in the centre. He grew increasingly frustrated. He then tried switching on the DAB radio, it was dead. He then began searching through the already preset channels, that once blasted tireless rock and dance tunes that had often upset his elderly neighbors. Tonight those channels were also now all dead.

He stood in front of the radio and scratched his head. This was annoying to say the least. Then he had a sudden idea of sheer brilliance, and pulled his mobile phone out from his pocket. He then threw it across the room onto the sofa, as the signal strength was at zero. This was tthe first time his mobile had ever let him down, except for that one occasion when the mobile phone mast had been vandalized a few years back. There was only one avenue left for him to check, and that was the internet.

The desktop was sat idle on his black glass desk. It was hardly ever used these days, but with it being hard wired and not reliant on Wi-Fi, it was the only thing in the house that was not reliant on either a mobile phone, or a weak electronic signal. He switched the power on and it seemed to take an age to boot up, and as the screen finally illuminated. It then asked for a password.

Daniel scratched the freshly trimmed hair on his chin. He was having something of a brain meltdown. He could not for the life of him recall what the password was. He typed in a series of letters, crossed his fingers, and breathed a little sigh of relief as the password was accepted. It was one of a seemingly endless amount of passwords everyone and everything require these days. He had punched in the name of Duran Duran (with capital D's), who were his favourite band.

Clicking on the internet icon, he was pleasantly surprised to see an internet address search bar appear in the centre of the screen. He searched for the words 'bright sky at night', and a multitude of options filled the screen. Some of the links pointed to some crazy conspiracy theory websites that he had seen before on occasion. He scrolled past full moons, aurora borealis, meteor showers and other natural phenomenon, he was sure that the bright sky was not attributed to any of these. Then he saw something close to the bottom of the first search page, which for some strange reason caught his eye.

He clicked on the 'Doomed Sky' homepage link, it loaded extremely slowly and as it finally appeared complete on the screen, he began to read. It was simply another end of age prophecy page, and yet as he began to read, the script on the page was simply compelling him to continue reading. It read

'The end of time commenced in 2012 as prophesized by the ancient Mayans and the great Nostradamus. The entity was projected toward our planet in December of that year. By our calculations, it will arrive at planet Earth on the 28th of October 2014.'

Daniel looked at the date on his watch. It was just as he had thought, this was the exact day. He was intrigued so he continued to read on a little further.

'All the major governments of the world are fully aware of the entity that is approaching, but they know that they are powerless to stop it. Nothing in our universe has the power to hold it back. On the 17th of October 2014, a secret space plane landed back on Earth, after almost two years in space. Its secret mission was to study the anomaly, and try to find a way to halt it, or at least deviate it from its course. The mission failed. Mankind, and every single animal on this planet, now faces total annihilation.'

The script would normally be dismissed as laughable, but Daniel remembered seeing an item on the news recently about a secret American space plane that had recently landed back on Earth. This webpage had surely been doctored mentioning the plane just to add a little credibility to the piece he thought. He then continued reading.

'Senior members of the royal family and selected politicians have already been evacuated from the Earth, and are making their way toward a secretly developed manned base on the planet Mars. As the end approaches, do not be afraid, as we will all face the same fate. The sky will become as bright as day, all radio, television and mobile communications will become lost. All will become silent as the entity turns the dark night into the light of day. Our days here have long been numbered and there will be no time to feel pain. The end will be quick. I pray for you all. Namaste.'

Daniel stood up from the computer, and walked back out toward the conservatory, he could already see that the brightness level had increased immensely. His glasses had chemically reacted to the intense light, and had started to turn a few shades darker. The crowd who had gathered had now become massive in number. All were stood in awe as they stared upward at the brightness of the sky above them.

Whatever this was, it wasn't natural at all. It was now becoming a little frightening. Daniel walked back into the living room and leant over in front of the TV screen. He looked closer at the static picture and focused as if he would on a hidden picture book, he was trying to defocus and make the hidden image appear. The word on the screen was now becoming clearer anyway. It said one simple word, and that word was 'Reboot'.

As he stared at the screen, a counter then appeared next to the word. It read 30 and began to decrease by one in value as each second passed.

"Oh shit!" He said, as a moment of sudden realization washed over him.

Rushing back out to the conservatory, he dared risking his eyesight to look skyward. He looked up directly toward the source of the bright light. The object was seemingly wider than the planet itself, and glowed with the fire of an intense summer sun. As the counter reached zero, Daniel could not move, he could not think about doing anything, he simply held his breath and accepted what was about to happen.

A single pulse of energy blasted down toward the Earth's core, and the force of the impact on the Earth was something that no one on the planet could had ever seen or felt before. As the Earth was instantly blasted into a billion tiny pieces, Daniel had no time to let out that final breath. The last thought he had was of massive warmth that now surrounded him.

The end of all life on the planet was swift, and as the Earth's crust disintegrated underneath Daniel's feet. The force of gravity that had held on life on the planet in stability, now failed to hold anything down. Everything that once existed was now escaping into the vast void of outer space. It may have been a dream, but the last thing Daniel felt, was a comforting feeling of floating that was to last for all of eternity.

A brief author's note regarding the next short story

I have lived in Andover since I was seven years old. Over the last few years, the town I have grown up in has seen more than its fair share of tragedy. It is heartbreakingly sad, that a number of young people for a number of different reasons have decided to take their own lives here. A similar series of events of multiple individual suicides had happened in Wrexham, Wales in around the year 2011.

All of the deaths that have occurred in Andover appeared to be unrelated, except for the fact that the cause of death in most cases, was by hanging. Two of my dear friends Jason and Emma were among those who killed themselves. Both of them had been suffering from depression as I understand, but both had young families who they were equally devoted to.

Whatever it was that finally pushed them over the edge, it must have taken them to such a dark place, that I can only hope and pray that no one else ever finds themselves in. I deliberated a great deal about whether or not to include this story, as it might cause pain to the families who have experienced such a tragedy. I only decided to include it, in the hope that it may help others who are suffering; to realize the pain that is left behind after a loved one ends their own life.

So I dedicate the next story to the memory of Emma and Jason, and to all of the towns lost voices, who have all been taken from us far too soon. May you all rest in peace.

Emma's Ghost

David lay rigid and motionless on his bed. With nothing much to do these days, most of the time he found himself just looking upward and yet again today he found himself staring blankly at the patterns in the elevated ripples of Artex that protruded from the ceiling. The light was switched off in his room and the place was deathly quiet.

Time now seemed to have lost all sense of meaning. He could not remember the last time that he had properly slept, or the last time that he had even eaten for that matter. Now there seemed little purpose in anything anymore. He hated his own existence. He hated life since the loss of Emma.

He missed hearing the sound of her talking to him. It seemed strange to him now that her voice was what he missed about her the most. He was surprised that it was not the touch of her skin on his, nor the scent of her perfume, or the suppleness and feel of her naked body, but he missed her voice and the way that she spoke to him on the telephone. She would just chatter away and occasionally breaking into the most insane laughter. Her voice and that insane laughter were the things that always made him smile the most.

He remembered the first time that they had met. She was all alone in a bar. She was happily dancing by herself on the dance floor to the repetitive music that the D.J. was playing. At first he had been apprehensive about approaching her. After all she had a very pretty face, and she seemed more than a little out of his league. Then across the bar he saw the occasional fleeting glimpses of her smile as she chanced a few moments of direct eye contact with him. She thought that he was really cute and he had also made her nervous too.

She was dancing around so energetically, despite the fact that she was holding a glass of wine in her hand. Every time she felt nervous, she sipped a little from her large glass of rose. He could see how the other men in the bar were sizing her up and he felt that if he waited much longer he might have blown it. He knew that it was the right time to take a chance, so he took a deep breath and made the walk over to talk to her.

He smiled as he approached her. He saw that her glass was running low of alcohol so he offered to buy her another drink. After a short pause, she finally accepted the offer with a smile and then accompanied him to the bar. She seemed genuinely nice and friendly, and after just a few minutes of talking to her, it almost felt as if they had been friends forever. In transpired that they both shared similar interests in films and music, and that surprisingly they lived relatively close to each other.

During that first evening together, they talked, laughed, danced and then even sang a song together on the karaoke system. In truth the song sounded awful, but they had both drunk so much alcohol, that neither of them cared a bit. At the end of the night they had walked home together and she had taken hold of his arm and rested her head against his shoulder. They stumbled drunkenly together toward her home.

They stopped just outside of her house, and under the bright and hazy orange blur of the street lights, they kissed for long and passionate moments. For quite some time afterward they became inseparable. It wasn't long before they ended up in bed together at his home. Embarrassingly they were almost caught as his parents came home early from a night out and they were half naked on the living room sofa. He had already taken her virginity earlier that night, and despite the slight pain she had felt, Emma was desperate to feel him inside of her again.

They stayed together for just under two years, until life managed to get in the way as it sometimes sadly does and then they both started to drift apart. It was not like they had fallen out of love though; they just seemed to spend less and less time together. They still remained close, until they both made the decision that they needed to live a little and both wanted to see other people, but the close bond that they shared still remained.

Lovers came and went for the both of them, but still they would confide in each other when things were going wrong. From time to time they would still secretly share intense passionate nights together. Then life started to go wrong for the both of them, and they confided in each other throughout their darkest moments. Now he was alone, and it hurt that she was gone. Life was dark and he had no one like her left that he could talk to at times like this.

He looked around the room and saw that his mobile phone 180was sat lifeless on his bed close to him. He was now a figure of deep sorrow and no one even seemed to call him anymore. He touched the screen of his phone and looked at his text messages. Only one string of texts still remained. It was a strand of texts messages between him and Emma. These words were the last remaining remnants of what they had, and now they were all that he had to hold. The last words he had shared with his long lost lover.

There last messages to each other were just simple electronic data in the form of a string of personal text messages between David Rees and Emma Jenkins, but they were priceless memories to him. He had reviewed the lines of text over again and again reading and absorbing every single word. These simple moments that they had once exchanged, they were so precious now that she had gone.

They had once been inseparable, but as distance had grown between them, they had still remained closer than friends and the very last text he had sent to her was to wish her well and for a speedy recovery from her anxiety and panic attacks. Those last texts they had sent to each other revealed just how dark they had both felt about their lives, and they would meet most nights to try and console each other. A week later, came that fateful night they had walked to the forest together. Then in that single moment, she was gone. She had disappeared from his life forever.

A single tear launched itself downward from the precipice of his eye without a hint of prejudice or remorse, and spent the moment of its short existence travelling what was an already well worn path down the length of his cheek. He had no idea why he felt the sudden impulse to type a message to her, but he reacted spontaneously by typing a response on the screen to his deceased lover.

He typed the words onto the screen, simple words that conveyed exactly how he felt. The words just said 'I miss you.' and then after a moments deliberation of trying to find any sense in what he was about to do, he still could not. He pressed the send button anyway. The sentiment that he was sending, was still a genuine one, even if she would never read it. For the last few months he had felt a deep sense of foreboding that had left him sad and lonely.

To him, she was more than just a former lover, she was also his closest friend, and if such a thing existed, she felt like she was his one true soul mate. The light on his mobile phone soon faded as the electronic message was sent into the ether. He then placed the phone back down by the side of his bed. He then lay back down on top of the duvet. He set the daily alarm to awaken him just five short hours from now (just in case he slept). It seemed pointless these days, but it was just a habit he couldn't break.

He closed his eyes, and tried once more to drift away, but sleep would fail him again tonight, as had often been the case recently. Instead he just lay there motionless on the bed, silently gazing up at the ceiling. His mind began to drift away as had happened to him almost daily now. Instead of sleep, his thoughts just drifted off elsewhere. Some might have called this having an out of body experience. To him the travels that he was taking were just tricks of his mind. After a few moments, his spirit had taken him far away from his body again.

He found himself walking alone along a long and barren motorway. The sun was blazing down from the heavens above. It was intense and he could actually feel the warmth bearing down on his skin. The heat was searing and the temperature was causing visible heat shudders to rise up from the grey tarmac on the road. It was like being on holiday on a foreign shore for the first time. The intensity of the suns power now seemed to feed his body with a new source of endless energy.

He stopped by the side of the road and then looked backward and forward along the motorway. There were no signs of life. Strangely there were also no vehicles of any sort in either direction. For some reason that was unknown to him, he was wearing a thick heavy black leather jacket. He took the jacket off, and without hesitation, he dropped it down by the side of the road and then he stood still watching in awe.

The jacket that had fallen from his hand seemed to sink into the heated tarmac and it was quickly swallowed up by the road. Within seconds it was completely gone from sight. It was almost as if it had blended in with the grey surface and become part of the road itself. After deliberating for a few seconds as to which way he should go he decided to walk forwards. There was no point in trying to walk backward he was sure of that.

He walked onward for what seemed like miles and his body was now visibly sweating from the intense heat. He decided that before he carried on, he should also remove his faded black t-shirt and black jeans. They felt as if they were just absorbing the heat. Once he was free of his clothes, he continued walking. After a short while, his skin started to blister from the relentless power of the sun above. It too had to come off. He started to peel back his skin, until his internal organs were bare, and then he felt the urge to carry on walking.

He heard the sound of a car engine somewhere in the distance. He turned and looked around to locate the source of the sound, and he saw that a car was approaching from behind him. As it drew nearer, David began to wish that he still had his skin. Whoever was driving the car might be freaked out by his appearance, and this might be his only chance of grabbing a lift. The black car was glimmering in the soaring heat and as it approached him, the driver noticed him walking alone on the road, and the car began to slow down.

The windows of the car were blackened out. The passenger window was slowly lowered. David leant into the car to talk to the driver, and he was surprised to see that the driver had no skin either. He looked just like David did. The driver then spoke to him.

"Don't be afraid, we're all the same underneath. Do you need a ride son?" The driver asked.

"Where are you headed?" asked David. The driver raised a bony finger and pointed forwards.

"To the end of the road." The driver answered.

"But I haven't finished dreaming yet." David answered "I'm still waiting for Emma, my lost lover. I need her to appear. I'll get the next ride that comes along." David said, and nodded his appreciation for the offer. The driver shrugged his shoulders and then pulled away at speed. David watched as the car sped off in to the distance.

David continued to walk forward. He carried on walking until the sky grew dark, and rain finally began to fall. As his body cooled, the dream ended, his eyes opened and he found himself back at home once more.

He was back on his bed. He had hoped that he would sleep instead of having these vivid out of body experiences, but three would be no sleep again tonight. The dream had sent his mind reeling and he could not understand the message behind what he had experienced. He tried to calm his constant mind chatter. Instead of thinking he stared upward at that same bland ceiling. He lay there motionless on the bed until he could think of nothing else, but Emma.

Through the seemingly timeless haze of an early morning sunrise, a sound of an incoming message echoed throughout a hollow and empty feeling bedroom. The phone vibrated throughout the top of the pine chest of drawers upon which it was sat. David reached out with a tired right arm and retrieved his phone. He imagined that he was dreaming as he read the name of the sender of the message. The name on the telephone told him that the message had come from Emma.

He opened the message up quickly and it said three simple words that sent palpitations coursing throughout David's chest. He sat bolt upright as he eyed the text. He read it over and over again trying to make any sense of what he was reading. The message was daunting. He read the simple line out loud; it just said 'Let me go.'

David had not been to work in such a very long time; such was the extent of his depression. It was almost as if his mind had refused to function properly anymore. He had pills still left in his bedroom, but he didn't want to start taking them again. He had been prescribed them a long while back. For a few months before her death, he had taken them on a daily basis. They had soon stopped working the way he hoped, so he stopped taking them. Now he felt as if his life was in such a mess that the days became blurred, and he often thought about taking all the pills. He felt so stupid that he could not even remember dressing himself in the mornings anymore.

Everything had so dramatically changed in his world since she had gone. Now he could no longer find any reason to eat or the ability to sleep, he seemed to be isolated from all his friends, and none of his work colleagues even acknowledged him. The only time he felt strong enough to go in to work, he had felt like a social leper, and after a short time he left building. Now he just barely felt as if he existed to anyone at all.

The message at least had given him a small but nonetheless ridiculous amount of hope. It wasn't time for her to leave. He had still felt such an attachment to her. Just a week after he had lost her, he first saw her apparition. The pain of her being gone had already torn him apart, and then when he saw her, just standing there as if she were still with him, it had really frightened him. Then she looked right at him and everything seemed to change in an instant. He ran toward her, but his fingers seemed to slip through her as if she had never really been there at all. She carried on walking, while he fell to his knees and sobbed, and no one even batted an eyelid.

Andover town centre was in desperate need of rejuvenation or at least an injection of life. The shops were lacking and limited in variety, and even most of those who lived closest to the town, chose to shop in the surrounding towns where the choices were much greater. Yet still the town itself had somehow still managed to retain a small amount of its former market town charm.

David had always dreamed of moving out of here to a bigger town or city, but his plans had always been pipe dreams and for some reason he had never found the strength to leave. These days he would walk the high street and around the single square of shops repeatedly. He had little else to do with his time, and as he walked amongst the busy shoppers he just seemed to disappear amongst the townsfolk and even his former friends. His sorrowful existence seemed just too much for them to bear.

Just days after the loss, he had started to suffer from a really deep sense of grief, and he found that people would look at him a lot differently now. Those he once knew well would sometimes look at him but would not register his presence; it was almost as if they knew him, and wanted to maybe acknowledge him, but they would no longer able to stop and talk to him.

At first it had bothered him. A few times he even shouted at people he once knew, after they had simply walked past and ignored him. He understood about the stigma attached to the illness he had. He knew that some would treat those with depression almost like lepers. Some people just didn't seem to know how to react to him anymore. In the end, he put it all down to sheer bloody ignorance of his condition.

He sank further and further down and after a few weeks, he just gave up trying. He would spend his days just locked away in his room keeping himself away from everything, including his parents. That would only change from the moment that he decided to brave the outside world once more, on a warm sunny day. That was the day that he saw Emma's ghost for the second time.

She was walking straight towards him. She was dressed in a summer dress that was a deep purple shade. That had always been her favourite colour. Her hair was long and curly, just as he remembered it. The gentle brown curls bounced around her shoulders as if she was really real. He closed his eyes for a few seconds and then opened them up again, he was expecting her image to fade, but instead her image still remained, and her face was as vibrant as ever.

He began to walk slowly toward her. As he drew closer and closer to her, her image suddenly became hazed. Perhaps it had all been a dream after all? He reached out his arms to hold her, but she passed straight through him once again. He stopped dead in his tracks. He could not feel his own breathing anymore. It felt as if some form of electricity had passed through his entire body, but this time he felt as if he had connected with her in some small way.

"Emma!" He shouted.

Emma stopped suddenly and looked back over her shoulder, but she stared straight through him. Her eyes looked empty and sad, and he called out her name once again, but she did not hear him this time. Instead of recognition, he saw tears now falling down her face. She looked so scared and confused. She started to run away and try as he might, the faster he tried to run after her, the further she seemed to slip from him. He just could not catch up with her.

To see her tears had made him feel sad. He sat down alone on a bench close to The George yard arch and pondered if he could help her spirit find its way home. The experience had knocked the wind out of him. He had never been religious, or had a moment that could be even considered to be a religious experience.

As a child, he had attended Sunday school once on the insistence of his parents, but the experience bored him a great deal. Perhaps it had something to do with his opinion that the idea of an afterlife or heaven and hell, was that it had always made great stories for television and films, but until now it had never been something that was really real to him.

He wondered why he had encountered her now, why today in the town. Had she been aware that he was there? Her face seemed so sad and distant, and it hurt him to see her in pain. Was he the one who was making her cry? There were just too many questions from this encounter that had been left unanswered.

A stranger then sat down next to him on the cold metal bench. The man looked as if he were homeless. His appearance was unkempt, and he looked as if he hadn't shaved or bathed in a long time. A young man walked past them both as they sat on the bench. He was wearing a black muscle top, with a swastika printed on the front. He was walking a Rottweiler dog that he held on to with a thick neck chain.

The dog suddenly went berserk for no apparent reason. David jumped a little as the dog began to snarl, and bark at the old man who was sat next to him. The old man smiled and went to pet the snarling dog on the head. The dog cowered down to the floor crawling away on its front feet, and the old man laughed out loud. The dog's owner, completely bemused by the dog's random behavior, then dragged the animal forward away from the bench.

The old man then turned toward David and smiled. As he began a conversation, it was as if he knew exactly why David was troubled.

"Sometimes when people take their own lives, they get caught. Sometimes they are stuck here, just...waiting." David was surprised at the stranger's words; perhaps he looked as if he had genuinely seen a ghost.

"How did you know?" David asked.

"Believe it or not, I'm here to help those in need. I've helped many pass on before." The man answered. David just shook his head.

"You're kidding me right; you're talking about ghosts and the afterlife?" He asked. The man nodded his head slowly.

"It's something like that. Each of us contains a mind with a body to host it on its life long journey. Now most people don't think of life like that. They think….well let's just say that they think things are the other way round. If you think about it though, everything that you do every day, the normal things like breathing and the unseen functioning of your organs, well that is your brain telling your body to do that. The brain is driven by thoughts, but where do thoughts come from? They come from the mind. The mind is thinking out loud and the brain reacts to it."

David thought about his words for a few moments.

"I guess that sort of makes sense." David said. He expected the man to be dumb and to be emanating a dirty smell, but he was surprised by the level of intelligence that this man had shown. Also he actually smelt really clean, which was totally unexpected. David looked at the man's hands, and they were also meticulously tidy, but there was something odd about them that he couldn't quite work out.

They looked if anything a little too clean, almost as if they glowed with cleanliness. The man offered David his hand.

"The name's Graham." He said, and after a moment's apprehension, David reached out and shook his hand. It felt extremely smooth, just as he had thought that it might. "Mine's David." He returned, and the man smiled at him.

"So what happens when people are stuck here? What happens then?" David asked. The man looked straight at him.

"Well there's a reason that some spirits don't pass on. In the past some would say that suicide was a sin, and that God was punishing them for taking their own lives. That is just pure poppycock though."

David smiled, Graham was either a little on the eccentric side, or maybe he had a point.

"Do you think that there is a God?" David asked him, he was genuinely curious about the question, but at the same time he couldn't help the little grin which had appeared on his face. He wasn't expecting the response that came.

"Of course God exists, he exists in any way shape name or form that you want him to exist!' Graham shouted. "You think your ancestors were damned monkeys?"

David had to admit that the whole evolutionary theory had never quite resonated with him, and if mankind had evolved from fishes, then why had we not evolved even further?

"So what do you think God is?" David asked. Graham grinned at him, as he regained his composure.

"It's like what I just said about the mind, the mind exists, but some call it the soul. It's the soul that tells you what to do when hard choices have to be made. It's that sixth sense that tells you not to take that turn down a dark alley late at night. The one that tells you where to find the things you misplaced. The thing which lets you know, that something bad is going to happen. God, to me is the greatest mind that ever existed."

David took a few moments to absorb the words he had heard. Again they seemed to make some sense.

Graham still felt the need to expand the answer even further. "God is mind, man is mind. When people pass on, parts of those people are left here for all to remember them by. Some can even communicate with those parts, and that my friend, is why you can't let her go. Part of you is still tied to her and you have to find a way to break that link. Only when you fully understand what needs to be done, will you ever be able to break the tie and to let her go." He said.

"Do you mean that it's my fault that I still see her?" David asked. He was more than a little puzzled by the words that he had heard. Graham lowered his head and thought carefully for a few seconds.

"You have to find a way to let go David. Find a way to break the routine, ghosts will follow the paths they always did in life. They follow a well worn trail of an electrical signature they left when they walked the Earth. Habits are hard to break. People are tied to places that they used to visit. To loved ones, and friends, they still walk the same routes they did in life. Some of them just can't ever let go, and they are stuck here forever. I've said all that I can say. Now you must do what you need to do." Graham concluded.

Graham then stood up from the bench and offered David his hand once again. "I just want to wish you good luck my friend." He offered. "This won't be easy for either of you."

Taking Graham's hand firmly within his own grasp David shook his hand with a good strong grip. Then he turned Graham's hand over before he let it go. Graham had no markings or palm lines on his hand or any fingerprints at all. He had completely clear skin.

Graham pulled his hand gently away and smiled once more as he walked away from the bench. David watched him leave and then turned his head around to his right. Something made him turn his head and now he could see Emma once more. Now she was walking away from the town and toward her old house. David was determined to try and help her this time. He stood up from the bench and started to follow her, but always at a safe distance. Graham seemed a little on the kooky side, but what he said had made sense. He and Emma had walked these steps so many times before, now it seemed as if she were following the familiar path back to her home.

His connection with her must have been really strong, as he never lost sight of her. Every now and again she would turn around, and it was almost as if she sensed that he was there. Every time she turned she seemed to stare straight through him again. Her face was now incredibly sad. Her expressions were now a mixture of both fear and anguish. David felt an overwhelming sense of hopelessness building up inside of him. He wanted to stop following her, but at the same time, he so desperately wanted to help her, and it left him torn as to what to do.

Her pace seemed to gather as she was nearing her parent's home. Then she turned the corner and he finally lost sight of her. He walked right up to her parent's front door. He paused for few seconds and just waited. He wondered if he was doing the right thing, he decided that he must at least try. He raised his finger to the doorbell, but then he paused again. How could he explain to them what he was doing here, they might have him locked up for being crazy!

He had never felt more insane than he did right now. Instead of using the doorbell, he lowered his finger and walked around to the side of the house. He peered through the ground floor window into Emma's former bedroom. The room was just how he had remembered it. Her parents had not changed a thing at all. Perhaps they never would. The wallpaper, the posters they furniture it all remained. Then he saw Emma in the shadows. She was sat on the bed and she was sobbing into her hands while she rocked backward and forward. She was in obvious distress. Now he desperately wanted to hold her and save her from this pain.

Emma suddenly became motionless. It was as if she had sensed him staring through the window at her. She stood up from the bed and walked toward the window. She lifted her right hand and placed her palm and fingers on the glass. David raised his hand up and placed it on the other side of the glass to match hers. For just a second, it felt that even though the thickness of the glass, that they had made a connection. Then Emma screamed, and he turned away from the window with tears streaming down his face. He felt her agony and the sound that she had made was soul destroying.

He could have walked away right then. He was about to leave, but at the last second he changed his mind. He could not let her suffer anymore. He had to at least try and talk to her parents. He walked back around to the front of the house, and placed his finger on the doorbell. The chimes of the doorbell echoed throughout the hallway, and then they slowly faded away to nothing. There was no response. He tried again, this time holding the doorbell down for a little while longer, but still there was no response.

He then felt as if there were someone stood on the other side of the door; were they just standing there silently, watching him? Why would they not answer the door? It made no sense at all. If it was Emma, perhaps she was afraid of trying to communicate with him. Maybe she just didn't know how to.

He opened the letterbox and whispered out her name "Emma, is that you?" He asked. There were a few moments of painful silence. Then a quiet response came from the other side of the glass paneled door as Emma's voice spoke.

"Let me find some peace, please!" She was sobbing as she spoke, and he felt the pain in her voice. If only she would open the door to him.

David was hurting too. He wondered if it might be better for them both if he stopped trying and let her be, but now after hearing her cries, he had never seen her in so much pain. He was truly torn as to what to do. Today she might not be ready to leave this place. He would leave her here for a little while longer. Mentally he himself could not go any further today anyway. Slowly he walked away from her house, leaving Emma to cry all alone in the hallway.

After returning home David went to the kitchen and looked inside the kitchen cupboards. There was nothing in there that he wanted to eat. They no longer seemed to buy the things that he once loved anymore, like they had forgotten him. It didn't matter though, he could not remember the last time he had actually eaten anything here anyway. He solemnly made his way into his bedroom once more and lay down on the bed. He thought to himself about how lonely his life was now. He no longer had visits from anyone. He truly felt alone without Emma.

He closed his eyes but again sleep would not come. Instead he lay there. He stared upward once more at the spiral patterns on the ceiling. The patterns started to twist and turn before his eyes as he soon found himself drifting into a trance like state once more. At first these experiences had scared him, but now he felt that he was learning from each of these spiritual travels of his mind.

His spirit rose up from his bed, and he projected his new form upward and straight through the solid roof of the house. He travelled high and wide, until he was far away from his room. His final destination would always be a mystery, and today he found himself standing all alone in a field of lavender. The colour purple was vibrant amongst the flowers growing in all directions around him, for as far as his eyes could see. The wind was blowing gently, and as he sat down the soft breeze blew across his face.

As he sat in the middle of the field, he drew the scent of the purple flowers deeply into his nostrils. The sweet scent resonated throughout his entire body, and it seemed to feed something like a new life force into every cell of his existence. The wind gathered pace and it soon whistled through the flowers. They danced around him as if they were now bowing down in honour of his very presence amongst them.

He sat cross legged silently in the field while time just passed him by. Clouds formed and then dissipated above his head, they were dancing to heavenly symphonies in the sky above him. Sudden storms broke, and the rain that then fell, soaked him through to the skin. Then the storms faded as quickly as they had begun. Still he remained motionless in the field. His eyes were closed as if they were sealed by time itself. He continued to just breathe in the scent of the Lavender. Life was so much better for him now. Now he was living without the confining boundaries of time to hold him back.

The animals and insects had watched him for a time and slowly they began to grow brave. They approached him inquisitively as they might approach a statue, but he did not mind them at all. They tenderly moved across his skin, examining him closely. He was now at peace with all of nature. The sun rose high into the sky and within what felt like seconds the sun had dried his sodden clothing. Still he remained here motionless while life went on with its business, oblivious to his presence.

Seeds then began to fall to the ground all around him. They sank deep into the soil and then they quickly grew into tall trees that surrounded and protected him. It was his dream and nothing could change this. He remained there for what could have been a thousand years, maybe ten thousand years, possibly it was even more. His body then slowly turned to dust. As the dust began to fall, it was carried away with the wind. Slowly he crumbled away piece by piece until there was nothing left of him at all.

Once he had faded, Emma walked into the field and knelt down where his body had previously been. She placed a small note on the ground that just said 'I miss you, I love you. I'm sorry.' And then she walked away. While she walked, she sang a sad song about a long lost lover who had never found his way back home. The sweetness of her angelic voice carried on the wind. Then it all started to fade away once more and he was back on his bed again with his eyes wide open, and tears of joy were flowing freely.

He never realized that seeing Emma's ghost would affect him so deeply. All he kept telling himself was that somehow she needed him to help her. He vowed to himself that he would do all that he could to end her misery. Seconds later brilliant spears of light in the form of rays of sunshine began to pour in through his bedroom window. He knew that even if he found a way to save her, Emma would always be with him. He walked out of his bedroom, but as he did, he left the door open. The shards of light in the room behind him quickly began to fade as he went.

There had to be someone that he could go to for advice. He had no idea about the spirit world or who he could go to for help. He knew that he had seen many books on the afterlife and ghosts in his local library. It seemed as good a starting point as any. He walked in the direction of the library. It was only a short distance to the town centre and he arrived in the library. It was so quick it was almost as if he had thought himself there.

Searching through the rows of brightly coloured books, he sought out anything that might hold some clues or hint of information that he could find useful. The paranormal section in Andover library was surprisingly large; and the search might take some time. His eyes were then drawn to a title that had instantly gripped him for some reason. He removed the book from the shelf and took it to a quiet reading corner where he placed it gently on the table.

The book was titled 'Talking to the Dead' By Christine Little. He thought that the name of the author sounded familiar, and reading the cover notes, it became clear that is was by no means a coincidence. It transpired that the author lived in a small village called Grateley, located just outside of Andover. It was not far at all from where he lived. He opened up the book and then began to read the introduction.

'At the age of twelve, I was involved in a terrible accident. Whilst in the car with my grandfather, I witnessed him suffer a major heart attack. He lost control and crashed the car through a bridge. We went through the wall, and sank into a fast flowing river beneath. The car quickly filled with water, and before I knew it, I was completely submerged and trapped without air. As water filled my lungs, all the days of my short life flashed before my eyes.

My grandfather came to my rescue in those murky waters. He released my seatbelt and swam with me to the edge of the river above. I was unconscious so he forced air repeatedly into my lungs. I then started to come round. I could hear sirens somewhere in the distance. As I sat upright, I was choking but I was able to spit out the water. I then watched as my grandfather turned away from me and he walked back down into the cold waters. I held out my hand to him, but he just turned and smiled gently at me, and then he slipped back under the water for the last time.

I was taken to a hospital where I spent the next three days. When the doctors thought that I was strong enough to hear the truth, my parents told me about my grandfather's death. They told me that his body was recovered from the car; and that he had died before he had even hit the water. I told them that they were wrong, and that he had saved my life, but they simply dismissed my story as a wonderful dream.

No one could ever fully explain how I got out of the car and on to the embankment that day. Only I fully understood and knew my story to be the truth. From that day on, I found that something had changed inside of me. Because I had technically died, the boundaries between life and death blurred and I became a channel to those who had passed. I found that I could now communicate with the dead.

At first I was petrified at what was happening to me, but most of the spirits that I encountered were friendly, and in time I came to accept this gift. I am now able to channel messages from those who have passed over, to help those who are suffering from a personal loss.'

The book then went on to detail various case studies and details of séances that had been held within Christine's own home. Some of the episodes seemed to bring closure and a sense of peace; some had ended in pain and heartache for those involved. The accounts appeared genuine enough though, and she seemed to be someone who might be willing to assist him with his mission of mercy. To David this was all that mattered.

He stood up and went to reach for his wallet. It wasn't in any of his pockets. He desperately needed to take this book home with him though. He looked around, but could see no one else close by. He tucked the book inside of his jacket out of sight and then began to walk toward the exit. He was relieved to see that none of the usual assistants were present at the desk. If he had taken the time to look around, he would have in fact noticed, that the library was completely empty.

As he walked down the cold marble library stairs, the lights behind him had begun to go out row after row. The darkness had started to follow him, but it was still at a fair distance away from him. It was biding its time, the darkness was not sure if he was ready to be taken just yet. The spirit knew that it had to be one way or the other for him, and the choice would have to be made soon.

He took the book back home to his bedroom. He lay down and then read the book from cover to cover. This woman seemed to either really know what she was talking about, or she was one of the most genuine frauds that he had ever encountered. He knew that if she was genuine, then he really needed her help, and he would have to find a way to get in touch with her in person. He reached for his phone and then he began to trawl the internet for her contact details. He soon found out all of the information that he needed to know. Clairvoyancy was a vibrant and lucrative business these days, or so it seemed.

He copied the number given on the webpage and pasted it into his phone. He then called the number that was showing online as Christine's home telephone number. It rang repeatedly, but there was no human response. Eventually the ringing ceased and the call was then redirected to an answering machine. He really hated talking to these things, but as this was so important, he would have to force himself to leave a message just this once.

'Hello…. my name is David, and I need your help to save my friend….' Before he could continue, the telephone made a clicking sound as it was being picked up. The other end of the telephone was silent for a few seconds, and then a woman's voice eventually answered.

'This isn't the way that I do things; you shouldn't have contacted me this way David.' Confusion filled David's face; He wasn't sure how else he could have contacted her, but he now felt really rude for intruding on her privacy.

'I'm sorry, I'm not sure what else I was supposed to do, I need your help though.' He said. The other end of the line then went quiet for what seemed like an eternity once again, and Christine then finally began to speak.

"I need you to come to my house as soon as you can, I will be at home tonight. At eight o'clock tonight, I will leave my front door open for you to enter the house. Come into the living room, and my friends will be there with me. There will be an empty chair waiting for you. I need you to sit in that chair, and tell us how it is that we can help you. Whatever happens, and this is important, you need to remain in the chair, no matter what. Do not leave unless I tell you to do so. You and I are now in a great deal of danger. This needs to be done slowly and sensibly. Please follow my instructions to the letter and I will do all that I can to end your suffering."

With that the phone then went dead. David felt his body temperature go cold. Her words had both shocked and scared him, and his skin now felt like ice. He stood up and stared out from his bedroom window. Dark clouds seemed to be gathering in the distance, and the weather fronts seemed to be battling each other for supremacy in the skies above. Today the dark clouds seemed to be winning the eternal battle, and the sky grew black as they storm clouds grew in strength and then they blocked out any visible signs of the sun in the sky.

Time slipped by until the moment that he found himself stood waiting patiently on the platform of the train station. Both of the platforms were totally deserted, he stood all alone. The train he needed to take slowly drew in and when it finally ground to a halt, he opened the door and stepped on board the train destined for Grateley. It was a short journey from Andover, but David was filled with apprehension. He had never even met a real life clairvoyant before, but his mother was a firm believer in such matters and would watch and read about these things religiously.

The train pulled away but for some strange reason, it felt as if it were travelling a little slower than it should. He sat facing backward and stared out from the windows at the scenery that had just passed him by. The train was unusually empty, but he put it down to the time of night that he was travelling. In fact unknown to David, he was the only person on board the entire train.

Feeling a little tired, possibly from his lack of sleep, he closed his eyes as the countryside just rolled on by. The sound of the train's wheels rolling along the metal tracks was soothing and they turned over and over again as the train sped toward its destination. He felt his mind begin began to drift away from his body once more. He wondered where he was going to find himself this time. His question was soon answered as he found himself at the foot of a clearing in a forest that looked a little familiar too familiar to him. He was sure that he had been here before, but he didn't recognize where it was. It gave him chills.

The entrance to the clearing was dark, but nonetheless he still felt the urge to explore. He walked over a large amount of uneven ground, without ever once losing his footing. Branches cracked underneath his feet as he walked deeper into the forest. At first the trees had been eerily silent, but now he began to hear the sound of the wind as it grew in strength until it whistled through the bare branches all around him.

For the first time since he had been having these experiences, he now felt uneasy. He was already deep in the forest now, and despite his fears he felt as if he were being urged to walk on just a little bit further. In the distance he heard the barking of what might have been a wild dog. The fallen leaves that covered the ground then began to rise up. As the ground awoke, all around the wind raised small whirlwinds of sodden leaves that now circled all about him.

As the wind grew even stronger in its intensity, the spirals were lifting up in an ever greater number from the floor. They seemed to be growing taller and wider. The he saw a lone figure that was underneath a tree, directly in the path ahead of him, and he swallowed hard as he now realized what was happening up ahead.

David became frozen. He stood rooted to the spot. Just up ahead the figure that he had just seen was trying to commit suicide. He was distant enough that he could not recognize the figure, and he was not sure that he even wanted to see its face. He moved toward it, and as he drew closer, he realized that the figure was still alive. Whoever it was, they were struggling to break free from the noose around there neck.

He had to act fast. He ran toward the figure to try and help whoever it was to break free from the rope. As he went to run forward, from out of nowhere a wild dog jumped up at him and slammed hard into his body. The impact of the animal striking him knocked all the air out of him and the speed of the collision forced him to fall down to the ground. He stood up quickly and faced the animal head on. The dog was huge, but it was not a breed that he recognized. The without warning, it lurched forward to attack its prey once more.

David fought against the creature as bravely as he could, but he struggled to keep the snarling dog at bay. Its teeth were exposed and it jaws snapped repeatedly as it tried to bite down into David's skin. David suddenly tripped over something that was buried in the ground. He fell awkwardly to the ground. The animal seized its chance and it was now on top of him. Saliva from the dog's mouth was drooling down on to David's face. Reaching out with one arm whilst the other held off the creature, David felt the ground around him. At first he found nothing that he could use, and then luckily David managed to grab a large piece of a broken branch.

Immediately he struck the dog around the head with the makeshift weapon. The first strike had little effect apart from temporarily startling the animal. The second strike had more of a swing to it and as it struck the dog fully around the side of the head, it yelped in pain. It rolled away for a few seconds seemingly stunned by the blow.

The sudden retreat gave David a few seconds to get to his feet. He now had to make a choice. He could either run forward and try and help the struggling figure, or he could try to get out of here as fast as he could. Even though this was only a dream, he was still petrified of the strength and ferocity of the animal. David decided to run for it.

He turned and made for the entrance to the clearing. The figure ahead now seemed to have stopped struggling, and as the figure swung slowly in the wind, he knew that he was probably already too late. He picked up speed as he ran further and further away. He looked back over his shoulder, and saw that the dog had recovered enough to realize that its prey was now escaping. It barked repeatedly, and then began to chase after him.

The Dog was incredibly agile for its size, David knew that it would soon catch up with him, and now he had no other choice but to turn around and fight the animal once more. No matter how much he dreaded the thought, it was the only way he was going to get out of this. It was either kill the animal or he would be at the animal's mercy.

As David turned to face his attacker, the dog was already upon him, and it jumped at his chest knocking him backward yet again. The impact forced David to drop the lump of branch that he had been carrying. David struck out at the animal with his fists, but the animal was too large and now it was proving to be just too strong for him. He fought with all of his might, but the dog was fast, and it was ferocious. Sensing victory, the animal bit down hard into David's left arm.

The teeth tore through his clothes and deep into his flesh. The grip that the dog now had on his arm made David scream out in pain. The dog was winning, and it was about to make a final fatal launch toward David's throat. He closed his eyes and waited for the inevitable end. At that exact moment the train pulled to a stop in Grateley station. The sudden braking as they had arrived at the destination had jarred David awake. Although consciously he was back on the train, he was still petrified by the reality of the encounter.

He quickly jumped to his feet. It was an odd sensation as he felt hot from an intense sweat, but at the same time he felt cold all over. This was the most insane nightmare that he had ever experienced. The train was stationary, and David realized that he had to get off the train before it pulled away again. He then made his way down toward the carriage door.

As he reached the door, he did not know why he looked back, but when he did, he felt the fear of God inside of him. The same devil dog from his dream was now walking slowly between the aisles of the carriage and straight toward him. It was still some distance away, but as the dog crawled its way forward, the lights in the carriages behind it blew out as the glass tubes explosively shattered one by one.

David jumped from the door, almost tripping as he landed outside, he quickly turned and slammed the door closed behind him. This made no sense at all. Surely this had all been just another part of his dream? Maybe he hadn't woken up yet? He moved back toward the door of the train, and checked the handle. It was safely closed. He then slowly raised his head slightly to peer inside of the window.

The dog jumped up at the glass, and the impact on the door scared David so much that he fell backward and onto the platform. The dog was not giving up on its intended prey. It was launching itself at the door and window repeatedly as it tried to smash its way out of the train. It launched itself again and again at the door and although it looked like the door would hold, there were no guarantees. David now wanted to escape from the very nightmare that he himself had apparently brought to life.

The door held fast, and eventually the train started to move off from the station. The door was still being battered by the dog over and over again. He watched the train lights rolling away until they were dimmed in the distance. At last he felt that he was finally safe from the animal. He breathed deeply but the air was so cold, that he could not feel it as it entered his lungs. In fact he couldn't feel anything except the numb feeling that now covered all of his body.

An explanation for the devil dog jumping out from his dream and in to real life would have been welcome right now. Since he had last seen Emma, things had turned from bad to worse. He prayed that the clairvoyant would have some answers for him. He certainly wished for no more out of body episodes if they were going to be anything like the last one.

The village of Grateley was small. There were very few houses here. That afternoon he had used street view to search the village and from the look of the properties that surrounded him, he knew the house that he needed was only a little way further. When he arrived at the house he was pleased to see that as he had been told the front door was already open. It was something you seldom saw these days with the amount of crime on the rise. To see the open door gave him a welcome sense of trust between neighbors.

As he stepped over the doorstep, he found that the house was exactly as he had expected it to be. It looked old and almost gothic inside and out. It was the sort of place that a vampire would feel more than at home in. He walked onward further into the house, constantly watching and listening out for any sign of the host.

As he walked the length of the hallway, the wallpaper reminded him of a tie with a purple paisley design that he had owned some years prior. This was of course before he had developed any real sense of fashion. Back then he thought that it would make him look more grown up, instead it just made him look like an extra from an old seventies television episode instead. He had worn it just once, and then it took up a lengthy residence in the base of his wardrobe. There it remained for a further two years before he re-discovered it. Eventually it found its way to a charity shop along with some other seldom worn items.

He had almost reached the end of the hallway. It was dimly lit, and the dark wood staircase to his right, only added to the sense of foreboding. He expected to see a mirror hung somewhere in the hallway. From experience he knew that women had a tendency to have a last minute look at their own reflection before leaving the house. Here however, he could not see even the smallest of mirrors being present anywhere.

He walked on further until he had almost reached the end of the lengthy hallway. He was surprised that the host had still not come to welcome him in to the house yet. In front of him in the near darkness, he could make out a kitchen. He could see from the tiny open plan size of the room, that there was no one present in that room either.

Slightly ahead of him on the left hand side of the hall, a door had been left partially open. Through the gap, he could see candlelight flickering and the shadows they threw across the room now danced on the walls. This must be the living room, he thought to himself. The place was eerily quiet, so he opened the door slowly and carefully, and then he stepped inside. He was totally unsure as to what he was to expect.

The scene in front of him reminded him of an act from Macbeth. Three women were sat together around a large round wooden table. He had half expected the women to be middle aged, but all three were probably in their twenties, and their age surprised him. One of the three women wore dark glasses which were a prominent feature, even though the top of their heads were all covered with veils.

The woman with the glasses was resting both of her hands on the top of a white cane. Clearly she was blind. As David walked further into the room, the blind woman seemed to suddenly become short of breath. She held her chest in momentarily and then exhaled fully before breathing in again more deeply. Then she turned her head toward David, as if she were looking straight at him.

"David is now here with us." She stated calmly, and then she waved her hand in the direction of the empty chair at the table. David assumed that the blind woman had heard his footsteps as he had walked along the hall. Knowing that the blind learn to adapt to using every other sense, it was unremarkable to him that she also knew where the empty chair was. Perhaps this was all part of an act, if so he wasn't particularly impressed so far.

He already knew all about Christine, and he recognized her from the dust cover on the library book. As for the other two women who were present, he had no idea as to who they were. Unknown to him one of the women was Katie Mulliner, and she had a growing reputation as being one of the most powerful psychics in the whole of the country.

At seven years of age Katie Mulliner had started to lose her sight. Numerous doctors and specialists were consulted in a frantic and desperate attempt to save her vision, but nothing could be done to stop her ocular degeneration. As her eyesight began to fade, she began to develop a gift and in place of her eyesight, instead she had welcomed another remarkable form of vision.

All of her other senses did indeed heighten along with another sense that only a chosen few ever learn how to use. It was daunting to others, but as a child she had welcomed her new power. She had developed a clear ability to communicate directly with the dead.

The third woman present in the room was Stephanie Crook. At only twenty three years old, she was still a virtual child compared to the other two women. Her friends had always considered her either to be eccentric or bordering on actual clinical madness. As a child she claimed to constantly hear voices when no one else could. She would often be found having conversations with what her parents assumed were just harmless imaginary friends.

As she entered her teenage years, the problem just seemed to get worse instead of better. These were not just imaginary friends at all. The voices she heard actually belonged to the recently departed. Stephanie had always been in direct conversation with those tormented spirits who could not find a way to leave this spiritual plane. Any other person may have been driven mad by these constant visitations, but to Stephanie, this was nothing out of the ordinary. To her, it was often like watching television, and sometimes she chose to just tune them out.

All three of the remarkably powerful women were now sat together around the table. David sat down in the chair that he was previously offered and placed his arms on his lap. The table was highly polished, and although he was no expert in antique furniture, David was sure that this table was well aged and was probably valued in the hundreds or maybe even thousands of pounds.

While he sat patiently, he looked all around him just examining the room. The rest of the decor in the living room consisted of mainly glamorous artifacts from various different cultures and an awful lot of crystals. It may all have been to add to the effect of the ceremony, however David remained unphased. He wanted some answers, and he wanted them tonight.

Christine then began to speak.

"Whatever happens, we ask you again that you do not leave the sanctity of the chair." She asked. David nodded in agreement.

"I count three spirits present with us in the room.' Stephanie added. The look on her face now showed fear and apprehension. The three women held hands to support each other, but none extended their hands out to meet David's hands. He was more comfortable like this. He would have felt uneasy holding hands with strangers and he assumed they had already sensed this.

The room was serenely quiet. A single clock could be heard ticking on a marble mantle piece above an electric effect log fire. The fire was switched off, but the glow from the candles that were sat on the table, flickered elements of artificial life down on to the plastic logs. Katie threw her head back and breathed in deeply. The other two women closed their eyes and tilted back their heads in turn. Christine was the first to speak.

'I have a tormented spirit present in the room who is seeking closure. The spirit is trapped among the living and seeks redemption.' Stephanie began to breathe in quick gasps. Then her head tilted forward.

'I am filled with serenity. The saviour of all mankind sends an emissary. He seeks closure for the tormented spirit. He speaks for the fisher of men, the divine intervention, he who is the whisper in the wind. He cannot interfere; he can only wait to hear if the lost one makes the choice to leave willingly.' She then threw her head backward.

David was now starting to feel uneasy. This all sounded too far-fetched to have any real meaning. What was it she had said? 'The fisher of men.' Where was that line from? He seemed to think that he had heard the saying before somewhere. Then as if things hadn't been quite weird and dark enough before, everything started to take a definite turn for the worse, and then things in the room began to get very ominous indeed.

Katie's head then fell backwards even further. She began to sweat and she was visibly shaking, this only grew in intensity. As her head fell forwards, the shaking abruptly ceased. She looked at the seat David was sat in and a look of dread filled her face.

"Oh no…." She remarked. Her voice was now trembling. "He is here. The dark one, the devourer of souls is present here with us!" She sounded petrified by her own words.

Upon hearing the words that were uttered, Christine immediately made the sign of the cross on her body. Then she quickly reeled off a few sentences. To David, the string of random words sounded like it was some sort of prayer but quite possibly it was being said in Latin. Hearing the words she spoke un-nerved David even further.

Christine then took command of the table.

"Sprits of both planes present here, we claim sanctity. No one here present in the room, in any form can be touched by you. This room is sealed by the power of Christ and the blessings bestowed on this ground from a time before. This is our protected circle. You have no power to hurt those here!"

The room went silent, and then what sounded like an almighty clap of thunder shook the walls.

"It is just a matter of time!" Katie shouted aloud. Her voice was no longer her own, but it sounded like the words came from a demented male clown. Christine began to sweat a little. This was far more serious than she had first thought.

"Reveal your name!" Christine demanded. Her body was now also shaking and David could sense something was now very badly wrong.

"We are Legion. We are the fallen. Here to claim the lost soul." Katie answered. Her voice had changed again. It now seemed to be that of a young and playful child.

Stephanie then began to speak.

"Still you try to take the things not gladly given. You have no rightful claim here. Still you seek the power and his glory. He offered you redemption, but you chose another path. I will fight to save this soul's salvation." Stephanie answered.

The two women were sat facing each other. On one side of the room the candles seemed to glow brightly, on the other the shadows seemed to grow thicker and heavier. The eternal battle between good and evil was one that had been waged for millennia. Now David felt scared for the first time since he had been here. Katie then snarled a response.

"You fool. You follow him blindly as I once did. His power weakens by the day. His churches are now empty, as his servants are replaced with mine. He is all but forgotten here. Yet he still chooses to try and save them? They are worthless figures who will destroy all that was created. They kill one another without thought or pity, and all for the love of monetary gain. I have taught them well. His time here ended long ago." She laughed.

"He offers them nothing but forgiveness. He only knows the power of his love. He offers them redemption. His churches will always remain, as does his eternal love for them." Stephanie offered. Katie suddenly roared with laughter. A single thick line of saliva drooled out of her mouth and hung down from her chin.

"You sicken me!" She shouted aloud "They reject him. Look at what they have done to all that he created! He made them in his image, and then they molded themselves in mine. They crave possessions and material wealth, forgetting all that he taught them. So much for the beloved book he gave them!" She shouted.

"He will never forsake them!" Stephanie shouted. Again Katie responded to this with laughter.

"They have already forsaken him! My army continues to grow, and this errant soul will be mine. Then I will truly rise from the flames at last. It is my time to rule over them. One more lost soul claimed by me, and I will rise upon the Earth and I will have my vengeance. This lost soul holds the eternal balance of power.'

"Love will save this soul, and no matter how large your army. You will never win." Stephanie concluded.

If David had turned around, he would have seen that the dog from the train had quietly entered the hallway of the house, now it was sat just patiently waiting outside of the living room door. Its teeth were once again exposed, but it dare not enter into the room.

The temperature in the room suddenly dropped and David was starting to realize that things were beginning to get seriously out of control. This was all too much to take. He wanted to get out of here right now. Then he looked down at the floor and noticed something that he hadn't seen before. When he peered under the table, he saw that the table itself was sat directly inside of a massive pentagram that had been drawn on the wooden floorboards.

He shot up out of the chair, afraid of any dark powers that may be at work here. He had seen numerous films on witchcraft and demonology, and he knew that the pentagram was a powerful symbol. Christine immediately shouted a warning to him.

"Do not leave the safety of the table!" She knew that she had little time as it was obvious that he was about to leave the safety of the circle. She shouted out another sentence, again which seemed to be in Latin, and then broke her grip with the hands of the other two women. David left the circle just as the sitting had been safely closed.

"I beg of you both, to grant the time for an errant soul to choose the path of the righteous, protect the spirit keeper of the flame!" Then she blew out the candle in the middle of the table and the rest of the candles in the room all died in unison. When she lit the candle again, the room was cold and the chair was empty. David was gone, and Christine began to shiver.

David was soon on the train and heading back home. He could not remember boarding the train, or even having made his way back to the railway station, and yet here he was. He looked between the chairs up and down the carriage nervously. He was glad that he could see no sign of the dog on the train this time.

He noticed a woman who was sat further along the carriage, and she was alone. David had been unnerved by the things that he had heard, but his mind was more confused than scared. He tried to recall all of the things that he had heard, and he went over them again in his head to try and make some sense of it all. The woman in the carriage had noticed him, and she stood up from her chair. She started to walk through the carriage and toward where he sat.

The woman looked blankly at David.

"Do you mind if I sit with you a while? I hate being alone on this type of journey." She said.

"Feel free." David then beckoned her to sit in one of the empty seats opposite him. He really needed the company of another person right now.

The woman must have been in her mid to late thirties. She had straight long brown plain hair, and was well dressed. She looked a little continental in that the colour of her skin was what he would describe as 'olive'. Her eyes were a haunting dark brown, and although she wasn't overly attractive, she had enough distinguishing features to be appealing to most men. David was just glad of her company. Tonight had been a little eccentric to say the least.

At the house in Grateley, the three women looked at each other. This was the first time that they had encountered the power of the two ultimate forces in the universe. Communicating with spirits of the dead was one thing, but to have such an evil presence in the house with them had unsettled them all. Katie was the first to gather her thoughts.

"I feel physically sick. I've never encountered the strength of such a spirit before. The power of the dark one was immense." She said.

"I felt such a feeling of love and forgiveness inside of me, I feel as if I could float. It's almost like I have wings." Stephanie remarked.

Christine had placed both of her hands flat on the table.

"I had real trouble containing the dark spirit. It was very powerful, and I know that it is growing stronger. What worries me is that the entity seemed to be truthful in its words, and that is unusual especially for such a dark spirit." The look on her face was one of sheer dread. "If he is going to rise, I don't think there is any power on Earth, or in any church that is capable of stopping such a force."

"What do you suggest we do?" Stephanie asked.

"We cannot interfere directly, that is clear. The lost spirit cannot accept leaving this plane. Something still ties it to this world. Until the link is finally broken, the power of darkness will only become more determined to lead the spirit toward the darkness. We cannot coax the spirit to choose its direction, it must find its own way to let go of life." Christine said.

Katie was visibly shaken by what she had experienced. The reality of the awful truth had finally sunk in and she knew that they were now all in very grave danger.

"When someone chooses to take their own life, it had often been said that this was an unforgivable sin, and that the soul could never find a way into heaven. This is not true. If the spirit dies for love, then it can still seek forgiveness for taking its own precious gift of life. If the dark one is allowed to claim this soul though, he said that his army would become complete. We cannot allow that to happen. If it does a gateway will be opened back to this existence. Demons will walk the Earth once more."

"You can't mean…" Christine started to interject. Katie cut her off before she could finish.

"Yes, the armies of the damned stand on the precipice of the final battle. Too many people have chosen to follow dark paths and the power of the eternal darkness has been fed by these errant tormented souls. Unless we can save this soul, the army of the undead will rise up and will walk over the Earth."

"But how can we stop it from happening?" Christine asked. Katie gathered her thoughts and then tried to visualize what needed to be done. After a few seconds, the answer came to her.

"We have to break the tie that binds the spirit to this Earth, then it must choose its path before the choice is made for it, and the soul is devoured by the darkness." It was a frightening thought.

The woman stared out of the train window. David was reluctant to talk for fear of interrupting the woman's peace. After all she has asked for his company, not for a lengthy conversation. The light outside had faded to nothing as the dark of night had drawn in quickly. It was now pitch black as David looked out of the window. He decided that maybe it might be better for him to initiate a conversation after all, and this at least may take his mind off of the previous events of the evening.

The woman was staring out of the window almost in a trance like state.

"Where are you headed?" He asked. He was trying to break the awkward silence between them both. For a few moments, the question was met without a response. He considered repeating the question once again, but then he thought better of it. Instead, he also stared out of the window into the darkness.

"I'm not really sure." She suddenly responded. "I just seem to find myself on this train every single day. I live this same damned journey over and over again."

David knew fully what she meant. Life had become tiresome and mundane. He could no longer watch television anymore and listen to the daily barrage of sad news of loved ones killed on foreign shores, the disabled committing suicide after inhumane sanctions or of some tragedy or another that had unfolded. Worst of all though, was seeing the pain of innocent children suffering across the globe. War was rife, and it took no prisoners in some quarters. It was just too painful to watch now.

He wondered where everything good in this life had gone. The simple childhood games and treasures that he had enjoyed had now seemingly been long forgotten in a quest for money and for faster evolving technology. This seemed to make life easier, but now it was far less challenging. Nothing seemed sacred anymore.

"I know exactly what you mean. It's a scary world outside of that window." David answered.

The woman immediately launched herself across the seat and grabbed a hold of his hand with both of hers.

"Do you?" She asked excitedly. Her grip was now just a little too tight on his arm. "Then can you save me from all of this? I just want to go home!" She pleaded.

The woman's touch was icy cold. David pulled his hand away from hers. Her sudden movement had startled him.

"What is it that you want me to do?" He asked. The woman now lowered her head and stared straight forward. She then stood up and adjusted her jacket.

"It doesn't matter anymore. This is where I get off the train." She said calmly. She then began walking toward the door of the carriage. It took a few seconds before David realized what she intended to do. By the time he had jumped to his feet and began to follow her, the woman had already swung the train door open.

"Wait!" David shouted. The words did not appear to register with the woman at all. She did look back. Instead she jumped from the open door of the fast moving carriage. As she jumped, she let out a scream that pierced his ears and then there was silence.

David reached up and pulled on the trains emergency stop chain. The brakes immediately locked into place. The train was now less than a mile from Andover, and it was grinding to a halt. David waited until the train was almost at a complete stop before he jumped from the open door of the carriage. He landed on stony ground just a few feet away from the carriages. He then ran back along the track trying to calculate where the woman might have landed. He desperately searched around the tracks and surrounding area, but there was nothing. There was no body, and no blood. Not prepared to admit defeat he frantically continued to search the grass embankment.

While he was still searching the area, the train suddenly started to move away. No one had even bothered to come and see what the problem was. David was not concerned about the distance as he was close enough to walk home, but he was surprised that no one on the train had come out to help. He once again scoured the area looking all around the track, and when he could find no sign of the woman, he finally admitted defeat.

He started to walk back along the length of railway line. There was no proof that the woman had ever existed. There was not a single trace. Then he came across something odd. To his right, he spotted that there were numerous bunches of faded flowers that had been placed at the top of embankment.

He climbed up to where the flowers had been placed. This looked to be about the same area that the woman had jumped. There was a jaded card underneath the dead stems of the flowers. David bent down and picked up the card. The words written on it were now pretty illegible especially in such poor light, but a photograph that had been attached to the flowers then dropped to the floor. David picked it up, and then he allowed it to fall from his hand. The flowers were in memorial to a woman, who had jumped from the train over a year ago. It was the same woman he had just witnessed jumping out from the carriage.

The walk home was full of dark thoughts. David had never felt uneasy. What was happening to him now? He never asked for any of this, and he felt sick of the thought of not just having seen, but also having apparently communicated directly with a dead woman. Did those three women bestow something upon him back at the house he wondered? It was evident that something was still tying Emma to him. To save her, he would have to find a way to break that tie between them forever.

The thought of Emma left here alone and in pain was starting to tear him up inside again. He would try and sleep on this tonight, and maybe tomorrow he would ring Christine for advice again. Maybe after the craziness of the night's events she might have some more sensible answers. The same thing happened to him again though, as it did every night now, and sleep failed him to happen. He would not let himself drift away from his body though. He was just too scared of what might happen after tonight's events.

Throughout the loneliness of the night, right up until the morning sun broke through his window, David remained deeply troubled. He kept playing the events of the previous evening over and over in his mind. He thought about the three women who were sat around the table. He wondered exactly what the conversations they had with him were really all about. One thing in particular kept coming back again and again into his train of thought. It was what the woman had said about the fisher of men. He had definitely heard that somewhere before, but where he wondered? He picked up his phone and typed the saying into a search engine.

The page loaded up, and the first link that he saw on the results, was a video directed at those who were considering the priesthood. He tried to watch it, but it just appeared to be some sort of commercial promotional video, and it bored him silly. The next thing on the list was a quote from the bible which read:

Mark 1:16-20 "As Jesus walked beside the Sea of Galilee, he saw Simon and his brother Andrew casting a net into the lake, for they were fishermen.'Come, follow me,' Jesus said, 'and I will make you fishers of men.' At once they left their nets and followed him. When he had gone a little further, he saw James son of Zebedee and his brother John in a boat, preparing their nets. Without delay he called them, and they left their father Zebedee in the boat with the hired men and followed him."

He read the lines repeatedly. Of all of the quotes from the Bible, if the séance had been a set up, then why would they choose this quote in particular? He then also decided to search for the word Legion and to see what came up. Again he also discovered a quote from the Bible that read:

And He (Jesus) asked him (the man), "What is thy name?" And he answered, saying, "My name is Legion: for we are many."

David spent the remaining hours of the early morning trawling through websites seeking anything that might be relevant to what he heard. Eventually he grew tired of the countless pages of information appearing in front of him. He placed his phone down once more and lay on his bed. The answers he sought only seemed to come from his out of body experiences, or from Christine. He reluctantly closed his eyes, hoping for something to guide him. Once again he felt himself being lifted away as his mind was transported almost instantly outside of his body.

When David opened his eyes, he was sat with his legs crossed over each other, but he was in the middle of a desert. There were mountains in the distance and the sun blazed overhead. This time he could only wish for a hint of a breeze. The heat was so intense and the humidity here was unbearable.

To David's left an old man appeared. He was walking toward him from out of nowhere. The steps that he took were painfully slow. He looked frail and beaten, as if he had carried the weight of the entire world on his shoulders for many thousands of years. His eyes were kind, but they were tired. He looked as if he were about ready to give up on life. To his right appeared another man appeared. He was young and virile and striding quickly toward David. As he drew closer, David noticed that his appearance was odd. It looked as if his face was constantly changing shape. Both men arrived with David at the same time. Then a chess board appeared between all three of the men. It levitated in the air as if it were held aloft on an invisible table.

The men now stood to either side of David and then began to play the game. As piece after piece was removed from the board David watched in awe. The younger man appeared to be winning. More and more of the old man's pieces were taken until one single white pawn remained on the board. The old man gently grabbed hold of David's hand. He looked deep into David's eyes, and David could sense that he was close to defeat.

The old man spoke in gentle tones.

"David. If the last pawn falls, the war is over. All life on Earth will belong to him."

The other man grabbed hold of David's free hand. His grip was tight, and David felt instantly sick at the feel of his touch.

"David. I can offer you a kingdom greater than you can ever imagine. I offer you a power unheard of. As well as this I can offer you your hearts one true desire, I can offer you Emma." David wrenched his hand away. The man held David's gaze and David knew that his offer was serious.

The dusty world around them all began to slip away from underneath them. David was sent spiraling downward with an avalanche of sand cascading downward all around him. It was filling his mouth and eyes and making him choke on the dry dusty substance. As he fell, he found himself endlessly spinning until the moment that his eyes open. His bed offered little salvation from the spinning effect, and his throat was dusty and dry.

All he had ever wanted was the chance to be with Emma again. His mind played the dream over and over again. After all this was just his imagination wasn't it? If he chose to accept the offer from the man with multiple faces, then what possible harm could it cause? More to the point, could she really be saved so that he could with Emma again once again?

That morning Christine was feeling restless. She had slept little, and her dreams had been filled with demons in field of flames rising up across the lands, and even from the depths of the oceans. They rose up in every corner of the Earth and mercilessly slaughtered every single living thing that they encountered. She woke up to the sound of her own screams, and the bed was soaked though with her own sweat. The previous evening had really shaken her up quite badly.

She decided to call Katie, just to see if she had had any further thoughts on how to rescue the errant spirit. She picked up her mobile phone scrolled through the contacts and then called Katie's number. The telephone rang repeatedly but there was no answer from her home. She then tried calling her mobile number. The telephone rang and rang until eventually it gave up from the ringing sound and was finally diverted to voicemail. Christine wasn't keen on leaving messages, but even though she was reluctant, she still did so.

"Hi, it's Christine. Can you call me as soon as you get this? I'm really worried about what happened last night. I have an awful feeling that something terrible is about to happen." She then hung up the phone.

She then walked from the living room and in to the kitchen. She picked up the kettle from the side, and she emptied out the old water, along with the deposits of lime scale that were so common from the local water supply. She turned on the cold water and then refilled the kettle up to half way on the water level. She then replaced the kettle back on its electric charging base. Then she turned it on at the switch and waited for it to boil. Christine looked out of the kitchen window, and she could see that storm clouds now filled the entire sky.

She took a mug from the cupboard, placed on spoon of coffee and two sugars inside it, and then returned to look out of the window once more. Katie's home was only a short distance from hers, and puzzlingly she could see that her bedroom light was switched on. Being blind, Katie had no need for light, and now Christine was puzzled. The light in the room now seemed to be flickering. The storm clouds also seemed to have gathered close by and they now appeared to circle in one place. They were directly over Katie's house.

Christine jumped as the kettle began to make the familiar whistling sound that signified that the water had boiled, but it was impossible though. The kettle took at least a minute to boil, and yet it was already red hot. She turned the power off at the power button, and it was then that the whistling sound turned into a much darker sound, the sound now became that of a woman screaming in agony.

Christine turned off the kettle at the mains and unplugged it from the wall, but the screaming still continued. She covered her ears to escape the haunting echo now filling the room. Suddenly the kettle exploded, as it did it sent shards of red hot plastic and boiling water flying across the kitchen. Christine was agile enough to avoid most of the exploding projectiles, but some of the water still managed to burn her right hand. Had she been wearing less clothing, her burns might have been much worse.

This was just too much of a coincidence, something was really wrong. She felt it deep in her bones. She looked out of the kitchen window, and then she realized why the light in Katie's bedroom had been flickering. It wasn't a light in the room at all. It was a fire that was burning wildly in the bedroom of her friend's house.

She gathered her mobile up and ran out into the street. The scald on her hand could wait. Whilst she was running towards Katie's house, she fumbled with her mobile phone. She tried to dial the fire brigade whilst she was running to help, but it was nigh on impossible. She had little choice but to pause for a few precious seconds and to dial the emergency number. After a few short rings, a woman's voice answered the call

"Emergency services, what service do you require?" She asked.

Now that Christine was connected, she was able to continue running whilst carrying on with the conversation. "Get me the Fire brigade!" She pleaded.

"We can't connect you now. While your friend is burning, I offer you a warning. Please be aware that if you don't stay out of this, you will be next. Now please try again later." The call was then ended abruptly. It was one of the same voices on the phone that they had all heard at the table the night before.

David now lay in a bath of warm water. He had no recollection of even running the bath. He was convinced that he really must be losing his mind. He searched the room with his eyes and then picked the phone up from the shelf at the back of the bath. He then dialed Christine's number again. When the phone connected it sounded as if Christine had been crying.

David was concerned, but whatever is was, he felt as if his need were greater than Christine's problem right now.

"How can I end all of this? How can I help Emma?" He asked. Christine was torn. She could not allow this to go on anymore. Her friend had just died in agony and for no reason, she was innocent. She knew that it had to be ended soon. Christine realized that she and Stephanie were now in mortal danger. Through her tears, she knew that the only way to end this quickly was to break her vow, and to communicate directly with Emma.

"Give me her number." She asked. David knew that it was pointless, but from his memory he said the number out loud anyway. Christine wrote the number down as he recited it, and then she ended the call. She took a deep breath, and then dialed the number she had been given. The phone rang a few times and then a woman's voice finally answered.

"Hello?" The voice was that of a puzzled woman.

"Is that Emma?" Christine asked.

"Yes. Who is this?" Emma asked.

"I need you to listen to me very carefully. What I am about to tell you will not make any sense, but I assure you, I speak the truth...." Christine then carried with the conversation, not really believing the situation that she had now found herself in.

Christine dialed the number that she had been called from earlier, but the line was dead. She then wrote a text to the very same number. She was hopeful, but not honestly sure if it would ever reach the intended recipient but it was the only thing that she could think of. It read:

'To end this, you must go to the place where your mortal ties were divided. Be there at the same time of day that you lost each other. At 3pm in the forest, Emma will be there to meet you.' She then pressed the send button, and the message disappeared from the screen. She then sat and waited patiently.

Five minutes later, a text message appeared on her phone, it was only a few words, but it was from him.

"I will go to meet her there. Thank you." Then after only a few seconds, that message also faded from the screen as if it had never even existed.

David was apprehensive about going back to the clearing. He had not yet found the strength to visit the forest, not since that dark day, he was just too afraid to. He sat alone with his thoughts for some time. As the clock ticked by and the time approached, he knew that this was the only way that this could all end. He left the house for what he somehow thought might be the final time, and began to walk toward the place where life had been so cruel, as it separated them from each other.

David had tears welling in his eyes as he approached the clearing in the forest. Emma was already stood there waiting for him. Christine was stood there with her. They were stood in the exact same spot that it had happened. He walked toward her, praying that this time she would be able to talk to him. Christine took Emma's hand and in the sunlight, Emma could now see David walking toward her. David was there with her once more. Tears rolled down Emma's cheeks as David stood before her. He reached out his hand to wipe the tears away. The tears continued to roll downward, as his interaction with her could not prevent them from falling.

For the first time in months the two former lovers found themselves together again. Emma reached out her hand to touch David's face, but the two were now separated by completely different planes of existence. They had formed a bridge between worlds that could never be fully crossed without one or the other passing over.

"Why are you here now?" Emma asked.

"I came here because you needed me. I came to save you." He replied. He felt a lump begin to rise in his throat as he could see the anguish appear on Emma's face.

"I can't be saved David. I just need to be at peace. I can only do that when you find peace inside of you. You need to accept what happened." Emma looked so lost and withdrawn that David tried to hold her, but his arms once more slipped right through her. Tears were now running freely down his cheeks.

"Tell me what it is I can I do to stop you hurting?" David pleaded with her.

"You have to let her go." Christine said.

"I can't, it wasn't meant to end the way it did. I still have so much love for you, and I can't let you leave here without me."

'It isn't me that has to leave here David…. it's you. You have to stop haunting me. You're killing me with your love for me. I can't eat, or sleep or even think anymore.' David had never seen Emma in so much pain, and it was tearing him apart inside.

At first the words had failed to resonate with him. He needed to find a way to end her suffering, and he would do whatever it took to save her.

"Tell me what I have to do to stop this?" He asked.

"You have to let go." She answered. The forest began to fill with a gentle light mist; it filled the area with warmth that was almost like a mothers embrace as it surrounded them all. It widened in gentle circular movements, as if ghosts were forming a ring to echo out a welcome. "That is where you have to go David." Christine said, and she pointed toward the light that had formed inside of the mist. David's face was now filled with confusion.

"But how will it help if I do that?" He asked. "Do you want me to take my own life?" He asked. He would honestly do it for her, if it meant that it would end her suffering.

"David..........that's what I'm trying to tell you, you already did. You killed yourself, and your ghost has haunted me ever since." Emma broke down in tears as she revealed the truth that David had failed to accept. He stood in stunned silence as the words echoed through his head. Then everything he had experienced all started to come back to him. It was almost like having a photograph albums pages being turned before his eyes.

All of it was created by messengers who were trying to guide him home. The dreams, the man on the bench, the woman on the train, the ferocious dog, and the feeling of solitude from everyone, they were all in his thoughts alone. Everything flashed before him and only then did he finally begin to fully understand. He was the ghost who would not leave her side.

This was why no one would talk to him anymore. Most people couldn't even see him. This was why he felt so alone, and why time had no meaning anymore. He was the one still trapped here. The message that had been given to him was to save Emma, but not in the way that he thought she needed to be saved, she needed to be saved from him. He now had to finally let her go. The tie that had bound them together had been words of love between them both stored as text messages on their mobile phones.

It was all that they still had left of each other to treasure. It had been enough to hold him here in hope. He pulled his mobile phone out of his pocket and opened the text messages she had sent. His finger hovered over the messages between himself and Emma. He touched the screen, and the delete question appeared. He paused for a brief second and then looked into her eyes and smiled at Emma. Then he pressed the button to start to delete them all. As the screen showed a circular pattern, all of the messages started to disappear, and his image started to fade along with them. It was time for him to go.

"Forgive me for leaving you alone." He begged her.

Reaching forward David put his hand to her face, and even though he could not feel the warmth of her skin, he hoped that she might have felt a slight tingle from the memory of his touch. He leant across and kissed her, but again he could not feel her lips. Tears rolled down Emma's cheeks as she knew that he would be leaving her for the final time. David raised his hands toward the light now emanating from the clouds, and he felt his body rising upwards. The warmth from the light embraced him fully, and his spirit began to fade.

The two women watched as he quietly drifted upward, now at last perhaps they could all find peace.

'Goodbye my love. I forgive you.' She said, and the ghost of David finally faded away.

As he walked into the light, he asked for forgiveness for his sins. He then felt as if loving arms were surrounding him, and then he was gone.

Emma's story.

They make it all seem so romantic in the movies. The fact of the matter is, that it couldn't be further from the truth. We were two former lovers who had made a pact with each other to end our own lives. We planned that we would do it together. We spent weeks deliberating just how we would do it. We considered pills, but the outcome wasn't guaranteed.

Then we thought about cutting our wrists, but that seemed too messy and painful, also it would be unfair on those who found us. Hanging seemed to be the easiest and cleanest option. So we chose the day and we wrote down our goodbyes. We cited our reasons for us both loathing this town and wanting to leave this life. It was all we could see to do to end our own misery.

What we were really doing though, we were wallowing in our own self pity. We were both depressed and unhappy with our lives, but we never took the time to stop and seek out the real reasons why. All we would do is swallow those pills they prescribed us day after day, letting them chemically suppress our feelings and numb our minds. We were like zombies.

So we decide to end our misery in what we thought would be a selfless act. We forgot about those we were about to leave behind, and all the suffering that they would endure. We couldn't see past our own misery to realize just what we would do to everyone else we left behind. It was just all about us.

We found the tree in the clearing, and attached the ropes to the branches. We made sure the nooses were tied correctly. Then we kissed each other goodbye one last time, and then climbed up high enough for us to jump. Together we leapt to our death. We watched each other as the life started to drain away from each other's eyes, but something then went very wrong. The branch that I had tied my rope to suddenly snapped, and I fell to the ground. In that moment I realized it had been a mistake, I now wanted to live. I could see David was struggling for air, and I knew that he needed to live as well.

I tried to support his weight and to lift him up, but as hard as I tried, I could not hold him. I had no choice but to let him go. I had to get help. In that moment I could see the fear in his eyes. I knew that time was short. I ran to try and get help, and fell at the feet of a couple who were walking their dog. Together we rushed back to the tree, but despite their best efforts they could not save David. The love of my life was already gone.

I was distraught, but there was nothing more that I could do. I was now so scared of dying, but at the same time I was filled with the guilt. I had let the one person that I cared about leave here without me. We expected that when we died, all of the pain would go away. It didn't. For the briefest of moments I was not of this world, and for the smallest amount of time, I felt the horror of the pain I would have inflicted on those who loved me. I never realized how selfish and cruel I was being to them. It was then I realized that I hated my life, but I didn't hate living. Nothing is worth taking that final step into the abyss. Everything can be fixed if you just open up.

Over time I realized it was my life that I hated because it was so mundane. I hated never having any money, and not being able to buy what others had. I hated being stuck at home living with my parents. I just wanted all the latest material things that didn't really matter anyway, and my independence. It made me realize that it isn't what you have in life, it's who you have. Life is the most precious of gifts, and you can be richer than anyone else in spirit by helping other people. Seeing a smile that you have put on someone else's face is priceless.

So I finally found a way to be happy, and I started to get over losing David, that was until the day that I started to see his ghost. The first time I was walking through the town centre, I thought I felt him passing right through me, and it sent me cold. Then when I was sat in my room and I felt him staring through my window, and then I heard him outside of my front door. It scared the hell out of me. I had never believed in ghosts before, until I found myself haunted by one that I had once loved.

It felt as if we are tied together. David was stuck with me, and I was running out of choices. We promised that we would be together forever. I began to think that the only way I might be free of his ghost, would be for me to try to end my again. If it wasn't for Christine, I may well have decided to try again. I'm glad that I didn't though.

I love my life, and I'm taking my second chance at living. I now realize fully what it means to really live. The world is full of sad people who are just so afraid of life and are just getting by from day to day. When did our lives become just about work and money and responsibility? The world around us is full of beauty but we no longer see it, we pass it by every day and we no longer choose to examine what is right in front of our eyes. We need to learn to open our eyes and minds to the beauty that surrounds us.

So now when I see that worker bee collecting pollen busily from flowers, or that elderly couple holding who are hands while walking along, then I stop and smile. I feel the lifetime of love and pain that they have shared in equal measure. I see a child playing happily and laughing at silly things, and I remember my own years of innocence once again. When did we forget our real purpose here? No one ever gives us a reason why as to we have to do the things we do just to survive.

I will be with David again, and now that his ghost has set me free, I won't be the one who chooses the day that I see him in that other plane of existence. I will live my life to the fullest every single day, and I will savor every breath that I take. Then when my time eventually comes I will be ready to face it, where I know that he waits for me. My love for David will always remain, and I know his love for me will never end. Time, will never fail us again.

The Reckoning

It was all bullshit apparently. The doom mongers who were telling lies and spreading those crazy twisted internet stories, and even all those videos that were posted on social media. They were warning us all about what could happen on the 23rd of September 2015. It was all complete bullshit the scientists said so. They told us that the machine was safe. They kept on saying it right up until that day, when they actually switched that colossal collider on and then they fired those tiny little particles together. It was only then that they had to try and quickly back track. It wasn't bullshit. It just happened to be far worse than anyone could have ever imagined.

The experiment that made 'it' happen, took place at exactly four in the afternoon. There was no major commotion, no devastating explosions to be heard, no black holes being formed, and no fireworks so to speak of. Instead there was a creation of something called dark matter. It came in the form of five miles of darkness that spread out across the land in all directions directly from the epicentre of the experiment.

Those crazy scientists, well they scratched their heads and had no explanation for it at all, it physically could not happen! They had assured us that it was safe, but it wasn't though. It wasn't anything of the sort, and in the place of where once stood the doomsday machine, now there was just a black void that had consumed everything in its path. The politicians had to know what was inside the void, so the Army were sent in with drones and cameras to try and see what was happening inside of the darkness, but anything or anyone who entered the void, would never be seen or heard from again.

So there we were with a five mile stretch of blackness that covered the land and the sky above it. People tried to rationalise it, and it was all over the television and Internet. Some said that this could just be a temporary void, and all the finest minds on the planet decided to work together. They began to calculate what had happened and start to work on finding a way to reverse whatever the hell it was that those scientists had done.

The first day was filled with sadness, for all of those who were missing inside of the void. The second day was different, the second day, well let's just say the second day was when the hysteria really began. At four o clock in the afternoon on the 24th of September, the void silently doubled in size. Everything within a ten mile radius of the epicentre was now inside the darkness. Naturally everyone just outside of the void soon realised that if events were to follow a similar pattern, then the next day, that they too would also be gone.

Thousands and thousands of families packed up their belongings and got into whatever vehicles were available, some even left on foot. They started to run as far as they possibly could from the dark. The scientists, well they were still just scratching their heads about what exactly was happening. There was still no rational explanation for any of it to be found. They were positive that there would be no further expansion of the void; they thought it had to have been losing its power by now. They assured everyone that this was the end of the event, and by the following day, things might be starting to return to normal. They were extremely disturbed when they realised that they were wrong.

They soon learnt that making such statements to the public was a very bad idea. The mob that attacked them in an angry panic had showed them no mercy. On day three at the exact same time in the afternoon to the very second, the void doubled in size yet again. Now it was no longer a case of blind panic, it was one of pandemonium. Families in their tens of thousands could see their homes were sitting on the edge of a dangerous precipice. They no longer cared where it was that they were going. They just knew they had to flee.

The armed forces helped to try and organise evacuations, while at the same time trying to maintain some sense of order. Riots and looting were occurring everywhere. How fragile the human spirit had become and how quickly the masses had fractured. Day four was a moment of realisation. We understood that we were all now in our end times.

Forty miles of dark void now covered the Earth. The speed that the void grew was yet again consistent. It took some time to realise the exact measurements, but the void had doubled exactly in size each and every day. Things then really took a turn for the worse. Day four was when the intense fighting started. It was only natural that people were panicking, but by now supplies of essentials were running short. The electrical power was now off in vast areas and water and petrol were now more precious than gold. People were now killing each other over food. Rioting was widespread and people now took anything they thought that they needed to survive.

Without electricity, forms of information were scarce. No one knew just what was going on anymore. Word would filter down to those who would listen, but stories became fractured and pandemonium ensued. A calculation had been made, and with it came a sudden realisation, if the void continued to expand at the same rate it had, then the Earth would be totally consumed in just another eleven short days.

A mass exodus of people were now fleeing as far away as they could, but it would only be a matter of time before they would realise that the void would consume them faster than they could run, but worse than that, within just a few days, there would be nowhere left on the planet for them to run to. Earth was now doomed it seemed.

Day five saw the void double in size yet again. By now some had decided that they wished to concede defeat, they had had enough. Many announced that they could no longer afford to or even wanted to keep running away. This was the first day of what was called 'The Reckoning'. On this day some of the people decided their own fate. This was their judgement day, and they were ready to face it head on. From very early in the morning people had started to gather at the edge of the void. Some would try to convince them to keep running, but there were many who could run no more. Those who were sick and tired, or just too ill to move any further, they had decided that it was futile to run from whatever fate had in store for them, today was to be their last stand.

As the day went on, crowds gathered in huge numbers all along the edge of the darkness. There were tears, sadness and laughter shared. Stories were exchanged and the people stood as one while they waited for the void to consume them. Seeing some of the small children who were playing without a care in the world, not knowing that they would soon be gone, it was truly heart breaking to see. To know that they would never grow up, and fully experience life, was daunting but in some ways the kindest choice their parents could ever make.

To end their lives before the Earth was finally consumed, most had viewed it as an act of kindness. It was a way to escape from the fear of imminent death, by standing tall and by facing it without fear. As four o' clock came, the end was swift for those families. The young and the old who had stood together, their faces would no longer be seen. The children's laughter would be heard anymore, for they too were now all gone.

On day thirteen, what remained of humanity, was nothing like anyone would have remembered just a few weeks ago. These were the very last people who were desperate to survive on planet Earth. They were hungry, thirsty, battered and worn, but resilient right up to the end. Tomorrow they would all be nothing. All the wars their ancestors had fought, all of the hard work they had ever done for the pittance that they had earned. The buildings they had constructed and lived in, the flashy cars they had once driven, they were all pointless now. All of this now meant nothing. The human race would very soon be just a distant memory.

On day fourteen we had reached humanities end. All those who were left now stood side by side, united as one. The people were not divided anymore. No one was safe from the end of the world. When they were no longer separated by wealth, religion, race, sex, colour, sexuality or creed, nothing could divide them anymore. All would pass over together. As four o clock approached, the last of mankind stood on the precipice. We were a dying ember of a once great world. Some held hands, some sang, some prayed, and some just held each other. Then as the darkness enveloped them all, the world became as nothing. Darkness now owned the planet, and it would do so forever more.

Helter Skelter.

The battery operated clock ticked away on the wall. Second after second it moved forward relentlessly. The sound was deafening, and nothing else could be heard throughout the entire flat. Ever since the day that the electricity went off, there was nothing else left in the flat that actually made a noise. The gentle hum of the freezer was now a distant memory, as were the pointless sounds that used to come from the television as it had once echoed all those tired voices and canned laughter out into the living room.

His tablet and mobile phone were long drained of power. Without electricity, everything that he owned and had come to rely upon for contact with the outside world, was now unusable. In the distance, he heard a scream. It gave him chills, but it was nothing unusual these days. Not now those things were outside.

He didn't bother to get up out of his chair. He would sit there through most of the days now, and he would even sometimes fall asleep there at night too. He had no desire to look out of the windows anymore. As for the world outside, well let's just say that it was just a different story out there now. He had no concept of what day it was anymore, the days had all started to merge into one. His supplies had now dwindled away to next to nothing.

The simple act of having to get up from the chair was a painful experience at his age, but he used his fading strength to raise himself up, feeling the strain in his upper arms as he did so. He did not like to move, but today his hunger was intense. He walked over to the kitchen and opened a cupboard door. He then started to search through the food cupboard. It was a pretty dire situation in there. The amount he had left in the cupboard was actually a lot worse than he had originally thought.

He was stood close to the kitchen window, and now he could smell something awful. The stench seemed to come from outside of the flat. He caught the scent of the world outside, and he was now sure that the smell of decay was getting stronger? He could definitely smell it a lot heavier in here today. Perhaps the heat was making it worse? It must have been at least 27 degrees outside. Inside the flat with all of the windows boarded up, it was even hotter in there. He looked across at the room at the now idle electric fan. It was now sat frozen in place, as it just gathered dust in the corner of the living room.

If only the electricity would come back on he thought to himself. He then opened the freezer door, and instantly he realised that doing so was a big mistake. Mould was now growing around the rim inside of the freezer door. The spores would not be healthy for him to breathe in with all this heat. The food inside of the brittle cracked plastic drawers had now all defrosted and was definitely rotten. He had to find a way to get it out of the flat soon. For now it would just have to wait a little longer. He closed the door, secretly intending never to open it up again.

He went back to the food cupboard to take another look. Inside the cupboard it was virtually bare, except for two tins of tuna in sunflower oil, and one tin of beans. On the top shelf, he found one packet of freeze dried noodles, and one tin of spaghetti. Even worse than that though, the water that he had stored in the plastic bottles, that was now all gone. The heat was making him thirsty, damned thirsty, and desperate times now called for desperate measures.

He opened the cutlery drawer and it squealed as it moved forward. It needed oiling, but this was the last of his worries right now. He removed a rusted tin opener from the drawer and carefully opened the tin of tuna. He then removed the sharp metal lid and raised the open can up to his mouth. He poured a little of the sunflower oil onto his tongue. It lubricated his throat as he swallowed, but it did little to quench his thirst.

He didn't mind the taste of the oil at all. He thought he would, but it was only slightly tainted by the fish. He took a fork from the drawer and slowly he ate the tuna directly from the tin. He savoured the taste of the tinned fish. He heard the sound of another scream from somewhere outside. By the sound of it, whoever had screamed was quite a way off in the distance. The next scream that he heard though, that was a lot closer. The sound caused him to freeze on the spot and he shuddered uncontrollably.

It had been one whole day without drinking any water. He wondered how long a human being could actually survive without it. If only the electricity would come back on, then he could search the internet for the answers he desperately sought. That wasn't going to happen any time soon though. How long had the power been off for now he wondered to himself? It must have been off for at least a month, maybe even longer than that.

Yes it must have been at least a whole month that he had been trapped in here all alone. The sound of silence was starting to deafen him all over again. Except that it wasn't completely silent was it? No, because he could still hear the ticking of that damned clock always clicking away, never ever ceasing in its solitary task of moving forward.

One more day, he thought to himself. He knew that he could survive without water, for at least one more day. Then he would seriously have to think about venturing outside of his safe haven. The very thought of leaving the flat then sent him into a worried frenzy. He walked from the kitchen, through the hall and into his bedroom. He closed the door and then immediately checked that the windows were still securely boarded closed. It smelt musty in here, but he felt so tired, that he no longer cared.

He allowed himself to fall onto the bed for the first time in what seemed like an age, and he lowered his face down into his soft feather pillow. He then placed his hands over his ears, and screamed into the softness beneath him. He just wanted this nightmare to finally end. Going outside was his worst fear. He wasn't sure if he would be able to do it, or if he even still had the strength in him to tackle the stairs. If he stepped outside, it would mean him having to face the creatures that now haunted his every waking moment, and they were the soulless ones who showed no mercy.

They were the stuff of his nightmares. They were relentless in their quest to get to him. Sometimes, they would find a way into the security door downstairs, and then he would hear them pounding away at his front door. At least in here he was safe from them. The door to his flat was solid, but he wasn't sure quite just how long it would hold them outside. It would hold for another day though, he felt sure enough of that.

The windows to the flat had all been boarded up months ago. He had used whatever wood he could find, even destroying the bookcase he had once made with his own hands. The windows were all screwed closed, boarded as well where he could, and only a small hole had been left so that he could still see outside. It had been a long time since he had peered out through a gap though. He never wanted to look out of them anymore. The one time that he had, he had seen them gathered there outside. They were screaming and pointing up at him.

Frustrating was the only word the he could use to describe his current situation. The stench now coming from the bathroom and filling the flat was now unbearable. Without water, he could no longer flush the faeces away. Nor could he brush his teeth, and that really made him angry. The kitchen, the bathroom, everywhere that was once so well kept in the flat they were now all smelly and dirty. He could see more dirty marks appearing everywhere that he looked.

For now, he was safely in his bedroom and he just wanted to sleep. He took a few deep breaths and then got up slowly from the bed. He secured the door to the bedroom closed, and then lay back on top of the bed and just stared blankly at the boards that covered the window. There he remained for the next few hours. He was petrified that they may find a way inside. Eventually, a restless sleep finally came.

He awoke at around seven thirty the next morning. Although he no longer had any idea what day it was anymore it somehow felt like it was the weekend. It was a strange feeling. He sat upright on the bed, and the heat from outside was already starting to rise. His throat was dusty and dry and his thirst was really becoming unbearable now.

He unblocked the bedroom door and walked out to the bathroom. The stench coming from the toilet was now really overpowering. He had no bleach or cleaners left that he could even try and mask the smell with. Flies were buzzing all around the cistern and cheekily walking all over the toilet seat. They were spreading filthy germs everywhere they went. He dry retched as he watched them all slowly walking over the excrement that was festering above the lime scale scarred toilet line. Tiny feet were walking in his human waste that was sat layered above where the water once used to sit.

He had to take a piss, but instead of using the toilet and risk even more disgusting smells emanating upward from the bowl, he opted to use the sink instead. Despite his urge to urinate, the fluid would not flow. He felt a sharp pain in his kidneys as he tried to force the urine to come out from his body. What did eventually come out from inside of him, were just a few drops of what was almost a thick treacle coloured fluid, it smelt almost sugary.

There may have even been hints of blood in the urine, it seemed that dark, but he had no real way of knowing for sure. Then he was startled as unexpectedly, the sound of the hands of those outside began pounding on the front door to his flat. He silently prayed that the door would hold out. He stood rigid to the spot as the banging continued relentlessly. He did not dare to breathe, as he feared that they may hear him inside. He had to remain absolutely silent.

If they sensed his presence, they may try even harder to force their way in here, he knew that they would be desperate to get to him. He stood completely still and as silent as he could be. He shook in fear and droplets of cold sweat began to run down his face. He cursed the fact that he was losing more bodily fluids when he was already dehydrated.

The pounding at the door continued for a while, but as they had not managed to get in again, he was positive that the door would hold, at least for a little bit longer. He had secured it with extra thick planks of wood that he had screwed across the door frame. There was no way that the monsters should be able to find a way inside here. He was now starting to grow weak with thirst, and his body was filled with what felt like a terminal pain that grew in his stomach. It was ferocious and he was soon doubled over in pain.

He sank to his knees, and then he fell backward against the wall of the bathroom. He sat in silence with his head in his hands. He was no more than three feet away from the toilet. He would not move from here though, not until he was sure that the demons at the door had gone away. The sound of the hands clawing away outside echoed throughout his head for what seemed like an eternity, and then just as quickly as it had begun, the creatures outside became silent once more.

This was his chance to try and get out of the bathroom, and away from that awful smell. He had already made up his mind, and there was nothing else for it. He had to make his way back into the bedroom and to hide away under the duvet once more. He stood up, and silently edged his way back to his bedroom using the wall for support. Once inside, he secured the door closed, and sat upright on the edge of his bed. He rocked backward and forward on the edge of the bed, for a very long time.

The last of the food had gone a few days ago despite his best efforts to ration them; it might have been three, maybe four days since he last ate. The days were now blurring into one another. Without water, he was also starting to hallucinate quite vividly. Ghosts were beginning to walk through the walls of the flat at random intervals. He thought that he had seen it all, until that one special day, it might have been day five of maybe even six that he hadn't even. Well that was the day that the king had arrived.

He woke up in the early hours to the sound of wonderful music. As he sat up, he had witnessed Elvis who was now singing and dancing live in his bedroom, right at the foot of his bed. The suit he was wearing was the famous white jewelled one, the very one that he wore in Vegas. He loved the exclusivity and Elvis he could cope with. He really enjoyed the serenades and he would applaud excitedly after each and every song had finished. It all started go wrong when his deceased family members started appearing. This made him sad and he wanted to hide again, but they would not let him rest.

The family gathered in his bedroom and they loved to sit at the bottom of his bed. They had returned from the void to hear Elvis as he performed his concert for the dead. One after one, they gathered, until they filled the room, and then it all became just a little bit too much. He had to leave the bedroom, the concert now just seemed a little too crowded for his liking, and he always hated large crowds.

He was growing weaker by the day, and he knew that it was now inevitable, that he would have to go outside and face them. The nearest shop was just ten minutes away on foot, and he prayed that he could make it to the shop and back, without encountering 'them'. If he were lucky, they would still have water there. He would have to take what he needed by force. He had nothing in the way of weapons, other than a kitchen knife, but he feared that would be useless. Outside they were large in number, and fearsome.

He had only once before seen them close with his own eyes, and the size of the monsters had frightened him. It was now or never though. It was finally time for him to leave the flat. He had to either face his fears, or he knew that he would surely die here alone. He suddenly realised that he was now sat in silence. The batteries that powered that damned wall clock had finally expired. Now there were no sounds now, none apart from the ones that were occasionally coming from outside. It must have been a sign he thought. Even Elvis was now silent, as he must have been taking a well deserved rest.

He had no idea of what time it was, but he thought it might be early morning, it was cooler and he could only assume that meant that it was early in the day. His body smelt of sweat, and his clothes were in a mess, but he no longer cared at all. It took all of the strength that he had left in him, just to unscrew the beams that he had fastened to the main door frame of the flat.

One by one, he took the wooden planks down, and he placed them carefully on the floor. Once the heavy wooden slats were removed, it was just the main door lock that he then needed to undo. He glanced into the hallway using the spy hole that was placed at eye level. It was dirty outside, but he could still see out of it. The hallway was empty, and his hands now shook uncontrollably with fear.

He steadied his hand as he selected the correct key from his large and varied bunch. They were attached to the good luck rabbit's foot key ring, and as quietly as he could, he placed the correct key in the lock. Slowly he turned the key around anti clockwise twice, and now for the first time in a very long time, he knew he was completely at the mercy of anyone that might have been stood waiting outside the door. He dithered for a few seconds, and then checked the spy hole once more. The hallway was clear; there was no one that he could see outside of the door.

As he pulled the handle down, it creaked slightly, but it was nothing that anyone would have heard, and then he pulled at the dead weight of the door. The door seemed to be a lot heavier than he had remembered. He cautiously peered around the corner and searched up and down and all around the hallway. Then finally, for the first time in months, he took his first step outside of the flat.

There were ten steps down to the ground floor level, and he steadied himself on the handrail as he gingerly walked down each one in turn. He walked with the stealth of an animal that was silently stalking its prey. As he reached the bottom of the stairs, he could see daylight shining in through the window of the external security door. Somehow the sunshine was reassuring, and it seemed to give him a little strength as he felt it touch his skin through the plain glass panel.

He was surprised to find that the door was locked. He wondered how the creatures had managed to open it quite so often. It didn't matter now though, he had to make a break for it. After a quick check outside of the window, he undid the latch and opened the flats security door. He took his first step into an outside world that was now a foreign nation to him.

The fresh air smelt almost heavenly compared to what he had endured. Perhaps it was now all over? With every second he felt his confidence was growing, and his feet were now unsteadily moving forward and in the direction of the shop. His smile widened as he walked each step, but then, just when he thought that he was finally safe, and that everything was at last going to be alright, it was then that he saw them. The monsters had still been hiding outside all along. They had been waiting patiently for him to emerge. He wanted to shout or scream, just so that he could unleash a torrent of uncontrollable anguish, but his mouth and throat were so dry, that despite his best efforts, he could not make a single sound.

He tried to run, but his legs were too weak, and his knees began to give way beneath him. He feared falling down and struggled to maintain his balance, but it was already too late. They were already upon him. The monsters had formed a circle that surrounded him, and in desperation, he sank to his knees and prayed that his end would be a swift and painless one.

As the monsters raised his body up from the ground, he looked at each of their faces in turn. He wondered what each of them had been like when they were children. What had happened to turn them into such raging and unforgiving hulks? His tears began to flow softly down his cheeks. He failed to understand the noises that they were making. In front of him about thirty feet away, he then saw Elvis once more. He was out in the sunlight, and dancing and singing once more, now it was an open air concert, and it was free for all, even the monsters.

The bailiffs then placed an eviction notice in his hand. The notice denied him access to enter the flat ever again. He had ignored the court orders, the disconnection notices, the final demands, and everything else that had been sent to him. They had all been ignored. They had remained piled up and unopened on the hallway floor. He didn't ignore them because he didn't want to pay them, after he lost his job, he could simply no longer afford to pay them. It was easier not to even look at them.

At sixty one, he was now considered too old by each and every employer that he had approached. His benefits had then been stopped when he could no longer attend any interviews. Each rejection had pushed him further and further into his well of misery and depression until he could take no more. Now the flat he had lived in for twenty three years, was no longer to be his home either.

As the ambulance arrived, the hallucinations had finally taken over, and he stared silently just watching Elvis as he danced and sang away outside the front of his flat. Elvis was now giving him the best concert of his life. As Elvis finished his last song, there was thunderous applause. He bowed and gave a lengthy wave to the only audience member who could actually see him.

A frail, afraid and hungry man was lifted onto a stretcher and up into the ambulance. He did not feel the needle scratch at his hand, or the fluids which were being drip fed into his body. He silently raised his hand upward, and just waved back politely to Elvis.

The paramedic looked down at the malnourished old man before him, and watched him as he waved to no one that he could see at all. Perhaps he was waving goodbye to his home for one last time he thought. The old man had been totally unresponsive to his questions so far, but still he had to keep on trying.

"Who are you waving to?" he asked. At last, the man turned his head toward him as he acknowledged his voice. He smiled a wry smile, firmly believing the words that were about to come out of his mouth.

"Elvis." He said "He just said that this is the time of Helter Skelter, and that.... humanity has now left the building." The paramedic just nodded his head and smiled. He recognised the severe signs of malnutrition, dehydration and extreme delirium, but at least the man would get the help that he needed now, if he managed to survive.

He closed the rear door and sat next to the patient. The ambulance driver turned on the blue emergency lights, and pulled quickly away on to the road from the flat. Time was of the essence right now, they had to get the guy into a hospital quickly. Sadly he knew the signs though, and there was every chance that this poor guy might not make it through the night.

The Spread

It started to rain much heavier than it had been throughout that evening. Everything seemed to be much calmer here when it rained. The man was now laid flat on cold, hard and unforgiving tarmac. He looked skyward as the rain fell down on his face. He had no strength left inside of himself, not enough to even turn his head. To his right, lay a puddle of blood that was thinning out with the water from the rainfall as it fell down increasingly heavier. He blinked his eyes slowly and deliberately until he could blink now more. The rain now began to sting his eyes which were opened wide with fear and expectation.

He knew that he did not have much time left. There was nothing more that anyone could have done for him. The pain started to rise once more in his stomach and then throughout his lower back. The virus had mercilessly ripped through his entire body and had relentlessly destroyed his internal organs. It was a truly horrific and inhumane way for anyone to die. Bile began to rise upward to fill his chest. The blood then mixed with the bile and formed clusters of acidic fluid that were burning his chest and throat as they rose upward.

As the man vomited, he tried in vain to turn his head to the side, but all of his strength was completely gone. In the distance, he could hear the sound of footsteps approaching, but it would be far too late for anyone to help him now. The fluid was choking him and he was drowning in his own vomit. It was very painful and death would now come as a welcome relief to him. He stared to the heavens with his eyes as red as an idyllic sunset, and watched as the rain appeared to fall down on to his face in slow motion. The light faded from his eyes, and his last thought was one of regret. He regretted leaving his family so very far away, and now he knew that he would never see them again.

This was supposed to be the way to a new life for them. Anything had to be better than being back at home in Sudan. Too much blood had been shed there over the years, but there was a place that he had heard of that was many miles away, a place that they called England. Here they could have a chance at a better life. Here they heard that they could make a great deal of money, and then in time, maybe they could find a way to bring their families to England too.

This trip had soon turned from an all consuming dream into the worst possible nightmare. Samir Garang, now saw his friend as he lay in the road ahead of him. He lay motionless on the ground as pouring rain battered down on to his lifeless body. Sensing something terrible had happened, he ran toward his friend. When he reached him, there were no visible signs of life. It was then that he knew his worst fears had been realised.

The trek for them both had been an arduous one. They managed to get through Italy and France quickly, but that had not been without incident. Then trying to move on from France to England had been a living nightmare. It had taken three attempts to stow away on a ship that was headed for the U.K before they actually had found a suitable hiding place on a boat. It was very dangerous, but they had to try. Tahir had been sick for days, but in England they would find him a doctor to help him.

Samir had been beginning to lose hope. The boat was his last chance to make it to England. He was missing his wife and son a great deal, and if this trip failed, then he decided that he would give up and return home to them. They stowed away safely, and the trip did not take long. On arrival in England they had managed to swim to and escape from the authorities easily. Both men spoke only limited words in English, and when they found themselves on the South coast of England, in a city called Southampton, both men soon realised that they were out of their depths.

When Tahir collapsed to the floor, he began to have convulsions. It was evident that he was now seriously ill, so Samir had run off in search of help. It was the small hours on a Sunday morning, and aside from the odd car headlights in the distance, he could see not a living soul out on the streets. He did not wish to stray too far from his friend, for fear of losing him completely in this unfamiliar place, and now as he returned to the dockyard, he saw that his friend was no longer breathing.

Samir placed his fingers inside of Tahir's throat. He cleared out lumps of congealed blood and vomit from his friend's airways. He then wiped his friend's mouth with his bare hands, and placed his lips directly over the cold wet lips of his friend. Forming a seal around the mouth, he forced air deep into his friend's lungs. He desperately tried to force life back into the unresponsive body that he now knelt beside. He repeated his ventilations a few times, and then began to compress the chest repeatedly. It was a futile gesture though, and there was no response.

He pleaded for his friend to breath, selfishly, he was afraid to be left alone here in this strange and unforgiving place.

"Please my friend, you must not leave me alone. This is my fault, please wake up!" He pleaded. Still there were no signs of life. He continued to try to resuscitate the body for another few minutes, until he reached the point of exhaustion. Then he realised, that there was no point in continuing any more. He punched down onto the lifeless chest, and then he wept openly over his friend's dead body. The rain yet again, seemed to once again increase in its intensity.

The weight of his recently deceased friend over his shoulder appeared to become heavier with every step that he took, as he walked toward the sea. The scent of the fresh sea air was strong here, and Samir breathed it in as deeply as his lungs would allow him. He could not let his friend's body be discovered. If it were, then he feared that he too might also be found out. They may already have been looking for them both. There were cameras everywhere here and it was impossible for him to know for sure. Paranoia filled his every thought. He so desperately needed this new chance of a life for his family.

He had to hide the body somewhere that it would not be found. He looked all around him in every direction, until he was sure that there was no one else close by. He then searched the surrounding area until he spotted something suitable that he could use. Dropping his friend's body gently to the floor, he then walked over and picked up an abandoned car wheel. The rubber was worn through and it was bald in numerous places it might be heavy enough to be of use. He then had to search a little further away to find something that he could use to tie the body to the wheel.

The abandoned strips of green plastic banding that he found, were not ideal, but they should be good enough for what he needed them for. Carefully he tied a few lengths of the bands together. He then tied one end of them through the car wheel. He stopped for a second as he realised that the rubber may cause the wheel to float on the water. He had to test it, just to put his mind at ease.

Using the bands he lifted up the car wheel and then carried it over toward the sea. He placed the wheel over the edge of the sea wall, and slowly lowered it down into the water. It quickly began to sink down into the darkness. It was just too heavy to be buoyant. He was confident that it would work, so he pulled the tyre back out of the water and there he left it close to the edge of the waterfront.

He realised that dragging the body would be a lot easier than carrying it, but Samir decided against this. He was too respectful for his deceased friend. So he lifted his friend's body up and carried it over to the edge of the water. He then placed him gently down at the edge of the sea. Carefully he then tied the plastic bands around his friend's legs. He could not risk the knots coming undone and the body floating back to the surface, at least, not until he had fled far away from here.

Once he was certain the bands were tied tightly enough, he began to say a little prayer. When he had finished the prayer for his friend, he was ready. He then lowered the tyre down once more into the water. The plastic bands pulled taught on Tahir's legs. He then pulled his friend toward over the edge of the sea wall. He then dropped him over the edge. The weight of the tyre dragged his friend's body down into the water.

For a few moments he witnessed air bubbles emerge from the water. They continued to rise as the body sank down further into the water. It was not that deep at the edge, but provided the bands held, it would still take time for the body to be discovered. The waves lapped against the concrete walls and they splashed waves of sea water upward. Samir looked downward into the sea. He could no longer see any air bubbles or any sign of his friend as he studied the dark waters beneath him.

The seawater splashed up on to his face. For a second he imagined his friend's lungs now being filled with the salty water as he was surrounded by fluid. This was how all humans come into this life, and it is now how his friend was finally at rest, the circle of life complete. He then coughed painfully into his hands, and the fluid that filled his palms was dark and sticky. It was blood, and that could only mean one thing, that he too was also infected. He had no choice, even if it meant that he was deported, he had to seek medical help right now.

He walked throughout the rain filled night and it remained dark for a few more hours. When the early morning broke, he then started to encounter other people. He did not know the English word for hospital. Instead he repeated the word 'Mustashfa' to everyone that he met, over and over again. Person after person backed away from this crazy man with a bloody mouth and bright red eyes. He finally collapsed in the middle of Southampton town centre and there he stayed until he was discovered by a policeman at ten o'clock the next morning.

Hundreds of shoppers had simply walked past the homeless vagrant. Some youths had even kicked and taunted him, as they to wake his lifeless body; it was only when the policeman arrived and had turned him over, that he noticed the dried blood that was all around the man's mouth. Unknown to them all, the new strain of virus that he had contracted, was now airborne.

Within a week, over five thousand people were infected by the virus. Within two weeks, and despite the best efforts to control the spread, it was already too late. A national emergency had quickly been declared. The virus went down in history as the biggest cause of death in the United Kingdom since the plague, and with no sign of a cure, those who had not been privileged enough to have fled the country could only pray for a miracle.

The infected were a lost cause. They were left to fend for themselves. The quarantine zone across the country widened daily. Fear spread among those who had not yet been infected, as they realised that it was just a matter of time before the virus finally reached them too.

Lady Ice

Giovanna was many different things. She was smart, beautiful and she also happened to be an efficient and ruthless killing machine. Some might say that she had a natural born talent for murder. It was a talent that had been passed down through her Italian family over many generations. She could swiftly and efficiently dispose of a target, at a reasonable cost and without regret, and that made her services very much in demand.

Unusually for an assassin, she had a certain code that she would adhere to, and that code allowed her to hand pick and choose her assignments carefully. Her mysterious employers soon came to learn that she would take time to consider their offers and that she would always research her potential targets. The more despicable the target was, the more likely that she was to take up the job.

Sometimes she would even donate some of her fee to her targets victims or their families, although the payments were always sent anonymously. Some said say there was no place for her in the business, that there was no room for an assassin with a heart. It was never spoken out loud though, such were her methods of termination that her name struck fear into those who knew of her. They only dared to say such things behind closed doors, when they were sure they were in safe company.

Whilst her methods were legendary, her face would always remain a mystery, even to her employers. Her fee was always the same; it was £50,000 per kill, no matter who the target was. The job would always be completed on time, and not a trace of evidence would be left as to who was responsible. Her latest target was an easy choice for her to make, and her method of killing the mark would be swift, painful and without any mercy.

Giovanna was now straddled across the lap of her target. Her tight dress was riding up her legs and he could see her ample breasts underneath the material. She had stripped him naked and now his large naked body was sweating profusely underneath her. As she whispered in his ear, he smiled with an inane grin in anticipation of the sexual act he thought that she was about to perform on him. The size of the man repulsed her, but she would show no hint of this at all. Instead she smiled as if she were about to have the time of her life. She swept her hair back and away from her face.

"Relax, lie back, and close your eyes." She instructed him. He did exactly as she asked him to.

Nadal Rahim was something of an arrogant man. A few years ago in his home country he had organized a military coup. There was an absolute bloodbath and anyone who opposed him was quickly put to death. Once he gained power he also killed those in the ranks underneath him who he had felt uncertain about. He then removed anyone he suspected would not remain loyal to him. Public executions were common for the most minor of reasons or suspicions. He used his power to rule without mercy or pity. Anyone who then dared to defy him, whether male or a female, would meet a swift and merciless death at the hands of his troops.

He soon grew bored of power and began to abuse his position even more. Rape became one of his favourite pastimes as countless young girls had been snatched from the streets and then delivered to his estate. He had arrived in London the night before to engage in diplomatic talks. They bored him, but were necessary for trade deals to continue. He made promises about human rights that he had no intentions of ever keeping. The next day he had been fed the finest foods and drank copious amounts of wine, and now a beautiful woman had been delivered to escort him. It was an unexpected gift.

He had excused his bodyguards for the day in anticipation of hours of pleasure with this high class lady. This was a standard extra that most countries he visited had often provided for him. He never expected it in London though. He always assumed the English were too upper class. He wanted the very finest of everything, and that included the women on offer. London did not disappoint him, the woman was very beautiful. The guards were never going to be very far away, and they were contactable by telephone if he needed them in the event of any emergency.

Now as he lay on the bed naked, he placed his hands cupped behind his head, and waited patiently to feel this pale woman's soft lips sealing around his naked member. As she moved her body backward, she moved her head down and toward his lap, and he kept his eyes closed in eager anticipation.

The moment she touched him felt truly intense, he felt a mixture of both pleasure and pain, and a huge rush of adrenaline as it flooded throughout his body. He enjoyed the experience of erotic pleasure and unusual pain combined, and this was something new. This was a trick he would have to teach other women. This woman was an expert or so it seemed. He had never felt such sensations in his groin before.

His head then seemed to be filled with a blinding white light and his body arched in rapture. This now felt more like intense pain, and the pleasure had quickly faded. He would now have to teach her how to enjoy him properly now. He opened his eyes to see a red spray rising upward and into the air. The blood flow was arching above his head and then falling back down on his body. It was only then that he suddenly felt the enormity of the immense pain that now filled his groin.

He did not feel the cutting edge as it was inserted, it was such a sharp blade that it sliced easily into his flesh. But now as he looked down his body, he could see something that he could not fully understand. His moderately sized penis was now gone and in its place was now a stream of blood that was pumping upward into the air above his body.

He tried to scream for help, but no sound came from his mouth. The knife that had removed his penis, had now expertly slid across his throat, and as blood pumped out from the two different areas with ferocious pressure, his felt his life force leaving his body. His vital organs had already begun to shut down.

Giovanna had leapt from the bed and run across the room. Now she was quickly ripping off her body hugging dress. She was narrowly avoiding the majority of the blood spray but speckles of the crimson fluid still managed to make their way across the room and onto her clothes. Spray from the incision in his throat had managed to splatter against the richly lavish designer wallpaper, and in a strange sense it seemed to add to the arty design. There was a great satisfaction in witnessing the death of a man like this.

In what felt like seconds, the tyrant's huge body was slumped almost lifeless on the bed. There was nothing but the occasional twitch in the legs as the nervous system reacted to the body shutting down for good. She looked down at her victim, without an ounce of mercy for the target. Now there was little time for her left. She had to carry out the cleanup session. Her routine was now such a familiar experience that she easily slipped into a different mode and began her cleansing ritual. She trusted no one to clean up her mess after her.

There could never be any evidence linking her to the body. The only way to be really sure of this was for her to clean the room herself. The victim deserved no respect in death. She removed a container of highly flammable fluid from her bag, and sprayed the fluid on to the body as well as the area surrounding him. The sheets began to absorb the fluid but it would remain highly flammable for a short while yet.

The body was still occasionally convulsing in the final death throws as Giovanna removed her blonde wig and fake fingerprint skins. She then threw them on top of the body along with her dress. She then used the remainder of the flammable liquid to soak her belongings. She took a replacement dress out from her bag and forced in on in a matter of a few seconds.

Taking a lighter from her bag she lit the bedding close to the body. There was no sprinkler system in the room, only in the communal hallway, she had already made sure of that. The time it would take for the body to fully ignite would give her the chance to exit the hotel. She then gathered up her bag, took out a pair of large dark sunglasses and gloves and put them on and then walked calmly out of the hotel suite. The body was already consumed in a mass of flames that was now spreading most efficiently.

Giovanna took very few risks at all. She walked past the lift and began her descent of the stairs. By the time she had reached the bottom of the stairs the fire alarm had already been echoing throughout the building for the last minute. People were now in a blind panic and were making their way out of their rooms as quickly as they could.

The scene in the lobby was just as she anticipated. Through sheer confusion and fright amongst the other hotel guests, she had been joined in the reception by many of the other residents as she walked toward the emergency exit. This would aid her in her escape, and allow her to remain unseen.

The sprinkler system that was installed in the hotel mysteriously failed, Giovanna had made sure of that. By the time that the fire engine eventually arrived and had managed to control the blaze, the burning lump body would be unrecognizable. It would take either dental records or D.N.A. to fully confirm the name of the victim. Even that would take some time though.

As she left the hotel, Giovanna waited patiently. She mingled amongst the ever growing number of evacuating guests and curious members of the public gathered outside on the pavement. She was waiting for the right time for her to exit the scene. Her escape plan should have been flawless. The kill had been perfect and rewarding. Now it was time for her to make her move.

The nearest security camera was situated on a building to the right. It was too far away to see her face at all. She walked to the left counting her steps. Thirty more and she would be ready to make another turn left. This would lead her to where she had left another set of clothes. They were hidden under the bottom of a filthy food bin at the back of a Chinese restaurant.

As she walked along the footpath away from the hotel, she noticed a small man who was now walking toward her. His features were strangely curious and it wasn't until he drew almost level with her that she noticed multiple scars across his face. Her instincts told her that something wasn't right about the man, but perhaps it was paranoia so soon after a kill. She remained wary of him anyway.

She kept her eyes on him as they drew level with each other, but now he was looking straight past her, toward the burning hotel.

"My God it's on fire!" He said as he pointed at the blaze. If she had to describe the man's features, she would say that his face looked almost rat like. Giovanna did not turn around. Instead she let the man walk by and she focused her eyes on the path straight ahead of her.

As he brushed past her, she felt a sharp scratch on the back of her neck. Placing her hand on the skin behind her head, there was a tiny trace of blood. Perhaps it had been an insect bite she wondered? She walked on for only a few more steps before her breathing suddenly became labored. The world began to seem distorted as if time itself had started to slow down. The rat faced man now had his arm wrapped around her and he was supporting her weight.

She turned her face the man to ask him what he was doing. She tried to speak but the words never managed to come out from her mouth. Her body now seemed to be functioning on autopilot. The man was leading her toward a car. All of the vehicles windows had been blackened out. She wanted to stop and fight the man off, but her arms would just not work in the way that they should.

She knew even through the haze, that she was in deadly trouble. The rear passenger door was suddenly opened from the inside and Giovanna was bundled hurriedly into the back of the vehicle. The engine was already running, ready for a fast exit from the scene. She was aware of everything that was happening to her, but she was completely powerless to resist.

The face of the 'rat man' was the last thing that she saw before a blow struck her forcefully to the back of her head. Then she was asleep for what felt like a very long time.

She didn't recall dreaming, but when she woke, her head felt as if it had been trapped tightly in a vice. The force of the pressure built inside her skull and it felt as if her brain itself were being squeezed like an orange inside a press. This was like the worst hangover that she could imagine, but she knew that she hadn't been drinking, as that was part of her strict code. So why was her head now feeling so painful? She could not recall how she got here.

Her eyes strained to fully focus, as the room she was now in was quite dark. She tried to move her arms and realized that they had been tightly restrained to what appeared to be a metal bed frame. She was laid down completely naked. Then with horror, she realized where she was. The metal bed frame was a dead giveaway. This was a torture chamber, one that was quite commonly used to extract information.

Now she was aware that she was in serious trouble, and it was highly unlikely that she would ever get out of this room alive. Pain was now imminent, and there was little she could do to prepare her body for whatever was about to happen. At that precise moment, all she could think of was her nine year old daughter Cecelia. She was now afraid that she might never see her child's angelic face ever again.

A single dull light bulb hung in the far recess of the room. It barely afforded any light though. Giovanna sensed there was someone else in the darkness, just watching her. She began to sweat, as she felt those same eyes examining her naked body. Gradually her eyes focused a little better, and shapes in the darkness of the room began to form.

She could make out a figure that was now moving toward her. It was the rat faced man, and he was carrying something in his hand. He slowed and then stopped directly in front of where Giovanna was secured. As he began to speak, the very tone of his voice sent shudders reeling right through her.

"I wish that I could tell you that your death will be quick and painless, but I just can't do that I'm afraid. My client paid for the whole treatment, and that is what you shall receive." He stated. His voice rasped as he stood in front of her.

As he grabbed hold of one of Giovanna's fingers, she tried to clench her hand into a fist. His grip was immensely strong and it didn't take him long to loosen up her hand. She felt the touch of cold metal clasp around the tip of her fingernail, and the pliers locked on to her nail and quickly wrenched it away from the flesh of the finger. Giovanna's scream filled the room as the pink painted part of her finger was now gone. The nail that was pulled clean now lay on the floor to the side of her. The pain felt as if someone had driven a metal nail right into the tip of her finger, and her body temperature rose instantly as it reacted to the pain.

Sweat beads were now forming on her body and were soon dripping down from her back. She wanted to show more bravery, but tears already streamed down her face. It was barely a few seconds before the man moved to the next finger and then proceeded to do the same thing with the next nail. One by one he removed all of her fingernails from her right hand. Each time he removed a nail, her screams filled the room just a little bit louder.

Giovanna could only think of one thing, and that was the face of her daughter. She prayed her daughter would remain safe, she knew that her family would always take care of her. Eventually they would avenge her death too. Unknown to Giovanna, Cecilia had been having quite a busy afternoon herself.

The walk home from school was short. Regardless of that, Cecilia always carried some form of protection about her person. The world was a dangerous place these days and considering her mother's choice of employment, Cecilia always felt safer with a knife about her body. Today it would come in rather handy.

They had followed the mother and her daughter for days. The window of opportunity was limited but workable. The girl took less than ten minutes to walk home from school. There were people around most of the time all along the route, and there was always the chance that some have a go hero would try and stop them taking her. It didn't matter though. They would soon deal with any threat. They had decided on the best place to drag the girl into the car, and it was here that the driver was now waiting patiently.

The client must have been some kind of sick freak. He wanted the mother tortured and then killed, and the girl...well God only knew why he wanted her kept alive. They had specific instructions though, and the client was paying extremely well. They would abduct the girl, take her to the place where her mother was being tortured, and she was to be forced to watch her mother die. Then they were to deliver the girl to him.

The girl was approaching the car. She was walking alone, as she always did. Cecilia chose not to entertain the locals and make new friends. She could ill afford to do so. Her mother never stayed in one place for too long, and safety was paramount. Cecilia had already realized quite a while back, that she was being followed. So far, she had decided to hold back on drawing her weapon. Ahead of her was a car with the engine running. It had all its windows blacked out, and that itself was a dead giveaway.

As the car door opened, a burly man in a dark suit stepped out from the car. He was wearing dark glasses, despite the fact that it was barely sunny at all. It was blatantly obvious he wasn't friendly. These idiots were amateurs though. The car door was held open as she approached, and the man who had been following her scooped her up and bundled her into the car.

She screamed like an insane child and kicked out as hard as she could. It was too late though, the man who had been following her had covered her mouth whilst the driver had sat back in the driver's seat and pulled away into traffic. Despite various people witnessing her abduction, no one had come to her aid, and it showed how cowardly society had become in dealing with instances like this. It didn't matter though. Her mother would soon deal with them.

The man who was holding her mouth felt sharp teeth sinking into his flesh.

"You little bitch!" He shouted and struck the girl around her face with an open palm. It stung her face as it connected, and a bruise started to appear instantly, but at least his stinking hand was no longer over her mouth. "Stop fighting me girl, we are taking you to your mother!" The man shouted.

"I don't believe you!" Cecilia screamed. "What have you done with my mother?" She demanded.

The man reached inside Cecilia's schoolbag, and searched around. He then pulled out her phone.

"Call her; tell her you are coming to her. We will take you there." The man instructed. Cecilia searched her contacts and dialed her mother's number. It rang for a few times until it was answered. The voice that answered the call was that of a man, not the one that belonged to her mother.

The phone vibrated on the table. Giovanna heard the ringtone, and knew instantly that it was her daughter. The rat faced man spoke to her.

"Wait." The male voice said. Then he covered the microphone on the handset and he spoke to Giovanna.

"You tell her that you are safe, and she will live. I give you my word. I can promise you no more than that. You tell her anything else; she dies before you see her for one last time. Do you understand?" Giovanna nodded her head. She struggled in vain against her binds. It was fruitless, but she refused to give up trying. The man then placed the phone back to his ear and he heard Cecilia's voice again.

"Mum, are you o.k.?" The male voice answered again.

"Your mum is here, I'm keeping her safe. Now you be a good girl and stay calm. I will let you speak to her now so you will know that she is fine." He then put the phone onto loudspeaker to be sure he heard the conversation, and then raised the phone up closer to Giovanna's ear.

"I'm fine baby girl. Just be good." She said. It was all that the man needed to hear. He then took the phone off loudspeaker and put it back to his ear.

"You are about five minutes away from us. Once you get here, I will tell you everything that has happened. Then we will see what happens next. Now promise you will be good." He said.

There was a slight pause.

"O.K, just please look after my mummy!" She pleaded. Then the phone went dead. Cecilia then started to cry.

In the basement, the pokers had been sat in the fire for some time. They were glowing red hot. The man carefully placed his gloves on, and picked up one of the irons.

"Beautiful. Isn't it?" He said as he held it in front of Giovanna's face.

"Fuck you. I'm going to kill you slowly." She replied, and then she spat into the man's face. He turned his face away in disgust, wiping the saliva away with his sleeve. Then he placed the hot poker on her chest, and drew it across her right nipple. At first there was no pain, not for a second or two anyway, but then, when it came, it was agonizing. Skin melted and bubbled as the heat was drawn across her naked flesh. The scream was deafening by the time her nipple had begun to swell and blister.

The drive was just over five minutes, exactly as she had been told. The car had pulled around the back of what looked like a small old industrial building. Timing was now everything. The words baby girl had told Cecilia exactly what she had needed to know. Her mother was in mortal danger, with little chance of escape. It was all down to her daughter now, and this was what she had been trained for.

The knife was hidden inside of her sock. It was rare that anyone would ever search a child that young. As the car was coming to a stop, she had to time everything as best that she could. The blade was six inches long once it was unfolded, and it was deathly sharp. Her tears had hidden the fact that she was working the knife up her leg and into her hands. Now it was unfolded, it was locked into place, and she was ready to use it.

The first wound punctured the throat of the man who had bundled her into the car. It had pierced the thick skin of the man's neck and had been driven deep into the carotid artery. Blood began to pump from the wound and the lack of oxygen now being restricted to the brain caused the man to panic. He held the wound with both his hands trying to stem the blood flow whilst he gasped for breath.

As the driver stopped the car and applied the hand brake, he saw blood splatter on to his rear view mirror. He tried to turn his head to see what had happened, but as he did so the blade pierced deep into his right eye. Cecilia pushed the weapon in as far as it would go, and then twisted the knife in the eye socket. The blade was cutting deep, straight through the eye and into the brain. The driver could only scream, but the scream was short lived.

As the blade was pulled back out from the socket, Cecilia turned around. The man on the back seat was now fumbling for the door handle. She jumped on his lap and stabbed him repeatedly in the heart. All the while that he tried to fend off her attack, the more blood was allowed to pump out from his throat, and now his chest was gushing blood outward too. Once she considered that the man was wounded enough, she turned her attention back to the driver. This time she slashed across his throat from right to left. He was already dead or dying, but by cutting deep enough she made sure he was definitely not a threat anymore.

The burns were agony. For the first time in her life, Giovanna wondered if she might be better off dead. The thought would not last for long though, instead a new thought had filled her head. Pain will always find a way to help you focus. The current now passing through the metal bed was making her back arch into an unnatural position. The pain from the high voltage was intense. Worst of all, it was unrelenting. As she fell back time and time again against the metal grid she was tied to, more and more of her skin was burning in perfect squares on her back.

The amount of blood in the car was incredible. She had never seen two men bleed the way that these two burly figures had. Her school clothes were now ruined. She searched through the jacket of back seat passenger despite the fact that he was drenched in the crimson fluid. In his jacket, he had carried a .22 pistol with a silencer. She checked the clip and it was full. She searched his pockets and found another clip. That was also full. It should be enough, if not she still had her knife. She took both the gun and the clip and sat patiently in the car. She remained patiently watching the building for any sign of movement from inside.

The car had been parked outside for too long. Ivan was already feeling a little edgy. Across the room another man was sat reading the paper, he was oblivious as to why Ivan might be worried. The men sometimes had a little fun with the victims, they seemed to enjoy the fear that they instilled. They found that it heightened the thrill of the kill.

"Alex! Go and check what's taking them so long. It's just a little girl for God's sake. Make sure they haven't touched her. The boss wants her alive!" He shouted. Alex threw his paper down on the sofa, and stubbornly got to his feet.

"Always me, always bloody me." Alex complained as he walked out of the building and in the direction of the car.

The engine of the car was still running. Alex was now positive that they were taunting the girl. He grinned as he walked up to the driver's window of the car, and tried to peer inside. The windows were just too dark to see through. He tried the driver's door, and it was locked.

"Come on guys, stop taking the piss." He said. Getting annoyed that he was even out here as rain began to fall in a sudden heavy shower. He turned up the collar of his jacket and walked around the front of the car. Then he tried the handle of the passenger door. It too was also locked. He tried to look inside once more. He was unaware that the back window of the car was now being slightly lowered. The last thing he felt, was the bullet enter his brain, and he fell down to the floor fatally wounded.

Giovanna was now really suffering at the hands of her torturer. He had used a pair of garden clippers and had cut the biggest toe off from her left foot. Blood was pumping out from the wound, but she no longer cared. If only the pain would end. She prayed that her daughter would not have to see her like this. She also prayed that Cecilia had remembered her training.

If it wasn't bad enough that those two had wound him up, now Alex was also taking the piss out of him. Ivan was furious. He saw that it was raining outside, took his gun from the drawer and holstered it and then he stood up and grabbed his coat from the coat hook. He put his right arm inside the jacket and reached across to put his left arm inside the other sleeve. By the time he had realized that the girl was in front of him, the second bullet had already entered his face. Both bullets had travelled out of the back of his skull and left blood and bone fragments impacted on the wall behind him. Ivan then fell to the ground with a thump.

Cecilia was not strong enough to hide the body outside of the car. Instead she had just left it on the floor. She hoped that she could get the job done quickly before anyone found her victim. She was pretty sure that there would be no others left in the building, but she had to make sure that it was safe. She walked from room to room. She checked around every corner carefully, always ready to take out any person she encountered. She only had one thing on her mind, and that was to save her mother.

There were very few rooms to explore, she checked them all thoroughly though. The last one was at the back of the building. It opened to a stairwell that descended downward. Inside the room at the base of the stairs, she could hear sounds coming from inside. The sounds were of a woman screaming in pain. Those sounds were coming from her mother. She slowly crept down the stairs. She tried turning the door handle gently, and it wasn't locked.

Just as he was about to remove another toe, Giovanna's phone started to ring once more. It was confusing to the rat faced man. It was Cecilia's number that was calling again. Perhaps they were telling him that they had arrived. He picked up the phone and pressed the answer button.

"Hello." He said. It was all the time that Cecilia needed. She had crept inside the door whilst the phone was ringing. Her mother had seen the door opening to her right. She remained silent though. There was one target in the room, and that made life easier, so much easier.

"Take him down." Giovanna shouted. That was a clear enough instruction. Down is down, and not out. Her mother wanted him alive. She rained bullets into the man's legs and arms and then one into his chest. He fell screaming to the floor dropping the phone as he did so.

Cecilia was already across the room to where the man had fallen. She knelt on the wound in his chest which left him struggling for breath. Cecilia then applied pressure as hard as she could underneath his jaw-line. It quickly rendered him unconscious. When he awoke, he realized that they had severely underestimated the woman, and her daughter. That would prove to be his downfall.

Giovanna knew that time was short. She he had to get to a doctor fast, but first she had to deal with the rat faced man. She used torn material from her bag to bind the wound on her foot, she screamed as she did so. It stopped the bleeding and that was good enough. The man was now secured to the bed exactly the same way that she had been. Cecilia was standing in the doorway keeping guard. Her mother wanted her to see what she was doing first hand. It was important that she watched him suffer.

The electricity flowed through the bed for slightly longer than it needed to, but it allowed Giovanna time to put the gloves on. She picked up the poker with one hand, and then switched the current off with the other. The man appeared to be crying and pleading, but she chose not to hear his words. Instead she placed the poker in front of his left eye, its glow was a fiery orange and the man now showed real fear as he realized what she intended to do.

Giovanna needed one thing from the man.

"Give me his name." She said. "Tell me the name of the one who hired you. Once you tell me, I end this quickly. I give you my word." Then without even giving him a chance to answer, she plunged the poker an inch into his left eye. The man was screaming as the hot metal was rolled around in his eye socket. He could hear the eye burst from the metal stake and the fluid from the inside of the eye as it bubbled before evaporating from the heat.

The man knew that his death was imminent. He was never going to get paid for this job, nor would he be able to enjoy the money from it. Instead perhaps this woman could avenge his death for him. It gave him little comfort, but facing death, he now had no loyalty to his customer anymore. The only thing he now desired was a quick ending to his pain.

He spat blood from his mouth as he began to try and utter a name. The words eventually fell out from his mouth.

"Kannis, Danny Kannis." He said. "Now keep your word bitch." He turned his head to one side, and for some insane reason, he now began to start laughing.

She had no idea who Kannis was, or why he would want her dead. That would come in time though. Now there was only one thing left for her to do. She grabbed the hot poker once more, and walked to the head of the bed. She pulled the man's hair back until his one remaining eye stared up at her.

His insane laughing continued. It carried on right until the moment the poker entered his mouth, and it was burning him inside as it glided down his throat and carried on into his stomach. As the body began to cook from the inside, he continued laughing, but not for very long at all. Cecilia handed her mother the gun and the .22 bullet was then fired into his forehead from point blank range.

The room now had to be cleansed. Giovanna picked up her phone, and it was still working, despite a large crack that was now in the screen. The fire was easily started using an aerosol can and her lighter. The clothes of the dead man lit up the room with an intense orange flame. Cecilia closed the door behind them and then led the way up the stairs; she would stop and help her mother through each room toward the exit, but she would always check first, to ensure that they had a safe exit.

As they exited the building, Giovanna took hold of her phone and called a number that she had previously stored.

"It' Gio, listen to me. I need an emergency doctor's visit. Cash as usual. Meet me at the safe house when I call you again." She said, and then she ended the call. She then dialed another number from her short call list.

"It's Gio, listen I can't give you details right now, but I need information. The target is called Danny Kannis. Get me everything you got. I will call you again soon," Then she ended that call too. "You did me proud today Cecilia. I'm glad you remembered all that I taught you." Her smile was weak and jaded, but it was genuine.

"Well you have been training me for this since I was five." She returned.

They both had a long walk ahead of them, but for now, they had to slip away into the shadows, and make sure that they lived to find the next target. Cecilia insisted that the next kill belonged to her. Danny Kannis belonged to Giovanna though, but to hear her daughters pledge to avenge her suffering, it had made her mother truly proud.

The Red Devil

He drove toward his home just a little above the speed limit. The music now playing was nothing but a background noise to keep him awake as he drove. The C.D. player stopped working over six months ago, but lack of funds, and a distinct lack of effort on his part, had meant that it had not yet been replaced. The radio would have to suffice for now. He wasn't really listening to it anyway. Instead he focused on maintaining the same speed as all the other traffic that was travelling on this god forsaken motorway. He would drive home and hide, but he knew that eventually it might come to find him.

Ahead the red rear lights of numerous cars slithered together. It was as if they were connected like giant illuminated snakes writhing along the highways of life. On the opposite side of the road, the white headlights shunted slowly forward and appeared to merge into a never ending circle of traffic that was moving round and around in circles. His eyes began to drift as the hypnotic dance of illumination bathed his eyes like night time starlight's twinkling.

The car rattled as it pulled over to the side of the road, and the wheels rolled over the rumble strips. He felt a constant shuddering on the steering wheel and instantly he awoke with a start. He grasped tightly to the steering wheel in shock, and he wondered just how long he had been asleep for.

"You bloody idiot!" He chastised himself. He was grateful that he hadn't crashed the car whilst he had been slept. There was a sign ahead, and although distant, he was sure that the sign said that the next services were close. He strained his eyes on the dimly lit road, and as he drew closer, he saw that he was correct. The next service station was only another three miles away. The traffic had suddenly eased, and now there were very few cars left on the road. He had to stay awake for just a little while longer.

Only the front electric windows of the car were still functional. The rear ones had stopped working before the C.D. player broke, but no one ever sat in the back these days anyway. He needed fresh air, so he lowered both of the front windows down to about half way. He also decided to turn up the radio up just a little bit louder, in the hope that something may grab his attention. If he could just hold on that next three miles, then he could at least get out of the car for a while and grab himself a hot drink.

The slip road to the service station was just up ahead, so slightly ahead of the third green countdown marker, he flipped the indicator wand downward. As he pulled into the services he gently applied the brakes, constantly slowing the car gradually until reaching the required fifteen miles per hour limit. The car park was almost deserted. He drove up as close to the door as he could and parked in the space directly outside of the entrance door.

As he stepped out of the vehicle, a cold wind blew hard against his face. It was so intense it almost knocked him backward against the side of the car. The wind had arrived from out of nowhere, and he zipped up his coat to protect him a little from the strong winds. He then climbed the steps of Fleet services and walked in through the heavy metal and glass door. He failed to notice the car that had just followed him into the car park.

He needed a hot strong coffee to keep him awake, but the need to pee was now greater. He saw the sign for the toilets and made his way toward them. The toilets here were always clean, but no matter how thoroughly they were scrubbed, there always seemed to be the scent of urine whenever he entered the toilets. He walked past the urinals and further on toward the cubicles. All of them were empty. He chose the middle one of five and locked the door behind him. It was for added safety he assured himself.

The relief was intense as the warm urine began to flow. He breathed deep and instantly regretted doing so, as the stench of urine was a lot stronger in this cubicle. There were pools of urine either side of the toilet bowl and he shook his head in disbelief. Some people either had no manners, or they just didn't care a damn. A lack of respect seemed to be the norm amongst the youngsters of today. He flushed the chain and zipped up his jeans. He really felt as if he could do with a bath or shower right about now, but it would have to wait.

As he walked out of the toilets, it was only now that he noticed that the services appeared to be completely empty. It was quite early in the morning, but there were always people around here, no matter what time of night it was. Adrenaline started to flood through his body and his legs began to shake. The bodies natural fight or flight reaction was kicking in, the only trouble was, at this moment he could do neither. He had been running away since 5am the previous day, and he badly needed that coffee just to keep him functioning.

He saw the sign for the coffee shop, and headed toward it. The lights at the far end of the service station started to dim as he slowly walked forward toward them. Still there was no one else in visible in the entire place. A dark figure then descended slowly from the roof of the service station in front of him. It was if a spider lowering itself slowly on its own web that it had spun. He froze to the spot in his fear, as the figure landed gently on its feet in front of him. It was the same creature he had encountered the night before. He wanted to run, but his body was trembling and refused to move.

The figure walked slowly toward him, seemingly aware of his inability to run away. As his eyes locked with those of the monster, sweat began to stream down his forehead and on to both of his cheeks. His breathing now became heavy. The figure was now less than three feet away from him. Try as he might, he could not move an inch. All of the stories, everything that he had heard about these creatures, he now knew that it was all true. This was some kind of vampire, but nothing like you saw in the movies. This was the first time he had seen this thing close up and it petrified him. The night before he had encountered the creature by accident, and now it had followed him all of the way back here.

He had spent the previous day in Liverpool. It had been a glorious afternoon watching his mighty Liverpool football club. They had stuffed their accursed enemy Manchester United by four goals to one that afternoon and it was the best feeling ever. It had then changed from an afternoon of watching sport into a heavy night out on the town to celebrate with the locals. The fans were all full of pride and more than ready to party after that drubbing. It wasn't everyday that you stuffed your biggest rivals.

This was a special moment. It was something that you may never see again in your lifetime, and it had to be celebrated. So celebrate was what he did, and he did it in style. He was worse for the wear but he was still singing his heart out to 'The Fields of Anfield Road', at four in the morning as he headed unsteadily back to his hotel.

Walking through a long and poorly lit underpass probably wasn't the cleverest idea at that time of the morning, but drunken bravery had won the day. It was here that he now found himself anyway, still smiling and desperately needing to piss. As he approached the middle of the tunnel, through a drunken haze, he spotted something up ahead of him in the shadows.

Two vagrants seemed to be fighting up ahead, and this was quite a frenetic battle. He kept walking, in the hope that his presence would either go unnoticed, or that it may shock them into ceasing their scuffle with each other. As he drew closer, one of the men used a single hand to lift the other cleanly up from the floor, and he held him up in the air with his feet dangling a foot from the floor.

With a single movement, the man who had been held aloft was now body slammed back down to the ground. Then the other man had sunk down to his knees to finish off the job. His teeth sank deep into the neck of the man, and fresh blood sprayed up on to the wall of the underpass. This was no vagrant. This thing was more like an animal that was now devouring its prey after the fresh kill.

For a moment he just stood in shock, and then the figure in front of him looked up as it finally noticed his presence in the underpass. The eyes of the creature seemed to stare directly into his soul, and a feeling of utter dread filled his entire body. The creature bellowed a deafening screech, and even with a stomach full of alcohol, he knew that he had to get away from here fast. So he turned around and he ran. He ran from that underpass faster than he had ever run before.

The creature might have been following him, but he did not dare to look back, instead he just kept on running. He had to get away from the creature. He ran as fast and as far away as he possibly could. He ran until he could run no more and it felt as if his lungs would explode at any moment. He then dropped to his knees as the sun rose in front of him. If this were to be his last sunrise, then it was a beautiful moment in which to die. The creature was gone though. It had not followed her here. He had just about managed to escape it somehow.

The next day, he had reported what he had seen to the police, and a thorough search of the area proved to be fruitless. There was no evidence that anything bad had happened in that underpass. Now he was almost convinced that his drink had been spiked and he had imagined the whole thing. Back at the hotel, he kept going over the scene in his mind. It wasn't a dream, it was real and he was positive of that. He began to search the Internet to see if anyone else nearby had seen anything that remotely resembled the creature that he had encountered.

There were numerous stories on the internet. Most of them had been reported by vagrants and drug users, who were always dismissed without any investigation and then they were ridiculed in the local press. He counted over fifty instances, over many years. All the instances had occurred on the exact dates when the heated derby between Liverpool and Man Utd was played in Liverpool. It had to be more than just a coincidence.

He checked out of the hotel later that day, and as he drove away, he had an awful feeling that he was being watched. The creature's eyes that morning seemed to have told him that it had some unfinished business with him. It was almost like having a sixth sense and he knew that he was in danger, even if no one else believed him. He knew in his heart that and if he could not get far enough away from here, then he might suffer the very same fate.

Now the creature was here in the services, and right in front of him. It was so close that he could feel it breath on his skin. It raised its left hand up toward his face. Its fingernails looked as if they were hundreds of years old, and its skin looked aged and wrinkled. Two small horns were present on the creatures head, and it looked somewhat demonic. He could feel the coldness of the creature's breath on his face, and the stench was that of rotting meat. It almost made him gag as the creature touched his skin.

"What the hell are you?" He asked. The creature tilted its head to one side as if it half registered the question that it was being asked. It did not respond though. Instead, it shifted its hand to grab its prey around the neck. His entire body weight was lifted with that one hand and he was now being held a few feet above the ground. It was only now, that he noticed the creature was wearing a Manchester United shirt. It hurt him to think that this might be the last thing he saw before he was sent to his grave.

He prayed his death would be quick, but he was certain that it would not be painless. He began to say the Lord's Prayer under his breath, and the creature started to laugh as it heard the words it had heard hundreds of times before throughout the centuries that it had existed. The creature stared straight into his eyes, then the laughing stopped, and an inhuman screeching began to escape from its mouth. The creature then released its grip and it dropped its prey to the floor.

As he looked up at the creature, blood began to flow from both of the corners of its mouth; the blood that now flowed was thick and black. He looked down and from the creature's chest and he saw that a wooden stake was protruding outward from where its heart should be. It was then driven further through the creature's chest and he was showered him with sprays of the creature's blood. Then the creature fell down lifeless to the floor beside him. A solitary figure now stood where the creature had been. The figure was wearing a Liverpool shirt, and this was all too much for him to take in.

The figure offered his hand and lifted him up from the floor.

"It knew where you were headed and it was waiting for you. I followed you from the hotel after I got a tip off for a friend of mine in the force. You're lucky it's only a loner, if you had chanced upon a nest, you'd already be dead by now. "The figure said.

"What the hell was that thing? Is it dead?" He asked.

"Some call them Vampires, bloodsuckers, Nosferatu, they go under many different names. Me, I call them what they really are..." He then kicked the creature over so that its shirt was once again visible. "There is a reason they call them fuckers the Red Devils." He said.

For some insane reason, and even though it shouldn't do, everything now made perfect sense to him.

What goes around comes around.

They had been watching him online for just over six months. The guy was becoming something to truly be admired. He spent a lot of his time collecting donations for charity, completing sponsored walks, even at one point jumping out of an airplane despite his morbid fear of heights. He always had comforting words for those in need, and he was always there both day and night to help those who were in need. It was clear that this guy had a heart of gold. The latest picture he had posted online was him handing over a cheque for two hundred pounds that he had raised for a local disabled boy. He was totally selfless in his acts, and this made Simon the perfect target to be murdered.

It had started just over ten years ago. At the time, Michelle had been a researcher who was working on a book for a local author. During her research she had come across a book which had captivated her imagination. Some believed the book to have never really existed, but somehow she appeared to have come across the sole copy in existence of the Necronomicon. It was more commonly known in black magic circles as 'the book of the dead'.

The knowledge contained inside the book was powerful, and she shared it with only a few close friends she knew that she could trust. From those early days, a dark cult was created amongst them. They were driven by the knowledge that was contained within those pages. The pages promised eternal life and unlimited power for those who would summon a dark lord. Their cult had been small at first and there were only four of them in number who had offered up the first of human sacrifices. Each life that they took was dedicated to a powerful demon they had discovered within the pages of the book. He was called 'Nefrante'. Over the years they had slowly recruited more servants who could be convinced to help them raise the dark Lord. Now the group had grown and numbered fifteen in total, and strength in numbers had made the abductions and sacrificial rituals much easier to accomplish.

They followed his every move for weeks, and soon worked out the pattern of his movements. They knew when he went out, where he shopped, where he went to train, and when and where he went out to have fun. They even knew the times that he got up in the morning, and when he went to bed at night. This guy wouldn't be easy to abduct though. He was big, and he was strong. It was going to take an awful lot of meticulous planning, or a cunning ploy. The reward though, for someone as kind and as giving as him, well they hoped that at last, his sacrifice might just be enough to finally resurrect the demon that they now worshipped so completely. This would be the seventh victim, and seven was always a magical number.

In the end, they had decided on a simple plan, as these had often turned out to be the best way to lure out a victim. He was a solitary figure without any family living with him, and they knew the times that he would be at home alone. His generous nature could be the very thing that would eventually lead to his downfall. The ruse was simple enough, and at half past ten of a rainy Friday night, they finally put their plan into action.

Simon had been surfing the internet. Social media had provided him with a new sense of purpose. Here he had a following, and it was nice to feel appreciated for all that he did for others. He never asked for thanks though, just to see the smiles of the people he helped, those were reward enough. It was enough to save him from a worthless life without any direction. He truly believed in helping others as a form of balance against all that was bad in the world. Now it was late in the evening, and he was considering an early night, when his doorbell unexpectedly rang.

Despite his size, Simon he was no fool. He checked through the spy hole and saw a petite woman standing outside on his doorstep in the pouring rain. He opened the door to see why the woman was at his door, he hoped she wasn't selling utilities at this time of night. The woman was slight, but he could see through her soaking wet white blouse that she was perfectly proportioned. He wondered why on Earth she was out in this weather without a coat.

"Hello." He said "Can I help you?" he asked.

"I'm so sorry to bother you, but my car has a flat tyre and I'm not strong enough to undo the wheel to change the tyre. Could I use your phone at all to try and get some help?" She asked.

"Come inside and out of the rain." He offered as he beckoned her into the hallway. She smiled as she walked inside the door and into the welcoming warmth of the house.

The house was decorated in a way she would never have imagined. It felt almost as if it had been designed to feel homely by an expert, and she immediately felt the warmth of the paintings that adorned the walls.

"There's no need for you to call someone, I will come out and change the wheel for you. I'll make sure you get on your way safely." He said. Then he handed her one of his coats from a coat hanger in the hallway. She placed it around her shoulders. It was way too big for her, but at least it would keep her dry for a little while. She was careful not to touch anything else inside of the house, the coat she could dispose of later though.

"Are you sure?" She asked, already knowing that he would respond this way. It was just too much in his nature to want to help a damsel in distress. "I don't want to put you out." She said. She was smiling all the time and just making it a little too obvious that she was slightly attracted toward him.

"Of course I am. I'm not going to leave you out by the road in this weather, am I? I want to make sure that you're safe. Now where did you leave your car?" He asked.

"Oh, thank you so much." She said. "It's so rare to meet someone so kind in this day and age. The car is just around the corner, this is the first house that I came across with any lights still on." She answered.

He put an old coat on. There was no way that he was wearing anything decent that might get ruined whilst working on the car. Then opened the door and showed the lady out first. The woman stepped outside and he followed her closely. He caught a hint of her perfume as she stepped back out into the air and she smelt amazing. Then he closed and locked the door behind him.

"You lead the way." He said.

For a short woman her pace was brisk. He managed to keep up easily though. She led him to a turning just around the corner from where he lived. The street was dimly lit, and close to the lakes that he lived by. There were no other houses here. He wondered what she was doing down this road all by herself?

"It's not very safe down here." He told her. "There have been a few attacks and robberies in this area; we even had a flasher here once." He told her. Her face looked surprised.

"Really?" She seemed surprised. "My God, I'm so glad that I found your house. I really do appreciate you helping me." She replied. "It's the front wheel on the passenger side of the car." She told him. He knew that it would be even darker around the other side of the car. Now he began to wonder if he should have had the sense to bring a torch with him. He made his way around to the other side of the car, and the tyre was completely flat. He then bent down to take a closer look.

The last thing that he remembered was bending down to look at the tyre. Then something solid had struck him hard on the back of his head. He placed his hand on the back of his head and as he held it to his hand, he saw the darkness of his own blood in his palm. Then he felt a sharp scratch as someone injected a fluid into his neck. He stumbled toward the woman and fell down to his knees as he tried to grab a hold of her. Dizziness, confusion and then eventually darkness followed. Three men then emerged from hiding places in the bushes and set about lifting the dead weight of the man up from the floor and into the boot of the car.

He would be unconscious for quite some time, but this still had to be executed quickly. He had to be back at the altar before midnight in readiness for his transition. While he was safely placed out of sight in the boot, the woman took a small air compressor out from the rear well of the car, and then inflated the flat tyre. Once it was fully inflated, she removed the compressor and replaced the cap on the valve. Then all four of them got into the car. They drove away at a comfortable speed, they were careful not to drive over the speed limit.

The moment that he awoke, he was still fuzzy and confused as to what had happened. The surroundings he now found himself in were unfamiliar to him. He was laid down on a cold hard slab that felt as if it were made of stone, but he could not turn his head far enough around to look at it. His head was tied tightly down. His hands and feet were also fastened tightly and he was completely unable to move.

His mouth was gagged and this prevented him from calling out for help. The place was abandoned, but occasionally someone would still chance upon the building. Tonight they had to make sure that they were not disturbed. Candles were lit all around him and they added sparse light to what strangely appeared to be an abandoned church.

From the limited vision that he had, he could see various Crucifixes that were hung upside down on the church walls, and large pentagrams were painted in red all around the church. There were also some strange symbols that he thought he recognized, but these looked very old, possibly Egyptian but he couldn't be sure. If all of these symbols were what he assumed they were for, then he knew that something bad was about to happen. He now felt very afraid of what was about to happen.

In the dim light, figures dressed in dark cloaks appeared from the rear end of the church. The figures then started to move toward him. As they moved closer, they began chanting and a long ancient rite of a ritual sacrifice had now begun. He had to try and stop them before it was too late. He pulled at the binds around his wrist, and became frustrated at how tight they were expertly tied. Despite his immense strength, the harder that he pulled, the tighter the binds became.

The figures drew ever closer until they surrounded him in a circle. They were still chanting some ancient incantations even when they had taken their places. One of the figures raised his hand up, and they all stopped chanting in unison. On the slab Simon continued to struggle. He had to try and warm them, to tell them to stop. Despite the pleading in his eyes, they would not remove his gag to hear what he was saying. To them it was just the muffled sounds of a mortal who was begging to be set free.

The lead figure stood at his right hand side and removed her hood. It was the diminutive lady who had appeared at his door earlier that evening. She leant over and spoke into his ear.

"You are one of the chosen. Do not be afraid mere mortal. Your sacrifice will lead us to a new world order, and the rise of the demon God Nefrante, the ancient Overlord of the Dark realm. It is he who has pledged to cleanse the Earth and assemble his army of the dark ones, he who will finally purge this world from the curse of mankind." He could only shake his head furiously to try and make her understand the mistake she was about to make. He tried time and time again to shout the word "No!" But his plea would not be heard.

Then he saw the blade, and he knew that it was too late to stop them. The silver sacrificial knife was now being presented to her. She took the knife and gripped it tightly. It was inscribed with something, but he could not read the word etched on to the blade. She then raised the knife above her head. She gripped it with both hands and now she was ready to commence with her final dark prayer.

Her words echoed throughout the church, and it was a surprisingly powerful voice for such a petite figure.

"Lord Nefrante, we offer you this human as a sacrifice. This is the seventh offering that your written word demanded of us. Seven heavenly bound souls no offered to you. As the blood of the innocent one flow's we offer you his innocence. We give you the power to rise from your ancient prison once more. We, your faithful servants offer you this. In return we demand our places by your side in eternal rule over the darkness on Earth, that will be for now and forever more."

The others in the room began to sway from side to side as they chanted louder and louder. The figures were becoming frenzied in the lust as they impatiently waited for the ritual to be carried on to reach its bloody conclusion. Simon could only watch helplessly as the knife swayed in Michelle's hands above his chest. He knew what was coming, and now it was just a matter of time before it plunged down into his heart. His eyes pleaded with the woman once more, but it was to no avail. The knife suddenly sank downward aided by the force of gravity, and it drove down into his chest with the force of a lump hammer smashing down into his body.

As the knife pierced his heart, it cut deep into the muscle. The serrated edge ripped at the walls of the heart as it was then driven further even down. The knife was then extracted causing even more damage as it was removed. Blood began to flow rapidly from the open wound and as the fluid pumped out from the hole in his chest his pulse grew weaker and weaker.

On the other side of the Church, the floor began to vibrate. The vibrations grew quickly in their intensity. The stone floor then began to crack until a hole in the solid stone began to appear. The light from hellfire then flooded upward and into the room. The hooded figures held each other's hands and watched in awe, this was just as the words of the book had prophesized. It was then that the Dark Lord began to climb up and out from the ever expanding hole in the floor that they had opened. They could only stand silently in awe as the figure fully emerged and then it stood upright in front of them.

Nefrante stood towering above the humans. Its height was around nine feet tall. Its head looked like that of a rabid Ram. It snarled spittle from its mouth that looked like black blood as it sprayed on the floor beneath it. Its body was covered in boils and sores, and it bore scars from battles that had been fought eons ago before his exile from the Earth. It looked around the room at the figures gathered before it.

One of the figures ran toward him ready to greet his new master, but the demon did not take kindly to the intrusion into his space. With sharpened claws, it made a single strike with its long and powerful left arm. The claws that adorned its fingers ripped straight through the neck of the oncoming figure. The body of the man fell down to the floor. His head was now separated from his body. It spun through the air and smashed against the church wall more than fifteen feet away.

The horned God roared aloud, and the gathered figures dropped to their knees in fear of the power of the demon they had just awakened.

"Who has summoned me from my slumber?" It roared. Michelle then stood upright, but wisely decided against moving any closer.

"It is us. We are your servants my Lord. We have summoned you here to cleanse this Earth. We are here to serve you!" She responded, bowing her head as she finished speaking. Nefrante moved forward toward the woman. He placed one of his fingers under her chin. She raised her head slightly and then looked straight into the Demons eyes.

"Serve me you will woman. You will be my bride, and your pain will be unbearable. "As Michelle looked deeper into his eyes, and she could see nothing but the suffering of humans this beast had previously fornicated with. She knew that she now faced an eternity of pain and suffering. It was at that exact moment, she fully realized the mistake that she had made. Now it was her turn to be afraid.

She started to back away, but the Demon sensed her fear. He grabbed hold of her and drew her back closer to him. She felt warm animal breath upon her face, and the stench of thousands of years of decay. She began to scream. Nefrante then pushed her backward onto the floor. "Scream for me woman, but it is nothing compared to what is coming later. Now you will wait, for I must feed." It said calmly.

Nefrante raised his hand and then pointed to each of the doors to the church, each of them slammed closed. They could not be opened again by human hands. Then he grabbed the closest man to him, and he started to devour him in front of all the others present. He started by taking off the man's head. The bite was clean enough to remove it in one mouthful, and his cloaked body then fell down to the floor juddering as it landed.

The church was now full of screams from both men and women alike as they tried to run, but Nefrante was agile enough to spring from one side of the church to the other in a single bound. Mercilessly he set about slaughtering the rest of the group. Michelle could only watch on in horror, blissfully unaware, that behind her on the altar, the once lifeless body of Simon had now begun to move.

As the crimson liquid had flowed out from his body, the ropes had been soaked in blood. The binds around his wrist had then become loose. He shouldn't be alive of course, but this was just going to be one of those days when nothing made any sense. There was nothing that he could do to stop the transition now. His hand slipped from the bindings and he reached for the knife that had been carelessly left beside him on the altar. He then cut the binding on his head and sat upright so he was then able to cut the gag and the ties around his legs. He was aware of the carnage around the room, but he did not let it bother him. He had more pressing matters on his mind. It was coming and the vessel had to be prepared in readiness for the emergence.

Simon stood upright at the back of the altar, and then turned to face the pentagram painted on the wall it had once been a much loved symbol of power and now it gave him strength. His body shook and his eyes began to glow red. When he spoke it was almost silent.

"I once again beg your forgiveness." He said. Then he forced the knife blade deep into the pit of his stomach and then slowly he drew the blade upward. He should have been screaming with pain, but instead of screaming, his laughter now began to echo throughout the almost hollow church.

Both Michelle and Nefrante stopped dead and turned toward Simon. They both heard the laughter as it grew louder and louder. Nefrante then moved toward the figure that now had his back to him.

"You dare to mock me mortal?" He challenged. The figure then turned to face him, and Nefrante stood motionless, he was the one now stood in fear.

Michelle shook her head repeatedly. She could not believe what was now happening. Her legs were parted slightly, and warm urine flowed down both of her thighs. She wet herself unable to control her fear as she witnessed what was now happening before her. She was certain that at any moment, she would wake up from this, and it had to be the worst nightmare that she had ever experienced. This was no nightmare though. This was all very real indeed.

As Simon turned around, his head had lulled backward. He was still laughing insanely, even though his head was in a position that no human head could ever consciously reach. From the open wound in his stomach a large red horned figure was now peering outward. It started to climb up from inside of his body and one leg after another it emerged from the shell of its former host. It stood around fifteen feet tall and it now towered over Nefrante.

When the demon finally emerged from the human host, it had run toward him. Nefrante now felt fear for the first time in his life. He knew exactly who the creature was, he was the ruler of the underworld, and he knew that this time he would not escape with his life.

The red horned figure had lifted Nefrante clean from the floor with just one hand. It squeezed the throat of the creature, and with its spare hand it repeatedly tore away at the dark lord's body. Nefrante howled in pain as it was ripped apart limb from limb. Just as quickly as the creature had emerged from the hellfire, so it would also be consumed by that very same fire. The ground opened up in instant portals to hell as each part of his body fell down to the ground, each part was devoured by the flames. Nefrante was soon completely torn apart. Now the figure turned its attention elsewhere in the church.

The Demon like figure now turned to face Michelle. It began to walk toward her. In desperation, she could only crawl backward through her own urine as the figure approached her. Then suddenly she could move backward no further. The small of her back was now against the base of the stone altar, and there was nowhere else that she could go. It was now too late anyway. The Demon was already stood right in front of her.

Michelle closed her eyes and waited for death, but death was not quite ready for her yet. She sobbed and held her head in her hands.

"I'm so sorry, I'm so sorry..." she repeated over and over again.

The Demon held out his left hand to her.

"I offer you life." It said. It was something that she had never expected to hear.

"What...why... Who are you?" She asked.

"My name is Lucifer. You may have heard about me over the last few thousand years." He said, and then he continued on. "Things are different for me now, and just as the good can sometimes turn to evil, everything is equal, and so evil can sometimes want to find its way back to being good. I have lived with the pain and hurt and hatred of mankind for longer than I care to know. Now I want to return to where I once was, to be as an angel back at his side. First I must do my penance to earn my place. My penance is a thousand lifetimes of good deeds, and this is the price that I must pay. Now I offer you the chance of life, do you accept the deal? If not, for your crimes, you will now die."

Michelle knew she had little choice if she ever wanted to get out of here alive.

"I choose life!" She screamed. Lucifer smiled as he then moved closer to her. He said just one more word to her, as he raised his hand up to touch the side of her face.

"Open." He said. Michelle found that she was no longer in control of her movement. Her eyes opened wide and rolled backward in her head. Her head then tilted backward, and her mouth opened as wide as it possibly could. As Lucifer's finger entered her mouth, she tasted the warmth of his skin on her tongue. Her mouth began to stretch further than she knew was humanly possible, and then Lucifer placed both of his hands inside her mouth and stretched it open wide enough to enable him to climb inside of her.

As Michelle raised her hand, the door to the church opened. She then walked out into the darkness of the night outside. Almost as an afterthought, she then turned and raised her hand and directed streams of fire from her hand all across the wooden beams of the building. This would be the last she remembered of the events of that night. The church would continue to burn for another twelve hours, until not even a husk had remained.

It was hard not to lose count, but such was the price of his salvation. She spoke under her breath as she walked toward her home.

"Five hundred and seven down. Four hundred and ninety-three left to go. "

She had no idea what that meant, or why she had even uttered the words. She just felt an overwhelming urge to now help anyone who might need it. It would all be worth it in the end though. She just instinctively knew it. What goes around comes around. Goodness will come back to you in the end she thought. It was her new mantra, and she liked it.

Keep Away From The Windows 2

The Dark Ones

The Dark Ones

Martin McGregor

The Banshee Dream

The day to day job of a window blinds salesman could often be filled with boring, uninspiring and thankless assignments, but every now and again it had its rewards. Today Chris Henderson was following a live lead, the type of lead which often had the potential to lead on a big sale, and big sales meant big commissions. As the top salesman in the company, he certainly had the track record for closing the deal on his initial visit.

The sat nav assured him that his destination was the next house on the left, and he slowed his speed down appropriately enough to safely make the turn into the drive. The Peugeot 308 was compact enough to make tight corners easily, but roomy enough inside that if often felt misleading to first time passengers. He drove slowly over the lowered kerb and carefully forwards toward the house. His initial impression from the exterior was that the house was looking a little run down.

The garden was a complete mess and wildly overgrown. This wasn't normally a good sign. It showed a lack of respect on the part of the home owners. He pulled up the handbrake and parked his car in the driveway. After cutting the engine, he pulled his briefcase over from the passenger seat, and climbed out of the car. From the outside, his second impression was that the house looked really dirty. He hoped that the office hadn't sent him on another wild goose chase. This month in particular, he really needed the cash.

As he walked slowly toward the front door, he surveyed the windows. It was clear that fresh blinds could make a welcome change. The house could like brighter. Instead of the old thick curtains that were drawn closed across each and every window, he knew that his sales patter could add some much needed colour to the drabness. It was 11.30 a.m, and all of the curtains on the front and side of the house were closed, it was odd but not the first time that he had seen this.

The residents of the house were either late risers, or they liked a bit of privacy, and didn't want anyone peering inside. He had encountered both types during his years on the job. If the inside were as drab as the outside, there was a good chance that he might be leaving earlier than he anticipated. You came across all sorts in this profession, and time wasters were nothing new.

He pushed the dirty sun yellowed plastic button on the face of the doorbell, but heard nothing. He waited for the count of twenty (standard response waiting time in case of elderly or infirm customers), and then he knocked the letterbox three times. It was either that the batteries were dead, the residents were hard f hearing or the electric connection was faulty to the bell, he decided on the latter. He guessed it would be fairly low on the list of priorities here.

He waited patiently, and then he knocked a little louder. It was almost a minute before anyone came to answer the door. He remained silently on the spot. When the door finally opened, it was only opened a short distance of the full length of the security chain that added the feeling of security. In reality the chain was so flimsy, it could be easily removed by a stealthy kick to the door frame. From behind the partially open door, a pair of darkened ears peered around the edge and a male voice emerged.
"Who is it, what do you want?" Shouted the male behind the door. He spoke rapidly, and his voice sounded stern.

Chris knew that he had to be assertive, he was a great salesman (one of the best the company had ever employed), and he knew that having confidence was always key to winning the sale. He breathed in deeply before answering.
"Hi there. My name is Chris Henderson, and I have an appointment about fitting you some blackout blinds." He said.
There was no immediate response. The door was then pushed closed and it slammed loudly shut. His immediate thought was that the door had been

closed in his face, but instead he then heard the sound of the chain being unlocked before the door opened up, but only about two feet.
"Come in quickly!" The man behind the door sounded impatient. The man remained hidden behind the door and there was just enough room for him to squeeze inside the open gap. Once he had stepped into the hallway, the door was then slammed closed behind him once more. Suddenly he began to feel uncomfortable.

The interior decor of the house was a completely unexpected surprise. Everything inside was immaculate, and tidy. It felt almost as if he had stepped through the door and entered into a parallel universe. The man stepped out from the darkness behind him, and as he became fully visible, Chris could see that he was huge. He must have weighed in excess of two hundred kilos, but he only stood about five and a half feet tall. His face although pale, was fully bearded and it looked very unkempt. It was obvious that he took very little pride in his appearance. He was wearing ill fitting tracksuit bottoms that were elasticated around the waist, but even the length of stretched waistband was straining to contain the man's large stomach.

Chris offered out his hand, and the man first viewed the outstretched hand, as if touching others skin was an alien experience to him, and then he reluctantly shook it. His handshake was strong and assertive and Chris felt the sheer enormity of his strength as the man squeezed his hand so tightly, it actually hurt him.
"Mark Jones." He returned. He did not appear the type of man who wanted to exchange unnecessary pleasantries. "Step inside the living room, and sit down a while." He said, and then he showed Chris into the room.

Chris stepped inside of the living room, and inside it was very dimly lit. It in the middle of the ceiling, there was a single unshaded bulb which had been set extremely low on a variable dimmer switch. He took a seat on the black leather three seated sofa. It was well worn with age, but it was still extremely comfortable.

He then opened his briefcase and started to remove his sample material books.

"Would you like a drink?" Mark asked. Chris was feeling a little dry, so why not he thought.

"Coffee. White no sugar please. Thank you." Mark nodded silently. He then walked to the door and shouted out in an unexpectedly aggressive manner.

"Selicia! Make the man a coffee, white no sugar." He instructed. There was no thank you; it was more of a demand than a request. It made Chris feel a little uncomfortable. The large bodied man then came back into the room.

"The woman won't take long. Well she better not." He said.

Chris, kept his head down, he did not wish to become embroiled in the couple's relationship. However this man spoke to his partner, it was none of his business. He was still sorting out his paperwork when Selicia entered the room. For some reason, he had expected the wife to be a large woman, but the creature that carried in his cup of coffee was nothing of the sort. He wasn't in the habit of staring at potential clients wives, but this time his jaw had dropped. She was one of the most stunningly beautiful women that he had ever come across.

Her body was supple and perfectly shaped, and her face was far prettier than any model he had ever seen in any magazine. He instantly wondered why they were together as a couple. He meant no disrespect, but this woman could clearly have any man that she wanted, and yet for some reason that he could not fathom, she was attached to this rotund thing that stood in front of him.

She placed the coffee mug directly down the table in front of Chris. Mark suddenly became livid and instantly showed unprovoked aggression toward her.

"Stupid woman, put it on a mat, you will mark the table!" He shouted. Selicia was timid and cowered. She looked so afraid of him. She quickly did as she was told, but all the while she kept her head lowered. Mark was still showing his unwarranted frustration with her.

"Get back out into the kitchen and get it clean woman!" He shouted.

He half waddled across the room, took hold of her arm and pushed her from the room and back out into the hallway. Then he closed the door behind her and shook his head.

"I'm sorry. You shouldn't have to see that. She always messes things up around the house. She ruins things and then I have to go and fix them." Chris felt embarrassed that Mark was now apologizing.

"It's really none of my business. Maybe you could go a little easier on her though." Chris suggested. Marks eyes instantly widened and he virtually spat out his response.

"Your God damned right it's none of your business! Now get on with it and tell me how much for the blinds, I want this over with so you can leave my house quickly." Mark was now growing redder in the face with every word that the vile creature uttered from his mouth.

Chris contemplated leaving right there and then. This was a big job, with what would add up to great commission, and to let it go would be stupid. He bit his lip, and instead he decided to try and focus on the sale.

"I need to measure all of the windows in your house, and then I can give you my best price sir." He said.

Mark sat his huge body down on to a chair, it sank down further than it should have, and he was visibly perspiring.

"Get on with it then." He instructed. He then switched on the television and soon became engrossed in a talk show that was playing. It left Chris free to walk about the house and to start taking all of the window measurements.

The front room window was a standard 1200 mm width. He had to go and measure in all the other rooms individually so he walked toward the hallway, and although he was being watched from the corner of his eye, it was clear that Mark had no intention of following him around. The effort would probably be too much for him. Chris walked into the kitchen where he found Selicia. She was on her hands knees on the floor scrubbing away at the linoleum flooring.

The TV could be heard in the other room, along with a new fresh additional sound, that sound was definitely that of a large male heavily snoring.
It was clear that Selicia was upset, as she was sobbing whilst she scrubbed the floor repeatedly.
"You don't have to let him treat you like that." Chris said.
"He cares for me, he took me in and I don't know any other way." Selicia said. All the time she continued to look down at the floor, it was if she were afraid to make eye contact with Chris.
"Why don't you leave him?" He asked. Then there was a slight pause before she answered. Her eyes looked up to match his gaze.
"He took me away from all that I know. Away from all my family and he brought me here. Now I cannot leave this house. I have nothing. I have no other place to go." She said. Then she stood up and touched his face, it looked kind. "Please, can you get me out of here?" She begged. It was just what Chris wanted to hear.
"Let me help you. You can come and stay with me for a while, just until we find you a new home." Chris was genuine in his offer to help her, but he also had an ulterior motive. This woman deserved far better, and a man who would not be afraid to have her on his arm. He would be happy to entertain her as his new lover, if she turned out to like him in the same way that he already knew that he liked her.

She put her mouth close to his ear, and then softly spoke. Chris could feel her breath on his skin and it sent a shiver down his spine.

"Come and get me tonight, I will gather some things and once he is asleep, we can get away from him." She said.
"What time do you want me to come?" He asked. She paused for a few seconds, as if the decision needed careful consideration. She moved closer to him, so that her lips were almost brushing against his ear.
"Come at midnight. I will be waiting for you." She said and then she dropped back down to her knees and continued to scrub the floor. She had heard the sound of leather rustling as Mark was lifting himself out of his chair.
Chris no longer cared about the sale; after all it was only money. It was more important to get Selicia out of here, and away from that thing.
He walked back toward the living room, and met Mark as he was walking out of the living room door.
"Ah, that is perfect timing. I'm done with all the measurements." Chris said. "I can get the quote out to you in the next few days. I estimate it to be around five thousand three hundred with fitting. Now, how does that sound to you?"

Chris knew that this was way over the top, but a refusal would mean that he wouldn't have to leave any further details. Mark looked at him, as if he was about to have a heart attack.
"Are you taking the piss out of me?" He asked. He was clearly livid at the excessive figure that had been quoted. "Get out of my house, and don't come back you vulture!" He shouted. He was already waddling toward the door ready to open it and show the salesman out. Chris was the one now smiling as he made his way toward the open door. He looked back toward the kitchen, but the door was now closed.

Chris was coming back for her later, and the woman was leaving with him. Tonight she might know how a real man should treat her. He squeezed out through the small gap in the doorway. Mark then unexpectedly pushed Chris fully out of the door, and into the front garden. He was an obnoxious fat fuck and Chris so badly wanted to turn and throw a punch at his puffy face, and maybe teach him a lesson.

Chris remained calm. Instead of showing his anger, he just straightened up his tie. He turned briefly to face his assailant, and at least gave himself the satisfaction of a few choice words.
"You are a rude fat fuck. You're lucky I don't take your head off. She deserves far better than a piece of shit like you!" He said.
"You think? You know nothing. One day boy, you might learn that beauty like hers often comes with an expensive price. Now get off my land!" Mark said, and then he slammed the door closed behind him.

He peered out from the door spy hole, and he watched as the salesman got back into his car, then Mark turned around slowly, and walked back to the kitchen. H opened the door, and Selicia was sat in silence with her head lowered.
"Did you say anything to him?" He asked Selicia. She remained silent whilst staring up at him, and then she shook her head. Now her body was visibly shaking in apparent fear of what was to come. "You better not have bitch!" He shouted and threw her down to the floor. He kicked her in the stomach while she was still on her knees. Selicia took the blow; she knew that it was her own fault. There would not be many more of these now. Tonight she would be leaving, and before she did, he would finally pay for what he had done to her. It had been a long time coming, and a move was what she needed right about now.

Later that night, the car drove up slowly onto the driveway. Its lights were dimmed, and the engine was fairly quiet. It was Mark's car. He was fifteen minutes early and had arrived at the house at a quarter to twelve. Despite the darkness outside, there were still no lights visible anywhere in the house. Chris switched off the car engine and he patiently waited. He hoped that she was brave enough to leave. If not, he was so wound up that he would go in there and get her out himself.

At precisely the stroke of midnight, the front door of the house opened and Selicia appeared. She was carrying a small solitary carrier bag in her hand. She walked calmly toward the car, and she was smiling as she approached the passenger door. Chris was puzzled by just how calm and happy she looked. He leant across and opened the passenger door from the inside, and then she climbed into the car. As soon as she had closed the door behind her, she then leant across the car and kissed Mark with her fully opened mouth. Her tongue was rampant in his mouth and her kisses took his breath away.

"Take me to your home, and to your bed." She said. Chris didn't need to be told such things twice. He sped out of the driveway, and floored the accelerator. They were at his home within ten minutes of leaving her house, and the kissing was becoming even more intense as they left the car and after fumbling with the door key, they both stumbled in through his front door.

Clothes were being removed by both of them all the way up the stairs of his home; this woman was frantic for him. Her kisses were covering his mouth and face, and her cries of expectation were becoming louder and louder as she did. She was intense and frantic and by the time they had reached his bed, he was already inside of her with her legs wrapped tightly around his waist. She arched her back and ground her body down against his, pulling him deeper inside of her. That night, they would not sleep at all. It was almost like a never ending sexual fantasy that just continued on and on.

She would not let him rest and even after he came inside of her, she would coax life back into him no matter what effort it took. It was one the most intense sexual encounters of his life, and the first time he had ever really felt his body being cared for and touched all over so tenderly. Her hands felt as if they were electrically charged and he could not get enough of her body.

It was Saturday morning when he awoke next to her. He examined her face, and even though it was still early morning and the light was dim in the room, her face was still enchantingly beautiful. She wore no makeup, and even despite how frantic the night's sexual escapades had been, her hair still looked perfect. She was stunning in every way, shape and form, and he could not believe how lucky he was to have her next to him.

Chris moved the heavy duck feather and down duvet aside. It was only then that he realised just how much the bedroom smelt heavy of sweat and intense sex, but it also smelt of something else, something sweet. He stepped onto the thick carpeted floor and walked over toward the curtains. As he approached the window, Selicia jumped up with a sudden start.
"Don't open them!" She pleaded. Chris was startled by her cry, and turned around to face her.
"What's wrong babe?" He asked, genuinely concerned by her cries.
"I.....I have a sensitive skin condition." She stuttered. "I can't be exposed to daylight. I have to stay out of the natural light at all times." She pleaded convincingly. She then pulled the duvet up and over her head just to be safe. Chris backed away from the curtains. He never quite fully understood what she had told him, but for the rest of that day, it wouldn't really matter. She kept him fully occupied, and neither of them would leave the bedroom unless they needed water or to go to the bathroom.

For three long weeks Selicia refused to leave the house, she said that she was afraid to go out in case they saw Mark. Chris used up his remaining holiday entitlement to stay at home and to keep her company, and surprisingly his boss had been very understanding. The house had been void of natural daylight for all of that time. He had personally sealed out any source of natural light from every single room. All the shopping had been done online and delivered to the house, and every day and night they would still continue to make love frantically.

Every time they had sex, it felt better than the last, and she was like a drug that he could no longer survive without. When the day came that he told her that he had to return to work, she had wept openly and begged him not to leave her, but finally she had accepted that at some point, he had to go out of the house and leave her on her own.

The moment that he had left, she began to clean. She would not stop cleaning until everything in the house looked spotless. Everything would be prepared for him before he returned home that night. She scrubbed every floor wall and side until they were pristine. Then the doorbell rang. She had to cover her head before she could open the door and invite the stranger in. He was perfect.

Chris walked into the office and quickly settled back in to his role. He started to catch up on his emails and live sales leads, but he could not stop thinking about Selicia . He had a lot of work to do, and he had to really try hard to focus. That morning he had three leads to follow, and unsurprisingly to him, none would lead to actual sales despite his best sales patter. He was rusty, but the sales would come again in time.

After the third rejection, he decided that it was time to head to back to the sales office. On the way there, he drove past the house where he had first met Selicia.
It was only the briefest of glances at the house as he drove slowly by, but what he saw, was enough to make him curious. He stopped the car and turned it around. The curtains of the house were still all closed. It was odd, and now he was wondering why they hadn't been opened yet.

Selicia was now living with him, and there was no way anyone would ruin the happy life that they had found together. This man still had a lot to answer for, and she must surely have left a lot more of her belongings there. Now it was the ideal time for him to deal with both matters. He drove his car straight up on to the driveway without fear, and he parked the car brazenly outside of the front door.

The house was silent. Not a solitary sound could be heard from inside. Chris walked toward the front door. He placed his ear right up against the thick wooden paneling, but he could hear nothing from inside. He drew a deep breath and then he knocked the door loudly. There was still no response. He waited a few seconds and then knocked once more. Again there was still nothing. He then walked around to the back of the house, and could see that none of the windows were open. He thought that maybe he should keep away, but his curiosity was too intense.

He tried the door handle at the back of the house. He gently squeezed the handle downward, and was surprised to find that it was unlocked. He thought long and hard before he stepped inside, but eventually he felt brave enough to do so. He pulled the door closed behind him and was almost sick. The smell was disgusting as he stepped inside of the kitchen.

The house stank of something rotten inside it. It looked almost the same as the day he had last been there. Everything looked as it had been left in the same place as the day he visited. It was all untouched and unmoved, except everything was dustier than before. He slowly and stealthily walked through the kitchen and then into the hallway. He was an intruder and he had to be prepared, just in case Mark suddenly lunged for him from out of nowhere. There was no one at home, or so it seemed.

He checked the front room, and there was no one in there either. He then walked to the foot of the stairs, and stared upward. Although daunted, he began to slowly ascend the stairs anyway. The stairs creaked on almost every step, and the sound of each footstep on the stairs made him cringe at just how much noise they made.

At the top of the stairs, there were three doors. One led to the bathroom, and one led to a single bedroom. Both of these doors were open, but both were dimmed by the lack of daylight from the closed curtains in the rooms. The third door was closed; he knew that this must have been the couple's bedroom. He placed his ear to the door, but heard nothing.

He took hold of the handle and pulled it down slowly. There was no doubt about it. This was the room where the foul stench was coming from. The smell hit him full in the face as he pushed the door all the way open. It wasn't pretty. Whatever he found inside, it wasn't going to be good.

He was almost retching as he walked slowly into the room. The bedroom was almost bare, save for a double bed placed exactly in the middle of the room. Chris's eyes were now slowly adjusting to the lack of light, and he could see that there was a lumpy shape underneath the duvet. On closer inspection, he could see that it was the shape of a human body. He crept slowly over towards the bed.

He was gripped by both fear and curiosity as he took a hold of the corner of the duvet; he pulled it back very slowly. He unveiled a human wrist that was covered in dried blood that had been tied to the headboard. He swallowed hard and pulled the duvet back fully. He then vomited all over the floor at the sight of what he had uncovered.

The body that had sunk into the mattress was yellow and gaunt. Mark's head was tilted back and his mouth was wide open, it was if he had died screaming. Parts of his body were missing, and huge bite marks covered the bloated corpse. Blood had soaked through to the mattress, and had formed a glue like seal that attached it to the body. Maggots were openly crawling over the wounds and were feasting on the rotten flesh of the body. Then he stumbled back in shock as he saw the chest rise slightly. Unbelievably, this deformed thing was still alive.

As Chris fell backwards, he almost landed in his own vomit. He quickly found his feet. His mind was racing in a mixture of confusion, revulsion and fear. Mark was trying to talk, and Chris, despite his fears, needed to know what he was trying to say. He moved his head closer to his mouth. Mark uttered a few words. His mouth was so dry; Chris could only just about make out what the words he was forcing from his cracked lips. He felt no pity for the man, but no one really deserved to be left to die like this. "See her... in.... the light." He said, and those were the last words that Mark ever uttered. It was almost as if he had waited for this very moment, before he finally passed away. The body lay in a pool of his body's own urine and feaces. His face now looked content and finally at peace.

Chris drove at speed toward his home. He had to hear it directly from Selicia. He had find out what she had done. She was supposed to leave him, not to try and murder him first! Now he felt unsafe and he considered asking her to get out of the house. He no longer felt sure that he safe around a woman who could do this to anyone. Tears were now flowing down his cheeks, and he cursed the weakness he was showing toward her. He genuinely felt in love with her, but she surely had to go. Didn't she?

He pulled up outside his house, and parked the car in the driveway. He locked the car, drew a deep breath and then made his way into his house. He slammed the front door behind him. Selicia was stood at the kitchen sink, and she was drying up. She had a large serrated knife held in her hand.

Chris felt uneasy seeing her holding a large sharp edged knife in her hands, especially now that he knew what she was capable of. He walked into the living room and called out her name. Selicia then walked into the room with a confused look on her face. He sounded angry with her.
"What did you do?" Chris asked. Selicia looked shocked. She then lowered her head and started to weep.
"I'm so sorry. I was hungry. I had to eat. Please forgive me. I love you." She begged.

Chris could not control his emotions. He was deeply in love with the woman and he himself then began to feel confused. He could never let her go. Even though he knew she had tried to murder Mark, he was now trying to justify what she had done. He then told himself that she might not have even been responsible for Mark's death. He might have got it all very wrong. She was now begging for forgiveness just for eating some food. He now felt shame at even thinking this tiny figure could have even done such an evil thing. Mark was a piece of shit. The world would be a better place without him anyway.

"Come here!" He said, and then she moved toward him gingerly. It was almost as if she was expecting to be struck. Instead he threw both of his arms around her and held her in the warmest embrace.

"I thought that you were mad at me!" She cried. Then she started to sob, and he wiped away her tears. He then kissed her tenderly until they were locked in another passionate embrace, and soon he had forgotten why he was even fearful of her at all.

She eventually broke off the embrace, and took both of his hands in hers.

"You are home a little early my love, but if you run a bath and I will finish preparing your dinner." She said. She then kissed him once more, but he pulled away after a few seconds. He felt the blood pumping furiously around his body and engorging his groin. He had to pull himself away from her before he got too carried away. He had suddenly forgotten all about Mark. He never thought of him ever again. He could no longer recall anything that had happened that day either, it was an odd feeling.

He spent a long hour soaking in the bath. All the while he could smell the lush scent of the roast dinner that was cooking. His mouth was salivating at the smells wafting up the stairs and filling out the upstairs hallway. When he could resist no longer, he drained the water from the bath and dried himself off. He then put on some light clothes and then made his way back down to the dining room. His dinner was already dished up and waiting on the table for him. He had to admit, that it really looked delicious.

Chris sat down and admired the meal in front of him. The meat looked so thick and tender; that he could not wait to try it. He picked up the gravy boat and poured the thick brown fluid all over the dinner. The gravy looked and smelt delicious, it was just like his mother used to make. Selicia sat down opposite him, and she smiled at him. They both raised their knives and forks from the table and then they both began to eat.

The food was sublime; it was the best food he had tasted in a very long time. That gravy though, well that was something else.
"How did you make the gravy?" He asked.
"I made if with the juices from the meat my love. Do you like it? I think it complements the meat." She said. The meat was an unusual flavour, but it was tasty and very filling. He devoured most of his meal quickly. He had only left a few peas to the side of the plate, as he was never too keen on them anyway.
"What meat was that?" He asked. She shook her head and laughed.
"It was Human meat; I find it the tenderest." She said. Her face told him that she wasn't joking; in fact she was deadly serious. The words echoed in his head, almost as if this were a nightmare that he was struggling to wake up from.

As Chris stood up from the table, he felt dizzy and nauseous. He felt like had to vomit, but his mind was stunned into submission by the words that he had heard. The realization struck him, that he had just tasted human flesh for the first time, and worst of all, he had enjoyed every single bite of it. He could hold the vomit back no more. He emptied his stomach all over the dining room carpet.
"Oh no, are you ill my love?" Selicia asked. She was now genuinely concerned for her lover. Chris stumbled over toward the dining room window.

It was still late afternoon, but he knew what he had to do. He retched once more and then pulled the covers clean away from the window. The daylight shone through the clear glass pane and the rays of light glimmered over Selicia's face.
"Why would you do this to me?" She screamed. "I loved you!" She shouted.

The face of the woman that he had come to love was now no longer the face that he saw in front of him. Her features became contorted and twisted in the sunlight and her body seemed to change shape before his very eyes. The woman that was now stood in the room with him was old and twisted. The creature looked just as how he imagined a twisted witch might look. Her nose was crooked and bent, and her mouth looked decayed and festering.

The creature had no bodily hair and only whisps of grey hair strands hanging down from its head. Its skin was grey and cracked, and the once supple body was now sagged and jaded. It may have been old, but the creature was still impressively fast. The thing leapt across the room in a single bound forcing Chris down to the floor. The thing was now on top of him, and he could feel it's breath on his face as its jaws started clamping down.

Ancient teeth sank into his neck as the creature had landed on top of him, its power was immense. It was not like a vampire's bite, sucking his blood through the wound it had inflicted. Instead it was a bite that was used to feed something into his body. It was the fluid that the creature naturally produced through its saliva glands that allowed it to control its drones. She knew how much fluid it would take, and when his eyes became glazed, she knew that the change was complete. The male drone was now hers to control.

She regretted the side effects of turning the drone into her slave. The sex had been really enjoyable with this male, but now it had seen her in her true form, it was unavoidable. There were so few of her kind left, she had to remain in the shadows of humanity. The drone's body began to swell up in size, and no doubt he would now be aggressive toward her and to any other male that came close to her. It did not matter anymore though; she now had him under her complete control.

He would now remain faithful to her until the next drone came along. The longest she had stayed in one place was close to a year. It was dangerous to stay too long. The next victim would be fond, and then she would shape-shift once more to become an image of his dream girl. She would shift according to the drone's desires and become the perfect image. Until that time, it was important that the light was covered up once more.

He had no idea why, but Chris did not want to leave Selicia's side ever again. He had to quit his job and watch her closely. He had covered up the window again just as she had asked. Then he had removed the body of the postman, the one that Selicia told him about. The postman had tried to take her away from him, and that could never be allowed to happen. So she had rightfully killed him, and they had fed on the best meat from the body. The meat was good. Chris was eternally grateful.

He had waited until night time and then took the body away from the house and he had buried it deep. She belonged to him, and she would never leave his sight again. The next few weeks he just felt tired and really hungry. He loved Selicia, but now sometimes he really hated her, but he didn't know why. He felt so confused. The next time that she angered him, he would show her he meant business.

God help anyone who ever tried to come between them. He loved her, but he also hated her for some reason that he never understood. Now she was making him wait for his food. He wanted another of those delicious roast dinners, and he wanted it soon.

For six months he had lived in virtual darkness. The letters had piled up in the hallway, and every now and again she would remove them. Once in a while, there would be a knock at the door. Today when the door rang it was a salesman, he was selling double glazing. He hated the look of the man, but Selicia had insisted that he came back later that day. It made him angry; he hated salesmen, and the way that he had looked at her. He hated the way she smiled at him; it had sparked a fury inside that he had never felt before. He had struck her across the face. She belonged to him, and she would never be allowed to leave.

At seven thirty that evening, the doorbell rang. Selicia licked her lips in anticipation. It was time for the circle to begin again.

Zombie Horror!

It was during the early morning of the 5th of September 2018 that the world as we knew it started to change. At around 3.25 a.m (Greenwich Mean Time), almost to the second. Well that was the moment that the skies lit up all around the world. It was a spectacle to behold as the meteor showers brought daylight to the night sky, and even caused consternation in the countries where it was still day-time.

As the showers of meteors burnt up in the planet's atmosphere, everyone watched in awe. Then, when the natural fireworks show was completed it was time for the grand finale. Showers of a fine powder glimmered as it fell down from the skies like bright stardust. It looked magical as it slowly drifted down to the Earth.

That powder was magical alright. Even though the scientists said that it was safe, it was anything but. It soon sank down deep into the ground. Then after a while it found its way into the water supply. No amount of filtering could remove every trace of it. The powder fell for days and covered everything like the thin layer of dust that appears on your TV screen. It took its time and buried itself deep.

It took a few weeks for the effects to start to take hold, but boy did we know it when they started to appear. Pandemonium ensued as the recently buried dead started to rise back up from the ground. The dead were now rising up in vast numbers and were walking the earth once more.

Global scenes of panic grew as the dead roamed the Earth. The zombie apocalypse (that we had all secretly feared might eventually happen), had now finally begun. Once the dust had found its way into the water supply, things got worse. Once perfectly healthy folk, then also began to fade away quickly. Roughly eighty percent of the global population had no immunity from the virus. Once they had passed, it was only a matter of hours before they would rise up like Lazarus and begin walking the Earth again as the undead.

For those of us who were left, well there was a great deal of fear and uncertainty. Christ, we had all seen so many films and TV shows about zombies, that we all thought that we were ready to deal with it. We knew what we had to do, and that was to take them down. We took up arms, and we were ready. After all, everybody knows how to kill a zombie, don't they?

Destroy the brain or sever the head. That's what the book writers and the movie experts had always said. That would stop them coming and put them back down for good. I wasn't quite ready for violence like that, and neither were most other folk. We were on lockdown for a while, and we just patiently waited for the government to sort the mess out. We were sure that the army would soon sort get things back to normal. So we just watched and waited. Then we waited some more. No one ever expected what was going to happen next.

The Zombies were still rising up and now walked in every single corner of the Earth. The undead were moving, but they were in a painful state of limbo. They wanted to return to the peaceful non existence that death had once brought them. They moaned and they cried out loud, day and night, and the sounds were never ending, but these Zombies were nothing like those that you saw in the movies.

No, these zombies weren't on a killing rampage or attacking the living. They weren't trying to attack anything at all. These undead walkers were just plain dumb idiots! I think some folks were honestly disappointed by the zombies, because all they did was walk, and often they walked headfirst into walls or cars, or even off the edge of tall buildings. Sometimes it was comical, but then you would remember that these were once someone's loved ones. That kind of made you sad after a while. You see they had no other brain function; they didn't want to eat or kill. They had no need for sustenance. Something was telling them to get up from the ground, to walk straight forward, and to just keep on moving, no matter what.

Some people (myself included), we were the lucky ones. We were naturally immune to the infection. We seemingly held the key to ending this mess. They started testing us, in the hope of developing a vaccine and it turned out, that it was purely just down to our blood type. The bad news was that now within just three short weeks, more than two thirds of the world's population were now dead from the virus, and believe me, that's a lot of people to be just walking forward day and night and moaning out loud.

The first night that I felt brave enough to try and sleep, well those damned walkers just continued to moan and walk into things all night long. They would walk into parked cars and were setting off all sorts of alarms. The dumb fuckers had no idea about the concept of glass anymore. They would see a space ahead and just keep on walking. Eventually enough of them would be pushing on to a shop window and the force would send them right through. Then the shop burglar alarms would go off and that would add even more noise. It was a living nightmare, and I hardly slept a wink.

Things got a little better once the electricity began to fail. That took about another week before it happened. At least then some of the noise stopped. Now we were left with another problem, and that was something that nobody had really thought about properly. We had to try and get rid of the vast number of walkers roaming the streets. Only then could we try and get back to something of a normal way of life. Not everyone was keen to help as we might have hoped. Some folks, well they were almost as dumb as the zombies themselves.

We were left with just a few types of people who had survived in the world. First we had what we called 'The Closers'. We called them that because that's what they did. They just closed their doors tight shut. They hid away in cellars or bunkers and just decided to wait it out. Some of em waited for God to come and save em, some of em hid in bunkers underground, refusing to come up into the light. Some of em even died of starvation as they were just too scared to open their doors ever again. When we opened those doors up again, well that just meant even more of the undead for the rest of us to deal with.

Then you had the type that we called 'The Chasers'. Those were mostly the young ones. They were thrill seekers who thought of more and more exciting ways to drive the zombies back to their graves. Some of em would shoot off their heads; some of em would run them down with cars and trucks like they were playing games of human skittles.

Some genius decided to devise a method of herding em in large numbers towards a cliff edge. Of course they just walked forward like lambs to the slaughter. Human lemmings, that just fell to their deaths once more. Except even after such a fall into the sea, most of them didn't die.

The undead, well they just sank to the bottom of the water, and then they got up once again. Then they would start walking through the sand and silt again until they reached dry land once more. The chasers, well they soon got bored. The walkers were just too many in number, and the thrill of such easy kills quickly wore off. It affected them mentally after a while. It just became too much for them to deal with. They thought they could cleanse the world, but they had no idea just how vast they were in number. Lots of the young ones became badly depressed by it all.

Next we had what we liked to call 'The Cuckoos'. These folk were just plain crazy. They would use grenades and explosives to take out large numbers of the walkers at once. I can tell you this from personal experience, more than once have I seen the effect of large numbers of bodies being blown to smithereens. It's not pretty, and it always left one heck of a mess. The cuckoos never got bored though, they continue blowing things up right to this day.

They group em up, fence em in, and blow them up high. Concert halls are ideal for taking out large number at once, and the chasers don't seem to mind rounding em up for them at all. They never clean up the mess after though; they always leave that for someone else to do. They are just running out of places left to blow up round here now.

Despite everything we were doing, it still wasn't enough. They were just far too many in number for us to deal with them effectively. That's where my type comes in. My name is Stan, and I'm what is known as 'A Grinder'. It's a Grinders job to clean up the planet. In every town and city, you will find ordinary folk just like me. We take our mechanical diggers and dig holes, and we make sure that we dig them deep. Then the machinery is put in place. The walkers are then herded toward the machines. As a Grinder, well it's our job to keep the machines going, and I got to say it isn't the prettiest job. No sir not at all.

As the walkers hit the blades, they get chopped up pretty fine. They don't seem to mind it though. They just keep on moving forward. Almost as if they are welcoming the end once more. As for what's left of the bodies, well those parts just come out of the back of the machines, and they fall down deep into the holes that we dug. On average we can get at least ten thousand in a hole, but then we have to cover it over and start again. It's like a landfill sight, only these are filled with organics.

As I said before, it's not pretty, but it's a job that someone has to do. Let's just say that I'm never short of a cold beer these days. When you're grinding your day away through the summer heat, well I got to say that most folks appreciate the effort you make. They tend to take care of you round here. They know what you have to endure, and to be honest, the only horror story I can tell you about these zombies, is the God awful stench that comes off em. They stink before and after they've been through the grinder.

Like I said to you before, its dirty work but somebody got to do it. They reckon that it could take us a good eighteen months before we clear the backlog, so I best get back to work. This is Stan signing off. Oh, if you ever decide to stop by and check out my work, please feel free to come and say hi. Those grinders are mighty fine pieces of machinery, but just be sure to wear a mask. If nothing else, it will keep away some of those damned flies!

Take care of yourself, and remember the Grinders motto, it goes 'Lead em to the machines, herd the sheeples in, chop em up, fill the hole, and then cover up once more.'

It's not exactly poetry, but it keeps us grinding.

Catch you later.

Stan.

The Unwanted

The telephone rang just three times before it was answered. The voice on the other end of the line was a female voice. She sounded quite well educated and polite.
"Hello. This is the Samaritans, how can I help you?" She said. The other end of the line remained silent for quite some time. "Hello. Is there anyone there? Please take your time. Can I help you at all?" She asked again. The dead air was finally broken by a response from the caller.
"I....I think I need some help." It was almost a relief to hear an answer finally spoken. The voice was that of a male. He sounded calm and collected. At least the caller was still alive and was reaching out to someone who would listen. The trouble with this type of call was that the outcome could sometimes be devastating to both the caller and the operator.
"Let's see if there is anything that we can do to make things better. Tell me, how I can help you?" The operator asked.

There was another slight delay, and then a slow but firm response eventually came.
"I'm debating....I'm debating, whether or not I should kill my parents." The caller's voice remained calm as he stated his intentions. The call was being recorded, but now the police would have to be warned in the interests of public safety. The operator raised the silent alarm via her keyboard. It was important that she remained calm and didn't alert the caller to her own fear. She had been trained for a great deal of different scenarios, but she never expected to hear anything like this.

She took a few deep breaths before continuing.
"I'm sorry to hear that. How about you tell me what is troubling you, and we will see if we can find you some help. How does that sound?" She asked. The response was slow but it was clear that the caller understood what she was trying to say.
"It sounds patronizing. To be honest with you and I had expected more." He said. The operator took more steady breaths. Then she tried to

communicate with the caller once more. This time she would be more careful not to offend or upset him.

"Alright, I will try not to talk down to you. Can you at least tell me your first name?" She asked.

"No! Now if you decide to talk down to me just once more, then they will both die. This I promise you. Their lives are now entirely in your hands. Do you get that?" He shouted, now he was sounding a lot more irritated and irrational. It was a dangerous sign.

"I understand. From where I sit though, what happens is all in your hands, not mine. No matter what I say to you, if you are deliberating murdering them, then you must have been considering this for some time. Now do you want to talk to me or not?" She replied.

There was a short pause before the caller replied.

"That's better. Now before we carry on, tell me your name?" He asked.

"No, I'm not doing that. I'm not playing any games with you." She said. She was a little annoyed about how the caller was trying to control the conversation. She had to try and exert some authority.

"Unless you tell me your name, then I'm not telling you mine. Now let's just forget about the niceties shall we? What exactly is it that you want from me?" She was stern, but careful not to overstep the mark. There was a brief silence, and then a little chuckle from the other end of the line.

"I just want you to help me to decide if I should kill them or not." He said.

The police had already been notified about the call, but they would take some time to respond and then to trace the caller. It was a withheld number, but they always had ways and means of getting around that. For now she would remain calm and at least try to keep him talking. It could be a crank call (and she hoped to God that it was), but he certainly sounded serious. This type of caller could turn out to be deadly if he wasn't dealt with correctly.

"Tell me about your parents. Where are they now?" She asked. The caller stalled his response slightly, and then laughed once more. It sounded almost ironic as he laughed. Then his tone switched to an almost

humorous one.
"Ha! Good old Irene and Frank. They are both asleep right in front of me now." He said.
"Have you harmed them at all?" She asked, now she was genuinely concerned for their safety. She was painting horrible images in her mind.
"I already told you. They are both sleeping soundly." He answered. Again he sounded slightly annoyed at the line of questioning.

The computer in front of her displayed a new email notification. The alert showed the first few lines of the content of the mail. It told her that the police were on route, and that it was important to keep the callers attention. She had to try and keep him talking on the telephone for as long as she could. He could end the call at any moment and she could not afford for that to happen.
"Why do you want to kill your parents?" She asked.
"Who hasn't in their lives? Who hasn't ever thought it would be better for them to be gone?" He questioned.
"I haven't." She answered. The voice on the other end of the line suddenly became more intense.
"I FUCKING WARNED YOU, DON'T YOU DARE PATRONISE ME!" He shouted down the line. "I swear to God, I will carve them both up into little pieces, right here, right now..."
"I'm sorry!" She shouted back down the phone. Alright, yes! Sometimes my parents pissed me off, sometimes I hated them, but I never wanted them dead!" She now had tears welling up in her eyes. She could not afford tears right now, so she wiped her eyes dry and fought the tears back them until they receded.

The caller on the other end was now silent.

The silence continued for quite some time, until it became deafening.
"Are you still there?" She asked.
"That's better. I needed to hear the honesty in your voice. Thank you." He said. His voice had now returned to a normal level. It was now back to the level of a calm spoken turn. "These aren't my real parents." He said. "They

adopted me when I was four years old. They were told that they would never be able to have children of their own.

 I never knew my real parents, but for a while things were good here for me. I had my own room. I had my own toys, and I had people who showed me love for the first time ever." He then went silent once again.
"So what went wrong? What changed?" She asked. The caller seemed to become irate once more.
"Somehow, against all of the medical expert's advice, they managed to conceive a child. Everyone was shocked.

 They had been going to church regularly, and had always prayed for a miracle. She did not even know that she was pregnant, but nine months later my baby sister was born into this world. I was now a big brother at five years old, and how I loved my little sister. Then things began to change."

 His voice sounded as if it was now becoming more strained.
"That often happens when a younger child is born. The older child can often become jealous." She replied.
" I loved that child, just as much as I loved my parents. They just seemed to stop looking at me in the same way they did before. Every time they looked at her, I could see that they really loved her. They looked at her in a way they could never look at me. I was only five years old, and this was all a painful game to me." He sounded as if he were now close to breaking point.
"I bet that really hurt to see. It must have been so hard for you to live with those feelings?" She asked.
"You have no idea just how hard it was. I wanted that same level of love. I wanted them to look at me the same way they had before. Instead they now only seemed to want her. I knew what I had to do though, I had to try and get rid of her before they became too attached.

 It was just a baby, and was only a few weeks old. I knew they would soon forget about her. Then they could love me like they did once before." He said, but now his words were spoken just a little bit too calmly for her liking.

"So what did you do to the baby?" She asked. Now she was worried that the caller may have already tried to kill someone before.

"I went to her room. Then I picked her up in my arms from her cot, and I took her to the bathroom. She was so tiny, and she was smiling at me. Then I ran the water into the bathtub and then when it was deep enough, I placed her into the water." The caller was now so calm, that he almost sounded happy to be reliving the story. "Then I went into my parent's room and I woke my mother up. I wanted to show her just how much I loved her. I took her to see her baby, and now the baby was silent, I was sure that she would love me the same way she had before. There would be no one else between us ever again."

The caller almost sounded delirious at the recollection, and it sickened her to hear what was being said.

"So are you telling me that you murdered a child?" She asked. The caller then laughed at the question.

"Well, I did try. Somehow when we got there, the baby was still breathing. I guess the water just wasn't deep enough, I didn't leave her long enough, or maybe I just didn't put the plug in properly. She was still alive.

My father beat me that day, for the first time in my life; I felt the pain of leather striking my skin. At first it hurt, but then I thought of the baby and I no longer felt it anymore. Then I was kept away from the baby. For days and days I cried and I begged my parent's forgiveness, but instead of forgiving me, they just pushed me further and further away from them. One day, it all got too much for them and they just drove me straight back to the orphanage where they found me.

I screamed and I begged them and pleaded for forgiveness, but they wouldn't listen. The only people in this world, who had ever shown me any love, had now both rejected me completely. My mother wouldn't leave the car. I could see that she was crying though. I could see the pain on her face, and it was my fault. I should have done the job properly. I was completely broken inside. I felt as if I would never feel loved again"

Another email notification popped up onto the computer screen. The operator viewed it from the corner of her eye. It told her that the police had traced the call, but she had to do her best to keep him on the line for just a little longer. They need her to stall him while they made their way to the address.
"I'm sorry for what they did to you back then. You were too young to understand what you did. People can be so cruel."

She sounded genuine, even though her voice was breaking under the strain of the conversation; she had still somehow managed to sound sympathetic. The caller hadn't finished yet though.
"I sat alone for months. I yearned to see my mother and father again. I prayed day after day that they would turn around and come back for me. My prayers were all in vain though. No one was listening to my pleas. Over the next few years, I was moved around from family to family. I always tried to make them happy, but all I really wanted was my parents. They never came back for me though.

I then stopped praying to a God who wouldn't listen to my cries. I was thirteen when I was found a place with a family who finally understood me. This family prayed to a different type of God. This one rewarded you for what you could do for him."
"Did they abuse you?" She asked.
"No. I hear all these stories about abused children in care, but I was welcomed into the fold. It was just one big happy coven. I found myself in embroiled in sex games, alcohol and drugs and my eyes were opened up to the wonders of the real world. To sacrifice another life, well within the coven it was more than just welcomed, I was fondly encouraged.

I worked my way up from killing animals, to murdering strays and vagrants. No one would ever miss them. My parents had made a fatal mistake. I should never have been cast out, I should have been embraced.

My new family showed me the way. The way of the dark arts, and from that moment on, I never looked back."

The police now had a confirmed address. They were on route, and it was just a matter of a few more minutes before they arrived at the callers address.

"So what happened to make you want to hurt your parents? I thought that you still loved and missed them?" She asked.

"Well, I did back then, but the new family helped me to find my old parents. Then I had to go and show them the error of their ways. I had to go and tell them they were wrong to let me go. They weren't happy to see me at their door. Old Frank and Irene had changed their names. They never wanted me to find them. In the age of information, things like that are just too easily done. I also found my sister on social media, and I found out where she worked.

I watched her closely. I found pictures of my parents for the first time in years. Yes they looked a little older, but I still saw the faces that I remembered. Only now, I could see that they had changed. So I went to their house earlier on today. I found Ian and Barbara and I made them lay down on their bed together." The voice on the end of the line now mattered little to the operator, as the real names of his parents had just registered in her head. The names he had mentioned were now alarming to her. She had to clarify what he had said.

"The names you just mentioned, Ian and Barbara, were those the names that you said?" There was a short silence, and then a child like giggling from the other end of the line. "That is the name of my parents! Is this some sort of sick joke?" She demanded to know. The voice on the other end was then quiet for a painfully long time. "Do you know me, are you trying to scare me!" She shouted, now more annoyed at just how much time had been wasted on this crank caller. She began to wonder just who would be sick enough to do this. She grew more furious by the second.

Whoever this caller was, he was probably some sick and twisted fantasist. She would not entertain his delusions any longer. She went to hang up the phone and terminate the call, when the caller spoke once more.

" I left them sleeping, Helen." Were the callers final words, and then the call was abruptly ended. "How did you know my name?" She asked, but it was too late, the caller had gone. The line was now silent.

"I never told you my name!" She shouted.

Helen dropped then phone down on to the desk without disconnecting the call. She picked up her bag from the floor and scrabbled around for her mobile phone. She searched through her contacts and then rang her mother's number. She was begging and pleading that she would answer. The phone rang a few times and then the call went through to her mother's voicemail. She could still hear her mother's voice asking the caller to leave a message when she ended the call. Without a second thought, she took hold of her keys from her handbag and ran toward the door to the cark park to find her car.

It was about an hour's drive to her parent's house, and she broke the speed limits all of the way there. She could see the blue lights flashing in the distance, quite a way before she had reached her destination. All the while her heart was beating faster and faster. Fear now filled her thoughts and adrenalin flowed through her entire body. She was shaking with fear and her legs felt weak.

She stopped the car as close as she could to the house. She had not spoken to her parents for five days, and now how she longed to hear their voices just once more. She prayed that this was all some sick joke that had got out of hand. It was soon clear that sickeningly, this was no joke.

Two bodies were being wheeled out from the house; both of the trollies were covered by black sheets.
"No, no, no!!" She shouted as she ran toward the bodies. A policewoman blocked her path. He was doing the best he could to prevent her from gaining accessing the bodies. She was incredibly strong as she fought to get closer. Her mind was refusing to accept that it was her parents until she

could actually see their faces.

"You don't want to see them like this. Please believe me. You're better off remembering them as they were." She said.

She was unable to get past the policewoman, so instead she turned and ran into the open door of her parent's house. She made the stairs in a few leaps, and stopped at the top of the landing. She stood frozen in a mixture of both fright and extreme pain at what she was witnessing.

The door to her parents' bedroom had been left wide open. Two human hearts lay next to either side of the headboard. Blood covered the off white bedroom furniture and fresh blood flowed down over the tacky silver plastic handles of the drawers. On the wall above the headboard, large words had been painted in the blood of her parents. They read 'For the love of my sister.'

Helen collapsed and fell down to her knees. She screamed an inhuman wail before any of the forensic officers had even noticed that she was there. For the second time in her life, she now felt as if she were drowning.

The Storm Riders

The storm clouds were gathering, and it was now or never. She had two choices. She could either make a run for it and hope to make it to sanctuary before they arrived, or she could just stay here and wait to die. Suzanne decided that she had to at least try and outrun them. If she could make it without stopping, she estimated that she should be able to reach the church before they caught up with her. It would be a close call though. If only someone had believed her story, she might not be so afraid right now.

The night before, she had been woken by the sound of an almighty thunder clap outside of her bedroom window. She checked the clock and the luminous red numbers were now nonexistent. She tried to turn on the bedside lamp and flicked the switch. Again there was no power flowing to the bulb. The storm had taken out the power to the entire estate.

Her watch lay on the dressing table and she edged over in the darkness, being careful not to stub her bare toes on the metal bed. The watch hands were barely visible, but she could just about make out the time. It was three a.m. She had to be awake and be getting ready for work in just three hours, and Monday mornings were already hard enough to face.

The room was suddenly illuminated by an extremely powerful flash of light. Despite the thickness of the fully lined curtains, the room was almost glowing with white light for a few seconds. Then the silence of the pre dawn morning was instantly broken by another almighty crash of thunder. This was much louder than the last one. Rain then slammed down onto the world outside of the window and the downpour became consistent.

The sound of the rainfall was calming, and Suzanne decided to lie back on the top of her bed. Then another rumble of thunder broke the serenity of sound of the rain fall. She kept her eyes open until the next flash of

Lightning. Then she made the count of five before the thunder broke through the air. This storm was definitely moving even closer.

A lot of her friends were so afraid of thunderstorms that she smiled to herself at the thought of them hiding underneath their thick duvets, shaking with fear as they waited for the end of the nightmare. It was unlikely that she was going to go back to sleep. Not until the storm passed anyway. So she decided to watch the storm. She knelt up on her bed and opened the curtains of the window behind her headboard.

The rain was pattering against the large square window pane. Silent rivers formed and ran downward at an ever increasing velocity. Then the sky lit up with the brightest white glow in front of her, it almost as bright as daylight. It was at that moment that she first saw one of the creatures. At first, she thought that it was her mind playing tricks on her, but she couldn't be sure. A strange creature had appeared where the lightning had struck the ground right outside of her house.

She opened the window to appease her own curiosity, and almost fell backward on the bed as a loud clap of thunder erupted once more. Then another flash lit up the entire room. She then started counting again. She was now at a count of three before the thunder clapped even louder. It was now so loud, that she felt as if the room were shaking. The storm was almost directly overhead by her reckoning. She breathed heavily as she looked back out of the open window. The lightning flashed once more and yet another creature appeared out of nowhere on the ground in front of her. She was now of the opinion that she might be dreaming all of this after all.

The creatures that she had seen stood around seven feet tall. They looked to be completely naked and seemed to have no hair anywhere on their bodies. Their skin appeared blue, but it might well have been the poor lighting playing tricks on her eyes. Each creature appeared to have razor like rows of teeth and a solitary central eye like the fabled Cyclops. There was also, an almost demon like single horn, directly protruding from the middle of each ones forehead. Thunder erupted once more and this time it was so loud that the walls of her house seemed to be actually moving.

There was another figure now stumbling along in the road. The figure seemed oblivious to the rain or the storm. As he juddered along, it was almost two steps forward and one to the side or even backward. She could now see that it was a man who looked to be in his early twenties, and whoever it was, they were now very much worse for the wear. It was a Sunday night, and she was positive they if they had work the next morning, then they would be cursing their own actions in a few hours.

Suzanne could hear that the drunkard was singing in a slurred manner and the creatures had now noticed him. One leapt toward him. In a single bound it leapt, and it covered at least thirty feet in distance. The drunkard seemed both shocked and amused at the figure that was now stood directly in front of him. If this was a costume, it was a fantastic one.

Using a single swipe with one arm, the creature tore out the drunkard's throat single handedly. As the man tried in vain to clutch his hands to the wound, he fell down to his knees, and rolled on to the floor. The creature knelt down over the body which was now convulsing in spasms on the ground. It then began to suck the blood directly from the wound in his throat. Suzanne could only watch on in horror at what she was seeing.

The creature drank its fill, and once it was satisfied, it turned to beckon the other creature over; it was already close by and had been keeping watch on the area. They swapped places and the other creature then began to feed. Suzanne was terrified at what she was witnessing, but she should not turn her eyes away from what she was seeing.

The creature that had murdered the drunkard then suddenly raised its hand up toward the sky. It looked skyward and a bolt of lightning stretched out from the clouds above and seemed to connect directly with its hand. The creature then flew upward faster than anything she had ever seen before. To the right of the back of her house, there was a railway line. The remaining creature was looking in the direction of the bridge that crossed the steel lines.

Once the second creature had satisfied its hunger, it easily picked up the dead body like a rag doll. Suzanne knew that the creature must have phenomenal strength, and it leapt to the top to the bridge in a single bound still carrying the body over its shoulder. She was rigid and almost afraid to breathe. She could hear a train now approaching from the distance.

As the train drew closer to the bridge, the creature dropped the body down straight in front of the engine.
Suzanne could not help herself as she shouted out loud.
"No!" It was a mistake that she instantly regretted. The creature looked directly up at the window where she had been watching in silence. It made eye contact with her directly and then it screeched out a sound so loud that it made Suzanne shiver in fear.

The sound of the creature was then drowned out by the noise of the train horn. It was sounding an alarm at the man who had seemingly just ended his life by jumping in front of it. It would have been a futile gesture, but the driver was in shock, and it was the only thing that he could think of doing. This was his third jumper, and it never got any easier to witness. The brakes were now engaged and locking on to the steel rails, but it was far too late to make any difference.

Her eyes were off the creature for less than a second, but when she looked back, it had suddenly gone from the bridge. Her body was now shaking uncontrollably. She leant over and picked up a scented candle from her bedside table. The grabbed the lighter that she had used to light it up earlier that day. She lit the candle and raised it back up toward the window. It illuminated the face of the creature. It was trying to reach her and it screeched again whilst trying to climb into the partially opened frame.

In a moment of sheer panic, Suzanne grabbed her hairspray from the dressing table that was next to the bed. She then sprayed it straight into the creature's eye. The spray itself was mostly ineffective until she had a brainwave and raised up the lit candle. The flame lit up the stream coming from the aerosol jet. The makeshift flame thrower did its job, and it burned the skin and eye on the creatures face.

The creature fell down from the window in sheer panic, and she watched it hobbling blindly back into the middle of the road. The creature looked as if it were badly injured and unable to see where it was going. Nevertheless, it still raised its hand upward and a shard of lightning made contact with its clawed fingers, and then the creature was pulled upward and back into the clouds above. At last it was gone.

She frantically closed the window and locked it tight. Then, she ran into the kitchen, and grabbed the biggest knife that she could find. She dived back underneath her duvet clutching the knife tightly in both hands. Whilst under the duvet, she repeated prayers over and over again, to a God that she had not spoken to for a great many years. In the distance, sirens had now begun to sound. The emergency services were now on route to the scene. The blue lights of the emergency vehicles flashed as they approached the bridge. Sirens grew ever closer. One by one her neighbours began to wake. They were curious and wanted to see exactly what all the fuss was about. Suzanne refused to get out from under her duvet. She would not leave the safety of the bedroom until it was daylight.

It was light outside by around six in the morning. The blue emergency lights were still illuminating the neighbourhood. Suzanne had not slept a wink, and only now did she begin to feel that is might be safe enough for her to leave the sanctuary of her bedroom. She was fearful that the creatures could still return. She was still wearing her night clothes, but she slipped on a coat and trainers from the hallway, and then went to the front room window. The police were still present, but there were no signs of the creatures. She took the knife, and placed it inside her coat pocket. Her hand remained firmly gripped to the handle at all times.

The railway line would not be open for another few hours at the very least. Scene of crime officers were present, and were busily taking notes and photographs of the death. They had taped off the entire scene. The woman walked slowly into the cordoned off area. She looked odd as she approached, and there was something not quite right about the way she was dressed. She had tears in her eyes and looked to be in some sort of shock as she approached one of the police cars.

She now stood outside of the vehicle and the officer in the driver's seat had already powered down his window, to speak to her.
"This is a crime scene. I am going to have to ask you to step back." He officer instructed her. He wasn't in the mood for messing around. His shift had finished hours ago, but he could not leave until the investigation was completed.

Her response was slow. Her body was shaking, and she gulped back her own saliva. Her fear was evident, and a trickle of urine began to flow down her leg. Eventually she spoke.
" I saw it. I saw the man. I saw him being murdered." She stuttered. The officer looked shocked at what she was implying.
"The man appears to have jumped in front of the train madam." He said. Suzanne stared at him. He eyes were wide and unblinking.

The officer began to wonder if the woman had taken any drugs. She was now frozen to the spot. She then shook her head for several seconds. It was almost as if she were struggling to recall what she had seen, unsure that it had really happened at all.
"No... He was thrown. I saw it. I saw it all from there." She insisted. She was pointing upward, toward her bedroom window. It was the perfect vantage point to see what had happened. Her voice sounded as if she was now becoming a little irritated.
"The bridge is about nine feet high. I doubt very much that any man could throw anyone that far upward madam. Are you sure, you saw what you think you did?" He questioned.

In the distance, a rumble of thunder echoed out. Suzanne instantly removed the knife from her pocket. The officer now reacted in fear for his safety, and for the other officers present at the scene.
"It wasn't a man, and it came for me too!" She then screamed. The full events of the evening now played over and over again in her mind. Now she could see the creature as close as it had been a few hours before. It was snarling in her face again. It was desperate to reach her, to silence her. She took the knife from her pocket and raised it up in front of her.

The officer had carefully opened the door, and had stepped out from his vehicle. His movements were slow and deliberate. His was calm, but firm. He was talking to her, almost the same way her father used to talk to her when she had done something wrong.
"I must ask you to put the knife down madam. Please drop it before you hurt yourself, or someone else for that matter. "The officer insisted.
Suzanne stared blankly at the knife that she held in her hand, and then she looked back to the officer. He was now holding a can of pepper spray in his hand, and he was pointing it directly at her. She realised that she looked like a crazed woman and suddenly dropped the knife. Then despite her protestations of innocence, they handcuffed her, but she was assured that it was for her own safety. She was then driven to the local police station. Whilst there, she was assured that she would have the opportunity to give a full statement about the previous nights events.

It was a few hours before she was interviewed, but the more that she told of her story, the more ludicrous it had sounded to both of the officers who were present. It was clear that the drunken man had indeed committed suicide, despite what she thought she had seen. The officers assured her that the evidence was clear. The man had climbed the bridge and in a drunken stupor. He had either jumped or had fallen in front of the train. There was very little of the body left to examine, but there was no clear signs of anyone else being involved at all. It was an open and shut case as far as the police were concerned.

The more the police told her it was not a murder case, the more irate she became with them. Now they started to believe that there may be problems with her mental health, or perhaps drug use might really be the issue. The woman could easily have been hallucinating. It was clear that this woman and her fear of nonexistent creatures could possibly be a danger to others. If they let her go, she may well be walking the streets armed with a sharp knife again. For her own safety, she was referred to see a specialist. Someone who might be able to diagnose exactly what was wrong with her.

Suzanne was growing angrier by the second. She wasn't mad! She knew exactly what she had seen, and now the officers were refusing to listen to the truth and what she was telling them. These creatures came out of nowhere. They had a taste for human blood, and they were hiding in the clouds. They were a threat to any man woman or child, who might be unfortunate enough to be caught in a storm. Why wouldn't they listen to her? In anger, she stood up and lifted the desk forward toward her interviewers. She had to try and get out of there. She had to be ready in case those creatures came back for her.

The officers fought to restrain her. She fought with the ferocity of a woman in fear for her life. It was clear that she believed her own imagination, and she really was a danger. It took the strength of both officers to hold her down. It was fortunate that a police doctor was present at the station, and after a continued struggle, he was able to administer a sedative. Suzanne felt the world blurring after the sharp scratch to her arm. She then drifted temporarily away to a shuddery world of dark dreams.

When she awoke, she had no idea of what had happened, or where she now was. It took little time to realise that she was now in a hospital ward, and that to her dismay, she had been restrained. She tried to pull at the wrist restraints, but they were tight, and it would take some time to work them loose. During that first night in hospital, a violent thunderstorm suddenly broke out. Heavy rain began to fall, and Suzanne was petrified once more.

Beads of sweat began to form on her forehead, and she pulled at her wrist restraints frantically. When the first flash of lightning came, it illuminated the entire sky and the ward lit up briefly, as if it were in daylight inside. She looked from side to side; she could almost sense that one of the creatures was close by. She raised herself up slightly in the bed, and then she saw one of the creatures appear at the window opposite her. She screamed, and as the next flash of lightning shone, another creature appeared behind the first. It was a secure unit and the windows were barred for security, there was no way that the creatures could get inside of there.

She still felt unsafe in there, as she knew the immense strength these creatures possessed. Suzanne then began to scream the place down. Her screams were frightening the other patients in the room, and the staff had no choice but to try and calm her down. As she was held down on the bed, it took four orderlies to hold her in place. She screamed as she looked out of the window again. The creatures were now pulling at the bars. They were testing just how strong the bars were.
"Please, please look out of the windows, they are out there!" She shouted. "They are coming for me!" She frantically tried to make them listen to her. She had no idea just how crazy she now sounded.

No one was listening to her cries. Instead, they were intent on forcing another needle into her arm. The world became hazy, and as she began to fade, she could still see the creatures looking in from outside. One of the creatures had burns on its face, and it was now pointing straight at her. The other creature was nodding in agreement. They would need another to remove the bars. They were coming for her; it would not be long before they would return. Nobody else knew that the lightning riders existed. She had to be taken care of. As the only human witness to their existence, she had to be taken care of.

The next day when Suzanne awoke, it was mid morning. She decided it would be wise to remain silent. Slowly she set to work, and after a while, she managed to work her wrist restraints loose. She had to get out of here. Then she had to find something she could defend herself with and to maybe find somewhere safe to hide from the demons.

The only place she could think that might be a safe place to seek refuge from these creatures would be a church. At least a vicar might understand. They wrote about such creatures in the bible. The ancients knew about the demons that she had seen. The church might be able to offer her some refuge. Getting out of the hospital secure unit was paramount, but that was still the tricky part.

As two of the doctors came over to tend to her, she kept her wrists held down and in place. She remained calm while the younger of the two men spoke to her.
"How are you feeling this morning?" He asked.
"I'm feeling much better. I'm so sorry; I'm not sure what came over me. I think it was the shock of seeing the guy jumping from the bridge." She said. She had reasoned that if no one was going to believe her, then she had to say whatever they wanted to hear. It wasn't safe here. Not now those things knew where she was. She had to get out of here at any cost.
"Shock can make you think terrible things. I think we had better keep you

here for just a little while longer. Just for observation you understand. "The other doctor said. She just silently nodded in agreement.
"That's alright. It will take as long as it takes. I trust you." She said, and then smiled at them both in turn.

The doctors then moved on to the next patient who was a little further down the ward. In the bed next to hers, an orderly was changing the bed sheets. He was making the bed ready for any new arrivals that day. His keys were attached to his trousers by a plastic doubled ended clip. She was positive that she could reach them. She leaned over silently, and gently unhooked the clip. Slowly she drew them back and tucked the small bunch underneath the covers and then into the top of her knickers.

It was a long and boring day. She was spoken to on numerous occasions, and was fed soft foods regularly. Her blood tests had come back fine with no sign of drugs in her body. Her restraints were not checked once as she was causing no trouble, and it was likely that she would be allowed to leave here after a few more days of assessments. The lights were turned off at ten in the ward. It was a long wait, but once the lights went off, the ward was much quieter.

The duty nurse was paying little attention to the ward itself, and was busy filling in paperwork. The solitary security guard was wandering the hospital, slowly walking from ward to ward. He would disappear every now and again and not return for at least fifteen minutes. Suzanne silently worked off the rest of her restraints from her legs whilst he was absent. The restraints on her legs were light, and meant to stop her from injuring herself, they were not meant to keep her secured. The nurses now showed little signs of interest in her as she was no longer considered much of a threat to herself.

She slid slowly and deliberately out from the bed, and dropped down on to the floor. She crawled on her hands and knees and made her way slowly around the beds and right up to the exit door. She pulled the bunch of keys out from the top of her knickers and then reached up and tried one of the keys in the lock. It didn't fit. She tried two others until she found the correct key. She slowly turned it until she felt the door latch drop as it unlocked. Then she pushed the door gently open, and she silently slipped outside.

The night air was cool. She slowly closed the door behind her, making as little noise as possible. Now she had to try and make it to the nearest church. She had no doubt in her mind that it would not be easy though. The skies above her were now beginning to fill with dark clouds. As the storm clouds began to gather pace overhead, she realized that these creatures were able to harness the power of the weather however and whenever they chose to.

It was now or never. She was barefoot, and it was at least a mile to the nearest church. There was no time to waste though. She started to run barefoot. The clouds began to open up behind her. It was night time, and there was no guarantee the church would even be open, but she had to try to make it there anyway. Her breathing was heavy, but she would not give up easily. Every step that she took, would take her closer to sanctuary.

The rain started to fall heavier, and the clouds began to rumble as the power of the storm grew in intensity. Her feet pounded one after the other against the wet pavement, occasionally she would slip or slide slightly and always had to adjust herself so that she did not come tumbling down on to the wet floor. Her heart was pounding as if it might soon try to escape from her chest. There was no stopping now though. She could see the church at the top of the hill.

She now began to sprint as fast as she possibly could. Then the first flash of lightning struck somewhere in the distance behind her. Then a second and then a third and final flash lit up the sky. Three creatures had transported on lightning strikes and were now at the hospital where they had come back down to claim the witness. They were soon checking the windows to locate the troublesome woman. They were now strong enough in number to remove the security bars if they needed to.

The creatures quickly noticed that she was no longer in the bed that she had been in the night before. One spotted the open doorway and then smelt the handle. It drew in her scent and then breathed in the air around it. It was a keen tracker. It pointed its claw in the direction of the church, and the creatures began bounding high into the air toward Suzanne. They would reach her in just a matter of minutes.

Despite her exhaustion, Suzanne climbed the steps that led up to St Mary's church. She ran up to the large archway and tried the metal handle. The wooden heavy doors were closed and locked tight. She pounded on the doors with her fists, but no one would answer. She placed her ear to the door. She was relieved that she could hear music from inside of the church. She banged on the door again as loud as she could. There was no response. She banged again, not prepared to accept defeat, but there was still no response.

She dropped down the steps and glanced back in the direction of the hospital, and it was then that she saw them. They were at the bottom of the hill, and three creatures were taking giant leaps toward her. She ran away from the creatures and around to the side of the church. Then she saw the side door, and she sprinted toward it as fast as she could.

To her relief, she found that the side door was open. Suzanne ran inside fearful that at any second one of the creatures may catch up with her.

Frantically she tried to push the door closed behind her. It was heavy and it took all of her strength to even start it moving. She turned her back against the door, and pushed at it with all of her might. The door stubbornly moved, and eventually it closed into place.

The key was still in the lock and she turned and closed it. It was only now with the door safely locked, that she could feel safe. She collapsed down to the floor where she now remained gasping for breath in a heap. She was exhausted, but at least she was in a place of safety. They could not get to her, not now anyway. She started to sob, but at the same time; she could not stop herself from laughing. This was a living nightmare and she had no idea if this was actually real or not anymore. The stone floor beneath her was cold, but she would not move until her heart rate had returned to normal.

The priest had been at the front of the church, and as the music from the speakers ended, he had heard the door closing. He had then stepped down from the Chancel where the altar stood, curious to know who was now in the church with him. He slowly made his way along the side of the church. He then saw the woman on the floor who was now sobbing.

He rushed over to help her. He was curious, but also a little fearful as to whom the stranger was. People were so different these days, and she might have been a crazed lunatic for all that he knew.
"My dear child, whatever is the matter?" He asked. Suzanne looked up at him, and saw that he now had his hands held out. He was trying to help lift her up from the floor.
"I have seen what I think are Demons father. They have come for me!" She cried.
"Let me help you up, you poor thing!" He implored. He took both her hands in his and then helped her up from the floor. He then sat her down on one of the padded church benches. "Now tell me exactly what is happening?" He asked. "Let me see if I can make some sense of it all for

you."

The story seemed crazy enough, but the priest was not about to judge the girl. She was in a desperate mess, and she was soaked through to the skin. The storm was still raging outside. He told her to wait on the bench a while he went to the church kitchen and made her a sweet cup of tea. In times like this, tea always seemed welcome and had a miraculous way of calming down people in stressful situations. He was not gone for very long.

When he returned, he handed the girl the tea in a white bone china tea cup with a saucer. He then sat down next to her for a while. All the while he continued to calm her fears. He assured her that God was afraid of nothing and that his power would protect her from her demons. Then there three large bangs on the side door of the church. Suzanne dropped her cup, and it smashed into what seemed like a thousand pieces on the floor. The priest then stood up and walked over toward the door.
"Don't open it!" She screamed. Her cries were now frantic.

The priest was already at the door. He held the key to the lock in his hand. He turned to face her and to reassure her that she would be safe.
"Don't be alarmed, you will be alright. I promise you. Whilst I was in the kitchen, I called for some help. You are safe my child. These people are here to make sure that you get the best help that they can give you." He assured her. Then he turned the key in the lock, and as he opened the door a rapturous clap of thunder shook the entire church. As he pulled the heavy wooden door open, two police officers were stood in the pouring rain just outside of the stone archway.

It was clear to the priest that the woman was unstable. Either that or she may have been on drugs and was hallucinating quite badly. Either way, he felt as if she needed professional help. So he had called the police for advice. The operator had advised him to remain calm and to keep her

talking for as long as he could. They were sending officers to the scene to detain her. As the officers entered the church, a female officer held a taser out in front of her; she pointed it directly at Suzanne.
"I came to you for help, and you betrayed me!" Suzanne shouted to the priest.

The female officer then spoke sternly.
"Please try to remain calm, I will use this if I have to, but please don't make me hurt you. Now get down on your hands and knees please." She commanded. It was clear that she wasn't in a mood for messing around. Suzanne turned to run toward the front of the church, and she felt metal hooks latch into her skin. A pulsing high voltage current then flowed through her entire body, making her muscles go into spasm. She fell to the floor and writhed around in agony.

When it was deemed safe enough to do so, the officers placed handcuffs on the woman, and then lifted her up from the floor. They then led her toward the side door of the church and despite her struggles; they forced her out through the opening, and into the torrential rain that was now pouring down. Once they were fully outside of the church all three stopped and stared upward at the swirling storm-clouds that swam like a tornado circling directly over their heads.

The priest was following them closely. He was making sure that the police were taking the woman far away from his church, only then would he be happy to lock the door and to make his way back home. Suzanne closed her eyes and tilted her head back. There was no point in even trying anymore. She waited for the eye of the storm to erupt.
"We are going to get you the help that you need. We will get you off to the hospital." The male officer told her. Suzanne kept her eyes closed and grinned.
"It's too late for that now." she said, and she started giggling insanely. She knew exactly what was coming.

The lightning struck the ground on either side of Suzanne; she leant backward against the priest and she grabbed a handful of his robes. She held on tightly and as the priest struggled to break her grip; his arms became locked inside of her handcuffed hands. The creatures then rode the lightning down and appeared on either side of Suzanne. The two police officers were knocked aside by the strikes of lightning, but Suzanne remained upright. She turned her head to see the priests face, and he was in complete shock at now seeing the creatures she had described, were now here in the flesh.

Suzanne smiled at the priest. He was panicking as he could not free his arms to run away from the creatures.
"You should have believed me father. Now you can see my demons. Perhaps now you might believe that they really do exist." She said. "I hope you're ready and that you truly believe in the power of your God. You see father, I need some protection, so I've decided.... that if I'm going to hell, then I'm taking you with me." She said. Then she looked at the creatures as the gripped hold of her arms, and without a hint of fear she spoke to them. "Let's go." She said.

The creatures gripped both of her arms tightly and raised their spare hands upward. They caught the power of the lighting, and Suzanne and the priest were lifted high into the clouds. In an instant they were gone. The storm clouds that had been swirling above them all began to disperse. The rains stopped falling, just as quickly as they had begun. Now the sky was silent and only a cool breeze remained.

The officers were dazed, but after a few minutes, they both managed to get to their feet. The priest and the woman were both gone, and neither of the officers had witnessed anything. It was impossible to explain. They tried the church doors, but they were both now locked and no keys were to be found on the ground. Then the sounds came, and they seemed to be coming from all around them.

They could hear the priest screaming, and the woman's insane laughter, but they were nowhere at all to be seen. Madly enough, the sounds seemed to be coming from the skies above. The woman and the priest were never seen or heard from again.

One Night Stand

"Wake up."

They were first words that Lucy heard. She opened her eyes, but everything seemed to be blurry. It must have been one hell of a night she thought. Her head was pounding, and her body ached all over. The voice that she had heard was a male, but it was not the voice of her husband. Lucy panicked and tried to sit upright, but her arms were tied tightly to the headboard of the bed. Her mouth was dry, and she coughed loudly to try to lubricate her throat.

"What's going on? Who are you?" She asked aloud. She genuinely had no idea what was happening.

A male figure was stood at the side of the bed. He was dressed all in black, and she vaguely remembered his features from the night before. His hair was dark, and it looked so slick and shiny that it could have been plastic. He was deeply tanned and his skin looked as if he were Mediterranean in origin.

"You asked me to take you home with me, so I did. Now here you are. You are a guest in my home." He answered.

"Why am I tied to the bed? Do you do this to all of your guests?" She asked. She was doing her best to hide her fear, but her legs were trembling slightly despite her best efforts to stop them moving.

"You seemed to enjoy what we did last night. Now I wanted to keep you here for just a little while longer." He answered. His expression was blank, and she found it hard to read his emotions. She had to try and get loose. Her husband would be more than mad when he found out that she hadn't made it home, and it certainly wasn't her intention to spend the entire night with another man. She would have to think of a damned good excuse for this one.

"Can you untie me please? I need to get home to my husband." She pleaded. The man was staring straight at her but only smiled in response. He now moved forward so that he stood directly over her.

Now he was just stood silently while he looked down at her naked body. She drew her knees upward to hide a little of her nudity, but she still felt too exposed by her lack of clothing. In her vanity, all she could think about was her belly being just a little too big. It was strange the way her mind was now working, even in a dangerous situation like this one.

"It's a little late to be shy now." The man said. He then ran his hand over her naked leg up and toward her stomach. "I already know every single inch of you." He said. The sound of his voice now began to frighten her. His touch was warm, but now she felt cold and afraid at how helpless she was.

"Alright stop!" She demanded. "Last night, I was drunk. I can't remember what happened, and I can only apologize. Now I need to get home to my husband, so can you please untie me?" She demanded.

The man leaned forward toward her face. He then knelt over her stomach, and his hand gripped tightly around her throat.

"You... Don't ask me for anything, understand?" His voice was loud, and he was visibly angry. As he shouted at her, spittle had ejected from his mouth and had landed on the side of her face. It made her begin to feel sick. She nodded in silent agreement, and felt tears slowly rolling down both her cheeks. Now she was absolutely petrified. The man seemed unstable, and she had to be wary of upsetting him again.

The man then kissed her on the forehead, and after a few seconds, he began to loosen his grip around her throat. He moved his head down to kiss her on the lips, and fearing his anger again, Lucie kissed him back but only gently. He then stroked her hair back, and away from her face.

"That's much better my princess." He said. His voice was now almost childlike as he spoke. "Now you must stay calm. No one will upset my special lady anymore." He then kissed her forehead once more, and then he lifted himself from the bed and walked out from the bedroom. He closed the door behind him.

Lucy was now petrified. She had stupidly cheated numerous times in the past, but now how she wished that her husband was here to save her from this nightmare. She began to look around the bed. Her phone was sat on the side of the bedside cabinet and she could see the display. The battery was almost flat, and the screen showed seventeen missed calls. All of which she assumed were from her husband. She then tried to reach out to touch the phone, but it was only just out of her grasp. She tried to pick at the binds around her wrist, and despite it being awkward she actually managed to loosen the binds just a tiny amount. **She would now be able to reach the phone.**

The door handle creaked as the man pushed it down, and walked back into the room. She quickly withdrew her hand back to where it was and lay frozen to the spot. She prayed that he had not seen her. The man was now carrying a towel and a bowl of water. Steam was rising up from the bowl which indicated just how hot the water was. The man placed the bowl down next to the bed, and then he removed a sponge from inside of the bowl. He started at Lucy's feet, and began to wash her body thoroughly. Lucy was now so scared that she wanted to scream, but she was afraid of what might happen if she did.

"My princess must be clean, or the mixture will not stay." He said.

His words made no sense to her. She welcomed the feeling of cleanliness, but not the feel of his hand now touching her skin once again. He started to kiss her legs slowly. He kissed her everywhere that he washed, and as he moved up her legs she had to bite her lower lip to stop herself from screaming out in revulsion. He forced her legs apart and she could feel his breath as his tongue slipped inside of her, and he began to taste her. By the time that he had finished, she was a shivering wreck.

"You are almost ready." He said. Lucy still had no idea what he was talking about, but now it was more important than ever for her to reach that phone.

The man picked up the towel, and dried her off. He was brisk as he dried her skin. Then as quickly as he had come into the room, he was gone again. Lucy reached out her hand. She managed to grab the phone from the side, and on the front of the phone she had an emergency call button. She pushed it, activating an alarm on her husband's phone. He would now know exactly where she was. She dropped the phone back to the bedside cabinet, and breathed a huge sigh of relief. Soon this nightmare would be over, and this sicko, would be behind bars where he belonged.

The man was gone from the room for a very long time. When he finally came back into the room again, he was wearing some sort of overall and a face mask. He was also carrying some containers filled with fluid, and this time he did not speak. Instead, he grabbed hold of Lucy's left foot, and tied it to the bottom of the bed. He then did the same with the other foot. Lucy again did not struggle. It seemed pointless to irritate him. She just had to wait.

Once her husband arrived, she was sure then that this guy was going to be regretting all of this. She would tell her husband that he had drugged her and brought her back here. He would have no reason not to believe her now. **Her husband was not a man to be messed with. It was quite likely that he would be so angry, that this man would soon be sitting in a pool of his own blood. The thought made her smile inside. It kept her going.**

The man opened the container of fluid and started to spread the liquid over her naked body. It felt like warm oil, but it stank like chemicals. He washed it all over her legs, then he moved upward over her torso and her breasts, then finally he reached her face. At first she feared that the fluid might burn her, but her fears were soon eased. That was until the fluid started to set. Within a few minutes, the fluid had set rock hard. She was now completely rigid, and unable to move an inch. **The only thing he hadn't covered was her eyes, and her nostrils.**

 The doorbell to the flat startled both of them as it rang. The man removed his mask, and placed the lid back on the fluid. He then slowly made his way out to the hallway, picking up an object from the side as he did so. He closed the door behind him as he left. Lucy was now completely unable to move. She could only shout out muffled cries, but she hoped that whoever was at the door, they might just hear her anguished sounds. It was highly unlikely though.

 She heard noises in the hallway, and she was positive, that she could hear the sound of her husband's voice. She heard her name mentioned, and then the sound of a minor scuffle. The door to the bedroom flew open, and her husband shouted out her name as he entered the room.

"Lucy! My God, what has he done to you?" He shouted. He stood motionless in the doorway. Lucy tried to scream out and warn him as she could see what was about to happen, but it was already too late. The man was now stood behind him and a lump hammer was being raised above her husband's head. Before he could turn around, it had been mercilessly smashed down on the top of his skull. He husband dropped to his knees and raised his left hand up to his head. His hand touched the wound and he began to sway as streams of blood flowed down his face. When he brought the hand back down in front of his face, it was covered in blood, bone and fragments of his own brain. It made him realise that his death was now inevitable.

"Oh my." Were the last words that he ever spoke. Lucy was crying, but the tears were unable to run anywhere. Instead they sat in pools at the edge of her eyes. They sat between her eyes and her cheeks. The tears were now stinging the edge of her eyes underneath her newly formed plastic mask.

The man stepped over the body of her now dead husband, and placed fluid over the hole in the back of his head. It should seal up the wound, but it may take a few more layers. He then turned his attention back to Lucy. He loosened her binds and then turned her over. He then covered her back with the fluid, making sure he smoothed over the seams. He covered her body, until she was completely encased. **Once it had set, he turned her back over, so she could see the body of her husband was also now being covered in the strange fluid.**

He applied fluid to the inside of her nose, and a thin layer across her eyes. No amount of blinking would take away the sting. The fluid had set fast in her nostrils, and without air, it took just a few minutes for her to suffocate. The last thing she remembered was the scent of a rubber compound and the chemicals had made her begin to hallucinate. When her brain shut down completely, her senses were flooded by the bodies' natural release of DMT, which amplified the chemicals effects much more vividly. Her eyes were now fixed on the wide open space in front of her.

It would take a few more coats to perfect the shell. Then he would have to do a lot more work on the male as well. It did not matter though. Now he would have another two mannequins for his collection. One was for the horror show; he now had the freak with half a brain. For the fairy tale section, he now also had his sleeping beauty. That mannequin would always hold a special place in his heart, and as long as married women found him attractive, he would always be able to add many more figures to his prized collection.

Mother Nature

Ever since they had bought the house, that old tree in the back of the garden had been something of an eyesore. Mark had often thought about chopping it down. Then it would just be a case of digging out the roots and levelling off the ground. Once that was done, there would be plenty of space for another carport. The only thing that was stopping him from removing it, was that stupid note that he had found.

The house had formerly belonged to an elderly lady who had fallen on hard times. It had been repossessed by the bank, and although they felt pity for the woman, Mark and his wife Louise, had paid a huge sum for the house and its land. It was almost perfect, except that at the moment they had to park one of their two cars outside of the garden, leaving it out on the main road. It was surely only a matter of time before some idiot managed to scratch or dent the car.

The tree was pointless, it looked ugly, and it was just in the way. The only thing on his conscience was the daft note that was left inside of the tree. He assumed that the old lady, who used to own the property, had left it there. He had found it almost by accident, whilst clearing the autumn leaves that had fallen from its now bare branches. A few feet up the tree, there was a small hole in the trunk, it was just large enough to enable birds to fly in and out of it. That morning, he just happened to notice something that was tucked safely inside of the hole.

The note had been carefully folded many times, and had been wrapped in clear plastic to protect it from the weather. He reached his hand inside of the hole and tried to remove the plastic bag. It was snagged on something inside, but he managed to pry it loose after a little adjustment to the angle of his hand. The plastic was old and weathered, and as he opened it up, it almost disintegrated. The note that was folded inside was yellowed and the ink had faded, but it was still just about readable.

He carefully opened up the note fully, and then held it out in front of him. A gentle gust of wind blew against the paper, almost as if it were trying to push the note even closer to his face. He read the note with interest.

It said. 'The ashes of my sister were buried with the seeds of this tree. She lays here undisturbed, and so she should forever remain. She is at one with nature, and held within the spirit of the tree forevermore. Heed my words, and leave my sister be.'

He smiled as he read the note. It was almost creepy to read the words, and by the style of the handwriting, this note was written a very long time ago. The paper had become thinner and weakened with age, but he thought that it was quite sentimental, so he tucked it inside of his coat pocket, and later when he went back into the house. Later then stored it in his study with the rest of his paperwork. There it remained, untouched by human hands for the next five months.

It was early on a Saturday morning that his wife Louise went out to her car to hoover out the insides. To her dismay she found that the passenger side wing mirror had been completely smashed. It wasn't just broken; the whole thing was now hanging off from the car. There were also deep scratches in the paintwork of the door. Mark had examined it closely, and he was annoyed that they now had to go through an insurance claim to get the car repaired. He was even more annoyed when he found out that he was liable for an excess payment of one hundred and fifty pound to pay as well.

The following Saturday, he walked out into the garden. He stopped and looked over at the tree. Sentimental or not he now had no other choice, it would have to go. There was no way he was going to go through all this hassle again. The tree would have to come down and then they could have some nice block paving laid. That afternoon, he started making enquiries about exactly how much it would cost to lay a new car port.

It would take around a week for the car to be repaired, and it was frustrating as the policy would not allow them use of a courtesy car. Instead, they decided that Louise would use his car, and Mark would take the week off work to oversee the driveway project. The first thing on the agenda was to buy an axe, and the next, was to chop the bulk of that tree down. It wasn't a huge tree, and he imagined that it wouldn't take long.

At first, he had considered using a chainsaw, but he did not feel very comfortable with such a dangerous power tool. Instead, he had opted for the axe. On Monday morning, he watched from the kitchen window as Louise left the driveway. He pottered around with a cup of coffee, and then he decided that he had better get moving. He dressed in some of his old sports clothes. There was no doubt at all in his mind that this job was going to get dirty and sweaty. He picked up the axe that was resting against the kitchen cupboards, removed the cover from the blade and then made his way out to the garden.

Mark stood directly in front of the tree. He sized it up, and it stood around fifteen feet tall. The trunk was not exactly thick, but it would still take some effort. He needed to cut down as close to the base of the tree as he could. The day before, he had spent the afternoon digging the soil out from around the base. Now the area he wanted to cut was clearly visible. He took the axe, and swung it hard and low at the trunk of the tree.

As the axe took its first bite into the tree, a woman's laughter could inexplicably be heard. At first Mark thought he had imagined it, but he looked around and there was no one else at all in the vicinity. Then as he took a second swing, he heard the very same insane laughter again. He carried on swinging the axe repeatedly, regardless of the laughter. Whoever it was, they sounded a little insane. If he was amusing them with his efforts, then so be it. The tree was coming down today.

The tree grew weaker and weaker with each bite of the steel axe into its trunk. It creaked and groaned against its own weight, and eventually it started to fall. There was a satisfaction in watching the tree fall down to the ground. The eyesore was finally going to be out of sight. Now he would just have to dig out the rest of the roots, and cut up the tree and feed it into the chipper that he had hired. He had earned himself a can of beer first though. Just to celebrate the effort he told himself. First, he had felt the sudden urge to take a piss though.

The bathroom was combined with the toilet, as was often the case, and he washed his hands in the basin thoroughly. His hands were already filthy in such a short time, and who knows what sort of grime was on his hands already. He took the nail brush from the side, and scrubbed his hands thoroughly. The mirrored cabinet was placed at head height in front of him. He stared in the mirror and saw that his face was also dirty too.

An unexpected pain then soared through his temples. He had suffered from migraines in the past, but this was instant and felt more intense. He opened the bathroom cupboard, and found some pain relief. He popped two tablets out from the blister pack, and placed them in his mouth. The water from the cold tap tasted a little warm, but it helped to ease the tablets down. Then he closed the cabinet door.

If Mark were a woman, he might have screamed at the sight that greeted him. The woman in the mirror had jet black hair, matted and wet. It covered most of her face. Her teeth were rotten and looked green. Her face, although not really aged, looked twisted and scarred. Mark was frozen to the spot in pure terror. The women then spoke.

"Now you have awakened me. I will show you the power of the dark ones. Prepare to meet the ten curses of the ages." Her head then tilted backward, and Mark heard that insane laughter he had heard when he began to cut into the tree. He was scared, but now ready to get this insane woman out of the house, and remove her from his property. He swung around with his fists clenched in front of him, but there was nobody stood there for him to fight.

It might have been his mind playing tricks. Perhaps the headache had caused a hallucination, whatever it was; it had shaken him up a great deal. He shook his head and checked the mirror once more. There was definitely no one else in the bathroom. Now he felt an overwhelming urge to pee again. If not, he was convinced that his bladder would empty itself. He unzipped his fly hurriedly, and then he lifted up the toilet seat.

As the warm urine flowed, he felt a massive relief. As the urine continued to flow, it then began to feel uncomfortable. For some strange reason, his urine was now stinging. He looked down, and then he shouted out loud 'Jesus!' His reaction was one of pure shock at what he now saw. Coming from his penis, and flowing down into the water, was a stream of dark red blood.

The tree would now have to wait. He telephoned the local doctor, and they advised him that he needed to attend his local casualty department. Without hesitation, he phoned for a taxi and then made his way to the hospital. That afternoon, he went through a plethora of different emotions. Most of all, he was frightened. Despite numerous tests, and needles and prodding, the doctors could find nothing wrong. They decided that it was safe to send him home, and assured him, that it may have been a kidney stone. He wasn't sure if he actually believed than, but eventually he began to calm down.

As he walked out from the hospital, he found himself stood all alone. There was an eerie wind blowing across his face. He stared out at the road ahead and took a few deep breaths deep into his lungs. He closed his eyes and breathed in the fresh air. Then he opened them up again, and it was at this point that he noticed that there was something wrong with the road. It was almost as if it were alive. He edged forward to take a closer look, and then he realised exactly just why the road had looked so odd. The road was filled with the bodies of thousands of dead frogs.

A local television news crew had already been alerted to the strange phenomenon and they had taken a camera crew to attend the scene. Mark was still at the hospital as they arrived and he unexpectedly found himself being questioned about the event on camera. He answered, but it was almost against his better judgement. A local fisherman soon appeared, and gave a logical reason for the phenomena.

It appeared that a local lake had experienced an unusually high level of tadpoles. As they had grown into frogs, the water had become polluted and the frogs had all been contaminated. They had left the water en masse, and all of them had died within minutes of leaving. It was a freaky event to say the least, but at least there was a rational explanation. As the camera crew were about to pack up, the sun beat down on the dead animals, and out of nowhere thousands of flies suddenly began to descend on the corpses of the dead frogs.

Mark was now being bitten all over. There were not just flies, there were also knats. Each of them seemed more than happy to bite down into human skin. The film crews were also being targeted too and the group was soon all running for cover. Mark joined them as they sought refuge in the crews van, and they made a speedy escape away from the area. As they drove Mark back toward his home, it was soon clear that the frogs were not the only victims of the chemical spill. All across the open fields, dead cattle were strewn everywhere. Not one creature that had drunk from the local river had been spared death.

As the crew was almost at his house, the knat bites had seemed to cause some sort of chemical reaction under all of their skins. Their faces and hands and everywhere that large areas of skin were visible were now beginning to swell up in large boil like lumps. Today was becoming too much to bear. Each of them would probably need a course of antibiotics, and as they looked at each other in disgust, all of them now looked hideously deformed.

When they arrived back at his house he thanked the crew for taking him home. Then as they drove away, the skies suddenly darkened. There was then a huge white flash of light that lit up the sky, followed by one of the loudest crashes of thunder that Mark had ever heard. The rain then followed and it was so intense that it felt as if it were solid as it struck his skin. This wasn't just rain though, it was hailstones, and they were getting bigger in size as they landed all around him. At least the rain had given him some temporary relief from the feeling of the itchiness of the boils. Then the hailstorm stopped as suddenly as it had begun.

The sky was now so dark, it felt like it were night instead of day. Mark looked upward at the sky, and saw that there was something below the clouds, something that was hiding the light. There were creatures hovering in the air the like of which he had never seen before. If he wasn't mistaken, then he could swear that these creatures were locusts. The creatures then descended, toward him, and his worst fears were confirmed.

Perhaps in some way they had been drawn here by all the dead animals, in the surrounding fields. Maybe they had been carried here by the sudden storm, but whatever it was that had brought them here, they were now descending as a group, and they were stripping everything in their paths, and as more gathered above above, the sky over his house became completely black.

Mark almost fell into the front door in panic and had to forcibly close it behind him. The locusts slammed against the plastic door repeatedly, but he was now safe inside. This had all been too much! He took a few breaths and then ran to the bathroom to throw up. As he walked inside the door in a hurry, he forgot that he had left the axe leant up against the bath. He tripped over the wooden handle and fell downward. His head caught the porcelain toilet bowl as he fell, and he sank into a dark and haunted sleep.

Louise was shaking him gently; her face was the first thing that he saw as he came round. She was pushing down on his forehead and it felt weird and unnatural. He lifted his left hand to try and move her hand from his head. She remained with her hand held firmly in place.

"I need to stop the bleeding; you've cut your head. You must have fell on to the bloody toilet." She said. She continued pressing on the wound for a few more minutes, then she took her hand away from his forehead. "I think it's stopped now. Thank God."

Mark tried to stand up, but she pushed him back down. "Stay there. Now as you are already sat down, I have some great news for us, and I should wait a little while but I have to tell you. I've done a third test, and I have had it confirmed by the doctor today. I can't wait any longer, so here goes...I'm pregnant. We are going to have a baby!" She said excitedly.

Mark was still dazed and confused, he started to try and list everything that had happened to him during the day. He was unable to form sentences but he started to mumble odd words out of his mouth.

"Tree...blood, frogs.....gnats, flies!" He mumbled.

"What on earth are you on about?" Louise asked. "Let's get you up and into the front room. We will get you laid down on the sofa. I think I better call a doctor out to get you checked over." She said, now slightly worried about his incoherent mumbling. She helped him up from the floor and she led him over toward the living room.

"Cattle....boils....hail...." He continued to mumble.

"Lay yourself down on the sofa. Let's get someone over here to take a look at you." She said, as she lay him down gently on the white leather sofa.

"Locusts....Darkness!" He said. Now it made sense, but it made no real sense to her whatsoever. Mark did not know the significance of what he was mumbling, but then he had a moment of realization from a movie had had seen recently. He realised that he was actually listing the ten biblical plagues. He grabbed a hold of her hand, but he was growing weak from the blood loss he had suffered. **His eyes began to close and he started to lose consciousness.**

"Fir...fir...first..." Mark was desperate to warn her about what he realized might be about to happen, but his strength had all but gone. He passed out where he lay, and released his grip on her hand.

Louise then felt a sudden warm feeling flowing outward from her groin. She reached her hands down instinctively and shook her head as she raised them both up in front of her face. It was devastating for her to see what was happening. They had both been trying for so long to conceive a child. Now she looked at both of her hands and they were covered in blood. She had lost the baby, and she began to wail in agony at her loss.

Mark soon came round, and Louise was sat sobbing with her legs pulled upward toward her chest. He tried, but he could not move toward his wife; instead he used his strength to utter the words he had been trying to get out."First son." He said. Louise then screamed, and raised her face to the heavens above, whilst beating her fists down on the wooden flooring.

"How could you be so cruel God?" She screamed out loud. This was not the work of a God though; this was the work of a witch who had been overpowered a very long time ago. Back then she had been burned by her own parents, and then her ashes were buried deep and marked with the planting of a sacred tree. Mother Nature had once contained her spirit, but now she had been set free.

Our Saviour

This was David's favourite time of day to go walking. The summer had been largely disappointing, and the infrequent appearance of the sun in the sky had served to dampen his mood numerous times over the previous few months. It wasn't that he didn't like the winter, as that would have been a ridiculous statement. He loved walking in the rain just as much as he liked walking in the dry warm summer air.

Now it was early evening, and there was a slight breeze blowing around him. The sun continued to glimmer through the trees and the birds were singing in the distance. His favourite walk was around the Anton lakes in Andover. The nearby estates seemed a million miles away from this place of solitude. On those estates he could never find peace of mind for very long. The area in which he lived had seemed relatively quiet until recently, but now the noise was becoming unbearable.

It had all started when his new neighbours moved in six months ago. He knew from the very first second he had laid his eyes on the family, that they were no good. They made noise both day and night, and Davis complained almost daily to the housing association. It wasn't long before they were forcibly evicted, and then peace returned. Then something awful happened. It was as if karma was punishing him. David had worked hard all of his life. For forty years he had worked like a trooper. Day in, day out, and he had one of the cleanest sickness records ever afforded a man. Then at fifty six years old, he found himself being made redundant from his employment through no fault of his own.

The pay off was a few thousand pounds, but it would not last for very long. He had put money away regularly into a savings account, but that in turn had only worked against him. Now he was no longer entitled to any benefits because of the amount of savings that he had put away for retirement. In four years time, he would have been moving away to a little plot of land in the sun, where he could live out the rest of his days away from the noise and hustle and bustle of modern day life. Now his dream retirement scenario had been cruelly torn away from him.

David had no close friends, he kept himself to himself and that was the way he preferred things to be. Since his mother had passed away, he had felt an extreme sense of loneliness inside of him. It was about this time that he started walking around the lakes. At first he struggled with the distance. The circuit around the area was around a mile and a half in length, and for many years he had done little in the form of exercise. Now he had not much else to do except for watch daytime television or to sleep.

Now he was becoming quite used to the little walks around the lakes. Of course he still felt the aches and pain in his feet and legs, but as his weight slowly began to fall away, the pains became easier to bear. When his mother died, the emptiness had overwhelmed him to the point where he made the decision to take his own life. He took a massive concoction of pills and then washed them down with an entire bottle of vodka. Then he wrote a good bye note to the world, telling them that he knew he would not be missed, and that he would now be at peace and back with his late mother again. She was the only woman in his life, who had ever truly loved him.

That night he lay on his bed and as he finished off the remainder of the alcohol, it burnt his throat and the world began to spin as the combined effects of the pills and drink finally took hold. He began to feel a sense of relief as he slipped into the longest of all sleeps. Eleven hours later, David sat upright in his bed. He had been spared. That night he had experienced long conversations with his dead mother, she had been furious with him and told him that it was not his time, that he had things still left to do. As he sat upright on his bed, he smiled for the first time in months.

A few weeks later the chronic pain started, and he collapsed to the floor in agony. One of his neighbours heard his cries of despair through the paper thin walls of his flat. The door was unlocked as the ambulance men arrived and they had let themselves in. David was writhing around on the floor in agony. In hospital, they had conducted numerous tests, and it turned out that the drugs he had taken had done some serious damage to his internal organs.

He had not died, but it was only a matter of time before one of his organs would almost certainly fail. Instead of depressing him, this actually made him realize that time his left here was short; he now had things to do with his life. He had been given a second chance to live, so that he could fulfill a special mission.

The hospital stay was brief, and he was given a new concoction of painkilling drugs and anti depressant tablets (upon the insistence of his own doctor). He took the pills regularly, and he found that he liked the effect the tablets had on his mind. The pills seemed to numb the past at first, and upon slowly increasing his dose according to how he felt, he realised that by mixing the tablets with alcohol, he was able to start to transform his mind. His body started to become thinner and searching the internet, as he often did, he could find a never ending source of information about what was secretly going on in the world.

He never knew about all of the things he was now discovering about the underbelly of the world. The secret societies, the bankers controlling the world's politicians, the government conspiracies, the existence of aliens and most disturbing of all was the effect that man was having upon the planet and the pain he was causing those of different races and religions. He started to make notes about all the things in the world that were wrong, the things that only he had the ability to discover and link them altogether. He wrote tirelessly. This was his masterwork. Once his volumes were complete, then he would show the world that he alone, could lead them on a path to salvation.

He had never once before considered the thought that he might be the savior of the human race. He always felt different. As a child growing up, he never felt as if he belonged, and as a sensitive child he had suffered a great deal. He would be struck repeatedly for being different, and this caused him to comfort eat. He soon grew in size until he was huge, but his mother still loved him. She realized that he was becoming hungrier, so she began to feed him larger portions.

If his father had been around, he might have put a stop to it. He never was though. He was the product of a drunken night from a dirty back alley fumble which had produced an unexpected result. His mother could love him enough for two parents though. A father was never a necessity. His mother loved him, and as long as she was around, she would protect and smother him with her love.

Being the size he was, women would never even look at him, except to laugh at his enormity. He wished that they could understand him, and feel the real love that he held inside of himself. He could make a great and loving husband and father. If only they could look past his enormous body. They never could though, so he spent his life alone.

He had paid for the company of women a few times in his life, but the size of his body meant that he could not perform in the way that he would have liked; in fact he could not perform at all. Still he would pay them despite his failings, and at least it gave him some female company, even if it was for just a short space of time.

When he had acquired enough information to realise that the world was on the brink of extinction, he now knew that the time was right to tell people about what he had uncovered. He decided that his neighbour would be the first person he would confide in. She would accept his gift of information.

He left his flat for the first time in months, and when he stepped outside the front door, he felt immediately sick to the stomach. The stench of what was going on in the world fed directly into his nostrils, and the power was overwhelming. He steadied himself on the wall and walked slowly across the hallway. The evil was growing stronger. Perhaps they were onto him. They might have even been using satellites to unsteady him.

David took deep breaths before he summoned the strength to knock on his neighbour's door. When he did, he knocked three times, and then waited. He stood at the doorway for what seemed like an age, and then he knocked the door again. He used his usual three knocks yet again. Still there was no response. He wanted to know why she wasn't answering. He knew that she would definitely be in at this time of day. He tried the door handle, and to his surprise the door was open. He gently pushed the door open and decided that he would let himself inside.

The smell coming from inside the flat was so intense, that he felt bile rise up from his stomach. He held his nose, but he was still curious to know what was happening. He walked further inside the flat, always being cautious. As he reached the bedroom, he looked inside, and instantly threw up inside of his mouth. On the bed, lay the body of his neighbour. She was decomposed and flies and maggots were crawling all over the remains of her body. He turned and ran back out of the flat as fast as he could.

When he was safely back inside of his own front door, he locked and bolted it. He ran to his tool box and took out the lump hammer. Then he ran into his bedroom and barricaded the door with furniture. It was then he knew what he had suspected was true. They had been watching him all along, as he had uncovered the truth. Now they were onto him. Her death was a warning for him to back off. He sat in fear on his bed, pulling the covers up around his shoulders for protection. Then the sweat began to pour from his body. He sat and silently waited for them to come for him.

He stayed in his room for a few days. Occasionally he would venture into the hallway to use the toilet, but by that point he would be almost bursting and could not wait any longer. He planned trips to the kitchen for supplies carefully, always keeping low from the windows. It would be easy for an assassin to pick him off if he strayed too close. He took his pills and water, and whatever food he could reach. Then he quickly made his way back to his room and wedged the door tightly closed.

After a few days he was awoken suddenly by the sounds of banging coming from his dead neighbours flat. They were in there, but for some reason they had not yet come for him. His tears flowed constantly as he waited. He knew that he would defend himself to the last, but if they came in numbers, he could only imagine the tests that they would run on him. He would be opened up alive, that he knew for certain. They may even have placed something inside of him at the hospital already. He shouldn't have trusted them at all. Perhaps they had even tainted his pills with something. Had they got to his doctor too?

The noises went on for days, and then they stopped. He had been saved. It was then that he started to question why he had been saved. Realisation came in an instant when he looked out of the window, and saw the sun shining down on his face. He had been chosen. He was indeed righteous. He was a God amongst men, almighty and all powerful. Nothing could kill him, and he knew that he was immortal. He dropped to his knees as the sense of power overwhelmed him. He had been placed here to save mankind. He placed his hands together and thanked the Lord above for granting him such an honour.

Leaving the flat was not as hard as it had been before, although he was still a little uncertain of what he would find. His neighbour's door had been freshly painted. He tried the door, and realised that is was now locked. He then made his way down the stairs, and out into the fresh air. He no longer needed to wash himself before he left the flat. Gods created their own cleanliness. He no longer needed much food either. He walked toward the lakes which was only a short distance from his home. It was a life awakening moment.

The stones felt hard under his feet. His shoes managed to absorb a little of the impact, but he could still feel the stones moving under him. The walk to the lakes took a few minutes, and the pathway laid him through a passageway of trees. Inside the overgrowing trees he felt the wind touch his face, and he closed his eyes. He felt at one with nature. As he walked around the lakes, he noticed the beauty of the nature surrounding him, which he had never truly witnessed before. He used his fingers to touch everything, and he felt the power of the universe in them all. This was all part of a bigger plan. He too would soon have the power to create.

He touched all the different plants and flowers that he could. He took in all the different colours and scents, and the sticky weeds reminded him of playing alone in fields when he was younger. He knew this was why he had been alone all of his life. He had been chosen at a young age and had never once realised why he was destined to be alone. He took in the sounds of nature as the water flowed in different streams around him. He placed his fingers in the water and felt the cold fluid flowing over his hands, and he smiled to himself.

"We are all one" He said to himself.

This was first time that he walked the lakes in a long time. He felt a little breathless by the time he had walked all of the way around. He would now return back to his flat, to continue to write his new scriptures, and then he could spread the word, that he was now among them. He slowly walked back to his home and smiled as he opened the communal door to the flats, he climbed the set of stairs to his first floor flat and it was then that he found out that they had arrived.

Music was blaring from the flat next door, and it was clear that someone was inside. He knocked on the door; he was going to warn them. Now he held no fear. There was no answer though. He grew angry at the lack of response, so he continued to knock the door even louder. Eventually the door opened, and a youth of about twenty years of age opened the door.

"What the fuck do you want?" he demanded.

"I live next door." Said David, rather taken aback by the way he had just been spoken to by a mere child almost.

"And?" Asked the youth.

"Can you turn the music down?" He asked. The youth just smiled.

"Dad!" He shouted "There's some prick at the door who doesn't like the music." David grew angry and leant forward to grab the youths shirt. The man who flew out of the door and pinned David to the floor was lightning fast. He couldn't have been human judging by his strength or speed. David could feel blow after blow now raining down on his face, and it soon became a bloodied mess. Once the onslaught had stopped, David lay in his own blood. It dripped from cuts to his mouth, his eyes were blackened and his nose bloodied.

"If you ever put your hands on my boy again, I'll fucking kill you!" The man said, as he stood over David. Then he kicked David in the ribs so hard, that it took his breath away completely. He gasped for air in a blind panic. The man spat in his face, and then he finally retreated into his own flat. He was laughing as he walked back inside. It was then that David looked up, and through his tear filled eyes, he saw the mark on the man's skin. He was tattooed with the number 666 on the back of his neck. His nemesis had now made himself known. Then the door was closed, and the music was turned up even louder.

It took David a little while to find out what he needed to know. He spent days searching for ways for him to defeat the demons next door. All the while he tried to research, the pounding sounds of music filtered through the walls and the pure filth of the lyrics seemed to drill directly into his brain. They had sent the demons to break him, and this was the way that they would get to him. David had to be strong. The battle between good and evil had already raged for thousands of years, and he was the latest in a long line of saviours who had come to save the world.

When the music got too much, he had his place of solitude. He had been given the lakes, and they were his alone, and from here, he could build his empire of salvation. Nature would surround him and feed him in his efforts. Of this he was sure. When the rain poured down, he would still walk, and now it was helping him become thinner still. He still felt the pains inside of him, but he knew that he was immortal, and the pains were those of his transformation.

There was just one thing holding him back from his quest. That was the demon and his siblings in the next flat. Day after day, he would sit and write his instructions for mankind, but day after day the taunting became louder and louder. The shouting, the screaming, and the cheap women the devil took inside the flat. The noises they made in bed, it was taunting him more and more. The child knew no better either, the obscene music he loved seemed to play at least sixteen hours a day, it declared his love for Satan through the dark lyrics. He hated every second of this loud filth.

Every day he fought the rage that was growing inside of him, but one day he realised that he had to do something serious to finally free his mind from all of the torment. Only then would he truly show the world his elevated form. He had to end the devil and his kin. It was for all of humanity, he would save them all. He stood up from his desk, placed down his pen, and walked out to the hallway. He then opened the tool cupboard and then unclipped the tool box that was inside it. Inside he found the lump hammer and a Stanley knife. Now he could finally end the torment.

He opened the front door and walked across the hallway. He opened the knife out fully, and held it in his right hand. The lump hammer was tightly gripped in his left hand. Then he rang the doorbell using the end of the knife. The child answered the door.

"What the fuck do you..." The boy started, but the sentence was cut short. The Stanley blade had slid down his right cheek and into his neck. The boy screamed, and cowered back inside of the flat, blood was running down his face, and the boy was doing his best to stem the bleeding, all the while he was still screaming in shock and pain.

"Dad! Dad! He attacked me!" The boy wailed. His father appeared from the living room and had a look of shock on his face. His first thought was to help his son, but then he saw the weirdo neighbour who was now just stood in the open doorway, staring at him. He was holding a bloody knife out in front of him. Even more infuriating though, was that he was smiling at what he had done to his son.

The man launched himself toward the attacker, and the hammer connected with the right side of his face. His cheekbone shattered under the hard metal, but he still lurched forward, grabbing the weirdo by his shirt. The man was insane with rage, and desperate to avenge his son's injuries. He then felt the knife plunge upward into his throat. When it was withdrawn, blood sprayed outward from the hole now exposed in his throat. He lifted his hand to stop the flow, and that was when the hammer struck fully him in the face again. His nose exploded inside of his face, and more blood sprayed across the hallway.

The man dropped down to his knees, and the third blow was the most painful. The hammer was smashed down onto his head from a raised height, and caved in a large part of his skull. The world became dark. He would soon be breathing his last breath.

Now the demon was under control, he could turn his attention back to the demons spawn once more. He started to walk toward the boy. After seeing what had become of his father, the boy was trying to back away and crawl away along the hall. The man quickly followed him. The hammer struck the boy in the temple, and he joined his father in a dark void of unconsciousness.

He dragged the father and son into the living room. They were both badly injured, but still barely alive. It was perfect. He tied gags around both of their mouths, and laid them carefully in position. Once they were laid out perfectly, he was about to return back into his flat when had a moment of realisation. The sunlight coming through the flat window had formed a shadow of a cross over the two evil ones. This was a message and he now knew this had to be ended. He would finish them in the same way that they had ended the last saviour. This was payback time for the demons.

He went back across the hallway and then returned with the smaller hammer, and enough nails to finish the job. Both men were still unconscious, and they would have been grateful to not have to endure the six inch nails being driven through both of their hands, arms, feet and legs as they were nailed down tight to the floorboards beneath them. Once he was satisfied that they would never be able to free themselves, he went back to his flat and gathered his books and then he locked himself out of his flat. He then went back into the demons flat and closed and locked the door so that no one could come in unexpectedly.

The boy regained consciousness, but his father (despite waking up partially), never properly understood anything that was happening to him. His brain was already far too damaged for him to fully understand anything ever again. For three days and nights, the man read to them from his own gospel. During the first night, the father died. The man then prayed over the body, and then he wrote some more.

When he finished writing his final words, he could only smile. The final chapter in his own bible, was an instruction on how to beat the devil and his kin should they ever appear again. He had survived and had beaten them both single handedly. He was truly a God and soon he would ascend to his rightful place. The boy could only wait and pray for his own death whilst nailed to the floor and soaked in his own urine. It would take longer than he could have ever imagined, and all the while he could see nothing but the crazed attacker on one side, and the body of his dead father on the other.

Lady Ice Part 2

The mailbox that she used was completely private. She had paid a reasonable sum for the privilege, but she deemed it worthy of the cost. The dossier inside was unusually thin, and that meant there would be little information with regard to the target. She placed it carefully inside of her bag and then took the envelope home with her.

Once she was away from prying eyes, she took the envelope out from her bag and then walked in to her study. Giovanna locked the door behind her and then carefully opened up the brown envelope. Inside there was a few A4 sized pages which gave her all the available information about the target. It was quite a surprising read.

Danny Kannis was a family man. He worked a mundane nine to five job in a factory. He had a mortgage, which he was slightly in arrears with, and if he wasn't careful, it was likely that his home might be repossessed. He also had a young daughter. He was in his early thirties, balding and overweight. The picture of the man was nothing like she had expected. It didn't matter though; he was to be her next target.

Something was troubling her though. Why on earth had this man ordered a hit on her? What was even more incredible to her though, was just how he managed to afford to do so. She knew the potential value that was placed on her head. This man was just so ordinary; it seemed unbelievable that he could be responsible. She called up her contact on her mobile. "Kannis. How sure are you that this is the right man?" She asked. "One hundred percent. I have details of the transaction, and the price that he paid. The price on your head was £125k. That sum was to be paid in cash." Was the response. "Thanks." Giovanna said and then she ended the call.

It was about a half hour drive to where he lived from her home. Giovanna carefully assembled all that she needed and packed them away safely. She placed the .22 in the holster which was discretely hidden on the inside of her jacket. Then she walked calmly out of the living room and out of the front door. She locked the door behind her and stepped into the car. She then started the engine and entered the details of her journey into her sat nav system.

Once the sat nav had acquired the satellite signal and calculated the route, she released the handbrake, put the car into gear and then pressed down on the accelerator. The pain in her foot was reminder enough of the torture she went through less than a month ago, but it was healing up quite nicely. Kannis would have some questions to answer, and then, when she felt satisfied with the reason that he had chosen her, he would then be terminated without any mercy. She reached her destination, and then parked close by to his house.

He barely had time to exit his car, when he noticed the woman approaching him. The woman's face seemed vaguely familiar as she strode toward him. There was just something about her that he couldn't put his finger on. When she pulled out the pistol and began shooting two silent rounds into his left leg, that he had a moment of realization. It was Giovanna, and the moment he had dreaded for over a month had suddenly arrived. She had come for him.

He had to make it into the house. He had to try and forget all about the pain in his kneecap and the blood now pissing out from his wounds and onto his trouser leg. He fumbled through his keys as he staggered forward. His nerves were getting the better of him, and he panicked. He almost dropped the keys to the floor, but caught them in mid air. He had seconds left before she would reach him. He found the right key to the door which was tangled in the middle of the bunch.

Giovanna was still walking forward as she held the gun out in front of her. The street was deserted, and this idiot was no match for a trained assassin. She allowed him time to open his front door, and then she leapt forward kicking the man in the small of his back. He stumbled forward into the hallway, and he fell to the floor. She was now in the hallway with him. He lay winded and unable to even beg for mercy. Another two rounds were then fired into his right leg. One of the shots obliterated his kneecap completely.

The man squealed in pain as Giovanna closed the front door behind her. She had waited far too long for this moment. Now it was all about her revenge. Danny Kannis was going to pay big time for what he had done to her, and to her daughter. She walked forward and kicked him across the jaw. Blood sprayed from his mouth instantly and showered the hallway wall paper. He raised his hand to his face to try and avoid another kick.

The next blow was to his groin. He wasn't expecting it. Giovanna stamped down and twisted her heal as she pushed downward. The pain of his testicle bursting was like nothing he had ever felt before, or ever wished to feel again. There was pain erupting from so many different areas of his body, that his tears were inevitable. He badly needed to go to hospital, but he doubted that this woman would show him any hint of mercy now. She was frenzied, and he only had himself to blame.

Her face was red with rage; as she grabbed him by the throat and shouted.

"Why me!" Giovanna screamed at him. He was trying to crawl backward away from the source of his unforgiving pain, but the woman was keeping a tight hold of his throat. He dropped flat to the floor. She knelt on his chest, and smashed into his right cheek with the butt of her gun.

"Please, no more!" He shouted. The gun struck his face once again though. The sound of his cheekbone cracking echoed throughout the hollow of his mouth.

"I said, why me?" She screamed once more. Kannis raised his hands up to his face again. He was now in a blind panic and fearful for his life. He knew that this woman would not stop hurting him until he told her what she needed to know. He had to tell her, or this would be his last day on Earth, filled with the pain of a woman's hatred fuelled vengeance.

"It was part of the game!" He shouted.

Giovanna was still knelt on his chest. The gun was aimed at his face and she never lost sight of her target. She raised her body up using just the muscles in her legs. All the while she maintained eye contact.

"What do you mean by the game?" She asked. People in fear of their lives would sometimes make up the craziest excuses, but this was something new, even to her.

Kannis managed to prop himself up against the wall. His trousers were congealed in a mixture of blood and his own urine. He took a few breaths, and then started to explain what he meant.

"I got involved with the wrong people. I started gambling heavier and heavier amounts. Before I knew it, I had lost almost everything, even my home. I couldn't tell me wife. Then they offered me a choice. I could join in the game, and I could wipe my debts clean." He said. It still made no sense to Giovanna.

"Who runs this game?" She asked. Kannis started coughing while the blood continued to flow from his mouth.

"I don't know. They took me out from the casino, blindfolded me and bundled me into a car. Then they took me to another place. It was dark, and I have no idea where it is." He seemed to be telling the truth, but she placed her foot down on his groin again and pressed hard.

"I swear to you, on my daughter's life, I don't know where!" He protested. Giovanna was silent for a few moments while she gathered her thoughts.

"Tell me more about this game." She finally asked.

"Well they took me into a room, and there were eleven other men there. Some of the men were just like me, others seemed like foreign men. We had a choice of key. We chose a key, and it opened a random locker. Inside of each locker was a briefcase. We were told to take the briefcases from the lockers, and follow the instructions inside."

Kannis seemed to become more and more agitated as he spoke. "I was driven home blindfolded and given a key for the briefcase. When I opened it and read the instructions, I refused to follow them. I locked the briefcase and tried to return it to the casino. I wanted no part of the game anymore."

"Which casino was it?" Giovanna asked.

"It was the Strand." He paused again. "It made no difference. There was no way out of the game. They took me out of the back of the casino and my wife and daughter were there." He now started to weep openly. "They put guns to their heads, and told me that I had to finish the game or they would die. I couldn't get out of it!" He pleaded.

"What we're the instructions for the game, what was in your briefcase?" She asked. He paused for a few moments before he answered further.

"I was to contact a man called Ivan Nuryeve. I was to pay him to torture and murder you. Your daughter was to be taken as well. There were instructions about your daughter, and what was to happen to her in a sealed envelope, but I never opened them." Kannis was now struggling from the blood loss that he had suffered. "I took the money to Ivan and the instructions, and even though I knew your murder would be on my conscience, it was either kill you or let them murder my family. I chose you."

Giovanna understood why he made the choice, but she had little sympathy for the man. He was weak and his lifestyle choices were of his own design.

"When I had arranged the hit, I went back to the casino to get my wife. They beat me down and then they dragged me into the yard again. I watched them gun down my wife in cold blood."

He was now weeping openly as he recalled the events he had witnessed.

"Then they took my daughter away from me. She was kicking and screaming, but I could do nothing. They beat me to the ground time after time." Giovanna finally understood about the type of people she was now dealing with. They were ruthless killers, just like her. Except unlike her, they had no morals. Now it meant that she had more targets, but these would be her last kills. After today, she felt as if she had reached the end of the line.

"They told me that if I went to the police, they would kill my daughter right in front of me, and then I would be next. I had no choice but to do nothing. I just had to wait until the game was finished. Only then would they let my daughter go." Kannis now sobbed loudly.

Giovanna had no sympathy for the man. This coward had lost everything in pursuit of money.

"You always had a choice. Unlike your innocent wife and daughter. I swear to you that I will avenge your wife's death, but you will not see your daughter again. She deserves better in life than a father like you." She then raised her gun and targeted his forehead. "This is for what you did to me and my daughter." She said.

Kannis closed his eyes and waited for death. The gun fired a single shot which singed his right ear. He opened his eyes as Giovanna leaned forward over him.

"I spared your life. If I ever have to come back again, I will come silently. I won't be so generous again. I will try to find your daughter, and bring her home, but when I do, you treat that girl better than you ever dreamed possible. Never ever gamble again, and be a real father to her. Do you understand me?" Her face was deadly serious, and he knew that she was telling the truth. He nodded his head fervently. Then Giovanna holstered her gun and then turned and walked out from the house.

The Strand was not exactly a small time casino, but it wasn't exactly Vegas either. The security was lacking, and making her way into the building was as easy as walking right in through the front door. She watched the security closely and soon worked out where the main office was. Those who were losing large amounts of money were often escorted to a back room down a hallway just past the toilets. She had armed herself with a new set of guns, and both were strapped to her inner thighs.

The security was small in number; she only counted two men going in and out of the back room. She waited patiently, just silently watching. The losing gamblers were in the room for a short period of time. Never more than ten minutes. The big winners, they were often out in five. Security escorted the losers; the winners exited the room alone. All she had to do was wait for the next winner. Giovanna made her way to the ladies toilets and drew her weapons ready.

She placed the guns in each of her jacket pockets and then waited with the toilet door left slightly open. From here, she could see if anyone were walking her way, but more importantly, she could see when the office door was opened. It was a few minutes before the door started to open, and by then she was already moving. The winner was smiling as he pocketed his winnings, and before the office door had even closed, Giovanna had already slipped inside the door.

The man behind the desk didn't register the intruder at first, not until both weapons fired simultaneously, taking out both security guards with single shots to the head. As the guards fell to the floor, the man behind the desk went to hit the panic alarm. The next shot went cleanly through his hand, and he pulled it away in pain.

"The next time you reach for the alarm, you take one in the brain. You understand me?" She said. The man nodded his head slowly. He looked livid at being caught out. Giovanna locked the office door behind her.

"Tell me about the game." She said. The man sounded Russian when he finally replied to her.

"Fucking bitch. If I tell you, then I will be killed!" He protested. Giovanna looked at each of the assassinated guards on the floor and smiled. She tilted her head to one side and shrugged her shoulders. The man seemed to understand that she really didn't care; she wasn't offering him any other alternative.

"Who runs the game, and where do I find them?" She asked. The man sighed, he was sat with two guns pointing at his head, what other choice did he have but to talk?

"Go and find the club called Barbarella's. In there you will meet the orchestrator of the games his name is Taylor. He organises everything. Now do what you must lady, but make it quick." The man behind the desk slowly closed his eyes. The bullet hit the exact target as always. It was clean and quick, just as he has requested.

Barbarella's was a huge eighties nightclub in Andover. She searched the post code, and entered it into her sat nav. She would be there around the same time that the club opened. The game was something that was held in a darkened room. It had to be either out the back of the club, or possibly in a downstairs cellar of some kind. The trick was getting in and then finding Taylor. For this job, she might need some bigger firepower. She had all that she might need already stored in a secret compartment in the boot of the car. This included her special weapons.

The circular object landed on the balcony of the club. The neon light sign glowed pink and electric blue, but they were nowhere near as bright as the light from the explosion. The grenade was standard army issue, and it took away a large chunk of the building as it exploded. Pandemonium ensued as the club goers began screaming as they ran out of the building. Giovanna slipped into the building through an opened fire exit.

The club had a neon glow throughout the hallways, and she calmly walked the building while people were screaming and running past her. People's minds always fears the worst at times like this, and self preservation was key. The security staff had their hands full trying to calm the panicked masses as they trampled each other trying to get out of the building. She spoke to one of the staff.

"The police are outside; they are asking to speak to Taylor. Where is he?" She asked.

The man looked annoyed, but he was too busy to start a long conversation with her.

"He is down the next stairs on the right. He's in his office." He said, and then he continued trying to deal with the manic crowd.

Giovanna carefully descended the steps and drew her weapon. The door suddenly flew open, and as the man ran out of the room, he almost walked straight into the gun. He dropped a case to the floor, and it was full of cash. It fell out into the hallway.

"Leave it!" Giovanna said sternly. "Get back in the room. Now." She finished.

Taylor raised his hands to try and keep the woman calm. He then backed himself into his office. Giovanna checked the blind spots before she entered the room. It was clear. She maintained the height of the gun while it was aimed squarely at Taylor's face.

She kicked the door closed behind her.

"If you want money..." Taylor tried to bargain with her.

"I don't want your money. I want information. Who runs the game, and what happened to the daughter of Danny Kannis?" Taylor now looked petrified.

"You don't want to get involved in the game lady, not if you know what's good for you." He tried to divert her questions, but there was no point. Giovanna walked forward and pressed the gun right into Taylor's forehead.

"Talk!" She insisted.

"The game is run by the rich. They use whoever they need to as go betweens. That way they keep their hands clean. Anyone can request anything from the game. A murder, a kidnap, a rape, anything they want. They pay a set price, and we arrange the details of who will do the job. Once someone is involved, the game has to reach its conclusion, and everyone wins." Taylor said.

"Apart from the victims." Giovanna answered.

"Expendable. Everyone has a price. Everyone has a reason; we never want to know why. We just get the job done." Taylor was smirking, and it was becoming annoying.

"A woman and her daughter. The woman is tortured before she's murdered in front of her daughter. Ring any bells?" Giovanna asked.

"Ah, now it all makes sense. You must be Giovanna. The one who got away. I don't know how you managed to kill five of our best men, but I must applaud you." He said.

"I only killed one. My daughter killed the other four." She replied.

Taylor looked shocked. He knew the daughter was fairly young. She had been well trained.

"Who paid you for it? Who made me a part of the game?" She demanded.

"His name was Robert Dossema. He was really annoyed that we failed him too." Taylor looked amused by it all. Giovanna felt light headed as she heard the name, it was hard for her to take it in. She had one more thing left to deal with though.

"And the girl, where is she?" Giovanna demanded.

"She was sold a long time ago I'm afraid. I have no idea where she might be now. It might be better for her father if she's never found again. She won't be his little girl anymore." Again that grin appeared on his face. Giovanna had heard and seen enough.

"Give me the key to your office, and your mobile phone." She demanded. Taylor reached into his pocket and threw his keys to her. He then slid his phone across the desk. There was a landline on his desk, and Giovanna ripped it out from the wall. She then began backing out of the room and she locked the door behind her.

Taylor took his gun from the draw and walked toward the door. He could see on the office c.c.t.v. that Giovanna was already running toward the main exit. He shot out the lock on the door and pulled it open from the inside. Taylor only made the first step of the stairs when he saw the object that was now at eye level. He had no time for any last words. The grenade exploded turning the top half of his body and head into a splattered mess that spread out into what was left of the office.

Giovanna had driven a safe distance away before she stopped the car. She stepped out of the driver's door and took in deep breaths. She shook her head not wanting to believe what she had heard. She now had a new target, just one more hit left before she could finally retire. Honour meant that she would not involve the rest of her family. A sense of duty to her daughter left her with conflicted feelings about if she should tell her. After all, her next target was her child's own father.

The Test

The voice was that of a female. "Kill them all." It said.
The voice seemingly came from nowhere. Darren's wife was changing the infants dirty nappy on the front room floor. The child was constantly crying. He was only four months old, but always seemed to be crying at all hours of the day and night.
Darren looked all around the room. The television was on, but it was barely audible over the sound of the infants screams. The noise pierced his ears. Then the brat also started.

The kid wasn't his. It was a responsibility that he took on when he married its mother. At first, the brat was alright, but then it started staying with its natural father. Whenever it came back, it always started.
"I hate you. You're not my Dad." It said. Then it kicked Darren firmly in the shin. It was testing his patience. It was an ungrateful little shit. It kicked him again and again, and then it started laughing at him too.

He was the one paying to keep a roof over its head, and put food in its belly, and this was his reward.
"Why don't you kill them all?" He heard the same voice talking again. It was definitely the same voice that he had just heard. His wife wasn't looking, so he pushed the brat down to the floor.

The brat then started screaming. It lay on the floor kicking its legs, almost like it was being electrocuted. It made Darren feel amused.
"You don't have to take any of this anymore. There is an easy way out. Why don't you end them all?" Came the voice again. Where the hell was that voice coming from he wondered?

Both of the children were now screaming in unison. His wife was visibly shaking. She looked as if she were about to burst into tears at any moment. She was growing redder in the face by the second. He pitied her

now. She wasn't the woman that he fell in love with anymore. He had left the army for this? She had changed more than he could ever imagine. He didn't even fancy her anymore.
"Can you please help me, instead of just standing there doing nothing?" She shouted.

There was no need for that. The brat deserved to be punished. It wasn't his fault it was crying. It shouldn't have kicked him. Then that voice spoke yet again. It was firmer and louder this time.
"Don't let her talk to you like that. Be a man. Stand up. Kill them all!"
Darren stood silently. The choice was made. He picked the brat up from the floor and carried him off toward its bedroom. Within a few minutes, the child had stopped crying.

Darren walked slowly back down the stairs. He was smiling. The feeling was more than satisfying. The baby was still crying though. He would help her out again. He would make sure that the child slept peacefully. He walked over to the infant and picked it up gently.
"I'm taking him upstairs for a while. It will give you some peace and quiet." He said.

His wife looked at him, as if his intervention was long overdue. He then carried the child up the stairs to place it in its cot. Then he took the pillow that he had used to smother the brat with. He held it over the infants face, and the crying was soon silenced. Darren stood over the cot in amazement. It was easy to quiet them both. He removed the pillow and stared down at the lifeless body. He then stroked the child's hair gently. He looked so peaceful now. Then his wife started to climb the stairs.

He did not try to stop her coming closer. She could tell by the colour of the child that something was badly wrong. Both children were silent, and this was highly unusual. She walked quickly over to the cot and tried to lean in

and pick up the child. Darren stopped her. He put his finger up to his lips to gesture for quiet.
"Shhh. The children are sleeping." He said. His face was somehow distorted. He seemed to be staring straight through her. He placed his hands lovingly on each side of her face. His grip tightened and he twisted her head to an unnatural degree and he snapped her neck cleanly.

The body of his wife fell down to the floor with a thud. Darren stood over the body and smiled. Then the voice spoke to him one last time.
"One more thing left for you to do now. Make yourself free. Be a man. Kill yourself. You know that it's the right thing to do." Darren did not to be told twice, the voices had made perfect sense. He wondered why he hadn't thought of this sooner. He slowly descended the stairs, walked into the kitchen and took out a large kitchen knife.

Without hesitation, he plunged the blade repeatedly into his own stomach. He collapsed to the floor, but continued to plunge the knife into himself until he had no strength left in him. Then the world turned black. Outside of the house, the black transit van started up its engine.

The experiment had been a complete success. Now they were sure that the method of mind control worked perfectly, they could take out anyone that they chose to without even being close to the target. No one could resist. They would go back into the house later to remove the hidden cameras. The family had been deemed to be a necessary sacrifice for the sake of national security. Their deaths might eventually save thousands.

The Rainmaker

The submarine had been sent to the area to examine the Anomaly. By the time they had arrived, the structure emerging from the ocean floor was already over a hundred feet in height. It was pyramid in shape, and the submarine captain could only watch on as the pyramid continued to emerge from the Ocean floor. By the time it had fully emerged, it stood over four hundred feet tall, and it began to propel itself toward the surface. Whatever it was, it had its own power source.

The structure began to rise from the middle of the ocean, on the surface; there were warships from America, Russia, and China were all watching on from a distance. None of the superpowers trusted the other. Each considered this a super weapon that another had created, and a show of strength was needed in case of an act of aggression. As the pyramid rose to around two hundred feet above the waves, it suddenly slowed. Then there was an eerie silence whilst everyone watched on to see what would happen next.

Underneath the waves, the lower half of the pyramid suddenly started to rotate. As it slowly rotated, it began to expand outward, and once it had reached its full extent, then it opened up its vents. The submarines now present were on high alert, and fully expected that something bad was about to happen. Then the object unexpectedly started to draw in the water from the ocean below it.

On board the warships, scientists had watched on in eager anticipation. This was a potentially life changing event, but no one had any idea of what was about to happen. It was roughly an hour before the first real expulsion occurred, and when it finally did, the whole world looked skyward.

The top of the pyramid opened up, and then expanded like an upside down umbrella. The noise suddenly became deafening as darkness was expelled from the pyramids apex. The blackness was forced high into the atmosphere, until it started to fill the skies with darkness.

It was a Chinese scientist who first realised what he was witnessing, and he could not believe what was happening before his eyes. He conducted tests, as fast as he possibly could, and only after carefully measuring the speed of the event, did he understand that this giant machine had to be stopped at all costs. He consulted the captain on the warship, and urged that lines of communication were opened with the other nationalities ships. Each agreed to listen, despite initial reservation and distrust. Professor Chung Lieng addressed the gathered ships to announce what was happening.

"I urge you to listen to me. I calculate that we have very little time to stop this from happening. If we don't stop, or at least slow this machine down, we will experience floods worse than biblical proportions. The machine is converting the sea water into rain clouds, but it is doing so ten thousand times faster than nature itself.

The sea water is drawn into the structure at an incredible speed, and then it is being forced high into the atmosphere where it will disperse along the jet streams, which are moving in the most powerful patterns that I have ever seen. As the water is dispersed, it will fall back down upon the Earth. It will be like nothing we have ever known before. We have to act right now, and destroy the machine, before it wipes out all human life on this planet. Whichever God you pray to, now is the time to do so, for if we can't stop this machine, only they can save us all." He ended.

There was a great deal of discussion over the next ten minutes. Frantic messages were sent back and forth; while world leaders looked at what options they had available. The American warship was the first to announce a call to arms; the captain announced his instruction to the crew as they readied battle stations to the highest possible level. The Captain gave his new orders to the entire crew.

"We have instructions from the Pentagon. Our instructions are to fire at will, and use everything we have got. Our orders are to destroy The

Rainmaker." Heavy artillery opened fire and was directed at the giant structure, and then it seemed as if all hell had broke loose.

The three warships battered the pyramid relentlessly. They threw absolutely everything that they had at it. For over an hour, it was targeted relentlessly. After the hour long barrage, they stopped to assess the damage to the machine. It was after sending drones closer to review the damage, that they realised that it had been a futile gesture. Apart from scorch marks on the surface, the structure was apparently undamaged. It not only continued to drain the water below, it now appeared to be accelerating. It continued to fire the dark vapour high into the atmosphere at a now unprecedented speed. The warships drew back and each captain had to concede that they were powerless to affect the structure in any way. For the next twenty four hours, the structure continued to drain the ocean, gaining momentum throughout the whole day.

The light from the sun was now blocked across vast percentages of the sky. Being unable to affect the structure in any way, the warships had been ordered to withdraw from the area, and to return home. The governments of the world then tried everything that they could think of to stop the event from happening. They tried using nuclear missiles, lasers from orbiting satellites and secret sound weapons that had been developed over the last decade, but each proved as ineffective as the last. Then the heavy rains started to fall, and global panic began to ensue.

The storms had a devastating effect across the entire world. Flooding of large areas occurred within a few hours. Within a day, vast areas of land were already submerged. The global sea levels were lowering, and the whole world experienced a polar shift. The Tectonic plates under the ground shifted by vast amounts, and the Earth itself began to crack open. Vast storms at sea battered those who had been able to take refuge on boats. Even the most expensive yaughts, were no longer a safe refuge. Those once safe in submarines, now found themselves unable to navigate properly and they were plunged into darkness. They would have to sit and wait out the storm whilst above them, the entire world was drowning.

It rained across the globe for eighty days and eighty nights. For those eighty days, the rainmaker continued to cleanse the Earth, it would not cease in its mission until almost all human and animal life on the planet was extinguished. Then just as suddenly as it had begun, the Pyramid powered down, and simply stopped.

The vents abruptly ceased to draw in water. Then, after last of the vapour was expelled high into the atmosphere, the top of the pyramid turned back to its original position, and it closed completely. The base began to contract and then rotated back into its original position. There was less now than a third of the ocean left below it. The pyramid started to descend back down into the water below, and when it reached the bottom, it drove itself down into the silt below. It had remained there for five thousand years or more, and would only emerge again if the planet ever needed cleansing once again.

As the rains finally ceased, the world now was an unrecognizable place. No continents that had existed before now remained. It took months for the waters to finally lower, and once they did, the small amount of survivors started to emerge. That next year they faced a real battle for survival, and without the natural ability to adapt to the new habitat, most perished quite quickly. For those who remained, it was a new chance to begin again. All of them were bitter at the way things had ended. Now every single day was a fight for survival, and only the strongest would stay alive. Famine and disease took its toll and humanity continued to decline.

Every single day it continued to watch them. Every single year it would review their progress. It would remain dormant under the Ocean until it was needed again once more. It only served one purpose, and that was to cleanse the world. It did so by making the rain. It slept, silent and unseen to those above, but it always did so with one eye open.

Before My Eyes

He punched and punched at the thick glass now in front of him, but it would not break. He watched as from the other side, people also seemed to be trying to break the glass, but it was just too thick. It was so dark in here, and it felt colder by the second. The cold reminded him of the first time that he had ever felt crisp snow crunching under his feet.

He was just seven years old, and was building a snowman in his back garden. The family had moved here the week previous and to the outside world, it may have looked as if they had brought the cold weather snap with them. The snow was around a foot thick, and it was ideal to make a snowman with.

His brother was only five, and as the older brother it was his responsibility to show him just how to make that snowman. Together they packed the snow tightly into a ball. They tried to roll the snow, but it soon became too heavy for them to roll it any further. This was where the snowman would now sit. They packed more and more snow around the body, until it started to properly take shape. They added sticks for arms, and there mother had donated a carrot for a nose, and two old mismatched buttons from her sewing tin, that they could use for eyes. The snowman was born. The brothers together had made it, but both of their hands were red and sore, it was worth it though. The cold now returned.

He shouted as he pounded at the glass. No sounds could be heard from either side though. He pressed his face up to the glass and it reminded him of his first real kiss. His mind began to drift backward again. Now he was stood back by the bus stop with his first ever girlfriend. He sat in his bike, while they waited for her bus to arrive.

He was a bit of a late starter, and his first real kiss didn't happen until he was sixteen years old. He sat on his bike and he realised that she was looking at him in a strange way. She was edging herself closer, and it was obvious that it was going to finally happen at long last. They both opened there mouths, and he prayed that he didn't mess up the kiss. He didn't, and she tasted of cherry lip gloss. A week later, he would lose his virginity to her and the following week, he was making his excuses and leaving her. He remembered her crying as she walked away and he felt heartless, but he knew that it was the right decision for them both.

He opened his eyes, and on the other side of the glass appeared a young child. He was also pounding on the glass with his small hands. The child took him back to when his first son was born. He was only twenty-one, and had nothing to his name. It was hardly the start he wanted for his son. It didn't matter though. He would still try to be the best father he could. Only that evening, he had gone to the pub and had drunk far too many beers.

He was called back to the hospital in the early hours of the morning, and he was still slightly worse for the wear. It soon faded though, when he realised that his son was actually on his way. The child's head appeared and it felt both hard to see his girlfriend in so much pain, but miraculous that the life they had both created was now about to take his first breath. He cried tears of joy as he held his son in his arms. It was something he would remember for all of his life.

He continued to pound on the glass, but the darkness was enveloping him. It just like the time the depression had started and he hit rock bottom. He left his wife and children. He started to recall all the pain and suffering he had caused the family with his affair. She was young and more than willing. He was drunk and stupid. It was a lethal combination. Now he could see his three sons on the other side of the glass. All three were the ages they were when he had left. All three were crying as they didn't want him to leave them. He cried for his sons, but his tears just faded away into the ether.

Seeing his sons in pain seemed to give him a new lease of life, and he wasn't prepared to give up on seeing them again. He beat repeatedly at the glass. He beat harder and harder until his hands began to hurt. Then he saw his mother appear on the other side of the glass. She was stood next to his late father, and she was crying as she tried to break the glass to reach him. She didn't want to let him go.

The pain on his mothers face was the same look as the day that his father had died. They had both watched him fade over the space of ten days. Each day they had faithfully travelled to see him, each day they had prayed together. Every day their hopes were dashed just a little bit more. When his father died, his mother looked lost. She looked sad, alone and afraid for the first time in her adult life. She had seen the man who had shared thirty years of her life perish before her. He held her then, and now wished that he could hold his mother once more, her embrace would help him to stop feeling so cold.

The glass did not break. Instead a light began to shine through the window, and it illuminated the darkness around him. To his left, he saw his late father stood next to him. His father held out his hands toward him. In the silence darkness his father spoke.

"Take my hands son. It's time. I've come to take you home." He stopped pounding at the glass, as it was futile. He knew that his father could not possibly be there but he reached out to touch his hands, and they instantly warmed his entire body. His father started to draw him toward the light, and in that moment, both of them felt forgiveness.

They had tried everything to break through. It was a desperate attempt to reach the man, but as he had fallen through, his body had been carried quite some distance. It had been twelve minutes since the man had fallen through the ice, and now he had long stopped pounding on the other side. The lifeless body floated away from them, and it would now be left to the emergency services to try and recover the body from the freezing water.

The Hidden Agenda

He knew only too well that the reptilians existed and lived among us. He had used an alias to remain anonymous, and he had told his many thousands of followers online. Today would be the day that he proved it to the world once and for all. There would never be any room for doubt ever again. Not after he exposed, and then murdered one on live television. It would be something of a world exclusive for Craig Khan, and one which would show the world what these things really were.

Charles Keenan was a rising politician. He had come from a fine family by all accounts, and he had always been given the best of everything. His family had accumulated so much wealth, that they were close to the country's top one hundred on the rich list. Money that the family had taken from the other families, whose lives they had destroyed.

The reptilians would take out entire households at the slightest hint of being discovered. Then they would lay claim to all their possessions by shape shifting into the victim's forms, selling off all their assets, and cleaning out their estates. They had no morals. They had to maintain their secret at any costs.

During his research, he had traced the race back at least two hundred years. There were many theories as to how they had arrived on Earth. Some had said that they had come from another planet. Some said that they came from inside the Earth itself. It didn't matter though. What mattered is that they were here, and they had to be exposed to the entire world.

Keenan's hidden identity was a shock to even him. He was a conservative politician, and some had even said that one day soon he would become the prime minister for sure. He was a rising star, who took no prisoners, and he was smart enough to negotiate his way out of any difficult line of questioning. He had made one fatal error though, and his hidden form had been caught on camera with his real lizards eyes exposed.

The program was called 'The Hot Seat'. Named after the fiery red leather chair the guests would sit in. Then they were subjected to an intense grilling, which many guests failed to survive without either losing their temper, or occasionally they would storm out of the studio. The broadcast was live, and Keenan was the first guest. Khan stood up from his seat to welcome the guest as he approached the hot seat.

Khan offered out his hand. Keenan shook it firmly. His skin was slightly colder than a normal human's body temperature. It was an assuring confirmation of what he already knew. Keenan stared straight into the interviewer's eyes and held his gaze assuredly. Khan could not wait to show the world this things true form. He was the Tory poster boy for a new generation, who women just could not resist.

After adjusting his tie, Keenan sat down. His suit was immaculate. The colour co-ordination was perfect. His teeth were the whitest shade of white, and his shoes were so highly polished, that you actually could see your face in them. His hair was perfect too. It made Khan a little jealous, as his hairline was now receding. At thirty two, he had hoped that hereditary baldness may have skipped his generation. It sadly wasn't to be though.

Khan had his notes already listed on an autocue. He also had an earpiece just in case he needed a nudge from the producer. They were going live any second now, and the floor manager began to instruct the audience. The cameras were all in place and the lights began to dim around the audience. Then the count of five descended from the floor managers mouth. They were now being broadcast live to the nation.

The audience was clapping politely. They had looked a fine cross section of the public. Some of the questions they would ask had previously been fed to certain audience members. It wasn't unusual to have plants placed in the audience of any political show now. It added a little spice to the proceedings, and Keenan was well versed in what the likely attack subjects might be.

Khan waited until the clapping had subsided (under the instruction of the floor manager), and then he began to speak.

"Good evening. This is Craig Khan, and tonight we welcome the rising Conservative M.P, Charles Keenan." There was a little light applause from the audience and Keenan nodded, and then he gave a polite wave.

The crowd looked hungry. He would soon have them eating from his hands though.

"Good evening." He replied. "It's a pleasure to be here." He then smirked. Khan was ready to get stuck in with his assault. After all, he had a reputation to uphold.

"A pretty boy, with a privileged background. Born with a silver spoon in his mouth. That's how one tabloid newspaper has described you. How would you respond to that?" Khan asked. He expected a slight grimace at least, but Keenan's expression remained the same.

"One would hardly describe himself as neither pretty nor a boy, but I will happily accept the compliments. Clean living helps the body stay youthful. I am a firm believer in looking after yourself. As for the second point, I can hardly be accountable for the circumstance of my birthright. I guess you could just say that I was lucky to have such wonderful parents who were financially astute."

Keenan smiled. He was now leaning back a little further in his chair. He looked completely relaxed.

"But your parents amassed a fortune by the exploitation of people who were vulnerable..." Khan tried to finish his sentence, but Keenan was now on the defensive.

"When people fall behind with payments on mortgages, they lose their homes. These people had every opportunity to not get into debt. My parents brought a great deal of these properties, and built a property portfolio. Now they have sold on many of these properties and rent out others."

Khan wasn't happy with his response, or being interrupted.

"What happened to the profits from the sale of these houses though?" He demanded to know.

"You already know the answer, after it was disclosed my father had funds offshore. He still did nothing wrong legally..." Now it was Khans turn to interrupt the response.

"But morally wrong, you must surely admit that?" He asked.

"No. Not at all. Millions of people have money held offshore. My parents donate to charity, and support local projects. My parents are very special people, and I reject that accusation and I ask you to withdraw it. "

He had his guest showing signs of being flustered. It was a fine start to the interview. He was going straight for the jugular, and it felt great. Now it was just about timing.

"O.K. So your parents made money from the misery of hundreds of despairing famines, but you don't see this as morally wrong. So, let me move on to the next question. You have been touted as a candidate for party leader. Do you honestly think that you have what it takes to run this country?" Khan asked, twisting the knife just a little bit more.

"I support our party leader one hundred percent. I have no aspirations to succeed him at all. I am flattered to have been mentioned in the same breath as him." Keenan was now starting to slouch a little further. Khan had to keep him on the defensive.

"A has been. Outdated and out of touch. Long past his retirement date. We need youthful blood to lead this country to greater prosperity. Were these not your own words, recently quoted in an article recently in a respected national newspaper?" Khan asked.

"You know damned well that my words were taken out of context, and I am seeking legal advice over said article. As such I cannot answer any further questions on the subject. As you already know of course." Keenan's face was now a little redder. He was becoming more flustered.

The gun was loaded in Khan's pocket. He reached into the inside of his jacket and took it out. He then pointed it directly at Keenan's head. Then he asked the question that he had been waiting to ask his guest all night.

"I know what you are. Will you now show us your true form before I end your life Reptilian?" His hand was shaking as he held the gun, but now Khan was ready to show the world that these creatures really did exist.

Keenan's head fell into his hands. At first Khan was unsure what he was doing. His shoulders were shrugging repeatedly. Khan leaned in closer to him. He could hear a strange muffled sound coming from Keenan's hands. Then he realised, that is was the sound of laughter.

"Boo!" Keenan jumped up suddenly. Now he was showing his true form for the entire world to see. Khan recoiled in shock at the sight of the lizard creature.

A pink forked tongue darted out from between Keenan's lips, and as he laughed there was a glimpse of his blood red teeth. His skin was dark green and covered in snake like scales. His eyes were bright yellow, and the pupils were now cat like. His fingers were now claws and his suit looked ridiculously baggy. Keenan then crossed his legs and his arms at the same time.

Khan had not expected such a rapid transformation, but now he could show the entire world that these creatures genuinely existed. It was a massive relief. He had lost count of the times that he had tried to convince close friends, workmates in the studio, and even family members, that these creatures were hiding right in front of them. They were hidden amongst workmates, celebrities, even in some cases like this one, as high flying politicians. No one would believe his stories, but now the proof was going out live on television.

He would not take the gun off the creature. The camera was still running, and it was taking close up shots of Keenan in his true form. The creature unbelievably was now playing up to the camera. It was smiling, and even more ridiculously, it was waving to the camera.

"You can now see for the first time ladies and gentlemen. These things are hiding in plain sight. They could be your partner, your neighbour, or your postman even. They can shape shift into different human forms, but once they are stressed enough, they cannot hold their true form anymore."

The audience in the studio then started to clap. It was the last thing Khan had thought that they might do. Then the cameraman behind him grabbed the gun from his hand. The studio doors opened, and Khan's friends and family all started to flood into the studio. They surrounded him, and lifted him onto the desk in front of his chair. Here he was held down by numerous strong pairs of hands.

"You can let go and reveal now." Keenan said. Khan looked around as everyone in the room started to transform. His family and friends included. They had not listened to his stories and not believed what he was telling them. They already knew the truth for themselves. He was one of a minority of humans left that was slowly finding out the truth. They were a dying breed.

Keenan walked to the side of where Khan was held down, and placed his clawed hands flat on his stomach. He then smiled at Khan.

"I'm sorry that you had to find out this way. There is no easy way to find out that everyone you know is actually in disguise. You have even been in relationships with our kind, and never even knew. Sadly for you, the human race is almost extinct, and it is not before time either.

We came here to save this planet from the scourge of humanity. Mankind has the most abhorrent tendency to destroy anything in its path to further its own self interests. We have taken thirty years to replace you with our kind, and now you are one of the few who remain."

Khan could not believe the words that he was hearing.

"So what are you going to do with me now?" He asked. "Will you let me go?" He asked.

It might have been Keenan that sniggered, or any one of the numerous people who were assembled on the stage. Whoever it was, it soon started a ripple effect throughout the audience. Soon the whole studio was laughing insanely. It took a few moments for the laughter to finally subside, and Keenan had to wipe his eyes dry from the laughter. He beckoned for the crowd to be calm, using his clawed hands and once the audience had regained control, he placed his hands back on Khans stomach, and then he replied.

"I'd honestly love to let you go, but I'm afraid you humans just taste too damned good!"

Another bout of laughter then started to fill the studio. The only person who wasn't laughing, was Khan. The reptilian had sunk its claws deep down through the skin of his stomach, and had ripped out a large chunk of his intestines. Khan could not breathe. His agony was intense, but there was far worse yet to come. His death would be slow and prolonged almost like a lobster being boiled alive, or an animal being skinned for its fur, the reptilians then started to eat him raw like sushi.

Keenan lifted up the handfuls of intestines, and the gathered crowd took polite bites of the blood covered tubing. Khan was starting to lose consciousness, so he had to be quick.

"I told you, I'd have them eating out of my hands!" He still felt the need for one final quip. Once again, the audience of assembled reptilians found the humour (and the raw meal), much to their taste.

Animal

It was the end of a warm summer's day. The sun had set as Mike Channing and his new girlfriend Tracey had sat together on the beach. It was the perfect end to a perfect day. The temperature had been just fine, not too hot or humid. The sea at Bournemouth beach had been calm, and they had eaten world famous fish and chips close to the sea front. Her appetite had surprised him. During the day, they had laughed, held each other close, and had kissed passionately numerous times. Now it was time for him to take her home.

This was only their second date in as many days, and he knew that she was determined to take things slowly. It was on the drive back that Mike decided he could use his charm to break down her resolve. He started a discussion that he hoped might take things a little further between them.

"So, would you like to come back to mine for a coffee?" He asked. She turned her face toward him and smiled. Then her eyes dropped so she was then looking down at her own lap. Her fingers were nervously twiddling. He might be pushing things a little bit too fast, but he wanted her. Perhaps he should try and change tact he thought. "Don't worry. If you're not ready yet, I am happy to take you home." He assured her. Her face was stunningly beautiful. Her blonde hair was shoulder length, and her eyes were a brilliant shade of blue. When she smiled, it was almost as if her whole face lit up. She was deep in thought for a few seconds, and then she turned to face him once more.

"Its fine, but Just a coffee though." She said "Then will you can drive me back home?" She asked. The smile was back on her face again, and she placed her hand on top of his as he changed gears. He took her hand and turned it over so he could hold hers for a few moments.

His ultimate goal was to try and get her into bed. Of course it was, he was a red blooded male and he had slept with hundreds of women before. He wasn't used to waiting around, but this girl was different. He had to put in some extra effort, but once she was in his house, then she might decide she felt comfortable enough to take things further. If not, then there were other ways that he could try to convince her.

The traffic was light at this hour and they were soon on the A303 and heading back into Andover.

"Are you sure that you are alright to come back with me?" He asked.

"I'm just a little nervous. My last relationship ended really badly. He didn't want to let me go." She now had a look of both sadness and fear on her face. It was almost as if the thought of her former partner was bringing up scars from the past that she did not wish to re-open. "Can we stop for a minute?" She asked.

Mike knew the perfect spot for him to pull the car into. He drove past the Picket Twenty roundabout coming into the town, and indicated to turn right. He drove the car into the side road and parked it up. Then he switched off the engine.

The road had no street lighting and only a few houses which were scattered all along the long length of road. It was nice and secluded. He had taken women here many times before. He took her hand once more, and tried to reassure her that everything was going to be alright. She stopped him before he could even say a word though. She undid her seat belt, and then she turned to face him.

"I have to warn you about something before we go any further. My former partner is an animal. He is jealous and controlling, and he still thinks that he owns me. He has probably been looking for me from the moment that I ran from him. If he finds out about you, your life will be in danger." She said. Her face looked almost frantic with worry.

Mike gripped her hand even tighter and smiled at her.

"You don't have to worry about me. I can look after myself." He laughed. It was relatively true as well. He had trained as a boxer for a few years, and he was pretty handy when it came to defending himself. He weight trained regularly, and had developed quite good upper body strength. Once he took his shirt off, most women loved looking at his body, almost as much as he admired looking at it himself in the mirror.

She was shaking her head at him, and it was confusing him. It was almost as if she had no faith in him at all.

"No, you don't understand. If he comes for you, then you need to get away. He won't stop until he has ripped you to pieces, and I don't want him to hurt you." She said. He was sure that he had seen tears in the corner of her eyes. It was now beginning to dent his pride.

"You don't have to worry about me. I will take care of it. I've dealt with jealous exes before and I will deal with him." He then pulled her close to him to hold her.

As he pulled her in close, her body was shaking uncontrollably. This was real fear. She was frightened to death of her ex, and that was clear. It didn't matter to him though. If this idiot was brave enough to confront him, he would quickly put him down. It would be embarrassing for him. There was no one who lived locally that he was afraid of, and he was sure that her ex would know of his reputation if he asked around.

"Let me get you home. I will take you back to your place tonight, and then tomorrow during the day, maybe then you can come to mine?" He said. She turned her head and nodded in agreement.

She had a look in her eye that he had seen before. She wanted him, he could sense it and it was just a matter of time before he got what he wanted. For tonight though, she was damaged goods and he would have to play it cool. Just until he found out a little bit more about her ex maybe. The last thing he wanted was some lunatic turning up at his house with a knife or even something worse. Then she leant across him started to kiss him passionately.

They kissed for long and enduring minutes, before the passion they were sharing between them started to spill over into touching each other's bodies. Tracey pulled away from him breathless. He hadn't been kissed like this by a woman in a long time. Now he didn't want to wait anymore. He had to have her.

"Take me home please. Then maybe you can come round to my house in the daytime." She said. Mike was a little annoyed now though. He was now sporting an erection, and would have quite happily fucked her in the car right there and then.

He tried to pull her close to him again, but she resisted his advances. He breathed in heavily, almost in a sulking manner. Then he realised that he might have a better chance if he backed off again until they got back to her house. She lived alone, so he might even get an invite inside. The mixed signals were driving him insane with lust though.

Mike knew that if all else failed, he always had a faithful vial of Rohypnol stashed away on his person. If he could convince her to have a few drinks with him, then he could easily spike her drink. It wasn't something that he particularly liked doing, but then he had his needs which simply must be met. He wasn't going to wait forever for her to give herself up to him. He felt that it was his right after she had messed him around so much. He hated the teases, and there were far too many of them in this town. He started up the car, and then drove her toward her home.

There was a long driveway leading up to her house. It was quite secluded and away from the main road. He pulled into her driveway, and parked right outside of the front of her house. Tracey seemed extremely nervous. She searched outside all of the car windows before she would even contemplate unlocking the door. The solitary street lamp close to the house was flickering on and off. It was long overdue for a repair. She now had sweat forming on her brow. Then the light from the street lamp died completely.

Outside there was complete silence. Tracey sat frozen. Then she slowly turned her head toward Mike, and whispered.

"Something isn't right. I think he's here. We need to go. We need to go now!"

The sudden impact that struck against the driver's side door was instant and ferocious. It rocked the car so hard it felt as if it were about to tip over onto two wheels. Tracey then screamed.

"It is him, it's Solomon, get us out of here!" Her expression was now one of blind terror. Mikes fight or flight response kicked in. He floored the accelerator and the car span on the slippery mud beneath it. As the car finally found traction, it lurched to one side and he almost lost control. Then another impact hit the passenger side of the car with more ferocity than the first strike.

The impact assisted Mike as he steadied the vehicle. He was now able to manoeuvre the car back out on to the main road, and he floored the accelerator once more. Tracey had caught sight of Solomon in the side mirror, and he now stood in the road some distance behind the car. She could see his eyes, and they seemed to be glowing bright yellow. Mike only glimpsed the figure in his rear view mirror, and the figure seemed to stand only a few feet tall. Even that small size though, this guy was immensely strong.

There was nothing else for it now. Tracey would have to spend the night at his place. He assured her that she could sleep in his bed, while he would be a gentleman and sleep on the sofa. That way he could be up and alert at any sign of danger. Tracey was reluctant to accept, but now she had nowhere else left to go. Now Solomon knew where she had been staying, he would soon find her once more. Mike was now in mortal danger, but he was now her only chance of getting away from Solomon alive. She had to at least try to start again.

Mike parked the car as close to his house as he could get. Tracey was a bag of nerves, and she had cried uncontrollably all the way back to his home. He struggled to open his car door, and when he had managed to work his way out, he could see why. There were dents in both front doors of the car. Each would probably mean a new door, they were that badly damaged. He put his head in his hands. The car was his pride and joy.

This guy needed a severe beating for what he had done. Now it was going to cost him a fortune for the excess for the repairs.

"We need to get inside now." Tracey said. She had made her own way out from the passenger side and was still nervously looking all around.

"Of course. Let's get you safe." He said. Tonight had been a nightmare. At least now she was back at his. He would get some sort of recompense, but then tomorrow, the woman would be history along with her lunatic ex. No woman was worth this sort of trouble, no matter how pretty she was. They were all just pieces of meat to him anyway.

The night air had cooled considerably. He fumbled his key into the front door, almost as if he were slightly drunk. Then once he had led her inside he locked the door, and pulled the security chain across. Good luck to anyone trying to get through there he thought. The door was thick and rock solid. He pointed the way forward.

"Go into the front room." He urged her. "Make yourself comfortable. I'm going to fix us a drink." He said.

He returned to the front room carrying two crystal glasses. Each was filled to the top. His was the one on the left, hers the right. He had to remember that. Tracey had taken off her coat and was now sat on the sofa with her knees pulled up toward her. Every little noise in the room was making her twitchy and nervous. He placed his glass down on the table. He placed Tracey's directly in her hand.

"Brandy and Coke." He said. "Just to calm the nerves." He then smiled as he sat down next to her.

"I shouldn't drink.." She began to say, but Mike insisted.

"Just trust me. You are safe here with me now. No one can touch you. I'm here." He reassured her. He then placed his right hand on her left knee. His hand felt warm and reassuring to her. Her leg felt cold to the touch.

Tracey took a sip of the drink. It was bittersweet but warming. She then took a larger gulp, and let the dark fluids warm her stomach. She had never touched alcohol before. It was a new experience for her. Solomon had always warned her about the dangers of it before. It was just another way of controlling her she guessed. She finished the drink, and then he went back out to the kitchen and poured her another.

He sat with her on the sofa for twenty minutes, just holding her and reassuring her that everything was going to be alright. It was then that her speech started to become slurred. The drug was working. Now he could have some fun with her. He had been patient for long enough. Her head began to drop to one side, and Tracey felt as if the world was spinning. She tried to lift up her head, but she was too dizzy. She felt unable to control the movement of her body. She fell over on to the sofa, and whispered a few words.

"What have you done to me?" She asked. She was now seeing nothing but a blur in front of her.

Mike loosened his belt and undid his trousers. There was no rush now, not now that the drugs had kicked in properly. Tomorrow she wouldn't remember a thing, but she would feel awful. He would claim that she had consented to sex, and that he had tried to convince her to wait. In her drunken state she had forced herself on him, and he thought that she was better than that. She was too easy. It was a good excuse to get rid of her. Now he had to take her clothes off though. Then he could get her into position.

He had to try and be as careful as possible. He had done this over twenty times before, and he had never been caught once. She was mumbling from time to time. None of it made any sense though. He had switched off the lights, and that would confuse her even more the next day. She shouldn't remember what happened but if she did, the darkness would help to mess with her head.

He lay her down on the front room floor, and made sure he had plenty of room. He then removed her dress carefully. He did not want to rip it. It pulled over her head easily. Then he removed her leggings, peeling them downward, and then throwing them to one side. He then pulled down her knickers, and placed them next to her.

The excitement was already building in his groin; he took hold of his penis and massaged it gently. When he was fully erect, he took a condom out from its packet carefully, and then placed it over his penis. He then pulled her legs apart and rubbed lubricant into her vagina. He did not want to leave any cuts or tears. Then he climbed on top of her, and forced himself slowly inside of her.

He moved in and out of her slowly. She felt tight and welcoming. She felt different to all the others. She felt cold inside, and it was a strange sensation. There was a scratching sound at the window behind him, but he paid it little attention. It was probably one of the neighbour's stupid cats trying to get inside the house again. Then it started to grow louder. Then she started to murmur.

"Solomon....Solomon.....Solomon!"

Mike was slightly annoyed that she was saying the name of her ex. It didn't matter though. She seemed to be enjoying it, and that's what he was telling himself over and over again.

The impact on the glass door shattered it instantly, and as it did, it sent shards of glass flying into his bare back. Mike screamed as his back was shredded by the flying shrapnel. Someone had smashed the window, and he knew damned well who it was. How the hell had her ex found his house though? He rolled to the side and instantly regretted the decision, as when he landed on the floor, he forced the shards of glass further into his back. Now he turned to face his attacker. He soon wished he hadn't though.

The creature stood around four feet tall. It was standing on its hind legs and hissing loudly. It had taken up an attacking stance, and it was ready to launch itself. Mike wanted to see what the hell Solomon looked like. He reached over to the front room lamp and switched it on. Then he saw Solomon in all his glory. Mike screamed at the creature that now stood in front of him. Solomon was not a man; he was a rodent like creature that had bright yellow eyes, and razor sharp teeth. Its dark black fur was dirty, and matter together.

Its mouth was drooling as it angrily hissed, and thick fluid was oozing from its mouth in anticipation of the attack that it was about to launch. Mike raised his hands up to protect his face, hoping that the animal would not destroy his good looks. Those teeth looked large and sharp. They were more than capable of scarring his face. It was those same teeth that Mike now felt, as the creature pounced forward, and it sank them deep into his throat.

Daylight flooded the room. Tracey put her hands up to her head. She had no idea where she was. As she sat upright, she realised that she was naked apart from her bra. Mikes naked body lay lifeless at her feet and she shook her head in disbelief. Then she thought she smelt a familiar scent behind her, and she slowly turned to see that Solomon was sat on the sofa behind her.

"This is why we do not take their form." He said. He had now shape shifted into the body of a man.

"I had to try to be like them, to live like one of them." She said.

"He gave you alcohol, he gave you drugs. Then he forced himself upon you. We are forbidden to mate with them. This is why we live in the shadows. Why we remain hidden from them." Solomon said.

Tracey shook her head in disbelief. She had made such a massive mistake, but the temptation had been too much for her not to try.

"Can you ever forgive me Solomon?" She asked. Her eyes now filled with shame and regret. He stared straight at her, with unblinking eyes.

"Maybe. In time." He said. His voice was distant. She had hurt him more than she would ever know. He was a proud creature, who had kept her safe for hundreds of years. Now it would take time for them to be normal again.

There was no need for the clothes anymore. They did not belong to her anyway. She had stolen them from a clothes line when she had first taken human form. The house, was not hers either. It belonged to a human who only stayed there for a few months of the year. It was information she knew from moving unseen in the shadows.

She now stood over the body of the man who had forced himself in her. He lay in a pool of his own blood, with a look of fear still evident in his face. He was still sporting an erection, only now it was on the other side of the room where it had landed after being ripped from his body.

"It's time for us to change back." Solomon said. He then took her hand, before changing back into his natural rat like shape. Tracey stood over Mike's body on the floor.

"They really are animals aren't they?" She said. Then she shrank back into her natural form. Her head hurt, but now she had to follow her mate. They made their way back to the open sewer grate, and headed back down into the safety of the darkness below.

Keep away from the windows 3

The world in my eyes.

KEEP AWAY FROM THE WINDOWS
VOLUME 3
THE WORLD IN MY EYES
MARTIN MCGREGOR

Take a bow.

"Where are we going Dad?"

It was a simple enough question, but one which I could not fully answer. Not just yet.

"We are driving up to Danebury ring son, so that we can watch something special." It was a painful half truth. We were headed to the ancient ring fort, but where we were going was an entirely different answer. It's something that I would have found very difficult to explain to him without breaking down in tears.

I have barely known my son. It's not been by choice either. His mother and I split when he was barely two years old. She then moved in the blink of an eye to another country with a new husband in tow, and I had no idea that they had even left. There was no note, no explanation, she left nothing behind. They just simply vanished.

I blamed myself for years, and I spent thousands of pounds trying to find him. It was a futile gesture though. They had gone underground. Then, nine years later his mother discovered that she was dying of cancer. It was a horrible thing to discover, even though she was someone who had taken my child. She was still his mother after all.

She had then returned to England to be close to her family. Her end was a slow and painful death, and her suffering lasted almost six long months. I had very little time to get to know my son in that half of the year. It was spent mostly comforting him the best that I could, as he watched his mother shrink to nothing before his very eyes.

When she passed, all that was left of her was a bag of bones. Her body was ravaged by the devastating disease that was eating her away inside, as it spread throughout her entire body. My son was broken. Even though I had no love for his mother, it was a terrible way for anyone to die. I was left to pick up the pieces of our broken family, and it was harder for me than I could have ever imagined.

During those last nine years, I had devoted my life to two things. The first was to finding my son, and the second was to my work as a scientist. Today, both of these devotions would collide with a life changing collision. I looked over at my son as I drove. He was beginning to look a little more like me now. It made me smile, but it also saddened me deeply.

"What are we going to Danebury ring for?" He asked inquisitively. He was just like his mother in that respect. She was always asking questions.

"We are going to have a picnic, and watch something amazing in the sky." I answered. Again this was a partial truth. Earlier in the day, I had visited a local supermarket before collecting him from school. I had bought everything that he enjoyed, and more besides. I bought a variety of things that I thought he might like to try, and junk food. An awful lot of junk food. This was a one off event that would never be repeated.

Looking at my son, it was heartbreaking not to be able to tell him what was going to happen, but in my heart, I knew that it would be better that he did not know. I realised, that for all those lost years, I could never get them back again, and now I never would be able to make up for them either. I was punishing myself again for not doing more. In reality, I really had done all that I possibly could.

We arrived at the hill fort, and then made a right turn toward the hill leading up to the fort. If my calculations were correct, then we had less than ninety minutes here. The car suspension recoiled repeatedly as we drove over the metal cattle grid that was designed to stop the grazing animals from escaping. This place had special memories for me, as when he was a small child, I had brought him here and he watched in wonder as we flew a kite high above the ground.

I drove to the car park, and parked the car. I switched off the engine and the whir of the air conditioning abruptly ceased. The air was still fresh and cool inside, but when I opened the car door, the warmth hit me. It was already starting, and I hope that my calculations were correct.

We took the treats from the boot of the car, and carried a bag each through the gate. We then started the ascent to the top of the hill. Neither of us were in great shape, and halfway up to the summit, we were both short of breath and sweating. The humidity was becoming unbearable, and I knew that things were going to become much worse in a short space of time.

"Can we stop for a minute Dad?" My son asked.

"I think we need to. It's higher up than I remember." I said. In reality, I remembered the climb well. It was my lack of fitness that I had conveniently forgotten. We stopped for a few moments, and looked back toward the car. When my son decided that he was ready, we then made our way toward the summit once more.

By the time we had reached the top of the hill, my back was covered in sweat. Both of us were now out of breath, but at last we could now rest properly. I checked my watch. There was about eighty minutes left. I took the chequered blanket out from my bag, and flicked it forward. It settled on the grass nicely, and allowed us a safe place to sit down and lay out our feast.

I laid out the selection of various items, cheeses, pies, biscuits, sweets and chocolates. I poured out the fizzy drinks, and even opened a small bottle of fine wine. I let him try just a mouthful of a wine, even if it was now slightly warm. For the next hour, we sat and ate, and we talked as father and son.

Even though he never remembered much from being an infant, he had kept a picture of me that his mother had given to him. It was touching to hear. He had always wondered about me, and had often asked his mother if he could visit me. She had always said that it wouldn't be possible until he was older. It was hard for me to hear, but it appeared as if he had missed me just as much as I had missed him. At this point I almost told him what was about to happen, but I had to protect him this one last time.

Four days earlier, I had been observing highly unusual sun activity. Across the world, we as scientists were communicating about what was unfolding before our very eyes. The sun had been unusually inactive for an extremely long time. It was too calm, and this really was the calm before the storm. We watched in awe, as a rift began to open on the surface of the sun itself.

A 21000,000 km rift opened across the surface of our star. It almost stretched completely around the sun, and appeared to virtually cut the sun in two. This wasn't visible to the naked eye, but astronomers across the globe studied the events with disbelief. This was an event that no one had ever witnessed before, and no one would ever witness again.

It would have been very different if everyone knew. The whole world would have gone into meltdown. There really was nothing that anyone could do though. What was about to happen was unstoppable, and unthinkable. That did not alter the fact that it was about to happen soon though.

You see, as the rift in the sun opened, we realised that the inactivity had been leading up to this point. This was an almighty event and we watched as the huge coronal hole opened, and there was an ejection of coronal mass that continued to be expelled from the centre of the sun. We plotted the course, and to our horror, we discovered that it was headed directly towards the Earth. There was nowhere safe left on the entire planet for mankind to hide.

My son and I filled up our stomachs with food and sweets and fizzy drinks. We then lay down side by side as father and son. Both of us lay with our hands behind our heads, using them as makeshift pillows, and we talked about life while we stared at the brightest clear blue sky high above us. Then the sky began to glow orange, which filled my son with curiosity.

"Why is the sky changing colour Dad?" He asked. He himself might well have decided to become a scientist one day, but for now, he was just an inquisitive twelve year old child, who was witnessing the full power of nature at work. I still could not tell him what was about to happen though. Instead I stood up and helped him to his feet.

"Look toward the sun, but not directly at it, and then close your eyes." I said. I then stood directly behind him, and embraced him around his shoulders and kissed the top of his head.

His eyes were tightly closed while I spoke.

"Keep your eyes closed tightly son." I was holding back my own tears while I spoke. "The sun sometimes let's off a little steam, and every now and again those plasma ejections come our way." It was true, but not the whole truth.

The impact was imminent, and I had little time in which to explain, for now it was just a matter of keeping his attention focused on my voice. "You can feel the warmth of the sun on your face is growing; and now I want you to raise your hands upward towards the sky, and if you try hard enough, you will be able to capture a real sunbeam in your hands."

His face was now covered with a little smile, and he knew that the truth was something else, but regardless, he kept his eyes closed and lifted his hands towards the sky. He became unexpectedly thrilled as he felt the sheer warmth of the sun between his hands, and he embraced the heat while I placed my arms around his neck and held him tightly. I shivered as I realised my own mortality. I had always feared death and now I had to face my own demise whilst telling my son the words that I felt he needed to hear.

In just a few seconds, all life on the planet would become extinct as a huge fireball would whitewash the Earth and pierce the ground with intense radiation that would make the soil infertile for thousands of years. I focused entirely on my sons smile as I held him tightly.

"I love you son." I needed him to hear it one last time.

"I love you too Dad." Then after a long pause, he asked "Is this what mum felt?" and with that short sentence, I knew that he had known the truth all along.

"Yes son, I think so. Now just keep your eyes closed, and feel the warmth of a new sunrise. We'll be with her again soon." I replied. There was a moment of silence as we felt the warmth spread over us.

"Will it hurt?" He asked. His voice was now slightly trembling.

"I don't know. I honestly don't. But don't be afraid. It's me and you now son. It's you and me together." In that instant, I felt the years of his potential future life that he would never see. I saw all those long forgotten memories. Before my eyes recollections of my own life were now flashing by. It was so painful, that it made me want to double over from that awful feeling of hurt that had now formed in my stomach. I had to be strong for just a little longer though.

After the moment struck, there were no more words, just two single tears running down both of my cheeks. In that briefest moment the sun instantly dried the tears that had fallen on my face, and then we were back with his mother once more.

Enemy mine

The dating site had proved to be a real blessing to Jonathan. It had made his life so much easier, in the sense that he could hunt his prey from the comfort of his tablet at home. The type of female that he was looking for was unique, but all of them had similar profiles.

He would always search for the same type of profile to find the women he was searching for. Firstly he would study all of the pictures carefully. The women would always be the slightly more attractive ones, and to find those normally took a little time. The next thing he would look for would be the way that the pictures had been taken.

The pictures would always be the self taken face or full body shots, not those distasteful mirror shots from across the room look. This would be one of his filters, and those with tacky pictures were a definite non starter. Most of the pictures taken that he sought would have been taken under artificial light, or maybe outside at night. He needed to find creatures of habit that tended to be nocturnal. Then it was down to examining the profile itself. His normal prey would have a standard profile.

Firstly they would profess to neither drink nor smoke or take drugs. They would be looking for a similar partner too. You can't beat clean living after all. They would also be without children, and they would be seeking someone similar. Their profession would often be vague, but the description would tend to show someone who liked to be close to home.

If the profile described all of the above, it made them prime targets, and the real eureka moment would be the suggested ideal place for a first date to happen. The description would always be of a place of solitude. This would either be something like a walk along the beach, a cosy evening picnic, or a wander through a secluded forest. It would be somewhere that they could be alone, together in nature's breath-taking beauty.

From time to time, especially in the early days, he had been wrong about his targets. He had turned up to meet people, who had blatantly lied in their profiles. Some had used pictures from a long time ago, some of the women were gold diggers with ulterior motives, and some had numerous children that they did not want to disclose on the site itself, afraid that it may put potential partners off.

These dates often ended in fast but unsatisfying sexual encounters, but they would never lead to a second date. He never gave out his number to anyone, and when he returned home, he would instantly block them from his profile. He had left numerous women in tears after blatantly using them for sex, and then removing them from his life without a second thought. They should have been grateful, as the alternative that he had to offer, was far less pleasant.

Nowadays, he spent a lot more time chatting before he would arrange to meet anyone. His targets would always show an unhealthy level of intensity in wanting to meet him. After all, he came across as the perfect date. Even though he was forty five years old, he kept himself fit and healthy, and looked not a day over thirty five. It had taken a few weeks to find a new target, but the moment he saw Gloria's profile, he knew that she had massive potential.

Her profile pictures were stunning. There were always a minimum of two pictures, and a maximum of three. Gloria had two. Both pictures showed off her amazing physique, and a perfectly flawless face. She had shoulder length blonde hair, and even though her age was stated as forty years of age, she looked as if she hadn't worn a day from her late twenties. Her profile ticked every single box, so he decided to send her a message.

'Hi. I'm intrigued by your profile. We seem to have similar interests, and like me, it appears that you prefer solitude to awkward social situations. I'm starting to feel as if the time has come to settle down, and these days, now my parents have both gone, and without children, it would be wonderful to find someone that I can communicate with. Please let me know if you would like to meet for a walk and a talk.

Jonathan.'

It was his standard template. It showed his solitary status in life, along with a slight hint of desperation of fear at being alone as he was getting older. It also showed that he was happy to be alone with the woman, and away from prying eyes. It was the bait that he needed to show her that he was meant no harm to her. It also never mentioned anything that was crude or offensive. He sat back, and awaited the response.

The alert of a message arrived at nine that same evening. It had taken her just over seven hours to respond. In his line of business, patience was the key. He had barely moved from the desk all day. Her response was friendly but direct. It already showed hints of desperation, but he would play on them for a little while longer before arranging to meet her. It read.

'Hey, you sound adorable and a perfect match! I've been on this site for just a little while, but it's full of freaks and weirdoes. It's unusual to find a man who doesn't have children or the crazies from his past. Do you not have any brothers or sisters? Listen, I need to get off here as soon as possible. I have a good feeling about you, and as you live close by, would you like to meet? I'm free tonight, and don't believe in wasting time. Do you know Chilbolton common, if you do, we could meet there for a walk around ten?

Gloria.'

He knew the common well. It was secluded apart from the odd grazing animal, and the occasional horse. A river ran directly through the middle of it, and it was an ideal place to hunt his prey. There were very few places to hide, as the common was open and exposed. It was perfect.

He waited for another half an hour before he responded.

'Thanks for the response. No, I was an only child, and I've never had children off my own. I've never been married either. I can't do tonight, as it's a little short notice, but I'm free tomorrow about nine. I can meet you at the gated entrance if that's good for you. Let me know. J.'

He had now clarified his solitude completely. It was true that he had no children, and if he never sired a child, then he would be the last of his bloodline. There was still time, to carry on the family trade, but this was a trade that was not for the faint of heart. From a young age, he was trained in the art of murder.

A new message quickly appeared in the inbox. He opened it and read her response.

'Sorry to hear that. I can see by your pictures that you have a kind face. I don't know why, but I feel as if I know you. I know its short notice, but please meet me tonight, even if it is just a little later. Say half ten maybe? I'm desperate to meet you face to face, and if we get on, then my house is close by. We can go back there and get to know each other better, away from prying eyes. Please say yes. I know that you won't regret it. G xxx'

He hadn't felt so sure in ages. He had indeed struck gold. She was desperate, and the covert lure of sex was designed to reel him in and offer him intimate company without any effort. He had already prepared everything in advance. Now he would meet her and it would be the final test. He breathed in deeply, and then responded. He was smiling while he typed.

'I'm a little unsure, as I am quite shy. However, I feel good about you too. I will be there at ten thirty, and we can talk some more. I'm looking forward to being close to someone again. It's been too long. See you soon. J.'

He sent the message, and then closed his laptop. He then picked up his sports bag and went out to his car. He was positive that everything would go to plan.

He parked his car a fair distance from the common. It was dark and secluded in the village, and no one would have seen his car where he left it. He took the sports bag out from the passenger seat, and hung it over his shoulder. The zip was partially undone, so that he could easily access the items inside. He then began to jog. He had to make sure that he arrived well before his prey did.

He slowed as he walked the final road leading to the common. It allowed him to regain his breath. He approached the gate, but to his shock, Gloria was already stood there waiting. He would need to change his tact. She smiled as he approached her.

"Jonathan?" She asked.

"Hi, yes. Sorry, I'm a little earlier than I thought. You look even better then you do in your pictures." He smiled. It was important to gain her trust. Play the part; he told himself, don't give away your true motives for being there.

"Thank you! Flattery will get you everywhere." She giggled to herself. He felt the urge to end her life right there and then, but it wasn't the time though. Instead, he approached her and kissed her on the left cheek.

It was a pleasantly warm summers evening, but her face was cool. Again it was another sign that everything was not as it had seemed. She kissed him back, and it was a gentle kiss on his lips, she then tried to pull him closer and kiss him open mouthed, but he pulled away from her. He could not afford to get too close.

"Let's talk a little first." He said. She smiled. He was obviously shy. He was coming across as the perfect date.

She took his hand and then led him onto the common. He felt that he fingers were icy cold.

"Your hands are freezing." He said.

"Cold hands, warm heart. Or so they say." Again she smiled as he looked at her. He had to hide his disgust. It was just a little further to walk before he could make his move. As they approached the river, he checked ahead and chanced a quick look behind him. There was no one around. It was time. He placed his hand in his left hand pocket, and took out the object. His closed his hand around it tightly. Then he stood still and pulled her close to him.

"Can I have that kiss now?" He asked. She did not answer, but moved her body to face him directly, and then she closed her eyes and opened her mouth. He let go of her hand and used it to pull her closer to him, holding the back of her neck.

As their lips touched, he opened his other hand and exposed the object. He placed it up to her face, and in a lightning fast movement, he held the silver cross on her cheek. It took less than a second for Gloria to register the pain. The skin on her cheek was bubbling on contact with the cross, and she wailed an inhuman scream. She was already turning.

He had to be fast. He reached inside his backpack and pulled out the noose. He had very little time, as the creature was still reeling from the shock, but the pain would not last long and then she would turn completely. He pulled the noose over her head, and then dropped down to the ground to drive a metal stake into the earth beneath him. The noose tightened and it pulled her down.

Her teeth were almost fully extended, and her skin was revealing its natural grey colour. Her grotesque features were now revealed and her true face was visible. He had seen hundreds of these creatures over the last thirty years. He had executed nearly all of them. He took out his secondary noose from the bag, and tied it around her feet. Then he pulled the rope tight and drove another stake into the ground. The creature was secured in place. Despite its intense struggle, it could not free itself. He removed the bag from his shoulder, and placed it on the ground. It was now time to end the creature.

As he went to reach for the wooden stake, he felt immense pain in his lower back. The wind had been completely knocked out of his body, and he struggled for breath. He had been knocked at least five feet across the ground as he was struck from the rear, and now his assailant was coming back for a second strike. He cursed his own carelessness when he saw the creature headed towards him. They were a pair, and he had not even considered this a possibility. His father had trained him better than that.

As he tried to gain his breath, he turned to face the creature head on. The creature was intent on freeing its mate, but to do so, he would have to kill Jonathan first. The second blow struck him around his waist, and the creature was now on top of him. This wasn't good. These creatures were powerful, and it had incredible strength. Jonathan was using all of his might just to keep the creature at bay. Its teeth were now extended fully, and saliva was dripping down into his neck as the creature sensed its feed.

In a moment of sudden realisation, he felt the cross was still in his hand. He managed to get his hand between himself and the creatures face. He opened his palm, and placed the cross on the creature's forehead. The creature started shaking uncontrollably. Its eyes both turned upward and inwards toward the cross. The silver emblem of Christianity was now sinking deeper into the creature's skin. The thing leapt high up into the air as it screamed. It gave Jonathan just the few seconds that he needed.

Reaching into his bag, Jonathan pulled out a folding crossbow. He extended it out fully, and aimed at the creature as it was about to land. As the creature impacted down on to the ground, it was shaking its head frantically as it tried to remove the cross. It then turned to face Jonathan with its face a mixture of rage and pain. The crossbow fired, and the shot was true as the impact pierced the creature's heart.

The wooden arrows were coated in garlic, and as the arrow pierced the creature's heart, it started a chain reaction within the creature's blood stream. Each cell within the body then began to explode, and Jonathan realised, he was right in the line of fire. He jumped into the river, and even though it was less than three feet deep, it still protected him as every single one of the creatures bodily cells exploded completely.

The water had been cold, but refreshing, and Jonathan was soaked, but he still had more to do. He walked over to the cross bow, and folded it back down to its compact size. He then located the arrow that he had fired. It had come to rest just a few feet away from here the creature had once stood. He retrieved it, and washed it clean in the river. Then he placed them both back into his sports hold-all. Now it was time to end this.

He took the wooden stake and a hammer out of the bag, and walked back over to where Gloria lay. She had now returned fully to her human form. A cross shaped scar was now visible on her cheek. Jonathan knelt down on the earthen floor next to her.

"Make it quick human, but know this. You cannot kill us all, and time is running out. My dark Lord has returned." She said, and then she started laughing insanely.

"Shut up." Jonathan replied. "You're not the first, and you won't be the last. There are plenty more fish in the sea. I love to kill them all, even the dark Lords." He said, and then he placed the stake directly over the creatures black heart.

Gloria did not squirm, nor did she try to free herself. She was almost welcoming or accepting of her fate. She stared directly into her killer's eyes and she spoke once more.

"You have never seen a dark Lord like this one, and trust me, he will end humanity, and the un-dead will claim the Earth!" She then spat in Jonathan's face.

He wiped away the spittle from his cheek.

"You talk too much." He said, and then he struck the stake with the hammer, driving the wooden implement down deep, right through the vampire's body.

He had already walked thirty feet away from the body before it exploded. The blood and body parts covered a large area, but quickly dissipated away to nothing. He waited slightly longer than he needed too. He then walked back and took all of his equipment and placed it back in the bag. He would have to wait a while before he would be dry enough to get back into his car. In the mean time, he stood on the bridge that crossed the river.

The moon was full, and it glistened on the softly rippling water. It was almost as if there were two moons now visible. The water continued to flow gently underneath him, and it lapped gently against the side of the bank. He knelt down and reached inside of the bag, and then he took out his gun. It was lucky that he was prepared for every eventuality. He walked to the edge of the bridge and watched the creature walking slowly toward him. It has over five feet tall when it was on all fours.

The creature stopped directly in front of him. It was growling angrily at him, but as it caught its scent, it began licking its lips. It was clear that it was preparing to strike. It was going to launch itself at him at any second. Timing was crucial. As the creature leapt forward, Jonathan was astounded by the size and majesty of the creature. It would have been over seven feet tall if it were stood on its hind legs. He fired three rounds into the creature, and once again he found himself rolling sideways back into the river to avoid the creature as it landed.

When he emerged from the water, the creature was slowly converting back to human form. It was a female that stood around six feet tall. The silver bullets had killed her instantly, and now she had a peaceful look on her face. This was a worrying sign. Never before had the vampires and werewolves been in such close proximity. It was clear that these three had been working together. They had been hunting the hunter. A powerful force must have been at work to forge such an alliance. He would now need to seek the advice of the elders.

For now though, there were more pressing matters. He had to move the body that now lay on the bridge. He would then have to place her in a secluded spot. Then there was the walk back to the car to retrieve the shovel, and hours to bury the body. On the plus side, it would help to dry his clothes, and there were three less creatures left in the world left for him to kill. On the negative side, it would be a long night, and her words about the dark Lord she served, were starting to worry him.

We Float

It was an unusual gift, to say the least. A two hour session within a floatation tank was something that Serena had never once considered in her life. Of course she had heard about these devices before, but a session inside of one, had never once been something that she had seriously considered purchasing. As a writer who was struggling for inspiration, her sister had suggested that this may be a way to stir up her imagination. It took quite a few hours of researching the subject, before she finally made the decision to abandon her inhibitions, and just try it out for herself.

Once she was inside of the tank. Once she closed the door behind her and she found herself in total darkness. As she lay down in the water inside of the tank, she let her arms drift free at the sides of her body. The water was heated at a comfortable ninety-five degrees Fahrenheit, and the high concentration of Epsom salts in the water allowed her body weight to float effortlessly. It was a strange sensation at first, but it was not uncomfortable in the slightest.

For the first five minutes, her brain would not switch off from the tasks that she regularly performed on the outside world. Her head was full of thoughts of her daily schedule, the social media chats, the emails, the phone calls and the horrors of hearing the distressing daily news bulletins. It was a constant bombardment of media that was assaulting her senses, and she had come to be a part of the news feed herself. Then she heard a soothing voice.

"Relax, be in the moment."

She turned her head to see any sign of where the voice had come from, but there was no one else in the room outside, and the tank itself was quite shielded from the noise outside. She wondered if she had created the voice with her own imagination, and decided to try to calm herself down. She really needed to find that inspiration right now.

She allowed herself to ease back down into the water once more. Despite the darkness of the room, she closed her eyes tightly shut. Now all she could sense was the beating of her own heartbeat, and the air escaping from her nostrils as she calmly breathed in and out. She then began to lose all sense of time. Her body itself now seemed unnecessary as her mind took over control. She wondered if this was what it felt like when you were dying. Was it just your mind roaming free across all of space and time for eternity?

Her hair appeared to be dancing around her shoulders in the water, and she finally succumbed to the relaxing sensation and to let go completely. The body, the water, and the space of air above her head were all completely regulated at the same temperature and Serena now felt completely absorbed into the tank. She no longer had any idea, of where her body ended, or where the water or air began. They were all now a single entity.

She had no idea if her body had been spinning around. Neither did she have any idea if she were still facing upright or if she was upside down. She might have even been standing up. She now had no concept of her position in the universe. There was no difference that she could feel anymore. She and the universe were now one. A myriad of colours flashed before her eyes even though the tank remained in total darkness. The colours were exploding above her almost like an endless stream of fireworks painting on a canvas in front of her. Then they were calm. The same voice spoke that she thought she had heard before, it said.

"The past is a forgotten country."

Serena arched her back and gasped as her entire life flashed before her eyes. She witnessed everything. From the moment of her inception, then back through the trauma of childbirth. She remembered all of the way through her childhood. Then the awkward teenage years, adulthood, marriage, divorce, pain, worries, love, hate, laughter, and suffering. Every emotion she had ever felt in life, all were recalled in less than three minutes. By the time the memories had replayed right up to the present moment, she was sobbing endlessly.

The tears fell from her eyes, and spread out into the water that she was floating in. The tears made the water seem to raise itself up higher in the tank, and she realised that if they continued, then she might drown in her own sorrow. She took deep breaths until her anguish had subsided, and then the voice spoke once again.

"The present. A reveal."

She then found her spirit was up above her body, looking down at herself as she floated in the darkness below. Looking down, she felt immense sadness at seeing herself alone. She looked as if she were a solitary child still cradled in her mother's womb. Inside, she was protected, but the moment that she would step out of the tank, the weight of the world would push down onto her shoulders again once more. She was alone, afraid and lonely, and without the child that she had so desperately craved. Then she found herself falling back down into her physical body, but she did not want to enter it.

She had been gifted a moment of release and with it came the realisation of how much she had never managed to achieve the things in life that she had always wanted. The voice then spoke for the third and final time.

"The future. Already written. The word is set in stone." The voice now sounded saddened as it spoke.

Serena then found herself outside of the tank. She was on her knees, with her head bowed down. There was sand beneath her legs and she cupped some of it up into her hands, and raised it up to her face.

She had been mistaken. It wasn't sand beneath her. It was something else. Something that now disintegrated between her fingers. She raised it up to her face to see more closely and then she realised that the material she was holding, was actually ashes. She let the ashes fall freely from her hands.

It was hard for her to stand due to the softness of the ashes that covered the ground beneath her. She struggled to maintain her balance, but eventually she found an uneasy balance. She looked around in all directions but all she could see was ash that was covering the ground in all directions for as far as the eye could see. Then in the distance, she saw what appeared to be some kind of structure. It was clear that this was the only direction she should travel in.

It took what felt like hours for her to reach the structure. It was the remains of a house that had been battered, but somehow it was still standing. The front door was hanging off from its hinges, and was gently swaying in the wind. Gingerly she stepped inside the open door and then she started to explore.

All of the windows had gone, but there were no signs of shattered glass anywhere. There were insects crawling everywhere. They were bloated and larger than any insects that she had ever seen before. She could not afford to be squeamish right now; for the sake of her own inquisitiveness, she had to discover what had happened here.

She moved silently from room to room. The downstairs floor of the house was completely empty. The house felt as if it had stood empty for thousands of years, and it made no sense that in a barren land full of ashes, that this single solitary structure remained. She decided to walk up the stairs, just to see if the top of the house was abandoned and empty too.

She slowly climbed up the creaking stairs one by one. If there was anyone up there, they would have already have been warned of her arrival. She reached the top of the stairs, but she could still hear nothing, except for the sound of the wind blowing freely through the open window frames.

She moved from room to room, and in the third room, she found what must have been the last two inhabitants of the house.

The body of what appeared to be a woman was sat on a chair. She was holding a child in her arms. She assumed that this was a mother and her young. The child could not have been more than seven years old. The bodies sat motionless, completely charred and burned where they sat. The end for them both must have been one of excruciating agony, as both mother and child had died open mouthed. She imagined the final screams that had exploded along with their dying breaths. They had been here for some time. There were signs that the bodies were now deteriorating.

For some reason, Serena felt an overwhelming urge to touch the dead woman's cheek. She leant forward and reached out to touch the woman's face, and as she made contact despite the fact that he woman had been dead for a long time, it still surprised her to find that the charred skin was completely cold. She shuddered and then moved her hand away.

"What happened here?" She said out loud to herself. As she withdrew her hand from the woman's face, the bodies of the pair instantly began to crumble. Within a few seconds, both of the bodies had crumbled to the floor. Both mother and child had now turned to ash.

Serena fell down to her knees once more. The ash that she has been walking on for hours, that was all that was now left of mankind. Everyone was gone. Not a single other person was still alive on the planet. Only she remained. She had been walking on the remnants of the human race. She shook her head in disbelief. Had mankind destroyed itself? The bodies of the mother and child drifted away as the wind started blowing even harder through the shell of the house. Underneath where the two bodies had been, protected from the heat, was a diary.

Serena felt as if she was betraying the secrets of the mother and her child, but she had to find out what had happened for own sanity. She opened the pages and moved to the last entry, and then she read the last words that had been written. They read.

'The truth was revealed to all, but mankind wasn't ready. Tensions have been rising for days. Each side pushed the other as far as they could. The warning has been sounded. We have no idea who fired first, but both sides have now declared war. We have no time left. My poor, poor child does not know. I will hold her close until the end. All we can do is sit here and pray. May God in his mercy save us all.'

Serena closed the diary. It was a nuclear war that had killed everyone, of that she was now sure. Then she stared down at the diary. The year was embossed in gold leaf on the front of the diary. It was the year 2020. If this image was real, then there was only three years left before Armageddon occurred. Suddenly she felt the world start to fall away around her. Her vision was melting away before her eyes, just as the glass windows of the house, had once melted from the heat of the nuclear blasts.

A light had come on inside of the flotation tank, and her eyes slowly opened as they adjusted to the light. She had used up all of the two hours. It was time to come back to reality. It was an insane wake-up call in more ways than one. Selena lifted up the lid of the tank, and stood upright. As she stood up, she felt the weight of the world pressing down on her shoulders. She no longer felt that this reality was safe anymore. She had to try and do something to stop the future that she had been told was already written.

She showered off the salt water, and dried herself. Once she was dressed, she took a single look back at the tank and then she opened the door of her room. She then walked out through the main door and into the reception area. The receptionist smiled at her as she appeared.

"Did you dream in colour?" The receptionist asked. Serena thought long and hard before she answered the question.

"Yes. I dreamt in colour. They were the darkest shades of black and gray." She replied. The receptionist looked puzzled by her answer.

"Do you want to book another appointment? Often there is much more to see on the second or third visit." The receptionist said. Serena answered with an unwavering amount of certainty.

"Once was more than enough for me, thank you. Have a nice day." Then Serena left through the front door, and never stopped to look back at where she had been.

The last days of Martusa

His eyes were closing, this was the end. Behind him, the wind was causing havoc. There was nothing but a fading track of foot prints, the only proof left of where he had once been. This was where the remnants of his body would now lay for all of eternity. It was not a fitting end for a King, but it was the end that he had chosen for himself. He would die here all alone.

It hadn't always been like this, he was once the leader of a proud race. There tribe was growing as the seasons changed, and now they numbered close to three hundred. From generation to generation, they had learnt from the old ways. They had survived the harshest seasons and they had grown.

They had developed writing skills and primitive speech had begun to evolve into a more complex language. They were more like an extended family than a tribe, and they shared equal values of peace and unity. They lived in harmony. That was until the day that strangers came. Then everything began to change.

The strangers came in shining ships that descended from the skies. They were Dran (three) in number, and they came with a dire warning. The language barrier was a problem; and it was hard to understand the sky people, one thing was certain though, is that they were already in a hurry to leave. They kept on pointing to the skies above, and it made the Kind nervous.

The King assembled his wisest aides. He was a strong hunter who provided for the tribe, but he knew that there were others who were far wiser than him. He ordered them to find out what the sky people wanted, and then let them have all they needed and then to ask them to leave. There was enough food for the tribe for the winter, but they could not feed all the extra mouths of the sky people.

The aides went to greet the sky people. They wore strange garments, completely unlikely those the Martusan people wore. They had a wondrous craft that could hover above the ground. They could create heat and light, without fire or the sun. They could turn night into day over large areas. It took some effort, but gradually, they explained to the aides, that they were here to help them leave.

The sky people were called Tularan's. They had come from another bright ball in the sky, many many travels away. The bright ball they had once called home, but there home was no more. A bright red ball had collided with their home, and they had travelled to seek a safe place to make a new home. They had discovered Martusa and travelled here. It had taken many sun sweeps across the sky.

They too had wise aides, but the wise aides knew that Martusa was not safe. It too would soon be impacted by the red ball in the sky. They warned that when the ball struck, no Martusan would survive. The land would grow no more, the sky, would be much hotter, and the rains would no longer fall. The Abasi (water) that they drank, would soon been evaporated and turn to dust. Nothing could survive after the ball collided.

The strangers needed more supplies; they tested the Abasi and knew that it was good. In return for the Abasi, they had offered to save the tribe and take them with them. They pointed to another ball in the sky. The closest ball that was safe enough to travel to. This ball they had called Ertera. They had only four sun sweeps before they would have to leave. The aides would now have to relay the message back to the King, and then he would have to make the decision whether to leave here or not.

When the aides returned, they began to explain all that they had heard. It was a fantastic story, like the elders had once told. Some truly believed that the lights in the sky were the same as Martusa. They believed that perhaps there were other similar worlds, where different people also lived a peaceful existence.

The King listened to the story, and the wisest aides believed that the tribe were in mortal danger, and urged the king that they should leave. The King would have to think long and hard. He dismissed his aides, but asked them for one sun sweep before he made his decision. He had to make the right decision, the one in the best interest of all his people.

As the light completely faded from the sky, the King sat on his favourite rock. He watched as the pool of Abasi reflected the brightness of the sky lights above. His chosen woman came out from the shelter that they shared and sensing that the king was troubled, she rubbed her hands firmly over his broad shoulders.

"Something worries you my King. Can I share your thoughts?" She asked.

This particular mate was his favourite. She was large of belly, and would soon enter the period of the blood screaming. From the pain of the ceremony, a new King would emerge. It was wondrous to behold the emergence of new life as a gift from the gods above.

"I have a decision to make that will affect us all." He answered.

She had never seen the King look so daunted before. It concerned her greatly.

"You are a wise King, share your burden, and lighten your heavy heart." She pleaded. The King pulled her closer to him, and then stroked his hand over her swollen belly.

"I felt him kick; the gift will soon be coming. He is strong and already he fights for the Gods to release him. He will become a great King I am sure. My strength and your compassion will make him a wise man." He said and the smile across his face was gentle. "The strangers wish us to leave our home. They say that a great tragedy will befall us. They say that if we do not leave our home, then they fear that our tribe will perish." He now had a great deal of sadness and confusion etched on to his face.

"Surely this cannot be true my King? The Gods will protect our lands I'm sure!" Her emotion was visible on her face and in the passion in her voice.

"We barely survived through the last cold season here. The crops were few and we lost some of the elders. I am worried or the tribe." The King had reminded her of the harshness of the winter that they had last endured, but she recalled it only too well herself. She could see that the Kings heart was indeed heavy.

"Can we trust the sky people?" She asked. The King sighed heavily.

"They have craft that travel to the other night lights. They need our help. They need to take some of the Abasi in return for safe passage for our people." The King knew that the Abasi was needed if the tribe stayed here then they needed it to survive the hot season coming.

His chosen then suddenly pointed up toward the sky above her head.

"Look my King, a sign!" She shouted. The King looked toward where the female was pointing. It was clear as a night stones glow. The red light was glowing in the black of the sky above, and it seemed to be getting bigger as it came toward them. He held his female close and they both watched the object that was now heading toward them.

The next morning, the King assembled the entire tribe. He had made his decision. He told the assembly, that he had spoken with the Gods, and that the tribe were to embark on a great journey. They were to help the sky people to deploy giant machines that would allow them to take as much Asabi as their crafts could carry, and in return the craft would each take one third of the tribe to a new land called Ertera. Here they would find plentiful crops, a new land of peace, and unity with the sky people.

Many of the elders were reluctant at first, but the people trusted the King and followed his orders without question. The sky people deployed the machines and set them to work. They gathered as much Asabi as they could carry. The tribe began to collect minimal belongings and the families entered holding areas on the craft. To the tribe, boarding each craft was like stepping into another world they were magnificent and the walls were unlike the caves they inhabited. They were smooth to the touch, and glimmered like the Abasi did in the sunlight.

Soon enough almost all of them were on the craft. It was a four month journey that they were about to endure and It would not be easy. The King thought long and hard before making his final decision. He then ordered his chosen one to gather her things, ready to board the craft.

The King then announced to his chosen and his aides that he was not going to be leaving on the journey with them. On hearing this, his chosen fell down to her knees.

"No!" She screamed. "You must come with us!" She sobbed openly as tears rolled down her cheeks. The final decision had already been made. His orders would be followed; and there was no doubt about this. He helped his chosen back to her feet, and rubbed her belly.

"He will make me proud. He will lead you wherever you may end up calling home." He said. "I have consulted with the Gods, and they have told me to welcome the red star as it arrives here. My time was nearly done, and this will be your new beginning."

The pains in his stomach had been growing for months. He knew in his own heart that he was dying. His father had also passed over in agony the exact same way. It would be better to not be an extra burden. One less number on the sky ship meant better odds for the survival of the tribe. A dying King, felt a duty to remain, he needed to witness the last days of Martusa for himself.

The chosen and his aides boarded the craft, and he sat silently watching from his favourite rock. As the door closed, he waved goodbye to his chosen for one final time. He watched as the sky craft lifted high into the air. He asked the Gods to afford the tribe protection. He stood watching until he could neither see nor hear the craft anymore.

For the next two days, the King watched the skies above him. The red star grew and grew. Now it was visible even during the bright sky sweeper as it passed. It was liked a winged red sister to the sun, and now he began to feel his chest becoming tighter. The act of breathing became harder by the hour.

The sky craft had travelled some distance before the impact of the red star, and they were a safe distance from Martusa and away from any danger as it struck. The scientists timed the impact to perfection, but they did not disclose the information to the Martusan's. Instead, they had left them with hope. They hoped that their brave and much loved King might have somehow survived. That the red star may have meant a new beginning and somehow the Kings bravery, had earned his salvation with the grace of the Gods.

After four long months of travel, the sky craft finally entered the atmosphere of Ertera. As the temperatures rose, each of the sky ships was damaged beyond repair. The atmosphere had been far hotter than any of their scientists had anticipated. Emergency pods were launched and over sixty percent of the travellers were saved. Each of the three sky craft crashed into the Earth.

As each ship broke into endless pieces, the Abasi that they carried covered vast areas of both barren land, and once inhabited civilisations. Atlantis was the biggest casualty, as it was sunk by the largest debris of one of the craft as it crash to the ground. Similar pandemonium ensued across the globe. The three sky ships were spread far and wide, and the people of Martusa would never be united as a tribe again. The Abasi from Martusa carried with it bacteria and life forms that over time would react and combine with those of the Earth. New life would be forged over many thousands of years.

As the red star impacted with the planet, the King was knocked from his feet. It knocked Martusa from its former position and sent it on a new trajectory around the solar system. The red star then carried on with its journey. It was now on a new trajectory itself, and the two planetary objects would never collide again. The King got back to his feet. He was determined to reach his favoured rock.

The King collapsed in front of his favourite thinking place. The Asabi was now all gone. The breathable air was also now all gone. He slowly let out the last of the air that he had held inside of his lungs. Before his eyes, he could see that his beloved home was now tainted red from the dust of the star that had left a residue behind after impacting with the surface.

The wind was intense and as he tried to inhale his lungs were immediately filled with the red dust. The trail of his footprints was now fading away, just as everything he ever known or loved had also vanished from his sight forever. The King of Mars was no more.

The End Game

It was going to be the biggest game release of all time. The hype building up to the launch day, had reached a frenetic fever. At nine in the morning, the game was finally made available and it was supported on every single mobile platform and device. The servers crashed multiple times during the morning, but Alan was determined that he would secure the game for his son. It took him until almost three p.m. to finally complete the download.

When twelve year old Joshua rushed through the back door of the house, he made straight for his mobile phone which his father had left on the kitchen side. He flicked through the icons until he reached the final screen, and the very last icon was a brand new one. It was the icon for the game called Zombie dead kill extreme live, and it was now ready to play.

Joshua clenched his fist in a triumphant gesture and said "Wicked!" His father then entered the kitchen. He had heard the back door of the house closing, and he was feeling rather pleased with himself that he had made good on his promise. Joshua was smiling and it was great to see. He had been quite down since his mother had left, and Alan was doing his best to keep his sons mind off what had happened.

It was barely three months ago, but every day Alan still thought about the day she left. He had come home from work on a Wednesday afternoon and in the kitchen he had found the letter. He recognised the handwriting as being that of his wife Eleanor. Before he even managed to open it, he felt a surge of adrenaline coursing through his veins. He had an awful feeling, that something inside the envelope was about to change his life forever.

It was perfect timing. Joshua always played football after school on a Wednesday, and he would not return home until seven at the earliest.

Normally Wednesday was steak day, but today there were none of the familiar smells of steak being cooked. The house was deathly quiet. It felt eerie. Alan carefully sliced open the envelope. He did not wish to damage the contents in any way. Normally he would rip open the post without a care, but this was different. He opened up the letter, and read the contents aloud.

'My Alan,

    Firstly I have to say to you, please don't blame yourself. We have been together nearly fifteen years, and we both know that things have changed so much in the last year.

A few months ago, I had an unexpected phone call from Nicholas, my childhood sweetheart. He had just split with his wife after a long marriage and had asked to meet up for a coffee. He gave me his number, and after a great deal of soul searching, I decided to ring him.

At first I had I had declined the offer to meet him, but after talking on the telephone for a while, I reluctantly agreed so that I might be able to help him through his divorce as he sounded very upset. When we met, he told me about how his life had become mundane and boring. How they had stuck to the same routine day after day, week after week, and how life was draining him mentally. He had tried to mention this to his wife, and it turned out that she had already been discussing a divorce with her solicitor.

It wasn't what he had planned or even wanted at first, but he reluctantly agreed. The more he told me about how desperate their marriage had become, the more I found that it mirrored our life together. I had been feeling trapped and unhappy for quite some time. We met up a few more times, and then the inevitable happened. We both realised that we still had strong feelings for each other that had never faded.

At first I struggled with my feelings, but I have to say, of all the things that I tried to make you notice me, the more I felt as if you never really saw me at all. Our marriage had become something that neither of us had ever intended, and I could not remain here living a lie. I love you and I always will, but Nicholas has made me feel alive again. I have decided that it would be better for us all for me to just leave.

Nicholas has sold his house, and we are going to start again in the South of France. We will be financially secure so please don't worry. Once we are settled, then I will ask Joshua if he would like to come and live with us. Until then I hope that you can explain things to him in a way that he understands, so that we don't disrupt his life unnecessarily.

I will call you in a few days, and I really do hope that you understand my decision.

Take care of yourself and our son.

Eleanor x

He found the final stupid little kiss quite offensive. Just a daft little unnecessary added 'X' to rub salt further into his wounds. He wasn't expecting this; he hadn't even seen it coming. To be honest he wasn't really all that bothered. It made the affair he had been having for the last three months with his secretary Paulina seem more than justified. He had walked upstairs and checked the bedroom; she had taken a suitcase, and filled it with some of her clothes. Everything else she had left behind. On the bedside cabinet was her wedding ring. It was laid next to her engagement ring. It made him a little sad to see them both.

It was true that he hadn't noticed his wife, because his train of thought had been solely focused on a woman who was twenty years her junior. She had the face of a model, the body of an athlete, and breasts that you would pay in excess of four thousand pounds for. He knew exactly how much they had cost, as he had paid for them personally. In return for his gift, there was sex. Not just any sex, but great sex. It was long and hard sex. It was enduring and sweaty sex. It was explorative, sensual, black silk, mind blowing sex. He was being selfish though. His thoughts then turned to their son. He was going to be devastated.

Joshua had cried tears of disbelief and then after the tears, then came a period of anger. By the time his mother had finally called, he had moved on to a period of resentment and he refused to speak to her at all. It had upset his mother greatly, and in a warped sort of way Joshua was happy that she was upset. She had destroyed the family with her reckless fantasy. They should have been a complete family, but now that would never happen again. Paulina had moved in after a few weeks, and she was a breath of fresh air.

Paulina was cool. She was less than twelve years older than Joshua, and they clicked right from the off. Of course it helped that she was beautiful and the amount of friends he had who wanted to come to the house, had suddenly made him one of the most popular kids at school. At night, he could hear her making love to his father for hours. It created strange stirrings within him that he couldn't fully understand just yet, but he was glad that his father was happy. She was also a video gamer. In that respect she was just like him.

The only thing that he didn't like about Paulina was that at most games, she was better than him. It was annoying to have to admit it, but it was helpful whenever he was stuck. She would always be on hand to see him through a difficult puzzle or end of level challenge. His mother had hated gaming, and told him he needed to get out more. Paulina actively encouraged him to play. His father had not stopped smiling since she moved in, and that had made him happy too.

Now the ex wife was long forgotten. It was almost perfect timing, as Paulina then burst into the back door of the house.

"Have you played it yet?" She asked him.

"Not yet. It's just loading up." Joshua said whilst raising a smile at her. She hugged Joshua before leaning over to kiss his father on the lips. She winked at him as she did so. Alan knew that she was horny just from that one little wink of the eye, and also the broad smile now on her face. Who was he kidding, she was always horny!

The music started to play from Joshua's mobile. The game had fully loaded and it was ready for him to play. There was a zombie stood right there in the kitchen, now he had to select a weapon and destroy it. Joshua chose the axe and gesturing with his phone, he sliced into the zombie's brain. It did not fall. He swung the axe once more sideways and sliced the head off of the zombie. The body fell to the floor, and the head rolled around. It was still groaning. Then both the head and the body faded to nothing, and his points appeared on the screen.

To kill an enemy in one strike was a major point score. His execution had been two strikes. He scored an impressive fifty points. It was ten points that were awarded for the first strike and then another forty points for the kill.

"Yeah boy!" He shouted as he beamed a huge smile. His father was totally unaware of the extent of the violence of the game, but he was sure that Paulina would discourage it if she had any concerns at all. As soon as Joshua had showered and changed, he was off outside and on a mission filled with hunting zombies with his friends.

For the next three weeks, both Joshua and Paulina became more heavily involved in the game. Each was finding more and more inventive ways to murder the zombies. The more inventive the kill, the higher the points score. Still that elusive one strike kill was avoiding them both. Paulina was often playing the game until eight or nine in the evening, but Alan didn't mind at all. It was essential that she bonded with Joshua, and when the divorce finally came through, he was determined that he was going to ask her to become his sons step mother.

The game started to lose a little of its excitement after a few months, but the game developers had already anticipated this. They were already working on a new updated version, and they were promising something special. Alan had received word from his solicitor that his wife had already started divorce proceedings. His ex wife and her lover were going to pay for the whole thing. It would be a clean split and she had not asked for a penny. It was a better result than he could have ever imagined.

The following Saturday, whilst Joshua was away at a football tournament and Paulina was working out at a gym class, he decided to go shopping for an engagement ring. He already knew what size she was by letting her try on the rings his wife had left behind. They had fitted her perfectly. She had blushed when he had called her Mrs Davidson. He just knew that despite the age gap, she would jump at the chance of marriage.

He had prepared everything. The decree absolute had arrived on a Monday morning, and he was ready to move forward. Joshua very seldom talked about his mother and still he refused to take her calls. The offer of spending a week on holiday with her and her partner had been met with utter contempt. He wanted a divorce from his mother in a sense. She had broken his heart and he had refused to allow her into his life in any sense. He was much happier now. On the night that his father proposed to Paulina, he felt incredible.

That night, he and Paulina and his father were off together on a special mission to a local playground. There was a new zombie loose in the park, but this wasn't just any old zombie. This was one of the founders. The founders had injected themselves with the original mutation virus, and as such they had started the epidemic. To kill a founder would mean legendary status amongst gamers. Joshua, his father, and Paulina were in the park just at the right time. There were only a few weeks until the new game launched, but this was a special moment.

The founder was less than twenty feet ahead of him. Paulina had joined forces with her camera phone and had crept around the back of the creature. She had struck at one of the creatures legs with a chainsaw, and had cut it off at the knee. It was a severe damage strike, but not enough to kill the founder. This would take something special. Joshua struck the creature with multiple objects.

Each strike had caused damage, but the founder had incredible abilities. Its leg was now growing back, and its wounds were healing as fast as they were inflicted. Joshua was searching for other weapons close by. There was a crowbar, another chainsaw, a first aid box, which he collected, and hidden behind the bushes, he caught just a glimpse of the weapon that he needed.

Paulina was working tirelessly with the chainsaw; she was determined to keep the founder grounded. Joshua moved toward the bushes. It was an amazing find. He clicked on the collect icon on his phone and picked up the weapon. As he turned around, the founder had taken Paulina out of the game. It was a near fatal blow. It would take her a day to recover.

It was all up to Joshua now. He started by throwing the first aid box using the send to player button. It was a selfless act which meant Paulina would be back in the game in less than two minutes. Then he selected the weapon and he ignited the flame thrower. The electronic flames covered the creature's body. It began to melt. Joshua continued to burn the creature. It was working!

Paulina quickly returned to the game and restarted the chainsaw. While the creature was burning in agony she cut off its head. The flaming head rolled around the floor, but then the unthinkable happened. It then started to grow a new body. This was a nightmare end of level boss to kill. Then Joshua saw the final item just laid on the grass. He had almost walked past it as it was so small. There was a tiny syringe on the ground. He picked it up and examined it. It was the antidote to the virus, and he knew exactly what to do with it.

It had to be the body or the head. The choice was where to use the antidote.

"Destroy the brain!" Paulina shouted. She was right; it had to be the head.

Joshua used the antidote, injecting it straight into the eye of the founder. It stopped regenerating, and then it started to vibrate while it screamed.

"Get back!" Joshua shouted. They had to be clear before the creature exploded. Other gamers were now descending on the area each of them now eager to witness a legendary event.

The head finally exploded, and every gamers screen began to glow. The white glow was really intense, and then it began to subside. JoshA1ze45 was the username that now appeared on every screen. He was the killer of the last founder. He had effectively ended the game. He had scored ten thousand points, and more importantly, he had won four free versions of the next generation event. It was ready for launch but it could only be released once the first game had been completed. He could not have done it without Paulina's help, but now Joshua was a legend.

Alan had been watching from the park bench. He was bemused by everything he had just seen. Gamers were still arriving in the park, and each was coming over to congratulate a fellow gamer. Joshua lost count of the compliments and the fist bumps and high fives he received. Paulina went and sat on Alan's lap, and hugged him around the shoulders.

"You made him the happiest boy alive." Alan said. Then he reached inside of his pocket, and pulled out a small black velvet box. He lifted Paulina upright and then took her hand. He dropped down to one knee and held out the box. "Would you make me the happiest man alive too?" He asked. Paulina's face was now beaming with happiness.

"Yes!" She said excitedly. She was almost jumping on the spot with excitement. More importantly, the ring fitted her finger perfectly.

The wedding was in a registry office, at Paulina's insistence. She had never wanted a big wedding; she had just wanted to be loved. It was important that they married quickly, and in less than a month of the proposal, they were man and wife. The reception was lavish and no expense was spared. It was the least Alan could do. Joshua agreed to stay with his uncle for a fortnight to allow the couple a dream honeymoon in Antigua, and on the day that the couple returned they looked so tanned, that he barely recognised them.

For killing the founder, the prize was due to be delivered before the day of the launch of Zombie Dead Kill: End Game. Joshua could not wait to see what the prize actually was. The courier was late with the delivery and Alan had to explain to his son, that sadly this happened all the time. When it did finally arrive, it had all been worth the wait though. He eagerly, but carefully ripped the box open, and inside he found that there were four new carefully packaged augmented reality combination headsets, along with all new electronic glove attachments.

These headsets were the ultimate design in gaming accessories. They had a new design installed that allowed any objects that you picked up in real life to be assimilated into the game. This enabled you to use anything close to hand as a weapon. You could actually feel the force in your hands, and the impact through the gloves which vibrated as you used them.

Joshua gifted one of the sets to Paulina. He kept one for himself and then gave two away to two of his closest gaming friends. He could have sold them on, but he decided it would be a good gesture if he were to give them to people who were less fortunate than himself.

For the initial trial of the game, all four of them travelled down to the local park where they all donned the headsets together for the very first time. The practice would give them a twenty four hour head start over all the other gamers, who were desperate to get their hands on this piece of gaming history. The headset enabled you to interact with the environment. The immediate locale would be assimilated into the game meaning that you could still walk anywhere safely without bumping into objects. It even warned you when you were about to encounter a kerb or a hole in the path. It was the ultimate 3D environment. In fact it was impossible to tell which of the realities was actually real until you removed the headset. The game was a trial version, but everyone agreed that it was immense in the way that it felt so real.

The headset retailed at less than a hundred and fifty pounds, and stores were selling out as fast as the deliveries could be made. For any child under the age of thirteen this was an essential accessory. The trailer for the games that were coming was sending everyone almost insane with excitement.

Each headset had a solar charging pack which stored power in reserve for night time use. This meant that the use of batteries was now obsolete. Each also contained a countdown clock. This was the countdown to the new End Game. It was promised that this would be a game unlike anything anyone had ever experienced before.

It was a Saturday and on every Saturday Alan always loved to catch up with the football scores in the afternoon. At three p.m. the game was released, it was exactly at the same time as most of the football games in the country kicked off. Paulina was determined to be out with Joshua when the game countdown clock reached zero. So they made their way to the nearest open field and once they placed on the headsets, the clocks were counting down the last few minutes to the launch of the full game.

Crystal clear images of Zombies flashed on the screen repeatedly and then they faded. Weapons appeared in all different guises and then they too faded. Simple tasks appeared, such as picking up nearby objects from the floor or kicking imaginary balls high into the air. Each helped to shape the environment, all in preparation for the game to begin. Then when the moment arrived, the counter reached zero and every single screen went black simultaneously. Then the game began.

Zombies were instantly appearing from everywhere. Joshua and Paulina were straight in battle mode. The first mission was to make their way home, but it was not going to be easy. They needed weapons fast, so they picked up and used anything that they could lay their hands on. They could pick up pieces of wood or branches, bricks, or anything solid. All of them could be assimilated into the game. These zombies were intensely lifelike as they attacked, across the globe over ten million children's hearts were pumping in a mixture of fear and adrenalin. The game was addictively scary, but hugely fun nonetheless.

Paulina was almost bitten as they approached the edge of the park. Joshua managed to spear the Zombie through the eye with a sharp branch he had acquired. The sights and sounds in the game were horrific. The noise of the other players screaming in fear and excitement only seemed to add to the thrill of the kill.

The pair battled homeward through wave after wave of attack. Some of the enemies would approach them with knives or other weapons. Once you had killed the oncoming attacker you could assimilate these weapons as your own and the gloves ensured you felt each and every impact they made on the enemy.

As they moved forward, they left a trail of dead zombies in their wake. The gamers could see each other, and were working as a united army against the un-dead. The game was simply the best thing in the history of gaming that anyone had ever experienced.

Paulina was the first to reach their home. She opened the door and ran inside. Joshua followed her in, and then heard her screaming. There was a zombie actually in the house. Paulina was trying to hold the zombie back from attacking her, and Joshua knew exactly what he had to do. He picked up the knife from the knife rack, and stabbed it down through the top of the zombie's skull. It dropped to the floor and groaned, but then it faded away. Their incoming next mission message flashed, and then it appeared on the screens.

They were to make their way to the local meeting point; it was the car park of a nearby supermarket. They both moved toward the meeting point with extreme caution. Once they had assembled a small army of gamers they went inside the supermarket, and it was in here that they encountered wave after wave of attack.

It was over an hour later before they had completed the second mission. The local supermarket had proved to be tougher than they had imagined. The zombies had emerged from the nearby pubs and houses in droves, and they had proved to be worthy opposition.

Paulina has started to feel exhausted, and the headset was now giving her a headache. She had also noticed a strange smell that was starting to unnerve her. She decided that she had to take the headset off for a little while. She undid the chin strap and paused for a few seconds, then was violently sick. She called out to Joshua, but he could no longer see her anywhere in the game. Where she was previously stood, there was now a foul zombie taking her place.

Joshua started an attack against the new foe. Paulina screamed at him.

"Joshua, it's me Paulina. Take off your headset please!" He was unsure if this was another trick inside the game itself, but Paulina sounded upset. He switched off his headset, and removed the chin strap.

Around them both was a scene of absolute carnage. Men, women and children were lying dead or severely injured. Blood ran red in the streets. Child gamers were attacking anyone who approached them, and dispatching them in any way that they could. Joshua shook his head in disbelief. Then the gamers started coming toward them. Without the headsets on they were now targets too.

Paulina shouted out to Joshua.

"Switch back on your headset but don't put it back on!" She knew it was the only way to stop them being attacked. Joshua instantly did as she had asked, and now both were now showing as live gamers and out of the targeting system. In the distance, sirens could be heard in all directions.

Now they faced a huge dilemma. How could they switch off the entire game? If they switched off the headsets on any of the players, then the players themselves would become targets. If they kept the headsets switched on, then the kill frenzy would continue.

This was a real life purge of the living that had been designed to have maximum impact on the most vulnerable. The game had been launched globally, so the most innocent and frail of the entire world were now under attack in supermarkets and other carefully plotted locations around the world.

There was just no way to turn off the power as the headsets were constantly charging. All they could do was to warn as many people as they could and then drag people out of the game one by one.

It was going to take an awful long time to stop everyone who was involved in the game itself. Then Joshua had a moment of awful realisation.

"Oh no.....we need to go home!" He announced. His face was now as white as a sheet. His stomach was churning and his eyes were filling up with tears. Paulina grabbed hold of his arm before he started to move homeward.

"No Joshua. You can't go home. You can never go back home again. It's not your fault." She took hold of him, and held him tightly. He sobbed openly into her arms. While all around them the End Game violently continued.

All Paulina was left to wonder was who would have the power to unleash such an evil thing? More importantly though, was the question why?

Multiverse

 The washing machine was always set on cycle number six. It would take a more than averagely drunk operator to turn the dial past the usual setting and up to number seven. Richard was far in excess of averagely drunk though as he started the machine and then stumbled back across the room of the open plan flat. The he collapsed on the sofa as the room began to spin. The rhythmic cycle of the washing proved to be very hypnotic. He would be snoring loudly within a matter of minutes. When he awoke, he would slightly more than a hangover to deal with.

 His mouth was dry, and it was almost as if his throat had been grated with the roughest grade of sandpaper. His eyes slowly adjusted to the light and to the surprise of where he had woken up. He had slept on the sofa occasionally and it always confused him when he awoke in somewhere other than his bed.

 The sun was blazing through the rear windows, and the heat inside the flat was stifling. He sat upright and then he felt the full force of his hangover pressing against his temples.

He knew that this was going to be more than a few hours recovery time. This was going to be a two day regret filled hangover. During those two days, there would be numerous promises that this would be the last time he ever touched a drop of alcohol.

 Right now, he knew that it was important that he started to hydrate his body. At the same time, he could pop a few ibuprofen pills and that would help to take the edge off things. As he stood upright he almost fell over his own feet. He was so unsteady; that there was a good chance he was still well over the legal limit.

He steadied himself slowly and then he noticed the anomaly. At first he thought that he might be hallucinating or that his eyes might be playing tricks due to the sunlight now pouring gloriously through the windows. He slowly edged his way toward the kitchen where the doorway was now visible.

He had no idea why or how the unexplained doorway was there. It might have been some kind of elaborate joke that his friends were playing on him, but the wooden doorway now in his kitchen, was very real.

He touched the frame. It was real wood, and the paint was flaking all around the edges. It was an old frame, too old to be part of this new build flat. There was no door hung inside the frame, it was just the frame itself. He had to walk through the doorway to access the sink, and right now he couldn't care less about where the frame had come from. Richard stepped through the frame, and went to the cupboard where he stored the drinking glasses.

He opened the door and went to reach for a pint glass. What he found though, were glasses that did not have any place being in this cupboard. Most of his glasses he owned been 'borrowed' from numerous pubs after nights out in the town. In this cupboard, there were lead crystal glasses. These were the very expensive ones that were seldom used. He took one out from the cupboard, and examined it. He had never seen anything so expensive looking. It was only now that he entertained the thought that he might still be dreaming.

He went to the sink and turned on the tap, he let it run until it was suitably cold, and then he filled the glass. Then he opened the cupboard to find some painkillers. There were no painkillers there. Instead, he found a stash of designer plates that had been stack immaculately. He shook his head in disbelief.

"What the actual fuck?" He said aloud. He shrugged his shoulders and then drank the water, and it tasted amazing. It was nothing like normal tap water should taste. Now his headache had completely disappeared as well.

He honestly had to be dreaming. He decided to go with the flow and see where this dream was going to lead him. He opened up and took a closer look inside all of the kitchen cupboards, and they were filled with expensive food and drink. He decided that he was going to enjoy this dream for as long as it lasted.

He turned around, and the doorway was still there. He decided not to step back through the door though, for some unknown reason he knew that he should squeeze him ample width around it instead. As he edged through the gap at the side, he saw that the decor throughout the flat changed. His worn material sofa was now a plush leather recliner. His thirty two inch television was now a huge eighty inch wall mounted monster. His eyes almost popped out from their sockets as he curiously examined all of his new toys.

His bedroom door suddenly opened. The woman who walked out from the room was ruffling her hair. About her body, she was wearing just a silk nightgown that left nothing to the imagination. Richards jaw almost dropped to the floor as he examined her entire body with his eyes.

"Hey sweet." She said, and then she continued walking over to the bathroom. She only partially closed the door behind her. He could hear the toilet seat being lowered and then the romantic sound of her peeing. It was strangely odd to be witness to this. After all, he had been single for in excess of six months.

He heard the toilet flush and then the sound of the bathroom tap running for a few seconds, the woman then re-emerged. She walked toward him smiling, and then placed a kiss firmly on his lips. She tasted of cherry ice cream. It complimented her smile. Very nice he thought.

"I thought you were going to be out for a few more hours?" She questioned. Richard had no idea how he should answer her but as it was his own dream he thought he might as well try his luck.

"I changed my plans. I thought that you were more important and that I could spend a bit of time in bed with you instead." He said. The woman looked shocked.

"I'm surprised that you have any energy left after last night's performance. I guess that you know by now, I'm not the type of woman who ever says no." She then grabbed his groin, and started to fondle him quite firmly. He pulled away in shock.

"I need to use the bathroom first. Nature calls. Give me a minute and I will be with you." He said. He was worried about his morning after breath, the effects of all the alcohol and even during such an intense dream he still wanted to give a good impression.

"I will be waiting in the bedroom. Don't be too long, I have other people to see today. Time is money. Don't forget that." She then flicked her finger underneath his chin, and she turned and walked slowly back into the bedroom.

The door was still slightly ajar as he walked past the bedroom, she was slowly lifting off her nightgown and her body was absolutely perfect. It was game on; this type of dream seldom happened these days, but this was so realistic that he intended to enjoy it! He quickly walked to the bathroom. At least his electric toothbrush was still there. He quickly squeezed out the toothpaste, and this wasn't his usual cheap bargain basement toothpaste he normally used, this was of a much higher quality.

After he had thoroughly cleaned out his mouth, and quickly washed down all of his essential areas he turned around out of the bathroom and then he walked back into the bedroom. The woman was laid on the bed. She was fully naked. The bed she lay on was an oak four poster. It was something that he had always dreamed of owning.

Again he saw that another huge television was fixed to the wall. He was loving all the detail that his imagination was creating. He sat down on the bed, and the woman was quickly pulling him backward until he lay flat on the luxury down duvet, and then she gently rolled over until she was on top of him.

She expertly took his growing penis in her hand, and massaged him expertly. It was an amazing feeling. When he reached the point that his penis was so hard that he feared it might cause some damage, she rolled a condom over the top of his member. Then she took his semi erect penis into her mouth. Richard arched his back in delight and enjoyed the sensations. Whatever it was that she was doing with her pierced tongue, it was sending shivers down his spine. When she unexpectedly stopped he was about to protest, but then she lowered herself into him and started to grind down against his groin.

"I have to make this quick, as I have another client at two. I need to go home and get myself dressed up for him."

It was now clear that she was a high class hooker and that when this dream ended he would never see her face again, but she did look strangely familiar. Perhaps his mind had pulled her face from his subconscious. Her face was possibly a remnant of memory long hidden. He lay back, and examined her face closely.

Her eyes were rolling back in her head, and even if she were faking the orgasm that she was seemingly encountering, he did not have a care in the world. They both came at the same time in a moment of total unforgiving ecstasy. Then her hands dropped forward until they came to rest on his chest. Her long blonde hair was almost covering her face as she tilted her head downward. She waited for a few seconds before letting out a little chuckle. Then she smiled at him.

"I have to go and clean myself up." She said. The smile on Richards face was so wide, that it probably made him look as if he might have been slightly insane.

"Feel free." He said. He just hoped that this dream might continue on for some time yet.

"That's an extra two thousand." She said.

"And you are worth every penny." He said, as he smiled that insane grin just a little longer.

She collected her clothes from the side and then made her way to the bathroom. He heard the shower running, and the thought of her body being covered in soap and water was making him feel horny again. He rolled over on to his right hand side, and his eyes slowly began to drift. She was in the bathroom for half an hour before she returned. He was gently snoring as she shook his shoulder. She tried a few times to wake him, but without success.

She was in a rush now and his snoring was becoming annoying.

"Hey. Hey! Wake up. I need my money. Hey! You owe me some money!" She shouted.

Richard awoke with a start. He breathed deeply as he came back to consciousness with a start. This was the weirdest thing ever. He was having a dream within a dream, and the woman was still here.

"It's in my wallet; the trousers are on the bathroom floor." He said. The woman went to the bathroom and reached into his trouser pocket. She fumbled through his wallet. She stormed back into the bedroom.

"Is this some kind of fucking joke?" She said. There was a five pound note in the wallet, and four pound twenty three in loose change. "You owe me twelve thousand. Ten for last night, and another two for this morning. Now where the fuck is my money? You said you were going to get it earlier!" She shouted.

Richard started to giggle. "I would have had more, but I had a kebab on the way home. Twelve thousand pounds, I mean seriously, I really do wish that I had that kind of money. I don't even have twelve pound to my name." He said. Then he laughed out loud. "This is an amazing dream." He said quietly. He then rolled back over and closed his eyes again. It was time to go back to sleep again and then he could wake up smiling.

It was then that the electricity surged through his body and in a shocking moment of realization, he understood that the idea of this being an insane dream was finally over. Now as the current ripped through his body, his fingers clawed and his back arched upward. This was actually a nightmare that was only just about to begin.

He had never even thought about how much pain a taser would inflict on his body. Now that he had experience it fist hand it was something that he never wanted to be repeated. When he awoke again, he knew that he had been unconscious but he had no idea how long for. His hands and feet were tied, and his mouth had been gagged. He was now no longer in the bedroom. Instead he had woken up in a bathtub, and he was cold. He was actually very cold.

He was naked, and his body was surrounded by ice. This was the most fucked up dream turned into a nightmare that he had ever experienced. Then the hooded man came into the room along with the hooker. The guy was around six feet tall, and he was carrying what looked like a picnic box. It was a messed up sight. The hooker then pulled the gag away from Richard's mouth.

"I need the PIN numbers for your credit cards." She then reeled of the name of every card in his wallet. He gave her all of the PIN numbers to each card in turn. They would not do her any good though; each card was already maxed out. Some were cards were over limits now too, thanks to the recent charges they had added for late payments.

The woman took all of the numbers down, and then turned to face the hooded man.

"Watch him while I go to the bank." She instructed and then she disappeared from the room. She was gone at least twenty minutes. When she returned her face was visibly furious.

"Not one fucking penny in any of them!" She shouted. Then she started throwing each of the cards, one by one into Richards face. Richard was still smiling. He felt dazed by the dream, and his body was comfortably numb from the effects of the ice. "You know what to do." She said to the hooded man and he nodded.

"You better leave the room; it's going to be messy." He warned her.

"Not a chance. I want to see every little thing. Every single little cut." Then she sat down on the edge of the toilet.

The hooded man turned Richard over. He was face down in the ice, and even when he turned his head fully to the side, he could barely breathe through the single exposed nostril. He no longer wanted to be a part of this nightmare. He wondered when his mind would call time on this episode and suddenly scare him awake. He hoped that it would not be much longer.

He did not feel the scalpel expertly slicing down into his skin. He still felt numb as his kidney was removed. He saw the man placing a bloodied ball of what looked like meat into an ice filled container. Then after a slight realignment of the body, his liver was also removed.

"That's more than enough to cover the debt." The hooded man said. The hooker smiled a wry smile. Then her face turned angry once again.

"I will tell you when to stop. Not before. Now take out his pancreas next." She said. Then she opened up her legs, and as the hooded man started making another incision. She started to pleasure herself. She was becoming more and more excited at the thought of how much money she was going to be making later that day.

Richard now badly wanted to wake up. He was now desperate to return to reality. At first he was numb, but now he was feeling every incision. The pain was quite unlike anything he had ever thought possible. As nightmares ranked, this was the absolute worst one he had ever experienced. The hooded man then carefully placed the pancreas into the ice box. He then turned to face the hooker, who was now moaning with pleasure from the self gratification. She was close to coming as she expertly worked her fingers inside of herself. "More?" He asked.

The prostitutes' breathing was heavy, and she was gasping for breath. She was experienced a powerful orgasm, but she nodded.

"The corneas." She managed to say in-between her gasps. The hooded man then tilted Richard's head upright slightly. Richard could see that the ice filled bath was now a dark red colour. It was his own blood that was now smothered over his skin. Then he saw the scalpel coming toward his eye and he desperately wanted to close his eyes to stop what he was about to see. Richard screamed as the hooded man dug straight through the eyelid, and then in turn he scooped out both of Richard's eyes from the sockets. At that point, Richard mercifully passed out.

The hooker had already reached orgasm twice more before the lungs and the heart were removed from the body. They had harvested everything that they could take from the client. Now she could probably afford to retire. She loved it when the clients were wealthy but refused to pay for services rendered. This was only the fifth total body harvest she had instructed, but this would definitely be the last. Now they would have to remove all traces of them being present. There were a few things left they had to do.

The hooded man walked into the hallway. He then returned in to the bathroom and pointed the shotgun at the man's head. A mass of teeth and brains exploded against the bath and sprayed a few feet up the wall. Chunks of tiles fell from the surrounding area, and the bloodied mess would take a while to properly identify. There was no way that any dental records could be used now.

They cut off both hands from the body and placed these in the box with the organs. Then they left the flat arm in arm. The hooded man was carrying the ice box with him. They had to get the parts to the doctors quickly. It would take D.N.A sampling before the victim would be identified, and that would take valuable time. By then, they would both be far away.

When Richard returned to the flat, he found that the door was open. He cursed his stupidity for leaving the hooker in the house alone. He thought that he would arrive back home much earlier, and if it wasn't for the stupid flat battery on the car he would probably have been back over an hour ago. He had her money with him and a little bonus for her for making her wait so long. He had hoped to use her again.

Now the chances were that she would probably have taken all that she could from the flat, and no doubt she had accomplices who would have helped her. He dashed into the front room, but everything seemed to still be in place. It was odd, but at least she hadn't robbed him.

He then walked into the bedroom, and found that the woman was gone. Her clothes were gone and the bed was still a mess. This is now slightly more confusing. Perhaps she had another client to see, but would return later for her reward. If she did, then he may use her again for the night. Then he thought that she might be in the bath! He hadn''t even looked there. He needed to pee, so he hoped that she wasn't locked in the bathroom. He walked over to the bathroom door and realised that it wasn't locked. He pulled down the handle, carefully so as not to surprise her if she was in the bath, but the bathroom was in darkness. He pulled down the cable that turned on the bathroom light, and then he saw it before him. The scene was like something from one of the worst horror movies that you could imagine.

Unknown to him, the police had already been called and they arrived shortly after he had made the discovery of the body. A neighbour had reported hearing something like an explosion in the flat above her, and with limited personnel on duty, they had responded as quickly as they could. When they entered the open door of the flat, they found Richard huddled in a corner of the hallway.

Richard was covered in his own vomit, and he was rocking backward and forward in the corner. He was muttering something to himself. One of the officers leaned forward so that he could hear the words he was whispering. "Look at his tattoos, look at his tattoos." He was just repeating the same thing over and over again.

The other policeman slowly and carefully entered the bathroom and he too almost vomited at the sight before him. Richard held his arms out in front of him and the body that lay in the bathtub was tattooed in exactly the same places. It was covered in exactly the same markings. Each of the two men had identical tattoos, even down to the minute detail. In the kitchen away from prying eyes, the wooden portal began to fade. There was no reason for the bridge to remain open any longer.

His guardians had reached out to another plane in the multiverse, and it had saved him from death yet again. This was the eighth time that they had saved him from himself. There were a finite number of other universes to take the others Richard's from. The guardians knew the best way to play the game, and they loved to interfere in the future of humanity.

The police entered the flat by breaking down the door. They searched inside every room, but there was no trace of the missing man. He had been reported missing after failing to attend work for eight days. His colleagues thought that his heavy drinking had finally taken its toll on his body, and in a way it had. In the kitchen, the washing machine flashed endlessly. Cycle seven had finished. The guardians had used this method of accessing duplicate universes before, and it was a strangely effective glitch. The policeman turned the dial to zero, and switched the machine off completely. The door to this universe was now completely closed from both sides.

New Years Eve

The party had been planned with meticulous care. No expense had been spared with the location, the food or the entertainment. They would also experience the most lavish New Year's Eve toast that money could buy. Only the finest champagne and caviar was to be supplied for everyone lucky enough to be in attendance. As for the crowd assembled in the suite, they were a collection of the wealthiest men and women in the world.

Tickets to this event were by exclusive invitation only. Each guest had signed a disclaimer, that whatever happened during the evening, nothing would be disclosed outside of the room. It was the sign of a potentially immense party. Knowing the host, it was essential that privacy was maintained both for himself and for the invitees. If the press were to get hold of what had happened at some of the past events he had held, there would have been reports that could bring down the very highest in power.

The host watched on in silence from a secluded corner. He was stood behind two way glass. He could see and hear them, but they had no idea that he was there watching them all. It was just as he had expected. Every conversation that he could hear was virtually the same. Diamond jewellery was sparkling in abundance, and everybody looked the part in designer dresses and suits. This New Year's Eve event would truly go down in history, he would make sure of that.

It was half an hour to midnight but there had still been no sign of the host. Suzanne Reinhold was anxious to see him in the flesh. She had heard stories about how fabulously wealthy he was but she had never once met the host personally. She was making conversation with the editor of a high class magazine; she had met her a few times previously at this type of event, but she could not remember her name despite racking her brain.

"When do you think we will get to see the elusive Stefan?" She asked. The woman who she was addressing was Sylvia Arkan. Her net worth had been estimated at around £740 million, but she was way down the list of net worth compared to the some of the exclusive crowd in attendance.

"My darling I am sure he will make himself known before midnight, perhaps then the party will begin. It's been a little bit of a slow starter." She had very little interest in continuing the conversation; this woman had bored her frightfully on the few previous occasions that they had met. She then excused herself and walked across the room pretending that she had just seen an old acquaintance.

It was just a few minutes to midnight when the host had seen enough. He adjusted his tie and cuffs. This was to be the grand finale, and he was ready to go out of this life with a bang. He took a few deep breaths, and then when he was ready, he stepped out from his private viewing room. As he entered the crowd, there was a round of applause for the host.

He had not been seen in public for more than eight weeks and he looked to have aged terribly. He was thinner than most remembered him, and his hair had turned completely grey. There were a few gasps as he walked out through the assembled guests. He shook numerous hands firmly and kissed expensive smelling female cheeks as he made his way toward the stage. The music started to lower as he climbed the steps to address the gathered guests.

When he reached the microphone positioned at the centre of the stage, the music had been turned off completely. Then he began to address the gathered crowd.

"Ladies and Gentlemen. If I could have your attention please." He started. The chattering rudely continued on for a few seconds more, but then the already lubricated crowd were quiet enough for him to start his speech.

"I have invited all of you here tonight for a reason. All of you who are gathered in this room, myself included, well we are quite simply the richest people alive on this planet." There was a loud cheer and applause and a great deal of laughter in the room at hearing the statement. The host was smiling; he was more than used to hearing this sort of pompous arrogance from his associates.

"I have come to know most of you quite well through social gatherings just like this one. Tonight though, I want it to be momentous. I want us all to celebrate just how rich we are."

At this point, there was an even louder cheer than the previous one. He smiled in anticipation of what was yet to come. He raised his hands in front of him, and gestured for the crowd to calm down. There was movement through the hall as trays of champagne were carrier on silver platters, to be distributed to each member of the gathered crowd.

"To see in the new-year as you can see, I have purchased only the finest champagne, and for those of you who are not drinking, of which I assume there are very few, there is a no alcohol option available. I will ask you to please to wait until twelve strikes before you drink from your glasses though. There is very little time left to wait."

The champagne was distributed to each and every person on the room, and then once everyone had a glass in hand, the host then turned on a huge projection screen. On the screen was a countdown timer, which was currently running at thirty nine seconds left until midnight. It was almost time.

"When the countdown reaches ten, if I could please ask you all to raise up your glasses together, so that we can toast the new-year in the exclusive club of ours, for we are the elite." Everyone now began holding up there glasses in anticipation of seeing in the new-year. As the clock descended down to just ten seconds to midnight, the assembled crowd joined together in counting down from ten to one. When the counter reached zero, it was midnight, and there was a loud cheer from all of those who were present, and the glasses were swiftly emptied while cheers erupted throughout the hall. The glasses were all drained dry.

It was around ten minutes past twelve, when the host returned to the stage and then began to address everyone present once again.

"May I now wish you a happy new year, and ask you for another few moments of your precious time." The crowd were now somehow subdued, and seemed a lot less energetic than before. "I would ask you all, if you could please take a seat while I explain what is about to happen."

Chairs were then brought into the hall by the waiting staff, and each of the guests seemed glad to be able to sit down. A few had glazed looks, and some even appeared to be blind drunk. It was a very unique glass of champagne that they had been given though.

"I need to tell you all a short story, and I know that you love to hear my stories. It was seven years ago, that I was travelling through Bulgaria when I came across a gypsy boy. He was begging me for money. He said that he was hungry and he was cold. How many times have we heard the cheek of beggars like this I ask?" A few of the crowd started grumbling, and a few nodded their heads in agreement. He then continued. "As most of you will know, I never ever carry cash about my person. I dismissed the boy and my aides moved him away from the path.

The next day he had the audacity to come back again. He was in exactly in the same dirty clothes, and he was begging me once more to help him. On my instruction my aides removed him again, only this time they threw him off the path. As his frail and skinny body landed, he smashed his head on the pavement, and it caused serious injuries to his brain.

Three days later the boy died in agony. I had his death hushed up. I paid off the authorities and then I forgot all about it, or so I thought. When I returned home a week later, I was awakened at night by something I could not even begin to understand. The dead boy was stood right next to my bed and his cold hand was shaking my arm until I awoke.

At first I thought that I was dreaming the whole thing, but I could feel how cold his skin was as it touched mine. He spoke to me and I shouted at him in fear and anger for him to get out, but he would not leave. He repeated the same words to me over and over again, he kept on saying 'I am hungry and cold, please help me to get warm'

I ran out from my house in genuine fear. I drove around London for hours, and I would not return home until it was daylight. When I went back inside the house, there was no sign of the boy. That night, I drank copious amounts of alcohol. I was sure that the apparition had been the work of my imagination. Then at three in the morning, I felt that cold hand on my skin as the child was waking me once again.

I closed my eyes, and covered my head with a pillow, but that small hand would not stop shaking at my arm. I left my house again, and I walked the streets. I was still too drunk to even contemplate driving anywhere.

Whilst I was walking those streets, I came across scenes of utter destitution. I had never seen the streets of my hometown at this time of the morning before, especially not on foot. There were homeless people everywhere. Men, women, and the occasional teenager and even children too. They were all desperate, all hungry, and all cold. Each of them would look at me with longing eyes. They knew that I could help them, if only I would choose to do so. I withdrew a few hundred pounds, and I gave it all out. I hoped that my kindness might see the spirit of that dead child appeased. I still refused to return home until daylight, and once again I found that the spirit was gone.

The next night, I stayed in one of my other apartments, but yet again at three in the morning the spirit of the child returned. I had to try and somehow find a way to communicate with the spirit. I told the boy that I was helping others and that I was sorry for what had happened to him.

I tried to assure him that it wasn't my fault. His eyes were now just sunken hollows, and he kept on repeating the same thing over and over, that he was hungry and cold, and that he needed to get warm.

Night after night the spirit would continue to awaken me. I tried using sleeping tablets but they did not work. I tried Valium, but that didn't work either. Every single night he returned over and over again. If I slept during the day, he would come to me and wake me in the daylight. It started to drive me insane. I turned to the church for help, then to doctors, I even organised a private exorcism, but no one could help me. The child's spirit was not evil. For some reason, it just could not leave my side."

The guests were now suitably comfortable in their seats. Some had wet themselves; some were dribbling from the corners of their mouths. Others were leaning back on the chairs and were just staring blankly at the ceiling. His audience were attentive and quiet. He liked the way that the idle chatter had now died completely so he continued with the story without interruption.

"Just a month ago, I was contemplating taking my own life. I had given away thousands and thousands of pounds anonymously to people on the street. I was always in disguise for fear that if anyone recognised me they might attack me, or my pictures would appear in the press. I could not be seen. I would wake to the feel of the child's cold arm on my skin, and then in a moment of sudden euphoria, I realised just how I could help him.

The glasses that you drank from earlier, I am sad to tell you that they were all laced with a deadly toxin. It is fatal in all cases. There is no known antidote. The only person to not drink from the glasses was me. Don't worry though I shall be joining you soon. The disclaimer that you all signed earlier states that you are a willing participant in a mass suicide event, and you have taken this toxin of your own free will, but none of you would have taken the time to read this. This disclaimer will also give my assistants access to all of your funds. The waiting staff have been hired from amongst the world's best ethical hackers. They will now be able to access your finances wherever in the world they may be hidden away from prying eyes.

All of this money will be redistributed to the poorest people in society. Of course I know that this won't stop the child from haunting me, but rest assured it will alleviate a huge amount of suffering in the world. A small amount of people, were never meant to have the enormous amounts that we have gathered at the expense and toil of the poorest."

Stefan then took a glass of champagne from the side of the stage, and then walked back over to the microphone. Then he raised the glass up to his face.

"I would toast your health but it would be pointless. Instead, I will drink to the health of those who we just walk past on the streets every single day. To those we fail to see or embrace. To those who never had a chance in life. Perhaps now they can learn to breathe a little more easily." He then drank the contents of the glass, and he smiled. His torment was finally going to be over.

A few minutes passed and his body slumped down on to the stage. It didn't hurt like he thought it would. When he had finally passed over the boy walked to the side of his body. Stefan's soul escaped from its mortal shell and once it was free, it met the boy's spirit.

"I'm cold and hungry, will you keep me warm?" The boy asked.

"I can only try." He said. He put his arms around the boy, as he tried to comfort him. He looked around the hall, and what he saw brought him little peace.

The hall was now full of lost souls, each of whom was now searching for a direction in which to move forward. Each of them was now without worldly possessions or money. Each of them was now truly saddened at the thought of the people that they had left behind. They no longer wanted money, they just wanted to see their own families for one last moment but that had now been taken from them. Each of them was drawn to the boy; each of them was also desperate for warmth.

The boy had no need for money anymore. He no longer felt the pains of hunger, but now he had plenty of company with nothing else to do, but to keep him warm.

To Stop My Bones from Rotting

The year was 1979 it will be a year that I will always remember as long as I live. Back then the world was a totally different place. I had encountered many unexplained events, and equally witnessed as many hoaxes. Nothing had prepared me for the encounter that was about to happen in a sleepy little market town called Andover in Hampshire.

It was the year that I was called to assist a family on a housing estate called Admirals Way, and on a quiet night in Collingwood walk, that was where I encountered the most malevolent spirit I have ever come across. He was known by the name of Eric. This is my story.

I waited patiently outside of the room. Emily Walters was laid down on her bed; this was the only way that the entity would agree to talk to her. I could hear Emily asking questions, and the gentle knocks on the wall, which seemed to respond quickly to each of the questions she asked. Then Emily decided that she would ask if I could join her in the room.

"Eric, Mr Savin is my friend, do you mind if he comes in to my room?" There was a single knock on the wall. This meant yes. Two knocks meant no. It was a simple code they had devised between them to enable them to communicate.

I walked slowly into the room. I was careful not to disturb the energy that I had already felt was growing within the bedroom. It was imperative that I showed no fear. I instantly began to try to communicate with the entity present.

"If you can hear me Eric, would you be happy for me to ask you some questions?" I was already prepared to be disappointed, but then the knock of response came. It was located right in the middle of the girl's bedroom wall. There could be a simple explanation, as the bedroom wall was above an archway above a footpath, and it was backing on to the next door neighbour's house. I would have to find a way to rule any mischievous neighbours out.

"Eric, can you knock on Emily's headboard for me, just so I can know that you are there." I placed my hand on the wooden headboard, and I felt an impact striking on the wood. The single knock was a relief to feel. This wasn't a hoax perpetrated by the neighbours after all, but there still might be another simple explanation.

"Can you please knock on the bedroom door for me please Eric?" I didn't have chance to move across the room, but the knock on the bedroom door was instant. It was much louder than the knock on the headboard. "Thank you Eric. Now can you tell me how old you are please?" I asked.

The knocking started back on the wall adjacent to the neighbour's house. I counted that there were twelve knocks in total. Each knock was slow and exacted with the same amount of force.

"Did you die in this house Eric?" I asked. There was a pause for quite a few seconds, and then there was a single loud solitary knock. It was a definite yes. Then there was silence. The knocking ceased completely despite Emily asked numerous further questions, there were no more replies during that first encounter. I was worried that I had asked the wrong question.

Emily was looking tired. The dark bags under her eyes made it appear as if she hadn't slept for a few days. I did not want to keep her awake, and it already looked as if it were past her bedtime. I decided to call it a night. I would return soon enough though. I wanted to investigate this case further.

The housing estate had been built in the late sixties. The houses were built to help house the influx of people heading down to the South. These people were part of an overflow from London. I could find very little information about the land in which the estate was built on. There appeared to be nothing out of the ordinary about the location of the house either.

There was nothing peculiar about the family as far as I could tell. There were two sisters Emily who was twelve and Marie who was ten and one younger brother called Nigel who was six. The parents and the three children were all living in the three bedroom house, and the only thing out of the ordinary, was that Emily was in direct communication with something that no one could comprehend.

Emily was a frail looking girl as I recall. She had very few friends and led quite a sheltered life. She was happiest when she was reading or listening to music, and she was not at all fazed by the communication that she had established with Eric. I always had the impression that she felt quite lonely, but she was quite content within herself. She was certainly intelligent, and had quickly established a way to talk directly with Eric just by using the knocking sounds he made.

The knocking sounds had first been heard when the two sisters had been laid in the bedroom on Easter Sunday. It was the day of the resurrection of Christ and the initial contact may have held some significance, but there was no way to establish this for sure.

At first, both the girls had thought the same as I had. They thought that the neighbours might have been responsible for the knocking, but then Emily had whispered questions, and there was no way that any neighbour could have heard the questions at the level she had asked them and Eric had answered them all by saying yes or no by one or two knocks.

The sisters had then seen this as nothing more than a friendly game, but only Emily would receive the answers from Eric. I felt that her age might have been a factor, as she was close to thirteen and coming up to what was a difficult age in any girl's life. The conversations with Eric had rapidly become a nightly event, and Eric had spelt out his name by knocks to represent each letter in his name. It was a lengthy process, but she found it rewarding for her to be able to communicate with the spirit directly.

I was called in by the child's father, when Emily had taken to spending an inordinate amount of time laid in bed talking to Eric. He was worried that her education might be starting to suffer from all of her late nights. The local police and even the clergy had both visited the house, and all of them had witnessed the rapping on the walls, but none were able to offer up any explanation. At this point, I was contacted by a friend of the family, because of my spiritualist connections.

On my second visit, I decided to take a former colleague of mine by the name of Margaret Simmons. As a medium Margaret hardly looked the part. She was a large woman in her later forties, whose face was adorned with dark thick horn rimmed spectacles. Her hair was cheaply permed, and she always smelt like animal fur (probably due to the fact that she had at least ten cats). There may have been more than twelve, but I never felt inclined to ask the exact number.

Margaret was feeling uneasy as I drove her to the house. My car was a brown Austin Allegro back then, and it always smelt heavily of petrol. It was late May and the heat was already quite humid, and she had to keep the window of the car wound down for the duration of the journey. Despite our best efforts, I had to pull the car over twice during the trip so that she could vomit at the side of the road. She assured me that she would be fine, but by the time we reached Andover her face was as white as a sheet.

The warm local air smelt of a heady mixture of chemicals and expensive tea. The scents travelled from the nearby industrial estate, and seemed to linger over the entire estate. Children were happily playing on steel climbing structures that in this day and age, would probably never pass a health and safety examination. It was a carefree time, and I miss those days a great deal. Writing this reminds me of how much I miss Margaret too.

As we approached the house Margaret became unsteady. I took hold of her arm to support her, and I allowed her to gather her breath before I knocked on the door of the house. Mrs Walters opened the door and welcomed us both into the hallway. I had not noticed the decor on my previous visit, but the house was painted brightly. It was welcoming and warm. Mrs Walters went to close the door and at that point, the door slammed closed all by itself.

Mrs Walters jumped back in surprise and I must admit that at that moment, my heart was pounding heavily in my chest. I was used to strange activity, but the unexpected shock would still send adrenaline coursing through my entire body. My legs were shaking by themselves and it took me a few seconds to regain control of my body completely.

Margaret was still looking pale and uncomfortable. I asked if she was alright to continue, and her eyes told me that she was afraid, but she insisted that she was fine. I was reluctant, but she assured me that everything would be alright. I felt an unusual amount of energy was already building within the house.

There were six chairs placed around the kitchen table; Margaret sat at the head of the table. I sat next to her. Emily was upstairs in her bedroom but her parents joined us to sit at the table. They both looked as if they needed more sleep. Both the parents were showing signs of too many late nights. Worry lines were etched onto both of their faces.

Margaret took candles and incense out from her bag and placed them onto the table. She then took out her lighter and lit them all one by one. The incense smelt sweet and rich and the air felt somehow cleaner and instantly lighter. I placed my tape recorder on to the table to my left hand side. I had placed fresh batteries inside the compartment. Once I was sure that we were ready, I pressed the record and play buttons down together. I had forty five minutes of recording time on this side of the C90 tape.

The room fell quiet without anyone having to say a single word. Margaret stared into the flame that was directly in front of her. Within a few moments her eyes became glazed. She looked as if she were hypnotised as she focused on the centre of the flame. Then she began to speak.

"I can see a child present. It is a young boy. He has been here for a very long time." She said. I started to make notes. I always felt the need to do this, in case the tape recordings ever failed.

There were a few moments of silence before she spoke again. "His name is Eric Colvin. He faced a violent death here. His body.....his body remains under the house. His body lies....there." She then pointed toward the corner of the kitchen floor. The mother and father both looked unnerved to hear that there may be the body of a child underneath the house that they had lived in for five years.

Then there was a loud bang on the kitchen wall, which made everyone in the room jump (except for Margaret who was seemingly oblivious to the loud bang). I decided to ask a question.

"Can we talk to Eric directly? Eric. Do you want to talk to us through Margaret?" Margaret's head fell forward and then after a few seconds she then spoke again.

"He's fighting me. He's hiding his intentions. There's something that he's not telling."

Two loud knocks on the wall were so intense, the floor underneath us felt as if it was moving from the impacts. Mrs Walters screamed and jumped up from her chair. She jumped on her husband's lap and hugged him tightly. There were tears in her eyes. By the look on his face, it seemed that her husband seemed equally as frightened of what he had just witnessed. Then Margaret spoke again.

"He wants to take over her body. He wants to feel alive again." Margaret then tried to talk directly to the spirit. "Eric, you cannot possess the living. You need to accept your fate and continue on with your journey. If you do not let go, you will remain trapped here forever. Do you understand me Eric?" There was a single knock on the middle of the wooden table. One knock that meant he understood. Margaret seemed a little relieved. "You must leave Emily and begin to move toward the light. Will you do that for me Eric?" She asked. The room was silent for a few terrible moments while everyone awaited the response. Then there was a knock in the middle of the table again. Less than a second later, it was followed by a second. The second knock came with such force, that it left a crack the middle of the table. It was clear that Eric was not ready to leave the house yet.

Margaret extinguished the flames. She felt entirely drained, and the whole episode had taken less than five minutes from start to finish. The energy of the entity had been intense. I turned off the tape recorder and then rewound the tape. I would listen to it on my stereo later that evening with the volume high enough to hear any voices that we might have captured other than our own.

The couple thanked both Margaret and I for coming to try and help, but I feared that I had actually made the situation worse. When we left the house and returned to the car, Margaret stopped me before I could unlock the car.

"I couldn't tell you in there, but we have to try and help the girl. Eric is fully intent on possessing her body. He wants to return to the living. He will do whatever it takes to get what he wants." She said. Her face was red, and it was clear that she was deadly serious.

"So what can we do to help her?" I asked.

"I have no idea, but we have to make sure that we do it fast. His entity is growing in strength. Every time she talks with him, the connection between the living and the dead grows stronger. We have to stop her talking with him." It made perfect sense.

I dropped Margaret back at her home. I declined her offer of coming into her home for a warm drink. Sadly this was due to my allergy to animal hair. She looked a lonely woman as she climbed steps on the path up to her bungalow. I could see cats jumping onto her window ledge.

It was almost as if they had already sensed the return of the woman who fed them daily. I wondered just how much of the feelings of loneliness those cats covered up. Margaret waved before she closed the door, and I waved politely in return. I would never see her alive again.

I sat with a hot cup of cocoa in my favourite leather chair. It was a single sugary luxury that I had afforded myself and it felt good to relax. I took the tape recorder out from my bag and uncoiled the thick headphone flex. I removed the tape from the portable tape recorder, and placed in to the cassette deck of my music centre. I then cupped the black plastic foam edged headphones over my ears and pushed the play button. I listened to the tape intently.

I heard the exact events of the evening. I replayed them over and over again. I rewound the tape numerous times but I heard nothing out of the ordinary. I started to doze off from the effects of the cocoa and the tape continued on past the point where I had ended the recording. I was jolted awake as I heard the voice which then echoed out from the tape. I rewound it back just a few seconds so that I could ensure that the voice was genuine. Then I heard the message again. It was a child's voice, it spoke calmly, it said.

"I'm taking her and I will end all who try to stop me."

I knocked the front door repeatedly. I had rung her phone maybe ten or twenty times during the following two days, and Margaret had not answered once. I had taken the time to drive to her bungalow and had tried in vain to get her to answer the door. I tried the door handle, and it was locked. I walked to the back of the building and I saw that her kitchen window was open. I pulled the dustbin over and carefully climbed up.

Reaching around inside of the frame, I managed to open the large side window. I cursed as I cut my finger on the edge of the window latch. I climbed uneasily through the open window, and I knew by the smell, that there was something not right within the house.

The smell was a mixture of cat urine, faeces, and of something else. The smell was of something much nastier. I walked slowly through the house, shouting Margaret's name as I left the kitchen and walked into the hallway. When I entered the living room, I found Margaret's body. The coroner would later estimate that she had been dead for around forty five hours. She appeared to have died less than three hours after I had left her. She died with a look of fright etched onto her face. Her eyes were still wide open.

Cats were sat comfortably on her cold dead body. Some had been toying with her corpse; others had started to bite into her flesh. The official cause of death was recorded as being a massive heart attack. If you want my personal opinion, I think that something scared her to death.

One thing I did notice in-between my bouts of sneezing that had become persistent due to my allergy, was that the name 'Eric' had been carved into the arm of her leather chair, along with the sign of the cross. Margaret had used her fingernails to scratch the name and symbol in the chair, and it had been her final ever act on this Earth.

I was scared. I will freely admit to it now. Back then it was hard not to admit it to the family. I felt as if I were out of my depth. Every day the family would call and they would leave numerous messages begging for me for help them. I was just too frightened to return to the house. I thought that if I just ignored them, then the whole thing might just fade away. It was too late for me to back out now though. I awoke one morning at three in the morning to see a young boy stood at the base of my bed. The boy was shaking my foot until I awoke.

I sat upright, and switched on my bedside lamp. I expected the figure to fade as every illusion does. The boy then said. 'Tag, you're it! Eric says that it's your turn next!" It said, and then the apparition was gone. I then realised that I had no choice. I had to see it through right to the very end, no matter what the cost to myself.

I seldom called on my brother for any favours. Tonight it would be a matter of life or death for me and I was positive of that. I just hoped that I had interpreted the last message that Margaret had left for me correctly. I explained everything to my brother and although reluctant to believe such a tale, he could see just how frightened I was.

He agreed to help me. Now I just had to convince the child's parents that I knew how to end their nightmare. In truth though, I had no clue if it would even work. I just had to try.

When Mr Walters opened the door, he looked as if he had aged ten years or more in the last few days. He told me how the banging on the walls had continued every day and night. Every time they had managed to fall asleep, the banging would wake them all up again. They had even tried staying with a friend for the night, and the entity had followed them there. It had slammed every door in the house simultaneously, and there friend had quickly asked the family to leave and never to return.

I explained my plan, and Mr Walters said that he was happy to help, but we first had to make sure that the body of the child was actually buried underneath the house.

The three of us lifted up the floorboards of the kitchen and then we took turns to dig. It was back breaking work, and the kitchen looked almost like a war zone. It was hours before we hit upon something solid in the clay. I jumped into the hole, and pulled at the solid fragment. It was a bone, and it looked as if it were from a leg.

The bone was not fully grown and probably belonged to a young child. Within an hour we had uncovered most of the child's remnants. Then we found the skull. It had been cracked, and it appeared that the child had suffered from a severe trauma to the head. Now I had to distract Eric long enough for my brother to do what he needed to do.

Emily was in her room and was laid on her bed. She had been pleading with Eric to leave the family alone. She herself was at her wits end and felt hopeless. Every time she asked to be left in peace Eric would answer no. He always knocked twice, no matter how much she pleaded with him. I climbed the stairs leaving my brother to get out from the house as quickly as he could. I gave him the keys to my car and it was only a short car journey to where he needed to be. I had to get Eric's attention. I entered the room without invitation and then I began to shout out loud.

"Eric, I think you are a bloody big fraud and a liar!" There was silence for a few seconds then followed two loud knocks on the headboard above Emily's head.

The girl appeared to be dazed and confused. She had been deep in conversation with Eric and it seemed that she could now communicate directly with the entity itself.

"Eric said that he loves me. That he's going to be with me forever." She said. There was no point trying to talk to the girl. I had to appeal directly to Eric.

"I won't let you take her!" I shouted. "There is nothing here for you Eric. You are just a fraud and a liar. I don't think you even exist!" The door then slammed closed behind me. On the far wall above the child's bed, the wall itself then seemed to start to pulsate.

A dark circular portal then began to open within the wall. It slowly grew in size. Then the decomposed hands of a child slowly started to reach out from the void. It was almost as if the hands themselves were extending the size of the portal, enabling the child to have enough room to exit the void. Eric was trying to cross the barrier and he was now ready to enter the world of the living once more. Eric climbed slowly out from the wall, and then dropped to his feet on the carpeted bedroom floor.

"What do you want from us Eric?" I demanded to know. The child looked up directly at my eyes, his own eyes appeared soulless.

"I'm here to rest and stop my bones from rotting." He replied and then he turned, and started to move across the room toward the bed where Emily lay helpless.

In the churchyard less than two miles away, a shovel was hastily being driven into the solid ground. The hole did not have to be very deep; it just had to be deep enough to cover the bag of bones that I had instructed my brother to remove from the house. The whole story and the events of the evening had been completely insane, and if he didn't get arrested then I would owe my brother at least a family tin of pale ale or a bottle of whiskey for this favour. The sweat was pouring off his brow, but still he continued to dig.

As the entity moved toward the girl, I had to think fast.

"There's no point in taking the girl. She's terminally ill. She has less than a year to live." It was a lie, but it was the best thing that I could come up with considering what I was currently experiencing. How I wished that there was a way to record what I was seeing right now. My words seemed to have the desired effect. Eric stopped in his tracks and turned back to face me.

"I want to live again. If not in her, then in whom shall I live in?" He asked.

"Take me instead." I insisted. I had every faith that my brother would soon finish the task at hand.

Eric walked toward me and as he did, I tried to back up toward the door. Now I found myself frozen to the spot. I fell down to my knees, and I was completely at Eric's mercy. As Eric reached where I knelt, he placed two of his bony fingers inside of my open mouth. I could taste the decay, and it made me want to gag. I was unable to do even retch. I could not move an inch.

I tried to close my eyes but it was impossible. I would have to face my destiny with my eyes wide open. I prayed silently to myself that this would be over quickly.

The hole was just about deep enough. He threw the bag of bones into the hole of the makeshift grave. The bones were now on hallowed ground and he started to shovel the dirt back into the hole covering the body.

Eric was not aware that he had been tricked. All he was now aware of was that parts of his badly decomposed body were now starting to fade away. His fingers had been swallowed by the new host, but it wasn't enough to possess the living. Eric fell down to his knees. He was unaware of what was happening to him. The dark portal on the bedroom wall then began to close, and I felt confident that everything was going to be alright.

Emily sat upright on her bed; she was now wide awake and fully aware of what was happening.

"Help me!" Eric shouted, and he held his hand out to her. Emily leant forward from the bed, and tried to reach for his hand. I shouted out to her.

"Don't touch him; don't talk to him. Break the bond. You have to let him go!"

Emily ignored my words and continued to try and reach for Eric's hand. It was too late though. Eric was going to find peace in death for the first time in ninety years. As his spirit disappeared through the bedroom floor, Emily began to cry. I wasn't sure if they were tears of joy or tears of pain. All I knew for certain is that the connection that they had would now be broken forever.

I returned to the house three months later just for my own piece of mind. Everything had been quiet ever since the events of that night. The family were happy and content and I was sure in time that the memories of those few months would probably become distorted and forgotten as the years passed by. I did not return to that house ever again.

My brother tried to research exactly who Eric was. He was determined that he should at least have a makeshift gravestone, but he never uncovered any more information about the child. If he ever asked me his name I would never tell.

As I reached my fingers inside of the man's mouth, my spirit entered into his body, his spirit transferred into mine and took my place in the afterlife. He tried to call out to the girl for help, but I stopped him. He was an unwelcoming host, and now I have a chance at life that I thought I had lost for almost a century.

My name is Eric, and I was murdered when I was twelve years old. Now I live again.

This story was based on true events. An entity had existed called Eric, who liked to rap on walls and developed a way to communicate with the living. For nearly fifty years the true story has been hidden, but there are those out there who know the whole truth. Emily actually exists, but her real identity still remains a mystery.

Rewind.

It was the strangest party, the weirdest dream ever. It was freaking him out big time. She was alive again. She was here in the bed next to him. The dream felt so lifelike, that it was already stirring up so many old memories.

The touch of her skin was real. He felt he warmth of her body next to his. The amount of space she had left him on the bed. He was positioned so close to the edge that he might fall. If he fell then the dream would be over, and he would wake up alone again. He didn't want to wake up just yet though. He thought back at all that had happened leading up to this moment.

Kate had been his second wife. She was ten years his junior, but it made little difference to their relationship. He loved her implicitly. He had believed that she had loved him too. He came home from work one day and found that she was gone. That was the end of the marriage. He was at his wits end with worry. He called her repeatedly, but her mobile calls just went straight through to voicemail. He tried every one of her contacts that he knew but they had no answers. She had simply vanished.

It was only later that evening, that he received a text from her. The text told him that she was happy and safe, but that she would not be coming home again. He sat down in his chair with a bottle of Bacardi at his side and he slowly drank himself into oblivion. He awoke in that same chair at five in the morning. The television set had turned itself off, and his head felt as if it had been pummelled by a heavyweight boxer as he slept.

As he stood upright, a pain shot through his lower back. It was a warning from his kidneys that although they loved the party, they were tired of dealing with the aftermath. He bolted toward the toilet and managed to hold most of the vomit that was now in his mouth. A little escaped and hit the side of the toilet bowl before he could even lift up the seat.

There was blood in the vomit, he was sure of that. Now the toilet smelt of acid and vomit mixed together and after he caught the scent in his nostrils he vomited again. When he was sure that there was nothing left in his stomach he sank down to his knees and then he vomited once more until he was dry retching. It was five long years ago almost to the day. When he found out that she was sleeping with one of his friends and then his mind began to descend into real madness.

He did not eat for weeks. His weight plummeted and he was afraid to leave the house. Solitude was his only friend. He could not risk seeing them together. He was afraid of what he might do to him if he saw them out in the street. Fate would soon decide the outcome for them both anyway. The next time he was to see her, her body was laid in a chapel of rest for the recently departed. He cried endless tears over her open coffin.

The couple had been on their way to a romantic weekend away at a theme park. A local hotel had been booked and they were singing away merrily in the car to a band they both shared a passion for. Her lover was driving the car. He had no time to react as the Lorry crossed the central reservation into the oncoming traffic. The driver's side of the car had been crushed completely. His wife had died three days later from serious head injuries. She never regained consciousness. It was a small blessing as her brain was a complete mess.

He may have been his friend once, but he had little remorse for the man who had run off with his wife. He just wished that he could turn back the clock and convince her to stay. He should have fought harder for his marriage; and never let her get into his car. He could not help but feel guilty about her death. After all he had been the one who had prayed to the devil that her new boyfriend would meet a painful end. He also prayed that he could have at least one last night with his wife. He had offered his soul, and it seemed as if the devil had accepted.

Now in his dream she was here once more. He would enjoy the dream while it lasted. He often dreamt of her recently. This dream was so vividly real though. He could smell the scent of her body. He could feel the curvature in her spine. He ran his hand all over her back, enjoying the sensation of her skin under his fingers. This dream was amazing.

Her face was now facing towards his, and she opened her eyes. They were a beautiful brown colour. They looked so real and alive, that it almost brought tears to his eyes. She smiled and he could see the slight gap between her upper front teeth, the warmth of her breath on his face. Then she pulled him closer to her, and they began to kiss.

It had been a harsh five years since she had died. In that time he had struggled to meet anyone that he would even consider dating long term. His confidence had suffered, and he could not help but to try and find someone as close to his ex wife as he could. His love for her had remained strong despite her leaving him, despite her death. The love he held for her had never died. Now his body was reacting to her touch, and as he entered inside of her, he closed his eyes and prayed that this dream would last forever.

The sex in the dream lasted less than four minutes, but still she smiled. He rolled over and lay on the small space left on what used to be his side of the bed. Then he closed his eyes once more, and dreamt that he heard her getting off the bed, and into the shower. He was snoring away merrily as her hand touched his face.

The dream was enduring, and as his eyes opened he saw that his dead wife was wearing his thick blue dressing gown. Her gown still remained hung up on the back of his bedroom door. She leant over his face and flicked his nose playfully. The flick was real. The slight pain in his nose was real. It was physically impossible, but his dead wife was actually in the bedroom with him.

He jumped upright and off the bed. The bedroom was now somehow different. Everything was fresh and new. He opened the curtains, and saw his car parked in the driveway. It was silver Mazda. It was the same car he had sold two years ago. He reached for his mobile phone on the side. This was one of his old phones too. He checked the date. It was a date five years and two days prior to the date that he had fallen asleep.

His wife looked puzzled by his behaviour.

"What the hell is wrong with you?" She asked. To hear her voice again was simply unreal. He walked over to where she stood, and threw his arms around her.

"Just let me hold you for a few moments. I've missed you." He said. Tears were now rolling down both of his cheeks. He turned her head to face him.

"Are you alright? I only went to the shower!" She said. She was wiping the tears away from his cheeks with her finger.

"Sit down on the bed. I need to tell you something." He had no idea where he was going to begin, but he knew that if this was real, then he only had only two days to make things right, and to stop her from ever leaving him.

She sat on the edge of the bed. He could see quite a way up her legs, and her tanned skin looked almost edible. He had to focus his thoughts though.

"I know this might sound nuts, but please listen to me. I had the craziest dream, but now I can stop this and turn things around. In two days time, you are going to leave me. You are going to leave with Owen my best friend, and leave all of your possessions behind." He said. His face was completely serious. Kate went white as a ghost. Her smile faded and now it was replaced by a look of anguish.

"How long have you known?" She asked.

"It doesn't matter. What matters is that I forgive you, and whatever it is that is wrong with us we can fix things. You will never want to leave me again." He pleaded.

"I don't know if we can fix things. It's already gone too far with Owen. I'm in love with him and I can't just switch my feelings off." She now had tears in her own eyes as she spoke.

Her words had cut deeply into him, but it was nothing compared to the last five years of anguish and suffering that he had lived through.

"A short time after you leave me, you will be driving to a theme park to stay there for the weekend. An articulated lorry will crash through the central barrier, and forty feet of steel will crush Owen in the car. His body will be so badly mangled that none of his family will be able to identify him. You will survive the crash, but with severe head injuries. You never regain consciousness. Two days later, you will die." His face was deadly serious. Kate was trying hard to absorb just how crazy this story was.

They had planned a quick exit; she was to leave everything behind. They had planned to visit a theme park together too. It was crazy just how much her husband seemed to know. She now began to doubt that she could go through with leaving her husband just yet. She may need some more time to think. She would have to call Owen later, and maybe they should cool things down for a while.

Perhaps it hadn't gone too far. Her head was still full of doubt. At least now she could make a proper choice. There was that minor chance, that as crazy as it sounded, her husband might actually be telling the truth. He had always been sensitive, and perhaps he had seen a glimpse of the future.

"I will call Owen. I think we need to sit down together and try and make things work. I still love you, but I thought that I loved him too. Now I'm so confused I just need some time to think. Can I please make the call on my own?" She asked. If she was going to stay, then it was the least that he could do for her.

He walked toward the bedroom door.

"I will take a shower. Take as much time as you need." He then stepped out into the hallway and closed the bedroom door behind him.

Owen did not take the news well. Not only had he betrayed one of his oldest friends, but now she had chosen her husband over him. It was the first time that he had ever truly fallen in love, and now it was all being torn away from him. He had already booked the theme park and he sure as hell wasn't going to miss out on that. He would go with or without her. Only now he had to make sure that she couldn't change her mind.

Owen was angry with her for choosing to stay with him. The best thing he could think to do was to block her from his life. He took the SIM card out from his phone. Now he would have to go and buy another one. There was no way he wanted his friend calling him right now, he had a fierce temper and it was worrying how much he seemed to know already. He had to lay low for a while.

The hot water ran in streams down his body. He used handfuls of shower gel to create a rich lather that cleansed him deep down. He smiled insanely to himself. He now had his wife back. It was an impossible dream, but sometimes miracles can actually happen. Or so it seemed. He rinsed off the rest of the soapy water and then switched off the shower tap. He used his hands to wipe the residue of water from his body, and then pulled back the shower curtain. His wife was now stood in front of him, except that this wasn't his wife anymore.

The woman in front of him had hollows for eyes; her skin had sunk away after five years of decomposition. Her body stank of rotten decay and maggots were eating at clumps of flesh that still remained. He fell back against the cold tiled wall of the bathroom, but he was unable to scream because of the frightening sight in front of him. He shook his head, unable to comprehend what he was seeing. Then her hand pierced through his chest, and squeezed his heart tightly.

"You promised me your heart and soul, in return for one more night. Now I come to claim my prize." Kate said.

This voice was not Kate's voice. This was a male voice. It was the voice he had once made a promise to in return for his friends death and one more night with his wife. In a few days time Owen would still make that fateful trip alone. The trip from where he would never return. In the bedroom, Kate had been so racked with guilt, that she had taken a month's worth of strong painkillers.

She had expected her husband to find her, and when he saved her life perhaps he would then fully forgive her for the harm that she had caused. Her husband would never make it out of the bathroom though, and his sleeping princess would never wake up from her dream.

In the bathroom, the devil released its grip on the man's heart. He had captured the soul he was owed and the victim had died with a look of sheer fright on his face. They would put it down to a massive heart attack no doubt. It would be weeks before the bodies would be found. The devil now had claim to all three souls, and all it had taken him was a simple rewind through space time. It was nothing compared to the eternity of suffering that hellfire for the three sinners that he was going to offer them all.

When the bough breaks

 The wind howled through the partially opened windows. It was mid August, and it felt like winter was in its firmest grip. It was strange how the weather seemed to flip as if the seasons no longer mattered. It was only six in the morning. He had just four hours of sleep. It was never enough, but it would just have to do.

 Richard reluctantly rose up from his bed. The need to pee was suddenly more urgent than the need to try and go back to sleep. It has been a tough week. Maria was still fast asleep in the bed. He softly walked around the room, desperate not to wake her. Her chest rose gently under the light summer duvet. As he reached the door and took his dressing gown from the metal hook, she gently murmured in her sleep but never woke. He opened the door and stepped out into the hallway.

 The television was on in the front room. It would be there son no doubt. The bladder issue was slightly more pressing though; such were the joys of approaching his fifties. It was scary and yet he felt as if he were still in his twenties. The aches in his legs reminded him otherwise. After he used the toilet, he flushed a short flush, and then washed and dried his hands. Then he left the bathroom and walked into the living room.

 Phillip was happily playing on the games console. The sound on the television was down, and he was grateful that his son was at least respectful of his parents need to rest at the weekends. His son looked up briefly and smiled at his father and then returned his train of thought to the game that he had been so engrossed in. Richard had bought the console for himself, perhaps as a desperate attempt to keep relevant and youthful. Instead his son had used it far more often than he did and no doubt a damn sight more efficiently.

Richard walked into the kitchen and emptied the stale water from the kettle. He then filled it with fresh water from the tap and switched the appliance on.

"Could you not sleep?" He asked his son through the open door.

"Shit Dad. I just died!" His son was annoyed that he would now have to go back and replay the entire section.

"Sorry! Mind your language though." He was sure that his son had far worse words already in his vocabulary, but it didn't hurt to keep him in check whilst in the home. "Do you want a cup of coffee?" He then asked his son out of politeness.

"Nah, I'm good." His son replied. He lifted a can in his right hand to show his father that this was his morning drink of choice to awaken him. He placed the half empty can of energy drink back on the table. His father had tried to discourage him from drinking those types of drink, but he had so far been unsuccessful.

Richard stirred the coffee in the cup. He had added two sugars, despite his promise to cut down. He was gaining weight month after month, but black coffee without sugar; well that just wasn't how coffee was supposed to be drunk in his book. He sat down on the sofa on the opposite side to his son. He slowly sipped from his favourite Liverpool mug and watched as his son set about hunting down victims in the video game. War was big business in the gaming industry, and one shot kills seemed to be particularly exciting.

By midday, Richard had cooked a full English breakfast. He had fed his wife a treat of breakfast in bed. Then he had washed up added a full load of washing. He had hoovered then entire flat whilst still in his dressing gown, and then he had showered and changed. All the while his son had barely moved from the same seat that he had occupied since very early that morning. It was only when his phone message sound bleeped to life that he became distracted. He read the message and then switched the game off.

Maria his wife had a yoga class at twelve thirty and she had asked Richard to drop her off. He needed some supplies from the town so he thought that he could kill two birds with one stone. His son Phillip also had to meet a friend in town, so he also asked for a lift down to the town with his father. They all jumped into the car, slamming the doors just a little bit too hard.

Once they had dropped Maria off, she had leaned into the car and kissed her husband gently on the lips. It was a quick kiss that showed little affection from a twenty plus year marriage. The excitement had long faded, but the devotion to the family unit was keeping them together.

To the outside world they were immensely strong as a couple. Except most of the outside world, didn't know about the affair that she was having with her much younger yoga instructor. Her husband would never discover that. She was positive it would always remain a secret. It had reinvigorated desires within her and that had seemed to make their marriage (and there sex life), much more adventurous.

Yoga had done wondrous things to her body so of course Richard was much happier for her to attend more classes each week. Now it was three times a week at classes that he knew about, and five times during the week that she would attend the private lessons with her instructor at his house that he had no knowledge of.

Maria opened the door to the sports centre, then turned around and waved before she entered the door. Richard smiled and waved back. The rear door of the car slammed again as Phillip jumped out from the rear of the car and made his way round to the front passenger seat.

What exactly was it that made the front seat of the car so much more desirable than the back he wondered, but then it had been a very long time since he had sat in the back seat of any car. The front door closed then he checked his mirrors and pulled out into the main road. He was now heading toward the town centre.

Andover town centre was always surprisingly busy on a Saturday. Despite the lack of many decent shops in the centre there was still enough variance to find all that you needed, it just sometimes took a bit of a hunt. Today the parking spaces appeared to be in short supply. Richard drove around two car parks until he found an available space. It was a bit of a trek into the centre from here, but it added to his daily step count and it would be nice to meet his daily target for once.

He handed Phillip some loose change from his cars change holder. There was at least three pound in loose shrapnel.

"Can you grab me a ticket for two hours please?" He asked his son.

"Can I keep the change?" His son asked.

"Yes!" Richard said. He knew that this question would come and he deliberately elongated the word, just to emphasise just how much money his son was managing to lever out of him on a weekly basis. Fatherhood wasn't cheap.

His son returned with the ticket, and Richard stuck it on the inside of his windscreen.

"Oh Dad, can I have a tenner please? I'm meeting Susan for a burger for lunch." Phillip asked. His eyes were pleading for parental financial support in a way that only teenage children can effectively use. Richard already had his wallet open before his son had begun to speak. He already knew the signs that the question was coming. His son had been just too friendly and chatty in the car today. He definitely wanted something.

Richard handed over the ten pound note.

"Another one you owe me." He said. If he added it all up it would have come to tens of thousands of pounds, he was sure of that. He was a good kid though; he was smart and tried his best at school. That made his parents proud. He had never smoked or drank alcohol, but fast food was his downfall. "And try and eat a bit healthier son. You can't just live on burgers you know. Get a smoothie in you."

"Sure. Thanks Dad. See you at home about six." Phillip said. He then placed his headphones inside of each ear, and walked off toward the town centre. Richard was heading in the same direction, but his son needed some space and privacy. He allowed him a few minutes before he too headed off to the town in the same direction.

After an hour of walking around the shops and talking with random friends, Richard's hands were now full of shopping. The bags weren't heavy but the plastic carriers were starting to leave indentations in his hands. He decided to grab a quick glass of soda outside of the Globe pub in the high street. He opted for a lime and soda and sat on the table at the front of the pub.

From this seat he could just watch the world go by while he used up some more of that parking ticket that he had paid for. He held the glass in his right hand and drank slowly while the midday sun began to glimmer.

The Earth itself then seemed to shake beneath his feet. Pedestrians had stopped at the bottom of the high street and were pointing to the left hand side of the shopping centre. Richard was both frightened and curious in equal measure. He dropped his pint glass and it smashed down on the ground in numerous pieces. Crazily, he picked up his bags of shopping. He was worried about losing the contents that he had just purchased. Now there were women and children screaming in terror. He ran along with his bags in hand toward the bottom of the high street.

He had not quite reached the bottom of the street when he chanced a look over his shoulder. The sight that he witnessed made him drop his bags in panic. He turned around to see a huge cloud was billowing skyward. It was unmistakable in its shape. Someone had done the unthinkable and had launched what he thought what could have been a missile attack. He knew what was about to come next and he screamed out loud.

"Run for cover!" He shouted. He was already running toward a nearby archway as he bellowed the instruction.

More blasts tore through the town centre. Everything was chaos and people were heading en masse toward the bottom of the town. Richard crouched down in the archway and prayed for this nightmare to end. He reached inside of his trouser pocket. He pulled out his mobile phone and dialled his son's number. He knew that he was in the town and probably scared and exposed. He had to try and get to his son and help him.

The phone failed to connect. He dialled his son's number again. The network still could not connect him. The masts would be down no doubt.

It took a few minutes for the chaos to die down a little before he could even think about venturing from the archway. The when he felt that it was safe enough to exit the archway, he ran out into the town centre and began frantically searching for his son. There were men, women and children strewn everywhere. Some were badly injured, some were entirely lifeless. Some were definitely dead. He wanted to help them but he had to find his son. Above all, he had to make sure his son was safe. He shouted his name out loud.

"Phillip, Phillip!" He repeated the name over and over again. It seemed a hopeless effort amongst all the screaming and crying that could be heard.

Despite the bedlam he then spotted his son. He was running down to the town from the direction of the burger bar. He was frantically searching for his father. "Dad. Where are you Dad?" Somehow in all the confusion, he had heard his father's voice. The made eye contact and both smiled with relief as they ran toward each other. They were within fifty feet of each other when a rain of hellfire descended down from the skies above them. Right in front of Richard's eyes, he witnessed his son torn apart by an aerial bombardment.

The explosions continued all around him. Pieces of flying debris were embedded in different areas of his body. He struggled to maintain his balance as the loudness of the explosions sounded from every direction. The fluid in his ears became unstable, and it was nearly impossible for him to remain upright. Nothing would stop him though. He was going to reach his son. No matter even if it meant his own death.

He collapsed down to his knees when he reached the boy. His son was still alive but barely holding on. His left hand side of his face was covered in matted blood. There was a wound deep in his head that was exposing the flesh underneath his skull. His son coughed and pure blood spilt out from the corners of his mouth. Richard leant down to cradle his son. His son's eyes were wide open with fear.

"I.....I'm scared Dad." He pleaded. He knew that he had very little time left. "I don't want to die Dad...please..." Tears now filled his eyes. Richard was in agony. Seeing the injuries to his son, he knew that there was nothing that he could do. He could only try and comfort his dying child, while the life ebbed out of his young body.

"It's going to be alright son. I'm here." He sobbed openly as he held his child in his arms. The body he held then started to convulse in his arms. "I love you son." He said. His child then stopped moving, as the last of the air left his son's body. He lifted his child's body from the ground and began to carry him toward his car. He was going to take him home. He was taking him back where he belonged.

Nobody knew who fired first. But the war raged on for months. Brothers avenged fallen brothers. Daughters avenged fallen fathers. Husbands avenged fallen wives. Mothers avenged fallen daughters. Fathers avenged fallen sons. Each of their victims was an enemy that they never knew. Each of them was fighting a cause that they would now gladly die for.

Somewhere in meeting room across the world, men in grey suits was gathered and they calculated how much they had made from the sale of weapons with weekly reports. The war raged on until they were satisfied that they had made enough money. Then they instructed the politicians that they should negotiate a cease fire.

The real horror of this story is that this happens every day. As long as it's in some other country or happening to some other nation, we see it on the news and say how awful it is for those people, but we carry on our days as normal, until the day comes when it finally happens in the country where we live.

This story was inspired by a five year old boy in Syria named Omran Daqneesh. His bloodied face and sad eyes inspired a billion tears. Yet at his tender age he was so accustomed to war that despite his injuries he shed no tears of his own. Omran I pray for your family and that you all find safety and peace from a war you never asked for.

The Dream Collectors

If it wasn't for the power of social media, then the group may have never existed. Mark was the first to post his dreams online. In July 2016, he had the same recurring dream for five nights in a row. The dreams all began similarly but each subsequent night after they would become more extended and prolific. The first night that he dreamt about the plane crash, he had woken up frightened in a pool of his own cold sweat. The second night he could actually remember the name on the side of the plane.

On the third night of the recurring dream, he had images of each of the passengers. There were men women and children and he saw them all. Each of them had perished in an immense fireball that had occurred just as the plane had landed. On the fourth night he knew which country the plane had taken off from and where it was attempting to land. By now he was sick of the sheer intensity of the dreams. On the fifth night he had taken a sleeping pill in the hope that this may subdue the dreams. The pill failed miserably.

On the fifth night of the dream, the images were so intense that he felt as if he were one of the passengers onboard that very flight. At the moment the flames surged through the plane he felt the intense heat on his skin and the plane exploded. He woke up trying to scream but he was so petrified by the experience, that he could not even utter a single sound from his mouth. His body was so breathless he was terrified into silence. He decided that he should take the story of the dream experience and share it on social media, but he had no idea why.

He opened up his account, and began to update his status. He wrote:

'For five days now I have had the same horrifying dream. A plane was taking off from Gatwick airport and it was going to be landing in Turkey.

Before it could land, an explosion ripped through the entire plane. It was absolutely petrifying.' He then posted the status in the hope that at least others may relate and help to assure him that the dreams were nothing that he should worry about. He was wrong.

About an hour after he posted an instant message appeared. It was from a girl named Kate, who he had known as a friend of friends. He opened up the private message, and began to read. It said,

'Hey, you're going to think this is crazy, but I've been having the same dreams all week too. A Simple-jet flight, number SJ25347, I think it's a Boeing. As it comes in to land at Antalya airport, it bursts into flames. I'm sure it's a bomb onboard. It's been scaring the life out of me all week!'

Mark read the message twice before he responded. 'We need to meet up for a coffee. Are you free today?' He asked.

'I am tomorrow about eleven if you are around?' She replied.

'Sure. I can meet you at the Blue Omega in town at eleven, if that's ok?' He typed.

'See you there.' He replied.

There were various comments posted throughout the day, but none quite as interesting as the one that Kate had written. Then at seven thirty that night another private message came through. It was from John, who one of Marks oldest friends.

'I've been dreaming the same dream as you. A flight that is landing in a foreign country, it blows up. I've been seeing the passengers too. It's bloody horrid mate. You think that it means something?' It was too much of a coincidence for Mark to ignore.

He decided to ring John instead of messaging him. The phone rang around seven times before John finally answered.

"Alright mate. Weird about these dreams isn't it?" He said.

"You aren't kidding mate. It seems like three of us have all been having the same dream though. A woman called Kate has been dreaming the same thing too.' Mark replied.

'Really. That's just crazy! We should all get together and compare what we've dreamt about." He suggested.

"That's why I rang. Can you meet us at the Blue Omega coffee shop at eleven tomorrow?" Mark asked.

"Yeah, it's a Saturday and I'm not working in the morning. I will meet you there." John answered.

"Great. We will meet you there mate. Be good to see you. It's been a while. See you tomorrow mate and we can catch up properly." Mark said. It had been a good few months since they had last spoken.

"Yes mate. I'm getting grief from my boss, so I better get back to work. See you tomorrow morning." Then John abruptly ended the phone call.

Mark had arrived ten minutes early. Kate was already sat outside of the front of the shop. She was drinking a latte. Mark acknowledged her and asked the waitress if she could bring him a decaf coffee. He ordered it white with no sugar. He also ordered a hot chocolate with sprinkles and cream. He knew that it was John's drink of choice, and if for some reason he never showed up, then Mark would happily drink it for him. He sat down opposite Kate and John arrived just as he had taken his seat.

"Hot chocolate. I've already ordered it for you mate." Mark said.

"Chocolate sprinkles?" John questioned.

"Of course I did." Mark smiled. John grinned in response and then took a seat opposite Kate.

Mark introduced the pair to each other.

"John this is Kate and Kate this is John." Mark said, and the pair shook hands across the table. John smiled at Kate as if he already knew her.

"You look familiar. I'm sure that I know you from somewhere." He said.

"I've seen you on nights out in the Town Mills." Kate replied. She didn't seem too impressed by John's attention and he reluctantly released her hand. Mark could sense that John was attracted to her. She was a good looking girl. He wasn't surprised in the slightest that he had taken a shine to her.

"I think you might know my boyfriend too. Dave Daniels." Kate said. It was then that the smile faded quickly from Johns face. He was hoping that she might have been single and now his hopes had been dashed almost instantly.

"Yeah I've heard of him." John said. "So what's happening with all these dreams?" He turned his head and asked Mark to tactfully change the direction of the conversation.

Mark was more than happy to start explaining what he was dreaming off just to get the story of the dream out of his head.

"It's been the same thing for five nights. It been expanding more and more every time that I sleep. I see the passengers waiting in the airport lounge. I see the flight number on the board. The gate is number seventeen. I see all of the different faces as they board the flight. Each and every face as they enter the plane. Men, women and children. Then I see the air hostesses running through all the safety checks. Then the flight is taking off. I even see the in flight movie that's playing.

Just before the plane is due to land, a huge fireball rips through the cabin of the plane. The heat is so intense that it melts everything in its path. The leather plastic and human skin, I can actually smell everything burning.

Then I wake up and night after night, I am seeing more and more. It feels as if I am actually on the plane." Mark finished. He looked visibly distraught at relaying what he had repeatedly seen.

Kate looked amazed at what she had just heard. She then pulled out a notebook from her handbag. She opened up the pages and showed them to Mark.

"My dreams were almost exactly the same. I wrote it all down. Have a read." She offered. Mark read through the notes. It was almost identical to what he had seen except for Kate had felt that she was in a female passenger's body during the dream.

"That's incredible." Mark said. John nodded in agreement. The notebook he was reading from looked about half full. "Is this all about the plane?" Mark asked. Kate shook her head.

"No. I've been making these notes about all of my dreams for the last few months. They have been growing in intensity so I decided to write them down. Some seemed strange and random, but certain dreams appear to have already come true. Nothing as spectacular or disastrous as this one though." She answered. She looked genuinely concerned.

John then decided to add his interpretation of his dreams.

"Mine are almost the same as yours but I see things from the back of the plane. It's definitely a bomb and it goes off from somewhere close to me. I see the whole plane engulfed in flames. I think I'm part of the cabin crew itself. I'm definitely stood up while everyone else is seated. As the plane is engulfed I feel a huge sense of anguish and then relief. It's almost as if I wanted this to happen. It scared the life out of me.

On the fifth night when I witnessed the explosion, I pissed myself before I woke up. The wife wasn't happy." John said.

The thought of John wetting the bed, added a little light relief to the moment and Mark could not help it as he found himself starting to laugh. Kate was soon giggling too, and after the initial embarrassment John even started to join in as well. When the laughter had subsided, Kate took her notebook off the table, and placed it back in her bag.

"Do you think we should tell someone about this?" She asked. After both men looked at each other in turn, Mark nodded.

"I think we should." Mark agreed. John thought differently though, and he was quite vocal in his disagreement.

"Are you nuts? You think we should phone someone and tell them that three of us dreamt a plane is going to blow up. I think they might lock us up for wasting time! Christ, people have dreams all the time but they don't go ringing the police every morning." John felt as if he had made his point with the statement. Mark remained silent with his thoughts for a few moments longer.

"You are probably right, but what if what we somehow all know what is really about to happen. What we say to them could somehow prevent it from happening. If we could save all of those lives, then I don't mind being made a fool of." Mark said. Kate nodded her head in agreement.

"I agree. I think we should at least try." She said. John shook his head.

"You're both nuts. I honestly think that I..." John did not get the chance to finish his sentence. Kate had grabbed hold of his shoulder and shook him where he sat.

"Look!" She said. She was pointing toward a television screen behind John that she had been glancing up at. There were pictures of an explosion on a plane playing on the national news.

Mark jumped up from his seat and turned up the volume manually. The waitress was confused by the sudden loudness of the television and went to ask him to turn it back down. As she approached the man the look on his face told her that perhaps she should leave him alone instead. The newsreader was commenting on the morning's events.

"Flight number SJ25347 left Gatwick early this morning. There were clear flying conditions and the flight was on time. As it was coming in to land the plane exploded killing all two hundred and fifteen passengers and crew on board. It appears that this might have been terrorist related.

Accident investigators are currently at the scene. They are currently trying to locate the flight recorder but debris has been scattered over such a wide area, that it could be sometime before we actually know what happened to flight SJ25347." Mark stood in stunned silence. Then he turned the volume back down to silence. He turned slowly and slumped back down in his seat. His face was now a pale white.

"Fucking hell." Kate said. The two men remained sat in stunned silence.

They then made a collective decision not to tell anyone what they had dreamt. It made no sense now after the event and all three had felt guilty that they had not told anyone before the explosion had happened. The faces of all the dead passengers would remain etched on their minds for weeks though. When the facts were made public, it became clear that one of the air stewards had managed to smuggle a bomb on board. He had worked for the airline for four and a half years, and no one had ever suspected any links to any terrorist organisation. It came as a complete shock to all that knew him.

Things remained quiet for a few weeks after. Then on a Monday morning at 5 a.m, Mark woke up from another nightmare. This one had made him so frightened, that he immediately picked up the phone to Kate. She answered on the second ring. Her breathing was heavy and it was obvious that she was also distressed.

"Don't tell me it's happening again?" She said frantically.

"I think so. Did you dream about the earthquake?" Mark asked. There was a stunned silence from the other end of the line.

"That wasn't just an earthquake. That was devastation." Kate said. She was now sobbing so hard that she had woken up her boyfriend. Mark could hear muffled noises from the other end of the line.

"Make some notes and I will call you in the morning." He said. Then he put the phone down.

On the tablet propped by his bedside a new message suddenly appeared. His eyes were still out of focus because of his lack of sleep but he picked up the tablet and opened the message. It was from John. It read.

'Mate I've just had the most fucked up dream ever. There was a massive earthquake, and hundreds of people died. I hope this isn't like that last time. I pissed the bed again it was so real. Call me in the morning if you had similar. John.' It really was happening again. Mark could relate to what John had said. It was such a realistic dream and it was nothing that they could even smile about this time.

The three met up at Marks house. It was a three bedroom place that his mother and father had left to him a few years ago. He had been an only child and both his parents were in there early forties when he was born. Both of his parents had passed away in there early seventies, and had left him a house and enough money to tide him over for quite a few years.

The money was quickly dwindling away now though and he had been seriously thinking about selling up the house, and moving to a smaller place. He could not bear the thought of taking in lodgers, but he also wanted to keep the only home he had ever known.

He convinced Kate and John that the best thing that they could do was for them all to stay in the same house that night. Kate was reluctant at first as she knew that her partner would be unhappy. However when she rang and discussed it, her partner appeared more than happy to not share his bed with a woman who woke him up screaming almost every morning at around five a.m.

That night they stayed up just talking and comparing notes until around twelve and then Mark showed them both to his guest bedrooms. Both of them were comfortable enough in the strange surroundings but at just after five, the whole house felt as if it were shaking, and all three were woken from their dreams but the apparent shuddering of the entire house.

Each of the three entered the hallway at exactly the same moment. Each look horrified at what they had encountered. Each felt relieved that they were now sharing the experiences together.

"Earthquake?" Mark asked. Both responded "Yes." At exactly the same time.

"Coffee?" Mark asked, again both agreed "Yes!" both nodded enthusiastically at exactly the same moment. This would take slightly more than decaf he thought. This coffee would have to be fully leaded.

The coffee was strong warm and welcoming. All three sat around the coffee table in the living room and discussed what they had dreamt. Mark started.

"I saw a huge Earthquake in San Andreas. I saw the ground cracking open. Cars were being swallowed into the ground, and into huge holes in the land." Mark began. Kate spoke second.

"I saw houses breaking in two. I saw supermarkets with shelves collapsing down to rubble. Cars were being swallowed whole into the opening crevices in the ground. People were screaming as they were trying to stop others from falling down into a huge chasm. It was definitely in America. I wasn't sure if it was San Andreas though." All the time, she was writing notes in her notebook. The more detail that she had, the better it would be.

John was the third to speak.

"I saw exactly the same. I saw a sign saying San Andreas so it was definitely there. I actually felt the ground moving. It was almost as if it was happening here. I saw devastation on a huge scale. We have to warn them." He said. He was deadly serious. Even though they might not be taken seriously, John was adamant that they had to try.

Mark agreed that something had to be done.

"Even if we only save one life, then at least we will have achieved something." He said.

"I agree completely. I think I know how to start as well." Kate agreed.

It transpired that Kate had been discussing her dreams on an online forum that was based in America. She had been in contact with an American news reporter who had been interested in the explosion in Turkey. Kate had sent all of her notes across to the reporter before the investigation had even been concluded.

When her notes matched the findings in the report, the reporter had been in constant regular contact. That morning, Kate mailed her contact and they agreed a time for a video conversation. None of the three would be going to work that day.

The conversation went better than any of the three could have expected. The reporter was taking the information seriously and she was prepared to add an independent report later that day. She just needed to speak to her boss in order to get the go ahead. In the mean time the three had agreed to the video interview to be aired.

It took a few hours before they had confirmation, but later that day the three dream viewers would become widely known across America. The three gathered around Marks laptop to enable them to watch the broadcast online. When the section started, there was a huge sense of excitement between the three.

"Three friends from a small town called Andover in Hampshire, England. Just a few months ago, all three of the friends experienced the same dream over five separate nights. No one was more shocked when the dreams actually turned out to be true. Now they have a dire warning for us here in America. For the last two nights, all three have been dreaming about an earthquake that occurs right here in San Andreas.

Experts have said that there has been no unusual activity in the area, but I spoke to the three earlier and I have to admit, I am actually convinced that these three know something. Earlier today, I spoke to the three ordinary folk from England; or as I like to call them, The Dream Collectors."

The video conversation then played out. It reached a huge audience across America. Within hours they had all started to receive messages, emails and telephone calls from all across America. Worried parents, friends and relatives were all asking for more details about what the three were expecting to happen. It was both frightening and exciting at the same time. People started to vacate the area, despite assurances that the area was completely safe. Then on the sixth day when the huge earthquake unexpectedly happened, the three dream collectors suddenly became a media sensation.

Over the next year, John Kate and Mark had all been offered relocation to America; each had turned down the offers. More and more money had been offered for insights into the future but they could not see the future on demand. They could only see potential disasters. Each time that the dreams began, they would use the power of the media to issue warnings. They saved hundreds if not thousands of lives. The minute they were able to warn of the events, they would issue statements online, and people were actually listening. Plans were changed, areas were evacuated and numerous disasters were avoided.

It was clear that the three had some sort of connection between them, so they decided to move into the same house. Some dismissed them as frauds but it wasn't long before the Governments scientists became interested in the link between the three. They repeatedly asked the three to come in for testing. They wanted to try and harness the power between the three but every time all of them had refused. They did not want anyone using the powers that they had for any other use.

One day, all three of them just simply vanished from their home. The three had all refused any sort of testing. They were just happy to continue warning others and saving lives wherever they could. It wasn't enough for some though and the Government wanted to try and harness the power that the three seemed to have. They had abducted all three from the house that they were all sharing.

When the lights came on in the room, all three were strapped down to chairs in the laboratory. Whatever they had been injected with it had left all three of them feeling drowsy. Mark was the first to come round.

"What is this place? Why are we here?" He demanded. Kate was now coming round, but John was still snoring loudly. The room smelt sterile.

There was no one else in the room and each of the three was now almost facing each other. There were cables and wires attached to each of them. Every separate body function was being monitored. Each of them had been fitted with catheters, and they felt uncomfortable. It was clear that they weren't going anywhere soon. Now Mark began to wish that they had perhaps co-operated when the government had asked them to.

For the next month the three were fed by drip after refusing to co-operate in any way at all. As much as the three tried to resist the tests, eventually they all began to dream the same dreams again. The scientists were recording the brainwaves of the three and each of the subject's brain activity was recording as off the charts. The first night after the dream, each of the three refused to discuss the dream with each other.

The dream was centred in the room in which they were all being held captive. Between the three of them, a dark energy force had been building. A swirling portal had been formed and a two way channel had been opened. Everything that was in the room had been dragged into the portal, and then something began to emerge. Every night the dream continued, and they felt the power growing stronger. Whatever was the other side of the portal, it was immensely powerful. None of the three could see what it was though.

On the fifth day they shared the dream, the lead scientist became worried. He went to the project leader with his findings. He rushed through the door and entered the office without knocking.

"You need to see this now." He demanded. The project leader looked at him with a puzzled expression.

"What is this?" He demanded.

"Look at it. I've been measuring the dreams. They aren't just dreaming. Somehow the three are manifesting the events. Whatever they dream, they can bring to life!" He said. His hands were shaking.

"My God." The leader said.

"It takes around five nights of collective dreaming for them to manifest the events. For the last five days, the brain activity has been so powerful that whatever they are about to manifest, it will have a huge destructive power. We need to stop them dreaming at all costs. We have to terminate the subjects right now!" The scientist shouted. He slammed both his fists down on the table. His hands were shaking as he lifted them up. He was frightened for his own life.

"Take a team to the test lab. End them." The leader instructed. Then the base alert sounded.

It felt as if the room itself were shaking. All of the power to the closed circuit television had been cut. The scientists could no longer see inside of the room. The escort soldiers were authorised to use deadly force. They hit the emergency button to enter the room, where they found that each of the three subjects was shaking violently in the test beds.

"Shoot them!" The scientist shouted. Each of the three was terminated by a single shot to the head, but the bodies continued to shake violently, death had no meaning for the three anymore. In the centre of the room the dark circle revolved. Then everything inside of the room was drawn into the vortex.

The last dream that the collectors had shared was of the creation of a black hole being formed on Earth. Now everything inside of the base was being swallowed into the darkness. The soldiers and scientists were pulled back into the darkness with the growing strength of the anomaly, and the only people with the power to end the nightmare were now lifeless bodies being drawn into nothingness. With every single second, the power of the darkness would grow stronger, and soon there would be nothing left.

The Sin Eater

I can tell you the exact moment that I became a sin eater; it was when I was just nineteen years old. It was somewhat freaky. I was walking through Andover town centre on a Saturday morning just after eleven. I wasn't doing anything in particular that day. I was just browsing the shop windows. I had received my first full month's pay packet, and I guess I was just looking for ways to stop the cash from burning a hole in my pocket.

I was working in a warehouse on one of the local industrial estates. With very few people in that department, I had volunteered to train in first aid in the hope of impressing my new boss. No one else fancied taking the task on, and I thought it might come in useful, so why not? I had no idea that I would be called upon to use my newly learnt skills, just twenty four hours later.

I had just passed the guildhall when I saw a small crowd gathered outside of the old Woolworths building on my right. There was an old lady on the ground. She was surrounded by concerned people; and she didn't appear to be moving at all. Her shopping bags had been dropped by her side, and her fruit and vegetables that she had just bought from the market stall were now rolling down the high street after escaping from the plastic bags she was carrying.

I was desperate to help so I rushed over to her side. I asked if anyone had called an Ambulance, but no one had. I sent one of the nearest bystanders to go and dial for the emergency services. He looked in shock, but he was one of the most agile looking people there. As soon as he was running off toward the phone box, I knelt down over the collapsed woman on the ground.

"Try not to worry, I'm a first aider. I'm here to help you." I told the woman. There was no response, but I still wanted to reassure her that she was now in safe hands.

I checked for signs of breathing but there were none. Her chest wasn't rising. There were no signs of a pulse either. This wasn't looking good at all. I tilted her head back slightly and I checked that her airways were clear. Then I breathed air into her lungs. Her chest rose as I forced air repeatedly into her lifeless body. Then I quickly moved over to start the chest compressions. It was difficult to gauge how much pressure I should exert. The old lady looked frail, and the last thing I wanted to do was to crush her chest bone. I exercised caution.

I repeated the procedure for a good ten minutes, until I was at the point of exhaustion. There was still no sign of the damned ambulance. Then the strangest thing happened and it was to change my life forever. As I went to start a new bout of chest compressions when time seemed to freeze. Everyone else around me became fixed to the spot, and there was the strangest sensation as the world around me became completely silent. An eerie glow then lifted from the woman's chest, and found its way up and into my hands.

The woman's soul was finding a way to enter through my body. Her life then flashed before my eyes. Every single sin that she had ever committed in her life was replayed as if I was watching a cinema screen. The woman had been a petty thief for all of her life. She had started stealing sweets as a young child, and the thrill had excited her so much that she had continued to steal throughout her entire life. Every single event replayed and I felt that I was taking on her sins. All the while, a single word was repeating over and over again in my head. The word was 'Absolution'.

That old lady had committed so many sins in her lifetime that it felt as if it would never end. She had done all sorts of crazy things, and never once repented for what she had done. She had never actually cared enough to ever worry about what she had done. Lying, cheating and stealing were just some the many sins that I now found myself offering her absolution for.

Then we reached the final moment of life. Her final sin was that she had filled her bag that very morning with some fruit that she had stolen from the market stall. After viewing the final sin her body became completely cleansed.

I was never a believer in heaven and an afterlife, not until that very moment. That was the first time that I ever witnessed a soul leaving a body. As the soul rose from her chest, I felt a surge of love and peaceful energy flowing through both of my hands. The soul was warm and caring, and it was heading toward a source of bright light that had appeared over her head.

I heard the words of the woman saying 'thank you', but only I could hear her words in my own head. It was very real, but without any physical sound if that makes sense. It certainly didn't make any sense to me at the time.

Then the world around me found itself moving in real time again. My hands continued to press downward onto her chest, and in the distance I could now hear the sound of an Ambulance siren as it sped toward the town centre. I continued to compress her chest even though I knew that the gesture was futile. The woman was gone, and I knew that for a fact. I still continued until the paramedics arrived and they then took over. I was filled with a feeling of sadness, but also a sense of hope in equal measure. It was the strangest sensation I had ever felt.

I had no idea why, but the children of the woman had asked through the local paper if they could meet me in person. They wanted to thank me for trying to save her life. I was reluctant; after all I had done nothing to bring her back. I knew the moment she had died as I had felt her soul leaving her body, and I knew that she was happy and at peace. There was no way that her soul would have willingly chosen to return to that frail and aching body. A week later at their own insistence I begrudgingly met her son and daughter.

I met the siblings in a local cafe. I had already ordered a cola and had sat down before they both arrived. When they turned up, both were wearing a look of extreme sadness and despair. I nodded to greet them both and they came over carrying a cup of coffee each. As they sat down, I could see sadness in both of their eyes.

"Thank you so much for trying to help our mum." The woman said. The daughter looked a little like her mother she and couldn't have been older than thirty five.

"There are not many people your age that would even stop to try and help. We both really appreciate it. "Her brother said. He was older than the sister. He was already mostly bald and probably in his early forties. They both looked as if they had seen better days. Both were in tatty looking clothes. The woman's hair was slightly unkempt, and her clothes looked dull and faded. They looked cheap. For some reason, I decided to open up and tell them a little about what I had felt that day. I had no idea why, but I thought that it might help in some way.

I had no idea where to even begin, but I just blurted it out and hoped that they understood why I was telling them what I had felt.

"I think you need to know. I'm not religious in the slightest but on the day that your mother died, something strange happened. I actually swear that I felt your mother's soul leaving her body." I said. On hearing these few words the daughter started to sob. The pain was still very raw for her and it was clear that she was hurting badly. I decided not to mention anything about all the sins that I had witnessed; instead I knew something that might help to ease the pain a little.

"Please don't ask me how but I know that your mother has left a considerable gift for you. In her dining room, you need to lift up the carpet in the right hand side corner of the room closest to the kitchen. There's a loose floorboard there. Lift it up, and look underneath." I finished. If what I had seen before her spirit passed over was correct, then the gift would be helpful for them at this time.

We talked a little more over the drinks and they offered to buy me another, but in all honesty I was feeling a little uncomfortable sitting with strangers and talking about a woman who I never even knew when she was alive, yet I had experienced her whole life flashing in front of my eyes. I felt that I knew her better than I knew my own mother, and I could recall every single one of her sins at will. It was a horrible feeling.

I soon made my excuses, we exchanged telephone numbers so that we could remain in contact, and then I left.

That night the daughter called me, and it was clear that she was in a much happier place. It soon became clear that the brother and sister were both very short of money. They had been struggling to work out just how they were going to afford the funeral expenses. That afternoon after the conversation we had, the pair had visited their mother's house. They had lifted up the carpet and found the loose floorboard, and then discovered a large tin that was hidden beneath. Inside they had found sixty three thousand pounds in cash that their mother had secretly stashed away.

She had told both of her children that she had never trusted banks. She had left no clue as to where she had kept her money, and in life she had been miserly toward both of her children. Now after my revelation they both had enough to have a comfortable existence.

If it wasn't for the information that I had given them, they would surely have never discovered the money and it may have sat underneath the floorboards until the end of time. It was a very rewarding disclosure for me, but it still didn't help to remove all of the woman's memories from my head. It would take a priest to do that.

I had not visited a church since I was young and I did not make the decision lightly. Night after night, I would dream about events in the woman's life. I was re-living all of her sins and her regrets. It was as if they were my own. I needed to do something to get them out of my head. I decided to take confessional, and it was such a relief that I did. In the next booth the priest heard my confession of all the woman's sins and absolved me of them all. I then felt the darkness building within by body as a force began to lift the sins out from within me.

It was a painful experience, but rewarding at the same time. My body began to shudder and I had to press my hands against the sides of the booth. My head dropped backward, my eyes then became completely black. The sins flooded out from my open mouth and up into the air above my head. Then darkness then arched and drove down into the stone floor of the church between my feet. It was like hot tar that was exiting my mouth, but it was a massive relief when it had all been removed. That was the day I realised the power I had as a sin eater.

I had no idea what this new found gift was, but I was determined to find out. I trawled through book after book in the library and just when I was about to give up hope, I found exactly what I was looking for. I found an article that told about a ritual that took place in the 18th and 19th centuries in Scotland. The families would place a piece of bread on the chests of dying family members. The families would then hire someone to eat the bread to try and absolve the sins of the deceased. The sin eaters then took ownership of the sins that the deceased performed. They were digesting the sins of the living or recently dead when they ate the bread.

The ritual started to become more popular, and the practice expanded. There was a strong belief that the sin eaters who performed the ritual helped to prevent the dead from wandering the countryside after death. The sin eaters were poor beggars who would be paid around half a shilling. In return the villagers believed that after every ceremony, the sin eaters became more horrible. They believed that the sins would remain trapped in the sin eater's body.

It was really confusing to read; after all I had just been absolved of the sins. Yet, I could still recall every single moment that the old woman had committed a sin. I had to work out why I still remembered them even though I had been absolved. The only way I could do this, was to try and eat the sin of another person. That wasn't going to be easy though. It took months before I was able to actually perform the ceremony again. I had to find the right place, the right time and the right person.

A change of career seemed like a natural way to use my new found gift. This was how I became a care worker in an old person's home. It was a sure fire way to be closer to those who had a good chance of passing over. It also meant that I could keep my gift a secret. There were two old men who were terminally ill in the home. One was named Dennis Leary.

I got to know Dennis quite well during the last few months of his life. He was in his late eighties and had no immediate family. I provided some company for him, and I watched intently as his health deteriorated. It was only a matter of time before he began to fade away.

During the last week of his life, his lungs were failing. His breathing was being assisted and on the Thursday night, the doctors made the call to switch off the machine. They were checking him regularly and monitoring his demise with sophisticated machinery. He was fading fast. As his primary carer I was allowed to be present during the final moments leading up to his death. I held his hand and told him that he was going to be alright. I was sure of it. Suddenly his breathing just stopped. An alarm sounded on the machine, but I turned it off. His hand suddenly lost all of the ability to grip mine.

I placed my hands upon his chest and waited. It took less than thirty seconds before time froze and his sins of his life were being relived through my mind. I could see every single bad event from his life. In total there were probably less than fifty.

Dennis had laid a pretty clean life. He had been quite clean living and his sins were few. They were hardly anything that a man should be condemned for. Once the sins had been fed into my body, his soul left the empty shell. It felt as if he was holding his arms around my shoulders in thanks. Then time began to move once more. He was cleansed.

I went to the church to confess his sins. They weren't mine, but I still wanted to remove them from my body. As I entered the church I caught a sight of my face in a window. My eyes were darkened underneath. It looked as if I hadn't slept for days. It wasn't good. I needed to take a break from work soon. I confessed the sins that weren't mine, and afterward the priest absolved me. My body began to shudder once one. My head tilted backward and the darkness left my mouth and fell through the floor once more. Yet I could now still recall the sins of the woman, and now the minor sins of Dennis as well.

I felt as if I had performed a ritual that had aided both of the dead. I wanted to try it one more time, and Geoffrey Hunter was the other resident of the care home who was also close to death. Every time that anyone had tried to get close to the man, he had pushed them away. He was the type of guy who would happily sit in his own urine and then laugh as the carer in charge would have to clean him. He often soiled himself and he wore an insane grin on his face as he did. No one liked having to deal with the man at all.

Every time his son had tried to visit, the man had begun to argue and shout. He did not want his son anywhere near him. He was so full of anger and rage at being put in the care home that he effectively disowned his son. Every week his son would visit, and each and every single time the arguing became more intense. It came as a relief to everyone when he Mr Hunter finally decided to end his own life.

He had stored up the painkilling pills that he had been given each evening. He had pretended to swallow them, but then he had spat them back out into his hand. When he had collected thirty, he knew that he had enough to end his life. He had left no note, but he had taken all of the pills at once. He died with a look of anger on his face. I was the one who found the body.

It was morning and the body was cold when I discovered it. The skin was starting to turn blue and it was rigid as a board. The room stank of urine and faeces as the bowel and bladder had both emptied after death. I wasn't sure if I could still absorb the sins but I still wanted to try. I placed my hands upon the chest of the cadaver, and closed my eyes. Time stopped once more and I instantly regretted my decision.

I relived every single sin he had committed, and there were many. I witnessed every cut that he had ever made upon innocent skin. He had once been a soldier. He had killed without mercy. He had tortured men, women and children. Anyone who ever crossed his path had paid the ultimate price. He had discovered a passion for murder. After the war had ended he had missed the thrill of the kill. So he had started to murder at random. No one was safe from him. He had travelled all over the world. He would kill totally at random. All of the murders were committed with deadly accuracy and without mercy. Every single death had been unsolved. They were just too random, and never in the same place or the same method of murder. Each time they were a little more inventive, each time a little more horrific.

The thing that left the body was entirely dark in form. It smelt more horrific than anything I had ever encountered. The shape that formed was not human; it was more like an animal. Then the darkness began to leave the shape of the animal and started to enter through my body through my open mouth. I was frozen to the spot and I desperately wanted to gag, as what felt like slime continued to slither down my throat.

The soul seemed to be drawing goodness from within me until it became filled with light. It was stealing my goodness and kindness I had ever shown to others. It was using the energy to enable it to ascend to a higher plane of existence. It was too late for me to stop it. I had released a killer from this plane, and I had unleashed an evil spirit to wreak havoc in a place of harmony and peaceful existence. When time started moving once more, I fell down lifeless to the floor.

I did not feel anything when the other carers open my shirt. I did not feel the compressions upon my chest. Nor the electric shocks that the paramedics had fired down through the paddles and into my body. I had already left. Now I was in a white room, in a single chair, and I was facing judgement. All of the sins had been counted; all of the sins had condemned me to an eternity of suffering. The pain I would now have to endure for all eternity is indescribable. I never believed in heaven, but now I know the reality that is hell.

Lady Ice Part 3

So this was how it was all going to end. At the hands of a man who had given me so much, but had taken so much more from me than anyone would ever know. I should have known not to underestimate him, but I thought that I could stay one step ahead. I thought that I had the element of surprise on my side, but I should have known better.

Now all I can do is to close my eyes, and wait for that single moment that comes to everyone. The moment my soul leaves my body. This will be the moment when I will finally face my maker. Despite everything that I have ever done, all of the lives that I have taken, I regret not one. The only regret I have is that I never got to finish this one last personal task. I should have put a bullet in his brains years ago. Instead I let him live for the sake of our daughter.

The ground is warm underneath me. My nose is broken, of that I am sure. The blood is running everywhere. It's running down my right cheek and drying out in the mid afternoon sun. It's also running down the back of my throat. I am coughing the blood out every few seconds. All the time I am waiting for the mercy of that trigger being pulled, but he will not let this end mercifully.

The gun is pointed at my forehead. I dare not try to move. My weapon is not close enough to reach. Even if I could reach it, my hand is ruined. The bullet went right through the hand when he fired and I will probably never be able to use it for anything again. I open my eyes to see his smirking grin leering down at me. It's almost as if this is how he wanted it to end. I wonder why he is waiting; I know that I will never see my daughter again. My tears are allowed to roll downward. There is no morning after; there is no time for redemption. I wait for death, and will welcome it with open arms. It is my time.

It was the same dream that she had woken from night after night for three nights that week. It could only mean one thing. She had to end this, before he ended her. It wasn't something that she relished. It was a job that had to be done. The sheets of her bed were wet with her sweat. She wasn't afraid of death, but she was afraid of seeing her ex husband again. She did not want those old memories awakened in her once more.

Giovanna was going home. It had been such a long time since she had been back to her home country that she had almost forgotten about all that she had left behind, but with good reason. She had left in the hope that she would never have to see her ex husbands face ever again. Now it was a different story. The next time that they met, one of them would not walk away alive.

Leaving her trusted weapons behind was regretful. She trusted in her own equipment. Once she was back home in her country, it would be a simple matter of purchasing new weapons, and then relying on them to do the job. It was roughly a three hour flight from Gatwick to Palermo, and back to her old home in Sicily. It was a year since she had been kidnapped and tortured, and it was surprising how much Cecilia had grown. She had insisted that she accompany her mother. She would not take no for an answer either.

Both mother and daughter had packed light. Fake passports, were par for the course. Fake identities and a reasonable amount of cash were required too. Too much would raise suspicion, if they were stopped for any reason, too little would be foolish too. There could be no cash point cards used. No risk of being caught on C.C.T.V. Footage either. Stay away from the mainstream movement of people where they could be monitored. This was a short trip, and purely for business only.

Giovanna had decided not to disclose the real reason for the trip, but she had assured Cecilia that this was the last ever business job that she would ever have to undertake. Then she was going into retirement. This was something that she had considered carefully over the last few months, but there was always the same worry in the back of her mind. The thought lingered within her that as long as he was alive, that they were both in great danger. He had paid to have her tortured and then murdered in front of her own daughter. Whatever his reasons for doing so, he was dangerous.

It was early in July that they had arranged the trip back home. Arriving at the airport, both mother and daughter had checked in separately. Both had only taken hand luggage onto the flight. They had both sat at different ends of the plane. The flight was comfortable and with little turbulence. It was an early morning flight and the views as they came in to land, were simply breathtaking.

As they exited the plane, the difference in temperature was incredible. When they had left a damp and miserable London, it was barely sixteen degrees. The temperature in Italy was thirty degrees and rising by the hour. It would take a little time for them both to acclimatise. Giovanna loosened the top of her blouse, opening up the top three bottoms. It did little to relieve the heat.

Cecilia had not returned back to the country of her birth since she was eighteen months old. They had fled the country with very little, but Giovanna had a set of skills that quickly made her a small fortune. Her child would never want for anything.

It was good to be home, but Giovanna was filled with a sense of dread. It was a lifetime ago that they had left, but now being back at this airport had stirred up some long forgotten memories. They were memories of the man who had tried to save her and her daughter. His face was still clear in her memories. He was gentle and kind to them both, but he had suffered a terrible fate for his acts of kindness. The day before they were due to leave, he had been stabbed repeatedly in his hotel room. Giovanna had been the one who had discovered his body.

She would have wept openly over the man's body, but she had to leave the country as soon as she possibly could. Her daughter was safe, but her lover had been brutally murdered in a dingy hotel room, without mercy. He had been her salvation from her abusive husband. They had planned a new start for the three of them. She should have known better. Her husband had eyes everywhere. Someone had seen them together and that had cost him his life. He had thought that by killing her lover, she would be too scared to leave. Instead it made her even more determined to run. It was years ago, but the pain of the memories opened up old forgotten wounds.

They collected their small travel cases from the carousel and left independently. They met across the road from the airport and headed for the nearest taxi. They needed a hotel that was comfortable and within easy distance of her target. They paid the driver in cash, and tipped him handsomely. The hotel was just outside of Altero, and had magnificent views of the Ionian Sea. Giovanna paid cash for the whole weeks stay and it was close to a thousand pound. They expected to be away from the hotel a few days sooner, but all eventualities had to be covered.

They spent the first day relaxing by the poolside. This was what it felt like to live a normal existence. Once this was done then perhaps they could live a normal life again. It was a thought that made Giovanna smile. Her daughter was chatting to a young man by the edge of the pool. She was quickly becoming a teenager, and then the years would go by quicker than she could ever imagine. She wished that her daughter would stay by her side for at least a few more years but she knew only too well that her daughter was already starting to drift toward her own life and the direction that personally she wanted to take.

That night when she was sure that Cecilia was asleep, Giovanna made her way down to the reception desk. The receptionist was more than happy to help and he organised a taxi for her. It took twenty minutes before the taxi arrived and the journey itself took another fifteen minutes. She had remained silent throughout the entire journey, despite the driver's best attempt at starting a conversation. When they finally arrived at the destination, Giovanna handed the taxi driver double the fare he had asked for in cash.

"If you come back here to this very spot in one hour's time, I will pay you the same again." She offered. The driver nodded. He would return. It would be a lucrative night, and a silent journey was not uncommon around these parts. Some people liked to maintain an air of privacy, and he had learnt over the years that it was best for him to keep his mouth shut.

The house was a short walk from where she had exited the car. Giovanna knocked twice, and then waited a few seconds. Then she knocked four times. The occupant knew that she was coming, and this was the signal that she was alone and safe. The door opened and Giovanna slipped effortlessly inside. The room was dark. Giovanna had a knife slipped safely inside of her sleeve. In her profession, you always had to have a back-up plan.

The light came on, and a gun was nudged into the hair at the back of her head.

"You are getting slack." It was a male voice. It sounded tired and old. It was comforting to hear nonetheless.

"Not at all. Look down." She instructed. She had removed the sharp blade from her sleeve, and it was now pressing against the man's left testicle. The man lowered the gun and then laughed.

"Giovanna. It has been far too long. How I have missed you!" The man said. Giovanna lowered the blade and turned to face her assailant. He had aged terribly in the last few years.

Leon had been more than a mentor. He had been her friend, and on occasion he had also been her saviour. He had helped her to escape the country, and he had made sure that she was safe. When she had called him out of the blue the day prior, he had been filled with mixed emotions. There was only one reason that she would return to the country she had once fled from. That reason would be to end her former husband's life, and Robert Dossema was a very dangerous man to try to assassinate.

Giovanna threw her arms around the man's neck. Marco was glad to see that she looked so well despite all that she had been through.

"You are so beautiful still." He said. He was genuine in his sentiment.

"You old charmer! You look fantastic too." She replied. His smile was wide and his face was so kind, and yet he had a darker side too.

"You cannot fool an old fool. I know that time has not treated me so well." He then looked down toward his left hand where he was holding on tightly to a walking stick. "The coffee is hot. Please come and sit with me." He offered.

The house was small and quaint. It was made of stone and rustic. It provided everything that he needed, and more importantly it was a safe haven. He had lived here for almost ten years since his retirement. The smell of fresh coffee filled the entire ground floor. Giovanna sat down at the wooden dining table. She would love to live in a simple house like this. Marco placed a hot cup of black coffee on the table. He then removed the gun from its holster and placed it on the table in front of her. It was a Beretta 92 handgun with a silencer fitted.

The gun was beautiful to look at. It was perfectly weighted, and the clip held fifteen rounds. He then placed a box of twenty spare clips by the side of the gun. Giovanna picked it up and examined the gun carefully.

"Marco, this is your own gun. I cannot..." She was not allowed to finish the sentence.

"Take it. I have no need for it anymore. I am an old fool with not much time left. One day my enemies will come, and when they do I will welcome them with open arms." He answered.

"You have plenty of time left in you yet!" Giovanna insisted, pushing the gun back toward him. Marco pushed it back in front of her.

"The disease is spreading. It cannot be stopped. I refuse to let them fill my body with radiation. Instead I wait. I am not afraid of death. I never was." It was true. His body was riddled with cancer. The sixty a day smoking habit that had kept him going during the seventies and eighties had finally taken their toll on his health. Giovanna understood. She felt a great deal of sadness, but she too was not afraid of death. In her profession, you could not afford to be.

"How much do you want for the gun?" She asked.

"You insult me." He answered, waving his hand to dismiss her offer. She had been like a daughter to him and if he had been thirty years younger, then he would have loved to have been her lover. He was realistic though. She was beautiful, and deserved the best in life. He could offer her security, but not the life she deserved with a decent man of her own age.

The two drank coffee for a little while and reminisced over old times. Giovanna wished that they had more time together, but the return taxi was booked. She placed the gun on her person and packed the spare clips away in her hold-all. When it was time for her to leave, she placed her arms around Marco and kissed both of his cheeks. He was a lot thinner than she remembered. It was sad to see him fading, but he was lucky to have reached the age that he had. There were tears in his eyes as he held her. In his heart, he knew that he would never see her again.

"You take care of yourself. Once it is over I can come back and see you before I leave." She offered. Marco shook his head.

"Once you walk out of the door. You don't stop you look forward and never look back for me again. Now go, and take care of your daughter." He then kissed her hand, and saw her out of the door. Giovanna stepped out onto the pavement, and she heard the door close behind her. It was a painful goodbye for them both.

The taxi was waiting where she had instructed him to. She opened the rear door and stepped inside. The night seemed unusually calm, and the moon was full. It seemed to light the roads as they drove back toward the hotel. Marco took the empty coffee cup from the table. He walked over to the sink and ran the tap. He liked to keep the house clean. It was a simple existence, and this was one of his two cups that he owned.

The front door burst open. It had taken an immense pressure to remove it from the hinges. Marco continued to wash up the cup. He did not turn around. Three men entered the open door and quickly stormed through the house. They located the man stood at the kitchen sink.

"Turn around!" One of the assailants shouted.

"Fuck you. Just make it quick." Marco said. There was no time to warn Giovanna that they might know she was here. He had trained her well though. He silently prayed for her. The hail of bullets tore through his body, leaving blood and flesh sprayed all over the kitchen wall and sink. The pain had ended. It was an amazing relief for him when all the pain was finally ended.

The taxi pulled up at the hotel, and Giovanna paid the driver the agreed amount plus an additional tip. It was a good night for the driver and it allowed him to finish his shift early for a change. Giovanna started to climb the stairs to the floor of her hotel room. She was reluctant to use lifts, as they were a potential death trap. When she reached the door of her room, there was an immediate sense of something being wrong. She drew her weapon before she entered the room.

She used the key-card to open the door, and kicked it open. A bullet hit the wall at head height behind her. She dropped to her knees and fired into the darkened room. A male voice shouted out in pain. It was a direct hit in his chest. It was luck more than judgement. She then reached up and switched on the lights. The two other men who were in the bedroom, both yelped in pain. Both had been wearing night vision glasses to give them an advantage.

She rolled into the room and fired off two shots, both hit the targets. One entered the front of the man's forehead, the other through pierced through the right eye of the night vision glasses of the other man. Both dropped down to the floor instantly. Giovanna rose to her feet and moved carefully toward the bathroom. She pushed the door slightly open with her foot, and splinters of wood exploded outward from the bathroom door. She fired wildly into the room emptying the clip except for a single round.

"Fuck, fuck, fuck!" She shouted. The man emerged from the bathroom with his gun raised. He was bleeding heavily, and applying pressure to the wound with his free hand. Giovanna pressed the gun to the side of his head.

"You should have learnt to count." She said before pulling the trigger and ending his life. She then dropped the clip from the weapon and placed in another full clip from her pocket.

The rest of the room was clear but there was no sign of Cecilia. She instantly thought of Marco. There's was no way that he would have told Robert that she was here. They must have been watching him. Robert was a devious man. His house might have always been watched, or even worse it may have been bugged. It was time to change tact. Robert already knew that she was here. Her daughter was now missing, and he knew that she had come to end him. His vineyard was not far from here. Daylight was imminent, and now it was time to end this for good.

The taxi dropped her less than half a mile away. The clips were stored all about her person. She was going in head first. As she approached the security gates to the vineyard, they began to open by remote. They knew that she was coming. Two men rushed toward her both holding rifles. They were trained on her face.

"Drop your gun!" One of the men shouted. They were both wearing bullet proof vests. It would require head shots or something more inventive.

"Wait!" Giovanna shouted. Then instead of dropping the gun, she turned it around to offer it out to the men. They both edged toward her slowly. As one of the men went to reach it, she threw it upward. Both men made the mistake of looking up at the weapon in the air. It took less than a second for the knives to be rammed into both of their throats. The knives were withdrawn, and the blood pumped out from the open wounds with a ferocious effort.

As she caught the gun, she pumped a bullet into each of the men's heads. Now she was two bullets down. There would be at least eight security guards here at the house, possibly more. She then noticed the security camera moving in her direction. She shouted out loud.

"I'm coming for you Robert. It's over." Then she shot out the lens of the camera. She moved around the grounds taking out every camera that she encountered.

Moving into the house, she carefully scouted every room before entering. A security guard was half way through the kitchen when she entered the room behind him. She placed a bullet in the back of his head and then continued to walk over the body on the floor. She hid in the toilet doorway in the darkness and she took out another two guards with single shots as they moved toward her. The house was deathly quiet. She moved on toward the living room, and it was there that she saw Robert. He was holding a gun to Cecilia's head.

Robert was smiling. His face was wide with that shit eating grin of his that made her feel repulsed.

"I would suggest that you drop your weapons. I mean all of them if you want our daughter to live. Then come and take a seat while we discuss the future." He said. Cecilia looked genuinely frightened, and Giovanna had to have faith that when the time came, her daughter would know exactly what to do. She dropped her gun to the floor and then dropped both of the knives that she was carrying.

Giovanna then sat down directly opposite her ex husband. They had never officially divorced, but that didn't matter. He was inhuman. He would never lay a finger on her ever again.

"Why did you take out a contract on me?" She asked.

"And now, after all this time you decide to try and talk?" Robert looked surprised. "Do you know the shame that I felt when you left me?" He asked. A little bit of spittle flew from his mouth when he spoke.

"I had no choice." She answered.

"There's always a choice. You didn't have to take my daughter!" He shouted. "Now I don't even know her, and she doesn't know me either. I wanted her to come into the family business." Robert smiled.

"I had to get her away from all of this. We wanted a new start. You had your chances, but every time you let us down. Remember all the drugs that you took. The hookers that you used and you thought that I never knew about, and let's not forget all the beatings that you thought that I deserved. Well I deserved better, and so did our child." Giovanna said.

Her voice was filled with emotion. She had always loved her husband, and she had genuinely wanted the fairytale ending. It was devastating for her when things had turned sour, and it took her a long time before she had made the decision to leave.

"And so you turned to Marco?" He angrily retorted.

"Marco helped us to find a new life away from here. He showed us nothing but kindness!" She replied.

"Well for his betrayal, he has paid the ultimate price." Robert said. Then he looked in the direction of his wooden dresser. Giovanna looked over at where he was looking, and there on the side was the head of Marco sat on a silver serving plate. Giovanna felt pain knotting in her stomach and the tears then began to fall from her eyes.

"Now, I have made the decision." Robert said. I want a fresh start in life. To do that, I need to remove all traces of my old life. That means you two. So now I end our daughter's life in front of you and then you can pay for your betrayal, with your own life." Robert then pulled Cecilia by the hair. He placed her head down into his lap and pointed the gun at the top of her head. Cecilia screamed.

"Daddy please don't. I love you!" She shouted.

Robert heard the words she said, but he was completely oblivious to them.

"Do you have any last words Giovanna? I would say them to our daughter now." Robert said.

"Don't do this. I will do anything that you want. I beg of you." She dropped down to her hands and knees and began to crawl toward him. "Take me, not her. Please don't hurt our baby girl." Giovanna pleaded.

The words registered in Cecilia's head. She had remembered the signal well. Her mother was close enough to grab the weapon she had to react quickly. Cecilia's teeth sunk down into her father's groin as hard as she could bite. Robert screamed at the ferociousness of the pain. Giovanna was instantly on her feet and bending his arm backward. He dropped the weapon on the floor behind the sofa. His wrist was probably broken, but the blood that was now pumping out from his groin was of a greater concern to him. Both mother and daughter were now raining blows down on to his face and head. She had trained her daughter well, better than he could have imagined. His world then turned to darkness.

The hole was around four foot deep. It was deep enough. His body was tied with whatever they had found in the house. Expensive silk ties bound his legs together. Small amounts of rope from the vines had bound his hands tightly. It was mid morning as mother and daughter dragged the struggling man over toward the freshly dug hole. It had been hard work, but it would all be worthwhile.

He knew that he was about to meet his fate, and now he was really becoming worried. Giovanna removed the duct tape from his mouth and Robert began to plead.

"It's not too late. You can still walk away from this. It's gotten out of hand but I can still make it right. How much money do you want? Just let me go, and you can take it all." He pleaded. Giovanna nodded to her daughter. Cecilia nodded in return. Between them, they dragged Robert to the side of the hole and then they tipped him in. He landed face upward. It was fitting that he could see his own fate. It was a courtesy that they had not afforded to Marco.

Cecilia spat on her father's face. Giovanna smiled as she leant over the trembling figure in the hole below her.

"It's not about money. It's about family and honour. We don't need anything that you have. We just want to live in peace." She said. Then she took the shovel and started to fill in the freshly dug grave. Robert screamed and screamed, but the area was secluded. No one could hear his cries for miles around. His lungs soon filled with the dusty earth, and then his muffled cries could be heard no more.

The clean up took longer than expected. There were a lot of dead bodies at the scene. The police did not uncover the body of Robert Dossema for another week. Very little effort was made to find his killers. To most, it was a great relief. He died with his mouth wide open. There was no trace of either woman who had checked in to the hotel, but they had left a bloody legacy in their wake. The hotel was a mess, the vineyard was a mess. The police had identified the head at the scene as that of Marco Ricci. He was suspected of being involved in hundreds of murders, and he had faced a nasty end. The rest of his body was never recovered.

The women had hired a boat and had moved along the coast. It took weeks before they arrived in France, and it was easy to buy a passage across to England. When they eventually arrived back home, they both felt a great sense of relief. For Giovanna, it was the end of an era. It was the end of her life as an assassin. Not many people had ever escaped from this choice of career. Now she could officially retire with enough money to keep her comfortable for life. No one would ever learn of her past. Perhaps wow she could even afford to fall in love again. That might never happen, but if it did then she was ready she was ready.

For Cecilia, she was growing up way too fast. For the life ahead of her and for the career choice she just had decided upon, it was just the beginning on a brand new chapter.

Never meet your heroes.

There are things in life that are beyond love, beyond even your deepest hearts desires. Sometimes you will catch a glimpse of the impossible. Sometimes you might even reach out and touch your deepest fantasy. You may even find that you can discover a way to achieve everything you have ever desired and beyond. A bond so pure, that it is forged by the gods themselves. This is my story.

I was an only child, and it goes without saying that I was also a lonely child. My eyesight was so bad that I would often walk into objects without even noticing them. From my early years I was forced to wear thick spectacles. I was bullied constantly from the moment that I set foot into a school, right up until the moment that I left. My constant tears were heartbreaking for my mother to witness. My father would be left shaking his head daily.

He always thought that you had to stand up to bullies. He tried to teach me how to box, but I had no wish to learn. The thought of being struck by another was horrific. The thought of hurting someone else was even worse. I just wanted to be left alone. I wanted peace. I wanted to live in a world of my own design. A world where my name would always be remembered.

My teenage years were a living hell. I was persecuted to the point where I wanted to kill myself daily. Then my mother passed unexpectedly and my father descended into an alcoholic wreck that would eventually cause him to drown in pool of his own vomit. He had been missing for three days when his body was discovered in a dirty back alley. I had not reported him missing. He seldom came home anymore anyway.

So at seventeen years old, I found myself homeless, loveless and parentless. The rope was already tied around my neck. I just needed another little nudge of heartbreak and I would have gladly jumped from the ledge. I had no choice but to find any work that I could, and a single room that I could finally find some solitude in.

I lasted just three days in that job. It ended with my modesty exposed to the world and my tears of anger and frustration. Back then it was a very different world. There was no Human Resources department to turn to. Everything was labelled as a 'laugh amongst the lads'. Even the shift manager had been involved in my humiliation. So it was on the third day that I found myself left out on the main road. Shrink wrapped naked to a street light.

You would have thought that someone might have taken pity on me. Instead I was ridiculed for hours. Cars would sound their horns at me. Young children would strike at me with broken pieces of wood and stones. The most embarrassing of all was the teenage girls. They saw me as naked as the day I was born, with nothing to hide my shame, and how they laughed at my shame. Eventually a policeman found me, and took pity on me. He placed me in his car and took me home.

I did not leave my room for six days.

Six days without human contact. Six days without food or water. Six long sleepless days of tears and anger and deliberation. I was going to starve myself to death and not a single person in this cold dark world would even care. There would be no point in writing a suicide note. Not a single person would even want to know why I had decided to end it all. Then as I lay down on my bed just staring at the stained yellow ceiling, I turned on the radio. Then I heard a song that told me I no longer had to be alone.

It was by a new artist called G-Lock. The song was called Lockdown, and it was the story of my life. It told of how he had been bullied at school too. How both of his parents had abandoned him as a child, how he had nothing in life, but he had fought back against his bullies and he had turned his life around. One by one he had shown everyone who had ever taunted him in life, that he was better than they would ever be.

I got dressed. I went down to the kitchen and made a sandwich. My landlady was sat in the living room. She was watching a daytime talk show where the guests were squaring up to each other every few moments. Then another guest would arrive and all hell would break loose. It was a tried and tested formula, but it made great television. She was smoking away merrily on a cigarette. The smell of these things made me want to retch. It did not even register with her that I was present. I sat down at the kitchen and ate, then I left the house as she ended her cigarette and then started up another.

I walked into the town centre and searched high and low. In the last shop that I tried, I found what I was looking for. I bought G-Locks new album on C.D, and placed it in my portable player. The next forty-seven minutes was to change my life forever. When I heard the song called 'Force of nature' it was almost as if he were giving me step by step instructions as to what I should do next. So I walked into the hardware store, and purchased a lump hammer.

I waited for two hours before my tormentor exited the building. It was dark and that would help. I pulled my hood up and over the headphones. G-Lock was providing my soundtrack. This was my force of nature that had been building inside of me all of my life. I approached him as he was trying to unlock his car. He sensed that I was stood behind him. As he turned and saw my face, he began to smile and he was trying to think of something that he could say to taunt me once more.

The only things that left his mouth were blood and teeth. The lump hammer connected with his jaw with such ferocity, that I was amazed at how little effort it took to half destroy his face with a single blow. It felt good. No, it felt intense. Those pent up years of anger and frustration had risen to the surface and I felt the power surging through my body. My legs were both shaking with adrenaline as I struck my former manager again and again.

He raised his hands to protect himself, but they were no match for the weight of the hammer. If his jaw had not been hanging from his face, then he might have been able to scream. The gurgling sounds he made were annoying me, so I turned up my music even louder. Blow after blow rained down on his skull. I had the power of life and death in my hands, and it made me feel like a God amongst men.

The bloodied mess did not disturb me in the slightest. The thoughts for his family were non existent. This thing had revealed its true form, and I had ended its miserable life in just a few moments. I smeared the blood on my cheeks, then I tasted it. The coppery tasting fluid tasted good. As the music played, I drank more of the blood of my victim and I felt as if I were absorbing his very life-force. Then as the song ended, I knew that I had to get away.

I moved away from the area and never looked back. The police had no clues, no motive, and back then D.N.A was in its infancy. I had left no prints at the scene, I took the hammer with me, and there was nothing to tie me to the murder in any way. I had a new purpose in life. I had to be closer to my new hero. I was going to find a way to meet him no matter what the cost.

Over the next few months I found a new purpose in life. I moved to a new town. I cut my hair short and dyed it to try and look like G-Lock. It was close enough, but not exact. I found another job which paid slightly more than I needed. I bought clothes that looked like his, I read everything that I could find that was written about him. I bought magazines and newspapers that mentioned his name, and as his career began to explode, I realised that he and I were inexplicably linked. Our rise was simultaneous.

When I first met him at a concert, he shook my hand and signed his autograph on a picture for me. He thanked me for my support, but he declined to have his picture taken with anyone. I knew what he was trying to tell me, right from that very first meeting. It would only happen when I was ready, when I was worthy He was my guide, and I was a more than willing student. No matter what happened, from now on in, I would follow him everywhere.

I knew every single word of every single song that he released. I watched him on music television and I eagerly awaited for each new video that he made. Recorded them on my video tape recorder, and I watched them over and over again. I could see myself in the videos. I so badly wanted to be him. To have the beautiful women surrounding me, to have the life without a care. To be elevated above all else. He showed me that it was possible to become him. Every day my transformation took me closer and closer to him.

I attended every show. I turned up at every signing session. He even knew me by name after a few signings. I had his signature on everything. On CDs on pictures, and magazines. His face adorned all my walls. This was my shrine to my God. Nothing else mattered. Then it happened. He agreed that I could have my photograph taken with him. It felt as if my life was almost complete. I had to have the film developed and that took a day. It was the worst day of my life. I paced up and down relentless outside the shop while I waited for it to open. Then when I finally had the folder of photographs in my hand, I began to shake.

I had the picture in my hand. It was an intense moment. I had to have the picture enlarged immediately. His arm was around my shoulder. My arm was around his. We were forming a partnership that no one else could touch. We were together. I took the enlargement and had it framed in a gilt edged frame. It was expensive, but it would be worth every penny. I placed the frame above my bed, and I touched it every single night before bed, and every single morning as I awoke. It became my ritual.

When the tour ended, my life was put on hold. It was hard to get information about artists. He was recording new material, and all I had was that first album and my poster covered walls to keep me sane. I waited patiently for months, but every day became more and more torturous. I would see the occasional glimpse of him on television and in the newspapers, but without tour dates to follow, I could not be as close to him as I wanted to be. The night that he was beaten in the award for best new artist, I smashed my television screen at the injustice.

Soon the news filtered through to his fan base. The new album was complete. The single was imminent, and that meant a fresh new batch of tour dates. I could soon be with him regularly. I suddenly felt happier than I had ever felt. When I heard the new single, I knew that it had all been worthwhile. When I held a physical copy in my hands, there were tears in my eyes. It was even dedicated to all of his fans. I knew exactly who he meant by that. I opened the case of the C.D single and saw the crowd picture from his London concert. I was there, clear as a day in the front row. It was clear now that I meant just as much to him, as he did to me.

The cycle began again. The album came out after the second single, and I had it in every single format that money could buy. My room was now filled with his pictures, so I had to begin scrapbooks to keep his clippings in. Then when the tour dates were announced, I bought a ticket for every single concert and began to plan how to get to each and every appearance.

At the first signing he seemed really glad to see me. It had been too long for both of us, of that I was sure. On the second day he seemed to be a little tired, and I forgave him for not feeling quite so friendly toward me. But the third day, well the third day just made me angry. I could not even get within thirty feet of him. There was private security at the event and for some reason, they would not even Let me get close to him. I called out his name over and over again, and although he waved at me, it was nowhere near enough. I was livid and began to write him letters to explain that for fans who were as close to him as I was, then the security needed to be made aware of us. That we needed to be allowed to get close.

The next night I managed to hand the letter to one of his assistants who assured me that she would personally pass it on to him, but still I was kept back away from him. My anger was building inside of me by the minute, and I knew that I would not be happy until I could have my picture taken with him again. I needed to feel his arm around my shoulder again. I needed to touch him. I had to be with him. There were only five more dates left of the tour before it moved to another country, and that would be a nightmare for me. Then it suddenly dawned on me. I knew how I could be closer to him to than anyone would ever be.

G-Lock was a man of habit. He had taste. He had style. He was already a legend. He would often book the honeymoon suite of a hotel, and I knew exactly where he would be staying on the last night of the tour. I booked the room well in advance. I knew that it would mean I would miss his last appearance in this country, but it would all be worth it in the end. I checked into the hotel the night before, and I prepared everything meticulously.

The clothes were exactly the same as he would have been wearing on stage that night. The make-up although minimal looked exactly like his. My hair was as close as I could get to looking like his. Money talks, as his lyrics had told me time and time again and this proved to be true as I managed to obtain the Polaroid instant camera and the one other thing that I needed for the night to end in perfection. I waited patiently and silently for him to return. He did not return to the hotel until four in the morning, it was the perfect time.

I watched through the spyhole in the door as he walked past my room. He had one security guard with him, and two women. They looked slutty and cheap. They were both blonde. He always had a thing for blondes. It wasn't fair. He never even saw how much I loved him, but he would share everything with the sluts and whores that he met on tour. Soon he would know exactly how much he meant to me though.

I waited. I heard the sounds of the drunken laughter. I heard the sound of the aggressive and loveless sex. I heard the sound of breaking glass and even more laughter afterward. I wondered if I would ever hear the door open, and then it did. The guard was leaving, and he was taking the women with him. He had to make sure they left before the press managed to take pictures of them to try and sell their rumour filled scummy lying newspapers. I waited until I heard the sound of the lift door closing. I knew it was time.

He had assumed that the guard had forgotten something, and opened the door without even checking who it was. He was naked as he opened the door, and he looked half dazed from the alcohol. The room behind him was in darkness. I switched on the light and moved into the room. He walked backward without saying a word. It's amazing the effect of a gun being pointed at your face. I walked into the room and locked the door behind me. This was the last time that we would be together. No one would stop this.

He was visibly scared as his leg hit the bed.

"It's cool man, you can take my money, you can take it all and just leave. Just don't do anything stupid" He pleaded. It was disappointing. I expected at least to be greeted like his number one fan should. I was an old friend after all.

"Lay down on the bed." I instructed him. There was a look of panic now on his face. I knew what he was thinking.

"I'm not sick!" I shouted at him, angry that he would think of me that way, after all that we had been through together.

"Just tell me what you want man, then please go." He said. His voice was full of fear. It saddened me that my hero would crumble and fold like this. He had suffered just like I had. He had survived and shown me the way. He had been my life for over a year. Now he was just like a scared child. This wasn't how I wanted to remember him.

"All I want is for you to lay down on the bed. I want to lay down next to you, and then you will take some photographs of us together. Then I will leave." I said. It was my plan all along. Just a few more photographs for my wall.

"Ok. Just don't do anything stupid." He slowly lay down on the bed. I kept the gun in my right hand all the time. I handed him the camera. Then I lay down next to him. I pressed my left cheek next to his, and I felt the warmth of his skin on mine.

"Take the picture." I raised the gun to my ear and waited. The camera flashed. "Again!" I instructed as the picture fell to my chest. His face was a mixture of fear and revulsion. The camera flashed once more. Then there was a knock at the door. The security guard had returned. There was little time to finish. "Again!" I shouted. Now the door was being struck by the weight of the guard trying to force his way into the room. It wouldn't hold for long.

There are moments in life where you make a choice that you will live to regret your decision. There are moments when you know that you made the right choice. I had seconds left. My image of my hero had been tarnished by his fear. He had inspired millions with his lyrics and videos. He was a God amongst men in the music industry, but he had ruined my dream. All I wanted was a solitary photograph of us together for one last time. Then I was going to leave, but now that was no longer an option. I had seen his true face, I had seen his humanity. I had seen what was hidden behind the mask.

No one else could be allowed to see what I had seen. His iconic status had to be maintained no matter what the cost. I would ensure that his music would live forever, and now I would always be associated with him. Nothing would ever come between us again. As the door burst open, I pulled the trigger.

The force of the bullet easily passed through both skulls. Fragments of bone and blood splattered up the walls. The end was instant for both men. The legend of G-Lock would live forever, and so would mine. Mine was the name of the man who had murdered him in his prime. The blood of both men formed pools of crimson red on the once bright white bed sheets. The guard was in shock, and never worked in security ever again. The photographs of the bloody scene were leaked to the press, and somewhere in the world a hotel porter suddenly had more money in his bank account than he could ever dream of. Someone somewhere was being tied naked to another lamp post, while others continued to gather around, and to laugh at the helpless victim.

Sleep won't come

For the seventh night in a row, Nathan had awoken with a start. Sweat dripped from his body, and soaked the bed sheets beneath him. It was only the beginning of April, and the air outside was still fresh and crisp. The dream was very real. He searched the room, half expecting to see a ghostly figure stood over his bed, but there was no one there. He looked over at the alarm clock perched on the bedside table. In was ten to four. The bright red illuminated numbers cast a soft glow across that darkened corner of the room.

The time was ten to four. It was a constant daily reminder of the past. It was at that exact time of the morning that his father had passed. It was more than three years ago now. It was confusing as to why this particular dream was recurring every night. He rolled over to the other side of the bed. It was a king size that afforded him space to do so. This patch of bed was dry. The sheets needed changing again, but it would wait until morning.

He closed his eyes and his mind began to slip into a light sleep. In less than three hours, the dreaded alarm would screech throughout the room and alert him to the need to prepare for work. When the alarm finally rang out, he felt as if he had not slept properly in months. He moved slowly to the edge of the bed and turned off the alarm. He allowed himself a few more moments rest.

An hour later, he opened his eyes. He had foolishly allowed himself to drift back off to sleep. Now he was going to be late, and there was absolutely nothing that he could do about it. He picked up his mobile phone from the side of the bed. He rang his boss and made a lame excuse about having a sickness bug, and that he had hardly slept all night. It was a half truth. At least now he could get some more sleep.

Two hours later, he was still in bed. He was wide awake. Sleep had failed him. Outside of his house, he could hear birds chirping away merrily whilst he stared blankly at the ceiling. He felt a little guilty at lying to his boss, as he had always looked after his employees. His sickness record would be tainted very early on again this year, just as it had for the last four years.

He decided to pick up his tablet from its chrome stand, and explore the world of social media. It was filled with the same old crap. Day after day it was the same gripes, recycled pictures attempting to inspire hope. Unfunny attempts at humour, and the occasional snippets of useful information that often turned out to be an untruth. If anything it was too much information on a perpetual cycle.

He then had an idea. He would run a search on his repeating dream. It was perhaps idiotic, but he wondered if it may have had a hidden meaning. He thought about what he should enter into the search. Then he typed in 'repeated visit of dead relatives in dreams' the search came back almost instantly.

He trawled through link after link. Most were stating the same thing. They believed that a lost relative was trying to stay in touch. He wasn't particularly close to his late father. The relationship had always been strained. His father had little time for his when he was a child, and when his mother past at twelve years old, his father could no longer cope. Nathan had spent the next few years virtually fending for himself.

He cooked his own meals, ironed his own clothes and kept the house as tidy as he could. It was during his regular cleaning sessions, that he started to find all the hidden empty bottles of vodka. Quite why someone would hide empty bottles was beyond him. If his father was trying to hide his evident drinking problem, then surely it would have made more sense to throw them away.

Nathan could never fathom out the irrational mind of an alcoholic. He tried to address his concerns to his father on numerous occasions, but he was always met with a series of ignorant grunts in response. The sound of the seal of the vodka bottles cracking open seemed to get louder and louder with each passing day. By the age of seventeen, Nathan moved out for the sake of his own sanity.

He did not see his father again for another twelve years. He would visit him at Christmas and on his father's birthday for the first couple of years, but his presence was clearly unwanted by a man who was being swallowed up by his own self pity. The visits stopped, but he still tried to call his father on the telephone. When the drunken slurs became abusive, then he stopped calling him as well. Nathan decided that he could reasonably do no more.

The next time he saw his father, he was in a hospital bed. He looked a shadow of his former self. His eyes and skin were yellow where the jaundice had ravaged his body. His liver and pancreas had both given up the ghost long ago. It was almost as if the shell of his father had been filled with poison and been left to rot from the inside out.

The end was prolonged for a few weeks. He visited his father daily, but there was never any sign of improvement. He watched as his father slid away into nothingness. It was sad to see, but hardly unexpected. When his father eventually passed, he was by his side at ten to four in the morning. He cried unexpected tears, and then he went home and slept like a baby.

The body was cremated on his father's instructions. The numbers were fewer than ten in attendance. Death was very much a part of Nathans life, but he did not cry at the service. He had no more tears left to shed. That fact in itself saddened him, but perhaps selfishly, he knew that he needed to move on quickly regardless of his loss of his last remaining parent.

Now it seemed that his father had waited until the grave to decide to communicate with his son, when it was far too little far too late. He recalled the recurring dream. His father would be stood in his bedroom. He would walk to the window and open the curtains. He could see the back of his father's head. Then the figure would shift instantly to each corner of the room always facing away. He would always mutter the same four words.

"Don't look at me."

During the week, it felt as if the figure had moved closer and closer to him. The previous morning, his father had apparently been stood at the head of the bed. Nathan could not help but to look at the ghostly apparition. The figure was sobbing in the corner next to the head of the bed. Nathan sat on the edge of the bed, and then stood upright he took a step closer to the figure and then placed his hand on his late father's shoulder. He turned his father around.

The ghostly figure was ashen underneath its hooded cloak. Its eyes were replaced with empty hollows, and as the cloak fell open, Nathan could see rotten organs through a charred open ribcage. He recoiled and fell back onto the bed in horror. The figure was then instantly over him and bony fingers were pressing down hard on both his shoulders.

"I told you not to look at me!" His father screamed.

The recollection of the dream was almost as frightening as them dream itself. Nathan knew that he could not go on night after night experiencing the same thing. He needed to find a way to try and communicate with his late father, and as he had no belief in an afterlife, it was going to take something that he had little belief in.

In the golden age of the internet, everyone and everything is graded on likes or performance. Likes afforded to an individual's status, to out of five star reviews to performance, everyone has become an unpaid critic. The performance of mediums was exactly the same. Nathan scoured page after page and review after review before deciding on whom to contact.

Christian Grimes lived only fifteen miles away from Nathan. He rang and booked an appointment, but it was fifteen days before Christian could see him. He was popular amongst his fans, and he had regular visitors to his home. Nathan could have chosen to see someone closer much sooner, but he was impressed with all that he had read about Christian, despite the fees he charged for private consultations.

For every single night up until the day of the meeting, Nathan continued to have the same dream. Only now, even in the dream, Nathan was too afraid to look at his father anymore. Instead he would listen to his fathers agonized tears, whilst he pleaded with his son not to look at him. By the time of the appointment, Nathan felt weak from a lack of sleep. He was now resorting to three or four cans of energy drinks just to keep him awake during the days.

Nathan felt a little uneasy as he drove to the address he had been given. He was almost expecting a gothic mansion, but when he reached the house, it was nothing more than a two bedroom terraced ex council property. Nathan parked his car on the private driveway, and locked the doors with the remote fob. The electric wing mirror motors whirred noisily as both mirrors folded inward.

It was around five to eight in the evening, and the air was unnaturally quiet. It was eerie to hear nothing even though there was a slight breeze. A cat darted out from a bush in the garden and bolted away from the garden as Nathan approached the front door. It startled him momentarily, and then he smiled at his own stupidity. It was a cat; cats often bolt away for no reason.

Christian opened the door. Nathan was a little surprised at the man who greeted him. He was a little over five feet tall, and wore thick round spectacles. He dressed smartly in a grey thick woolen jumper and crisply ironed denim jeans. They had an unnecessary crease ironed into the front of both legs. To top it all off, he was wearing burgundy slippers. The man clearly had no colour co-ordination.

Christian held the door open and beckoned Nathan inside.

"Do come in please." He instructed. Nathan did as he was asked and stepped inside the thick white PVC door. He suddenly felt a little uneasy as the door closed behind him.

The entire house appeared to be painted in magnolia. It looked clean and fresh, but a little bring. No pictures adorned the walls at all. There were no ornaments on display of any kind. It was as plain as any house could be. The carpet was light brown throughout, but a thick pile type and immaculate. Nathan took off his shoes as a courtesy. He left them in the hallway by the door without being instructed to do so, but by the wry smile that had appeared on Christians face, he knew that he had done the correct thing by the host.

Christian led the way through the house through a dining room, and then out into an extension to the back of the house. This was the sitting room. This was the only room in the house that was painted dark. Soft candles lit the walls, and incense burnt with a heavy scent.

There were four chairs in the room, and a small round table between them.

"Take a seat." Christian offered. Nathan duly obliged. The padded seat was comfortable. He felt a little more relaxed now. "I hate to do this straight away, but I take my fee before we begin, just to avoid any confusion. You'd be surprised how many people try to haggle down the price after a sitting, when they don't hear what they expect to." Christian explained. It was almost as if there was a hint of anger in his voice. Perhaps it was frustration? It was difficult to say.

"Of course. It's understandable." Nathan said, as he took the wallet from his trouser pocket and took out the two hundred pound fee. He counted the notes onto the table, all in twenties. The last one had something unreadable scribbled in biro on the queen's head. Christian watched intently as the money was counted out, and then he took it from the table and placed it in his right hand jean pocket. It was a lot of money; Nathan just hoped that it was worth it.

Christian began a series of deep breathing exercises. Then he took some leaves of sage and rubbed them on the table in front of him. It looked odd to say the least. He then turned on a soft red light above his head.

"I'm going to start with a protection spell, but don't worry. You are quite safe." Christian assured him. He then began to recite a well practiced verse.

"Are there any spirits present? If so would you make yourself known to us?" Christian instructed. Nathan searched around the room with his eyes. In the corner of the room, a cloaked figure appeared to form. It then started to move slowly toward Christians back. Nathan sat with his eyes wide. It was the same apparition from his dreams. It was definitely his father.

"I will allow you to communicate through my body. I ask that you keep my body free from harm while I allow you to enter my being. "With this instruction, the spirit began to merge into the body of the reader. Now it was Christian whose eyes became wide. "Oh no." He exclaimed.

"What's wrong?" Nathan asked.

"How I have missed you my son." The voice returned. It was the sound of his later father's voice that was now talking to him.

"What is it that you want from me? You never had time for me in life, but now in death you won't leave me in peace."

"You left me to die alone. You watched me fade to nothing." The spirit groaned.

"No! I won't have that. You don't deserve my pity. I sat with you every day until you died. I was the one holding your hand!" Nathan argued.

"You don't understand son. I died long before my body did." The figure was now reaching out its hand toward Nathan. "I want to hold you once more son." He remarked.

Nathan was in disbelief at what he had heard. Reluctantly he stood up and leant across the table. "Dad...." His voice was now quivering. The one thing that he wanted in life was his father's love and affection, and now in the most bizarre of circumstances, his father was reaching out to him from beyond the grave. He felt warmth in his chest, and a sudden rush of blood to his brain. The hand of his father was now on his chest, but it did not stop there, the ghostly hand had continued to move straight through his chest. The ghostly hand was squeezing his heart, and stopping the blood from pumping.

Nathan was now gasping for breath.

"A father should always hold his sons heart!" The figure cackled. "I've spent what feels like an eternity alone. Now I want you with me." He said. He squeezed tighter and tighter on Nathans heart muscle, until it could pump no more. Nathan wheezed his final breath, and his body fell forward on to the table. He died with a look of fright on his face. The spirit then left Christians body, and he too slumped forward unconscious.

It was the next morning before Christian awoke. The room stank of excrement and urine where the dead man had emptied his bowels and bladder. Nathans lips were blue, and the look on his face, was one of sheer fright.

The coroner could not determine the exact cause of death. The energy drinks were thought to have probably caused the heart failure. Christian was cleared of any wrong doing whatsoever. He had no recollection of what had happened on that fateful evening. He also had no idea that he had not performed a closing prayer, and that a benevolent spirit was still free to cause untold harm amongst the living, and now he was not alone.

There are sights that should never be seen by human eyes.

Glimpses of the future can be bestowed upon ordinary human beings.

Those who at first appear ordinary can often be anything but.

Do you dare to take a look through these windows and see the darkness behind every single different pane of glass?

Keep Away From The Windows!

You have been warned.

Printed in Great Britain
by Amazon